MANACLED HEARTS

AN AGE GAP MAFIA ROMANCE

BY LILITH ROMAN

AUTHOR'S NOTE

They're feared. Powerful. Ruthless.
And they don't just love... they worship.

Welcome to The Sanctum Syndicate series of interconnected standalones. Manacled Hearts is book 3, an age gap mafia romance that challenged my writing skills in such a satisfying way. I've never written slow burn and angst like this before, and I know it will make you scream at your screen for them to kiss and wait all at once. I hope you enjoy Finnigan and Evelyn's story. Happy Reading!

Love,
Lilith

Start the Series in Kindle Unlimited:
Book 1 – Dangerous Strokes, a Dark Mafia Romance
Book 2 – Reckless Covenant, a Second Chance Mafia Romance

CONTENT WARNING

Due to recent publishing guidelines, the list couldn't be included here, however I would never want to put a reader in an uncomfortable situation. This dark mafia romance is a work of fiction, and it contains violent and sensitive situations which could be triggering for some.
For a full list, please go to:
https://lilithromanauthor.com/lilith/books/warnings/

MANACLED HEARTS

THE SANCTUM SYNDICATE BOOK 3

LILITH ROMAN

PLAYLIST

Dirge - Death in Vegas
Your Hands - GRAE
Daylight - David Kushner
Chokehold - Sleep Token
Alkaline - Sleep Token
Burning Sea - Daniel Spaleniak, Tomasz Mrénca
Iron Sky - Paolo Nutini
Left Me for Dead - Rob Dougan
Daddy - Ramsey
Running Up That Hill - Placebo
For You – HIM
Vermilion, Pt.2 - Slipknot
Lullaby - Low
In Bad Dreams - Crippled Black Phoenix
Shadows of My Name - Emma Ruth Rundle
Marked for Death - Emma Ruth Rundle
This Will Make You Love Again - IAMX
Dead Flowers for Her - Skywatchers
Shadows & Light - Saudade, Chelsea Wolfe, Chino Moreno
Depraved - Mammals
Cities - Toby May, Two Feet
The Kill - Thirty Seconds to Mars
Be My Man - Nostalghia

Unfurl - Katatonia

It Will All Make Sense in the Morning - Halou

Bitches Brew - † † † (Crosses)

16 Psyche - Chelsea Wolfe

The Space in Between - How To Destroy Angels

Secrets - Omido, Ordell, Rick Jansen

Phantom - Kaphy, BLVKES

Good Looking - Suki Waterhouse

Like U - Rosenfeld

Looking for the Summer - Chris Rea

*To all of you who believe you don't deserve to be loved...
Remember seeing those mugshots of ridiculously hot convicts you
swooned over and thought, "I can fix him"? How about you
fix yourself first, because if you think they deserve love,
then you're worthy of so much more!*

PROLOGUE
Evelyn

One month earlier

THE SCREECH OF THE CONTAINER door plays on a disturbing loop in my head. Hours must have passed since the last time I heard it, closing with a shattering bang that held a finality to it. The loop is never-ending, an excruciating background noise to the whimpers and cries currently reverberating against these walls.

It took me a while, but I finally understood why it plagues me so. My subconscious is demanding retribution for my failure to save Maya from the bastards who took us. Who locked us in this godforsaken place, along with so many others like her.

I had one job—protect my little sister.

I failed.

Miserably.

As if becoming homeless, unexpected orphans, and evading CPS wasn't enough, now we're kidnapped. Stuck in this hot, metal box with thirty other children, suffocating in the smell of urine and God knows what else.

Only, I'm the odd one out. I'm not a child.

I'm just shy of turning eighteen, still a minor in the eyes of some laws, but my childhood ended with our mom's sudden death. Overnight, I became my sister's guardian, and without siblings, grandparents or other family, we had no one else in the world on our side. Almost two years have passed since she became my whole life.

Sometimes it's like I'm trapped in a Lemony Snicket novel. Event after unfortunate event seems to have taken a horrible hold of us, and the passing of years did nothing to improve our situation.

It didn't start with Mom, though.

In reality, it all started with the events that took Dad from us.

The container jolts. Terrified cries erupt from the children, serving as a reminder that the unlucky events haven't ceased.

"Hold on to each other. It's all going to be over soon." I try to soothe them with empty promises.

Still, the cries never stop. Like the little light that used to shine in their souls, they quiet down to fear-stricken murmurs.

Tightening my hold around my sister, I whisper words of reassurance to her. She wasn't one of the kids who screamed. Maybe that's why I'm holding her harder. I'm hoping her silence stems from my comfort, but the alternative plays in my mind. Is she in some sort of catatonic state from the trauma?

I yearn for a sliver of light in here. At least then she could look into my eyes with her pretty green ones and see the promises in them. I will never fail her again. I will protect her with all I have and make sure she will be safe. Since they took us and locked us in here, those vows haven't touched my lips. I'm afraid I won't be able to keep them. So, words of reassurance are all I can provide. I'm a coward. A failure.

I failed when I chose to park on the dark side too far away from the school—all so I could hide that we live in our car.

I failed when I didn't immediately notice the men following us, after I picked her up. When I didn't get her to the car in time.

I failed when they yanked me by my hair, struck me in the ribs, then pushed me away from her. When she screamed my name with such terror in her sweet little voice, it clawed into my soul. I jumped on the man who grabbed her, erratically punching him in the face, aiming at his eyes until he finally dropped Maya.

Then I failed to hold on to her. They ripped her out of my weak arms, punching me hard enough in the gut that I almost threw up before my head even hit the ground. But I got up and ran after them like the pain didn't exist, following my sister's muffled cries deeper into the darkness of the alley. I ran even as the worn soles of my shoes gave out and the rocks gouged my socked feet.

When I saw my sister being shoved in the back of the black van, I pushed my way in without thinking. I couldn't get her out. Instead, the men spit their curses at my hysterics and decided it was safer to take me, too.

Since then, there have been no opportunities to attempt an escape, but I refuse to accept that none will come. There is no other choice. No more room for failure.

With guilt fogging my mind, my exhaustion takes me before I can stop it, and I drift into a restless sleep.

I drift in and out, frequently woken up by the metal screeching or the kids. Even when I manage some sleep, I'm woken up by the children. Some require calming, the really young ones need help to relieve themselves, and I need to make sure they all eat the cheap bread that's provided. Before closing the doors, the bastards who took us threw in sealed bags of sandwich bread and bottles of water. I tested them on myself before I let any of the kids touch them, and I was fine.

I'm not sure how much time has passed since we've been here. The absence of light creates deceit, but I think at least two days have gone by. Although, my measuring system may be flawed. I can't truly trust my stomach since it's used to such little food, but I've been keeping track of Maya's hunger. So far, she's asked for food, albeit reluctantly, six times. I can't fully trust this method. It's not like we've been sleeping well. We drift in and out, caught in a daze that sometimes gets interrupted by the movements of the container.

I'm convinced we're on water, but I've been praying to all the gods I know that we're not leaving the country. It covers a vast continent, so maybe we're going to a different side of it. The alternative is dire. Even *when* we escape, it will add many more challenges. Requesting asylum with a child who isn't in my custody will be a sure way of losing Maya to the system. But at least she'll be out of here.

More time passes by, more meals for Maya, more screams, more cries, more begging for mamas and papas, more drifting in and out of sleep.

Until the jolts come.

I urge the kids to huddle together and protect each other while I keep Maya curled under my arm and the other kids hold on to us. My sister is the happiest, most easygoing and trusting kid, and the fact that she's been so quiet is unbearable. I've talked to her and soothed her the best I could, but even now, as the container jolts in all directions, she barely whimpers.

The exhaustion is almost debilitating, but when the container stops moving and thrashing us around, adrenaline kicks in, pumping new energy back into me. Not the good kind of energy. No, the kind of jittery energy that makes me shake with the fearful anticipation of what's coming next. I hope that when the time comes, I'll find the physical strength to do what I need to protect her.

Muffled words sound outside these metal walls, and the cries of the kids grow.

"Shh..." I attempt to calm them. Only some of them listen.

The side of the container rattles, and my sister finally makes a sound, yelping as her small body flinches.

When the noises intensify, I squeeze her tighter. "I'll keep you safe, Maya."

The metal box jolts again, and it feels like we're being lifted. Controlling my fear is proving so much harder than I thought it would be. When my sister groans, I realize I've been squeezing her a bit too tight.

My thoughts stray to this unbearable helplessness, to our dad, and to the fact that no one will search for us. Maybe Maya's school will contact the police when they discover that the address they have for her is fake. That could be our shot at having someone to look for us, but the people who took us are highly professional, so I doubt there's even the slightest trail.

We're screwed.

I don't realize the container has stopped moving until the door cracks open, and the screeching pierces through my eardrums. All at once the kids throw themselves back against the walls.

Squeezing Maya to me, I brace myself for the worst.

* * *

From the moment those doors opened to what seems like a vast warehouse, everything has been happening so fast, and I'm struggling to wrap my mind around things. Initially, I thought we reached our destination, but the shock and disbelief in the expressions of the men looking back at us made it clear these were not the same ones who took us. Those types of emotions cannot be faked, not by men who look as hard as them.

Slowly, pity bled through their gazes.

I counted eight people walking around, running their hands nervously through their hair, talking heatedly. Though a few of them seemed to only stand silent and take orders. Some were dressed for combat—boots, cargo pants, casual T-shirts—but others gave me grave vibes in their black, tailored suits. One in particular seemed to be in charge, and the man stood out in his three-piece suit, ordering the others around to do things for us.

They gave us food, more water, and asked the kids if they were hurt.

But they didn't let us out.

Instead, they left the doors cracked open so we could get some air and light.

I tried to peek around for an escape route, but I'm too deep into this space. Even so, running while herding thirty kids will be impossible. All I could do was sit, wait, and listen.

Now, something is changing.

More footsteps approach, and with them, another spike of adrenaline surges through my veins. Though it prickles up my spine more like fear.

"This is one thing I won't work with, and I'm convinced you won't agree with it either."

The container opens fully again, and I grab onto my sister, trying to peek from the darkness—four new men stand in front of us. Their features are grim, but there's something about the look in their eyes that doesn't just remind me of anger. It's something more.

Darker.

My gaze flickers to the wavy-haired blonde one who asked a question I didn't hear, and I can't tear my eyes away. I can't see his from here, but that expression... It's different from the others.

Parts of their conversation breaks through the haze. It sounds like this container belongs to someone they made some sort of business deal with, only, they weren't supposed to be transporting people.

The moment I hear someone say that they have to close it back up, heat fills my chest. I want to scream, I want to shout at them and beg them to reconsider. But the words don't come. My mouth falls open, yet the sounds don't even reach my throat. I manage to rise and lean toward the men and their plan to seal our fate.

The discussion turns heated, kids begin crying, covering their ears as they likely struggle to understand what they're hearing. I barely can.

"That's complete fucking madness!" someone shouts.

I think it was the man who towers over all the others. He looks ready to pounce and fight them all, angrily swiping a hand over his buzz-cut hair.

I agree, it *is* complete madness! My sister and all these kids need to be saved. They have to save us. They have to let us go. I want to shout at them, demand they free us. But the blonde one speaks again, and my thoughts pause all at once when his voice breaks through my own raging thoughts.

"Are you fucking saying that we're supposed to close these doors and let them go wherever the fuck those assholes are taking them?!" He shouts those words with so much rage woven through each syllable, that I almost miss the emotion at the base of it—*pain*.

There's something deep within his chiseled features, behind those golden curls, which hold a particular type of pain. I can't take my eyes off of him, and he looks like he can't bear to look at us. Maybe he's disgusted. I wouldn't blame him. However, his outrage is unmissable.

"We don't have a choice," the man with black hair, who is dressed from head to toe in the same color, says. "They can't know we're aware of this. This is the quickest way to find out where they're taking them, because this operation might be bigger than this one container. The hydra has many heads, and we need to cut the root and find all of them. Saving just them will not save all the others. If there are any others."

Oh my god, there could be more kids?

I've been so wrapped up in our circumstances—our fate. I didn't even think about the possibility that there are more. That we may not be the first *shipment*. How many more could there be? Before us... after us? How many children are missing their parents, their grandparents, their siblings? Children stolen from their beautiful lives, maybe even unfortunate ones, now made so much worse.

"We need someone on the inside. But none of Katya's employees would fit in. None of them look remotely young enough," someone else says.

My mind reels with images of what those men are doing to these pure souls. Countless missing posters holding the faces of the kids surrounding me flash behind my eyes. Some of them aren't even in school yet, young enough that it wasn't long since they stopped wearing diapers. There are others like them taken by the same scumbags. They're abusing them... raping them.

Oh, my god.

Tears well in my eyes.

They're raping them!

A visceral shake erupts from deep within my bones, and I squeeze Maya closer. God, why does she have to hear this? Why do all the other children have to hear this conversation? But there could be many more like them who are actually experiencing all these horrific things.

I could do it. Right? I could be their person on the inside.

No, no, no! What if something happens to Maya? Or to me, and I'm unable to protect her? I can't do this. I have nothing to offer them.

But they're sending us anyway. Whether I volunteer myself or not, they said they need to make sure there aren't others, and I'll end up in the same place. At least this way, not only do we have a better shot at being rescued, potentially not being hunted down again, but more kids might be saved.

Bending down slightly, I whisper to my sister, "I think I'm going to help them."

"But it sounds dangerous," she whispers back.

"I'm going to be fine, sweet girl."

It's not technically a lie.

"Is it true? Are there others?" she asks, her voice shaky.

"Maybe..."

I feel the bobbing of her head against me, and I have to let go of her, because my trembling seems to increase as the decision sinks in. Two deep breaths don't seem to help. The third one doesn't even reach too deep. But this is the only way... the only control I have over this situation.

"I'll—I'll do it," I say out loud before I can talk myself out of it.

I struggle up to my feet, urging Maya to stay where she is. The tall man with a buzz-cut rushes to me as I force my weak legs to move forward. He's moving too fast, his eyes fierce as he reaches for me, and I scurry back.

The whole space falls silent—both the container and the men watching us. My gaze drifts over each of them, but no one says a word.

I've already made a horribly poor choice this week by parking in that alley. Am I about to make yet another one by offering myself up and trusting them? It could be a stupid move, but the anger and disgust at our situation bleeding out of their gazes, gives me confidence.

They will rescue us, even if it's not happening right now.

It's a choice I will likely regret, because they can't guarantee our safety once we're out of their hands. And something about these men screams of a world I loathe, illegitimate business affairs, and danger. Yet, between the two evils currently in my life, they might be the better one.

One deep breath later, I reach over to the man who, in this confined space, looks like an absolute beast, and he takes my hand, leading me out of the metal box. There's no missing the wet spots my broken shoes leave on the floor. I would crawl into a hole if I could.

Will they know what that is? What I'm leaving behind?

It's silly to ponder, but surrounded by all these well-dressed, clean men, I experience an incredibly overwhelming sense of inferiority.

Someone brings a chair, and I'm urged to take a seat. I stifle a groan when I settle on the basic wooden structure that shouldn't feel like anything special, but after sitting on the floor of a shipping container for God knows how long, this is heaven.

"I'll do it. If there's more," I glance toward the inside of the container, "I want to find them. But it has to happen fast. I can't risk them getting… I can't." I sigh, forcing the images of what could be done to them out of my mind.

"I know. I understand," the one dressed in all black answers.

When I look at him, I swear my soul stalls. He has black eyes, too, like a dark devil. He stands here, and the anger simmering just beneath the surface is all kinds of wrong. Disturbing.

He says something about a tracker and my gaze wanders to another man I only catch a glimpse of before he turns on his heels and rushes toward a door.

"We're going to put a tracker on you. It's going to be small. You might have to swallow it or—" The black-eyed man stops short, as if he's thinking.

"It's okay. I'll do whatever it takes. Slice me open and put it under my skin. I don't care. Just... help them."

Guilt has a louder voice than my logic, and I think it's why I'm so driven to sacrifice myself now. Closing my eyes, I take a deep, centering breath, but I startle when someone asks my name.

"Evelyn," I answer, though it comes out more like a whisper.

My gaze wanders around the space but settles on the blonde man with sun-kissed curls, and I have to swallow one too many times as his broken, blue gaze pins me in place.

"How old are you?" he asks.

I wasn't mistaken before—sadness definitely hides behind his anger.

"Seventeen." I turn toward the container. "My sister is seven." This is not a piece of information I thought I would share, but it might work as motivation for them. Appeal to their compassionate side—if they have one.

"Fucking hell." His voice lowers with a different type of fury. An uncontrollable one. Maybe I was successful.

"We'll get you all out. That's a promise. But you have to be strong. I just don't know what will happen as soon as you'll arrive wherever they're taking you," the black-eyed one says. He's convincing in his uncomfortably honest tone.

I flinch when he reaches over and attempts to soothe me, his hand touching my shoulder. I'm not sure why, but my gaze shifts to the buzz-cut man who stands firm next to me. Maybe I'm going crazy, but for some reason, I think I'm looking for reassurance from him. How bizarre.

Yet, I get exactly that. His eyes reveal the gentlest, most tragic gaze. He's built like a beast, but all I see is compassion and warmth in his gaze.

"Will they—will they get to the children?" I all but whisper. I don't want the kids to hear me.

"I really hope not, but I don't want to lie to you."

It was a stupid question I can't believe I asked. They're not psychic. How are they supposed to know?

"I understand."

"Where did they take you from?" the one standing beside me asks.

"Various places. We're not all from the same city... They just brought us all to the same place. My sister and I, they took us when I was picking her up from school after work."

"What about your parents? They must be looking for you."

I hesitate. We need to be saved, but we can't be sent back to Fleeton. Not until I figure it all out. Will they hand us over to CPS? I'm over-thinking this. I need to take it one step at a time.

"They, um—It's only us two." I stop to wipe from my cheeks tears I didn't realize were falling. "I can't fail her."

"You won't. We'll get you out before anything happens," the blonde one promises, and once again, I'm fully trapped in his gaze.

It's so different from everyone else's in this room. Emotional and tragic. Why is he reacting so differently than the others, even though they all look cut from the same cloth?

Something inside of me, a stray piece of my soul, wants to reach out and find out why. It's a visceral need, inappropriate too, but it demands his comfort. To give and receive.

Jesus, this is—it's wrong. I'm... wrong.

The men talk between themselves now, and I quietly ask the one beside me where we are.

"Queenscove," he answers.

"On the South coast?" I'm filled with a bit more hope.

"Yes."

Thank God! We're still in the country. Just... around twelve hundred miles away.

The man who left earlier returns, walking toward me with determined steps.

I sense the blonde man's gaze, like the brush of heat over my skin. Even as everyone in this room have their eyes on me, only his touch me. It burns. It stings. It almost hurts. Although, that hurt might be self-inflicted by my shame at the pleasure of the heat.

"This is the tracker." I'm handed a pill. *This* is a tracker? "It won't dissolve, it's specially made. But it will pass through. Keep it in your mouth for as long as you can. Swallow it only if they try to check your mouth, okay?"

I nod, looking at the pill in disbelief before sliding it between my cheek and molars.

The man next to me helps me up and guides me back into the metal box that threatens to be my demise. I won't let it, though. I refuse to have anything happen to my sister—to any of these kids.

The metal doors grind my eardrums as they screech behind me, and I flinch, memories of the first time I heard them scaring the soul out of me. But it's different now. These men are trying to save us. They might be seeking their own goals, but a lot of effort seems to be put into us. So, I decide to entrust them with something else.

I stop and turn just before the door swallows the light.

"When it's done," the door stops and the men watch me and wait, "I can't have the police knowing of me and my sister. It's only us, and they'll split us up. I'll lose her to the system."

The buzz-cut beast nods, the promise vivid in his eyes.

Then, the world turns dark.

The fear returns with a vengeance, but at least now I have something else to balance it—hope.

If only it lasts.

Half an hour passes by. The doors open again, and dread fills me with such force, bile rises up my throat. Especially when my eyes land on the man who took us. He stands next to a new guy who points at me as we're urged out of the container and into the back of a truck.

The new guy watches me with far too much interest for my liking, but I get it—I wasn't supposed to be here. I'm too old.

Which means that they might try to get rid of me. I'm no use to them.

The insoluble tracker-pill sits against my cheek, and it grounds me peculiarly. It's a reminder that I have to stay strong for Maya. And for the other kids.

The urge to grab my sister and run is so strong, my legs shake and fingers twitch. But we're pushed and forced to move faster, and the truck door closes behind us before the urge settles.

I can't even process how much time passes until the drive ends. I've spent it all going through likely scenarios in my head, whilst holding onto Maya for dear life. She's still quiet. In a way, I'm happy. Maybe she's dissociated somehow.

What should I do?

How do I protect her?

I just have to stall. I have to keep an eye on her. Just until the men who own this tracker come for us.

And they will come.

They will come on time.

The curly-haired blonde one promised.

"Take them all to the assessment room!" a man shouts over the voices of crying children as we're *herded* out of the truck and into what looks like an abandoned factory.

I stumble but catch myself just as the same man who was watching me before, turns to look at me. He was the one shouting. He leans in toward the guy beside him and whispers something into his ear, his eyes never leaving mine.

I don't feel good about this. At all.

Driven by instinct, I swallow the tracker pill I was holding in my mouth.

"Evie?" Maya's voice startles me. "Evie, what's happ—"

"Not you." A hand wraps painfully around my bicep, hauling me away with enough force that I lose my feet.

"No! Let me go!" I shout, thrashing to break free as another guy grabs Maya from behind.

All the kids turn, and at the sight, a cacophony of fear fills the space. They cry and yell, some of them shout in pain when the men who watch them hit them to silence, and tears of frustration and fear blur my vision.

I fight the one who holds me, kicking and punching in a whirl of untrained moves that don't take me anywhere. But I do it anyway, aiming for low spots, for his belly and groin, anything that could make him lose his grip.

With the loudest of thuds, my ear rings. It takes a second to register the pain that comes with it.

"Shut the fuck up!" someone shouts, but the threat sounds muffled.

"Let me go! I need to be there with them! With—"

"No. You're coming with me. I need to find out what you're worth."

I turn my gaze to the man who spoke those heavy words. It's him... the one who seems to run things. The one who watched me.

"Although," he continues, "I might keep you all to myself, regardless."

My lungs heave with quickening breaths, and the visceral scream that breaks out of me is followed by furious thrashes in an attempt to escape once more. But he grabs me by the hair, my messy ponytail so tight in his hand, my skull burns.

It takes but two seconds more, then pain shoots on the right side of my skull, and my world falls into darkness.

CHAPTER 1

Finnigan

THE FLOWERS WEIGH STRANGELY HEAVY in my hand. As heavy as the uncertainty weighing me down.

What the hell am I doing coming here with flowers?

I already knocked, damn it. Footsteps approach behind the door—it's too late to throw them away.

The lock clicks and Katya greets me, but she's not alone. A little figure squeezes between her and the edge of the door, looking at me with green doe eyes.

The sister.

"Hennessey. Come on in," Katya greets, dressed much more casually than her usual pantsuits. "Maya, go on, let him in."

"Who are you?" she asks before she dares to move.

"I'm Finnigan."

The little girl narrows her eyes on me, scrutinizing my

presence, though it comes across as more cute than menacing.

Her eyes seem to sparkle when they notice the flowers. She's around seven years old, if I remember correctly, yet she seems untouched by the events that almost took her on an unthinkable path.

"Are those for me?" she asks.

"Maya," Katya warns.

"Yes, sugar." She gives me a way out, and I'm gladly taking it, leaning in and handing her the bouquet.

"Lilacs!" she exclaims, looking back at me in awe. "My favorites! How did you know?"

I realize that I'm fidgeting with my fingers, and I shove my hands in my pockets to stop myself. I'm not used to interacting with such small humans, even if I do have a nephew roughly her age. Granted, I've never met him. But Maya's smile is infectious, and one pulls at my lips too.

"Lucky guess," I answer.

"Thank you!" She jumps in excitement and disappears inside.

Katya shakes her head, gesturing me in, her expression as composed as ever. I don't miss the amusement in her dark eyes, though.

"How is *she*?" I ask.

"Not as well as she tries to make it up to be." She knows I'm not referring to the tiny human.

We walk into her kitchen, and I prop my elbows on the central island, looking into the open-plan living area. Katya fills a vase with water and takes it over to the coffee table. Maya carefully places each flower stem in, looking at the scented greenery like they're the greatest gift.

"Were those for Evelyn?" Katya asks when she returns next to me, watching me intently.

"No."

The answer comes too quick and one of her perfectly plucked eyebrows quirks. But she doesn't press. She knows better than to do it.

"Where is she?" I ask.

"In the bedroom."

"She trusts you with her sister?" I ask.

"No. She doesn't trust anyone. Though I think she acknowledges I'm not a threat. But whatever they did to her in there is still coming out of her system. She drifts in and out, no matter how much she fights it." Katya sighs, crossing her arms against her chest, and looks over to the little girl. "And she really is a fighter, Finnigan."

I have limited information about the girl beyond her name—Evelyn Shaw—but based on what I've witnessed, I am convinced that she is a fighter. She didn't hesitate to throw herself in the deep end in order to save all the children. One hundred and twenty-three souls are alive because of her sacrifice.

"Can I see her?" I ask before I can stop myself.

"Why?" Katya narrows her eyes on me.

Why, indeed. What am I looking to achieve?

"If she's up for it, I have some questions."

"She's already been asked questions by the others, Finnigan."

"We have more."

No, we don't.

She sighs and points to the corridor leading to the bedrooms. Only, we're both taken by surprise when we turn that way. Me more than Katya.

Evelyn stands at the entrance to that hall, holding her sister against her front, arms slid protectively over her chest. Her fierce gaze lingers on me. She's watching me closely, not like prey, but equally ready to flee at the first sight of danger.

She hasn't blinked yet.

Neither have I.

There's an internal struggle happening, bleeding through her distant gaze. She's tired. Still alert, but on the edge of disorientation.

No words leave her full, berry-colored lips, but she looks weary. Almost scared.

"It's okay, Evelyn. He just came to check on you and Maya," Katya says, breaking the silence.

"I'm sorry to wake you," I say to her, forcing my voice to steady so I don't make her more uncomfortable than she already is.

Only... I can't break eye contact. I try, but the little voice in my head tells me she might never look me in the eye again if I do. For some reason, that bothers me.

"Did something happen?" Evelyn asks.

Christ, her voice is so soft. The tonality like cashmere, brushing dangerously pleasant against my ears. Her gaze is more focused—but luckily still fixed on me.

"Nothing happened. I wanted to see how yo—*both* of you are doing." I think I forgot how words work.

She notices, and I swear she looks a shade brighter.

There's no denying she just woke up. Her wheat-colored hair is messy and wrapped in a bun above her head. Stray strands fall around her delicate, slightly gaunt features. She looks sun-kissed with her medium-toned olive skin. It makes her eyes pop—golden sun-burst seeping into ash, followed by a thick, dark ring.

She is...

She's quite something.

I shake the thought away before it has a chance to linger. This is far beyond dangerous territory. It doesn't just touch on the forbidden, it's smack bang in the middle of it.

"He brought me flowers!" Maya exclaims, pointing enthusiastically at the bouquet on the coffee table and pulling all of us out of this tension.

Her sister isn't impressed. On the contrary—There's suspicion in her eyes.

"We're okay," she adds. "Ekaterina has been good to us.

We're the reason why Katya has been good to them, we arranged it all, and made sure they were taken care of and provided for.

But I say nothing to her.

"If you're here to find out how long we'll be staying, we will leave as soon as we are able to. I just need to—"

"I'm not here to make you leave," I interrupt. "Stay as long as you want. We can find you a place of your own when you feel safer—"

"No. We'll be fine. Thanks." She cuts me off before I can continue.

Her gaze finds other interests, like the top of her sister's head, or the floor. It flickers from her feet to me. Almost like she's stealing looks.

A discomfort seems to settle in her.

Considering what she's been through, I can't blame her. Though, she hasn't shared much about that. Only details about the kids, what she saw and heard, but nothing about herself. She brushed all those questions off like they were irrelevant. Maddox was the one who found her that night, and in the chaos of the rescue, I didn't lay eyes on her. He said if she has anything to share, she will, but we won't force it out of her.

"It's no bother at all. We're more than willing to help."

"We don't need any more help from people li—We're fine." Her tone is firmer, with an edge of disdain, and her eyes don't meet mine anymore. I don't fail to see the aversion in her expression, though.

Well, what the fuck was that?

To say I'm a little confused is an understatement. Seconds ago, she was watching me like a hawk. I could have sworn her cheeks even flushed.

I take a step around the kitchen island, and she tightens her hold around her sister as her eyes shoot to mine, but it's for a few moments and she averts them again.

Those moments were enough to send all the wrong sensations through me.

"Right. Well, if you need anything…" I take a couple of steps away. "I have to go."

I rush to the door and grip the handle.

"I thought you had questions," Katya says behind me.

"Later. I realized I have a previous *engagement*."

"Date?" Katya raises her voice after me.

"Yeah, a date." It's a lie, but right now, I think it's exactly what I need. A woman to take my mind off of… everything.

I'm out in a split second, snapping the door shut behind me, and I exhale so loudly, one would think I held my breath the entire time I was in there.

What happened in that apartment?

And do I actually want the answer to that question?

Evelyn

I STOOD PINNED IN PLACE in Ekaterina's living room for far too long after the blonde man—the man I now know as Finnigan—left. Only when Maya began to forcefully wiggle out of my grip did I snap out of the daze I was trapped in, and I realized I was still watching the hallway leading to the front door.

Why?

He looked like he couldn't bear to be here anymore. To see my pitiful self. Like my presence was a stain on his pristine image. He walked out of here so fast.

Then why is his image still lingering in my mind?

Because it never left.

Not since the first moment I saw the cracks in his blue eyes. They stayed with me after the container doors closed for the last time. His image was burned into my retinas as my kidnapper separated me from the children. And it turned sour when his promise was broken... when the man with the lisp asked the others to pin me down so he could find a good vein. Even as I stared at my attacker, Finnigan's face appeared like a mirage before my eyes, their faces blending together.

We'll get you out before anything happens...

His words lost all their meaning then, as my reality began to break after the needle left my arm, and I was flipped to my front. His was the last face I saw when I closed my eyes as my pants were being yanked down. When my ass cheeks were being pulled open and spit hit the tight spot between them.

His beautiful blue eyes were watching in my mind as tears spilled from mine, and searing pain ripped my scalp and body before the colorful, confusing darkness took me away.

That's why I can't move. Because seeing him again feels like he's still watching me as he repeats his broken promise to me. Over and over again. Through the haze of my attack... he's there.

"Evelyn? I think you should come sit and eat something." Ekaterina's voice is soft as she gently attempts to grab my attention.

The frown pulling at her arched eyebrows doesn't match the tone, though. She's worried.

I'm not even sure how long we've been staying here with her. Two, three days? No, it can't be. It's been longer than that. Maybe a week. The drugs, whatever those men filled my veins with, should be gone by now. Then why am I still so hazy? So broken? So... thirsty?

Sweat drips down my spine, my hands turn clammy, my muscles heat beneath my skin, and my blood vessels... they scream at me.

They scream for that sickly rush. The disgusting pleasure it brought with it. For the haze that pulled me from reality, into a place far, far away, where my body wasn't mine.

Where I was... not in pain.

"Evelyn?" Ekaterina's voice is louder, and I flinch.

My whole back is wet now. My temples too. Air spasms in my chest.

"I'm sorry. I just need a minute."

I stumble backwards and turn to rush through the short corridor. I reach the bathroom just as the bile sears my throat, and my knees hit the cold tiles.

I retch repeatedly, but there's nothing to throw up. Only this foamy thing that burns too much.

Delicate hands pull my hair away from the toilet, and the blood freezes in my veins. I want to scream, but bile comes out instead, and a fierce tremor takes over my body. I manage to swat the hands away from my hair, and I fall on my ass, scrambling backward until my back hits the wall.

I know it's Ekaterina. I am aware that it's her squatting before me. Yet my brain, my heart, my lungs aren't acknowledging it.

Her gaze softens—I'm not sure what she thinks she knows about my reaction, but she understands. Her eyes shift down, and I realize I've gathered all my hair to the side and I'm holding onto it like it's made of threads of pure gold.

She doesn't linger. Instead, she moves to wet a washcloth and approaches me slowly.

I let her.

She wipes my face gently and hands me something. When I look down, she holds a silk scrunchy. Funny how a silly hair tie has so much power in this moment.

I take it and wrap my hair into a low bun. It's quick and messy, but it doesn't matter. It's out of the way and I'm... safe.

"Come. Let's have some food. You need some meat on those bones."

I smile at her. The idea of being able to eat enough to put meat on my bones is enticing, and I'm definitely going to take her up on it. Lord knows this privilege won't last. I need to make sure Maya experiences it all before we have to move on.

"Thank you, Ekaterina." I take her hand and rise, my body

feeling more like it's mine again. The shivers haven't left me though.

"Please, call me Katya."

Katya. Like Finnigan called her.

What does she call him, I wonder?

Boss? Friend? Business partner? Lover?

That last one sounds wrong. And I truly hate myself for even thinking it does.

I follow the stunning redhead through her apartment, back into the living area where Maya quietly sits and watches an oldie cartoon on TV. She seems oblivious to it all. To our situation. To my failures.

"We can't stay here," I say as I take a seat at the kitchen island, suppressing a wince when I put my weight on my bottom. At this point I'm not sure if it still hurts or if it's the memory of my assault that does.

"Of course you can."

"No. You have your own life, and my sister and I need to get on with ours."

Katya quirks an eyebrow.

"It's not my place to question this, but I have to. What life is that, Evelyn?"

I'm both surprised and insulted. I'm aware I'm doing a shitty job at caring for my sister, but this doesn't mean I'm incompetent. We *do* have a life.

"You're right—it's not your place."

She doesn't react. Either she expected my reaction, or she simply doesn't care. She's not taking me seriously.

There's no way I'm going to show my weakness to this woman, to anyone for that matter, but... lord, she is right. What life? My sister cannot return to her old school. They probably already reported her as missing. The police would arrive as soon as she stepped over the threshold. She'd be taken away from me.

Katya is oblivious to my erratic and panicked train of thought as she slides over a deep plate with a soup that doesn't smell like any soup I've ever had.

I can't even bring myself to lift the spoon.

What will I do? I'll be eighteen soon. I'm not sure what date it is, but it must be a few weeks away. They can't take Maya from me then, I'll be a legal adult.

Yes. That's it. We can return to our home.

Home?

We have no home. My car has probably been towed by now. Social Services wouldn't allow Maya to stay with a homeless person. What if the men who took us come looking for us?

"Eat, Evelyn."

I attempt to shake all those thoughts away.

"But Maya."

"She's eaten already. Two bowls."

I shouldn't take her word for it. I should ask my sister myself. But this woman has done nothing but take care of us, of her, since she took us in.

Focusing on picking up the spoon, I take a whiff of the strange soup, and maybe it's the heat, or the blend of flavors, but it seems to calm my mind. It smells delicious.

"What is it?" I ask, dipping my spoon in.

"Borscht. It's like a sour soup. I made a leaner one, so as not to overload your stomach."

Do I truly look so malnourished? I don't remember the last time I looked at myself in a mirror from the bust down, when I wasn't drowning in my old, tattered clothes.

"Borscht," I repeat in a whisper.

The first sip of the *borscht* warms my whole soul in one swallow, and nothing can stop the moan vibrating in my chest. Either I'm really hungry, or this is one of the best dishes I've ever had. There are egg noodles in here, some finely sliced veg, potatoes, and delicious herbs that make me want to moan some more.

I dig in so hard, I don't even notice a shadow has fallen close to me until I've swallowed the last of the sour soup. It takes a lot of force not to fall off my chair when I turn toward the gigantic man standing at the end of the island—Maddox.

"Sorry, I didn't mean to—" He lifts a hand to excuse himself.

My memories of the night are fuzzy at best, but his strong, scared face floats there. He rescued me that night. Or he was one of the ones who did; I'm not sure if he was alone.

The day after, I woke up and screamed the house down for my sister. I still remember the terror in her eyes. Not because she was in danger, but because my screams scared her. She was... fine. Sleeping soundly on the sofa next to my bed, her head on the lap of this bear of a man.

He didn't quite know what to do with me apart from... being there. Quiet. Trying to make himself as nonthreatening as possible. After I calmed down slightly, he brought a doctor in. A female one, thankfully, and she checked us both over. I don't remember much of that interaction, apart from that fact that I didn't consent to more than a general checkup. He waited patiently outside until we were done, then came back in and asked me a bunch of questions about everything that happened.

There's something about his presence, about the way he looks at me and Maya. It seems very similar to the way I see my sister. There's comfort in that gaze, but I have questions, too. It's not my place, though.

"Sorry, I'm just a bit..."

"No need to explain. A few days have gone by, and I thought I would check up on you. See if you need anything," he says, pulling out a chair and taking a seat.

He's so tall, the bar stool looks like a normal chair for him.

"You too?" Katya asks.

He cocks his head and looks between us.

"Finnigan was here. Not even half an hour ago." She answers the unasked question.

He nods but doesn't add to that. For some reason, he doesn't seem that surprised, like it makes sense to him. To Katya too.

"How are you doing?" He turns to me.

"We're okay. Maya seems to be doing good, thanks to Eka—Katya," I say, quirking a lip at her. "It's strange, like she almost forgot what happened to her."

"What about you?" he asks again, and I'm a bit confused by the question. I just answered it.

"Like I said, we're okay."

For some reason that answer doesn't satisfy him, and a brief glance is exchanged with the redhead.

"Did you find them?" I ask, changing the subject.

"Not yet. Their operation is big. Established. You're safe, though. Do not worry about that, okay?" He says it with such conviction, I almost believe him.

I'm not sure what safety is anymore. The feeling of it is foreign now. I nod and push the empty bowl away from me, thanking Katya, before I step off the stool and walk toward my sister. She snuggles into me, laughing at whatever *Scooby Doo* has been doing. She's barely spoken about what happened to us, and this truly worries me. Is this how her trauma manifests? Did she compartmentalize in such a deep way that she has no idea what happened?

Maybe...

I sigh because the thought is ridiculous, considering my situation.

Maybe she needs a therapist.

I try not to laugh at myself. What am I gonna do? Get my

ass to the doctor and tell her that my sister and I are homeless, that we got kidnapped by a human trafficking ring, rescued by something that looks a lot like a crime syndicate, and now I'm worried my sister has repressed trauma? I'm sure the therapist will just be like *okay, let's crack on then*, and they're not going to call CPS and the police.

But I have to do something. She needs to have the best care. I can't fail her again, especially not when it comes to her mental health.

The last thing I want to do is ask these people for help. They took us in, but I do not want them to give me much more than this. Not when it might come at a cost I cannot pay.

I know nothing of this organization. They're probably just as bad as the people who took us in the first place.

No, not as bad.

Otherwise, I wouldn't be sleeping in the most comfortable bed in the world every night.

There has to be another way to get Maya into therapy. I will make it happen somehow. Maybe some homeschooling too; I don't want her schoolwork to suffer.

But I cannot accept more help. I refuse to sell my soul to them. I need to find a way out of this limbo. Regain some strength and then... get a job, I guess.

That thought makes me even more uncomfortable because it implies some sort of permanence here, in Queenscove. And that just can't be.

I cannot stay. *We* cannot stay.

We have something to return to back in Fleeton.

CHAPTER 2
Evelyn

Two men stand before Katya and me in her kitchen. Ice fills my chest, spreading over my lungs as far too many scenarios go through my head as I stare at the bald men. The instinct to run, find my sister, and hide with her, is straining my muscles.

But it's Katya's nonchalant presence keeping me in place as two pairs of brown eyes watch us with straight faces.

They look so similar.

"Evelyn, this is Brinn"—she points at the shorter, stockier man—"and this is Jay, his brother." She nods toward the taller, leaner one, with softer features.

Ah, that makes sense.

Yet my nerves haven't calmed. Fisting my hands, I try to hide my apprehension, but I don't think it's working.

"They look out for me," Katya continues. "They're usually

either here, the apartment next door, or walking about the building. They've been staying out of sight while you two got more used to your environment, but it's about time you met since you'll see more of them."

My chest staggers with heavy, strained breaths. Having these strangers around me is not my idea of security. Logically, I know that Katya's ease around them should help me calm down, but... they are still men.

Visions of the man with a lisp snap into my mind, and a shudder ripples through my spine at the lingering disgust.

"It's okay, they're here for my security, and now for yours and Maya's, too," Katya says quickly, noticing the sudden shake in my bones.

I don't think my sister and I are in enough danger to require *security*. What worries me more is the fact that I seem to have stumbled into a world where these people deem it normal to have their own security... just lingering about.

I shake my head. "Thank you, but we don't ne—"

"There are others that will come and go as well," she interrupts. "They will always report to Brinn or Jay, whichever one of them is here. They both have instructions to introduce you or make you aware of their presence until you remember who is who. Okay?"

Her words caught a stern tone toward the end, leaving no room to argue. I debate it for a few seconds, but in the end I nod. I understand that Katya and the others live a vastly different life than me, even compared to when my parents were still around, but on the clock security who have their own apartment next door?

Who is Katya? Who are all these people?

And why are we being given this privilege?

"If I'm not here and you feel unsafe, call for them." She shows me a shiny phone and places it on the island counter.

"This is yours. The red app on the first screen is a direct signal to them. If you want to go out and neither me nor one of the guys are around, use Jay or Brinn. They can drive you around, show you shops, cafés, the beach—anywhere you want, so you can get accustomed to Queenscove."

I scowl, finding this situation rather ridiculous. First of all, we're a bunch of nobodies. Two homeless, pretty much orphaned girls who got stupidly unlucky. Having a security escort is preposterous. On the other hand, I also want to burst out laughing at her mention of shops and cafés. Like I have money or can afford to be shopping around. I'm uncomfortable lounging in Katya's clothes, but even if I had money to spare, it would still be spent making sure Maya has everything she needs. I don't actually remember the last time I bought clothes for myself. And every time these people offered to do it for me, I refused.

I've taken too much from Katya already. I can't accept this too. Hand-me-downs are fine for now. Not for Maya, though. She got some new clothes from her.

"I appreciate it, but they should stay focused on you. We don't need any *security*." That word tastes wrong on my tongue.

"Evelyn, they are focused on me. And you and Maya are here, so they are focused on you too. You have everything you need in this apartment, but we both know that you will burst out of your skin soon, being cooped up for so long. It's not my place, but you've been through hell all on your own. This way, you won't be alone as you see the city and get used to it. You'll be safe."

But being alone is exactly what I want. She's both right and wrong about the whole bursting out of my skin business, but it's not a matter of the future. I'm already there. The shivers, the cold sweats, the gnawing somewhere in the hollow of my chest is screaming at me. I want to go out. I want to be alone. I want to search the seedy streets of Queenscove to find something. I don't know what it is, but my veins are begging for it either way. I'm afraid I may be willing to risk too much to find it.

Sinking my teeth into my tongue, I try to push the perilous thought away. But it's been with me since I woke up from the daze. When I forced down the groans that came with each movement that made my body burn with pain. When I wondered who pulled my clothes back up? Who cleaned me, wiped the blood from between my legs? *Was* there any blood?

A few more memories came back to me, though they feel like disjointed nightmares, not things I experienced. Just over a week has passed, and I'm done remembering. I don't want the memories to come back. I can't... I can't have them back.

I want oblivion.

"Hi, I'm Maya." My sister jumps out of nowhere, startling me.

A drop of sweat trickles down my spine, and I'm itching to jump into a shower. A cold one.

"Hi," the men say in unison. "It's nice to meet you, Maya."

Looking at my little sister, I realize that it would be stupid of me to fight this and refuse the privilege. It's not about me. I wasn't able to protect her, so why risk not having the extra hand that is so much more capable than mine?

"It's my turn today," Jay says, "but we wanted to drop by together to introduce ourselves. Get acquainted."

"I have to leave for the day. I have quite a bit of work to do. But I will be back tonight," Katya says, turning to grab her expensive looking bag off the bar stool. "I don't think I'll be here in time for dinner, but there is food in the fridge and the boys know the good take outs in the area as well."

"Thank you," I say, already knowing we will be eating whatever is available here.

I feel sorry about this. She hasn't left this apartment since we came here. Not while I was awake, anyway. We've kept her away from her work, from whatever responsibilities she holds. I should ask her what she does for a living.

She's only around mid-thirties, and this apartment cannot be cheap. Even if she rents. And the way she's dressed—a tailored dark green pantsuit hugs her slender, tall body, and shiny high heels that must cost more than all the clothes I've ever worn are wrapped around her feet. She's important, and I kept her from whatever fuels her lifestyle.

"We appreciate this... Brinn, Jay," I say, finally addressing the men. "Thank you, Katya."

Brinn nods and follows her out.

"I'll be outside if you need me," Jay says with an almost cold, impersonal expression in his features.

I want to ask him what he means by that. Where outside? Literally standing in the corridor? Will he stand or sit? I feel bad, but I don't know the man, so I don't ask a thing. He leaves a moment later, and for the first time since we were taken, Maya and I are alone. Not just that, we're in a *home*. Albeit a neatly manicured one, but a home, nonetheless. No car. No shoddy motel. No... danger.

Looking around, it takes but a second to realize that I have no idea what to do with myself.

"Do you think Katya will mind if I take out one of her books?" Maya pulls my attention, standing in front of a narrow bookcase.

I head her way and glance at some of the titles—classics. Foreign titles, too. Kafka, Dostoevsky, Orwell.

"I'm afraid none of these books are for your age, honey."

The complexities of the works are unsurprising for a woman like Katya. There is warmth in her, but it's hidden under cold, hard layers only she can peel. She's done it for me—briefly. She does it for Maya more.

Everyone does it for my sister, though. She bears our mother's soft eyes, but not her personality. None of ours, actually. Maya's a social extrovert in a family of introverts, and not only that, but people naturally gravitate toward her. Then she pries them open and doesn't even acknowledge *no* as a valid answer. Or one that exists. She understands limits, but I swear she can see right through a person and notice that the limits they set are not the ones they truly want. So, she feigns ignorance and pushes on. She's going to be a force to be reckoned with when she grows up.

I spot something familiar on the bookshelf. A book that looks out of place amongst the others, not because of the subject matter, but because of how cracked the spine is— *Twenty Thousand Leagues under the Sea*, by Jules Verne. I reach for it and carefully slide it out.

"This one, Maya. I think you'll like Captain Nemo's adventure." I flip briefly through its pages to make sure it's still in good condition, then hand it over to her.

She reaches over, eyes sparkling with excitement, and turns it carefully in her little palms like it's some sort of treasure. In two seconds flat she's throwing herself on the sofa, the world around her lost. I won't get a word out of her until dinner. But I can't help but smile at her joy. Yet the muscles in my cheeks seem strained at the movement. Like they haven't done such an exercise in so long.

* * *

Lights flicker from an overhead bulb. Two men speak around me—it's him, the one who took me. The one who...

"You're my glory hole now," he speaks into my ear, his pronounced lisp sending tiny splatters of spittle along with the words.

I say nothing. I can't. My tongue is numb and heavy in my mouth. It's not clear if those words were actually spoken, or I imagined them. They float in my world of colors like they were thrown into the universe, and I happen to encounter them here.

Something sharp breaks through my skin, and an uncomfortable heat fills my body. Even after the weight of the man with the lisp leaves my back, the heaviness lingers. I want to reach for that sensation, wrap it in a soft cocoon, and nurture it back to something beautiful.

I can't get to it, though. In this kaleidoscope of colors, that one is a void, and I can't latch onto it.

"I think I'll ask the boss to keep you. All to myself." His voice echoes.

My mind reels. It doesn't feel like it's mine. My veins carry a fire in them, a comfortable one that tickles all my nerves, sending enough pleasure through the fibers, and the void seems to be pushed farther in the background.

I don't understand what's happening. It's heaven and hell, beauty and sickness all at once.

A new person appears in my line of sight. Older, walking with a limp, and ordering everyone around.

"Vassallo," I hear someone say. What a strange name.

I try to focus on their conversation, but the words don't register. They're looking at me now. The voices grow louder.

"Why is she still alive?" the limping man asks, sending a deep shiver down my spine. "She's too old."

Too old? Oh yes, they're talking about me. They were only interested in kids. Like my sister.

My sister! Where is she?

My brain begins to register who it belongs to, but those signals don't reach my limbs. They refuse the connection with their nerves, but I need to find Maya.

Tar has my arms trapped, but a cold thread zaps through one of them. It moves, but I'm not sure I'm the one controlling it. It doesn't feel like it.

None of this feels like me.

I can't tell if my body is mine anymore. There is no longer a sense of being connected.

But when the limping older man presses his thick boot against my shoulder and rolls me over ever so slightly, I know that I don't want to be me right now. Not when evil pours out of his gaze and spills onto me with such disdain, I don't understand.

A scream driven by nothing but fear lodges in my throat. Something hot trickles at the corner of my eye. The younger of the two men drops on one knee next to me, leans in slightly, and reaches over. Stings rip my scalp as my head is yanked up by the hair, and a seedy grin contorts his face as he stares at me.

"I want to keep her," he says to the older man standing next to him, his gaze fixed on me.

Then Vassallo cocks his head, and with one simple grin, he chills my bones.

"You might have to share this one."

The scream bursts out of me at the same time my limbs are released, and my whole upper body shoots up. Only, I'm no longer in that warehouse, but sitting on a soft bed, surrounded by ridiculously fluffy pillows.

"Evie?"

I follow my sister's voice, turning to my right, and lit up by the faint moonlight is her pretty face, marred by worry and slight fear.

"I'm so sorry, honey. It was just a bad dream. I'm sorry." I lean over to kiss her soft forehead, then lie down next to her and scoop her in my arms.

"But you—you were crying and saying some things."

The sleep leaves me in an instant and my eyes widen with

the impact of her words. I'm scared to ask what I was saying.

"I'm sorry I woke you. It was just a nightmare. Everything's okay."

Only, it's not.

I can't do this to her—bleed my trauma onto her innocent soul. And the talking? It simply won't do. I have to find a solution for this. A different arrangement. If we continue sharing a room and the nightmares carry on, it could traumatize her. Especially if I talk in my sleep about things that should never reach her innocent ears.

"What did I say?" I risk it because I have to know how grave it is or could be.

Maya hesitates for a moment. "You were mumbling about keeping something, then you kept asking for me. Where I was, I think."

"I'm sorry, honey. Go on, go back to sleep."

A soft knock sounds at the door.

"Yes?" I answer, but I can't hide the apprehension in my tone.

It opens slightly and Katya peeks through, light streaming in with her. Brinn stands behind her, his expression stern.

"Are you okay?" she asks.

"Yes, sorry, just a bad dream. I'm sorry I woke you."

"No need to apologize. Do you need anything?"

"I'm okay. Thank you... I'm sor—"

She raises a palm to stop me. "I'm here if you need... anything."

There's an implication there. An invitation to be comforted, to talk if I need to. I'm grateful but talking is the last thing I wish to do. Talking means rehashing, and all I want to do is forget.

Not that I remember that much anyway.

I nod and she leaves, closing the door and returning us

into darkness.

One thing I'm grateful for is that our experience didn't take away from me the comfort of the shadows and replace it with fear. Whether dimly moonlit or pitch black, the absence of light brings me a sense of calm and security. It's ironic, I know.

Why do I feel guilty that those horrible people didn't take this away from me?

It shouldn't be like this. Right? Other vic—No!

I will not say that word.

I am not *that*.

Stroking Maya's hair, I urge her to fall back asleep, only I notice that the faint light I was seeing wasn't moonlight at all. The sun rises slowly, and I urge myself to fall back asleep, even if just for another hour or so.

Only, my mind wanders. It wanders back to the man who came here with flowers he never gave me and left with ire in his eyes.

He confused me, and I've been trying to understand what happened for the last two days. He was eager, then a switch flipped, and he couldn't distance himself fast enough.

But unfortunately, that's not all... my mind wanders to the brightness of his blue eyes, his messy, blonde curls, and to his high, defined cheekbones.

It's all flavors of wrong.

Yet, I'm curious of the taste of them all.

CHAPTER 3
Evelyn

KATYA WAS RIGHT—I'M BURSTING out of my skin in this apartment. I have more space here than in our old house. Much more than my car or the shoddy motel rooms. Still, I'm beginning to feel claustrophobic.

There's an ache beneath my skin, an itch I can't scratch, and thirst that I fail to quench no matter how I occupy my time. Maybe getting out of here is the solution. I have to.

I need to.

Jay is here today. We're alone again as Katya had to go to work sometime around nine this morning, and I still didn't ask about her job. The opportunity came, but I chickened out. Even confined to this apartment, it's not hard to piece things together and understand the type of world I stumbled into. And I fear I might judge her when she reveals it. I don't want to resent her for being part of what's clearly an organization dealing in less than legal endeavors. Even if she's been helping us selflessly.

At least, I think it is selfless. Nothing has been asked of me—of us—so far.

If I'm right about her and their world, it might be better for mine and my sister's safety to remain oblivious.

I shake my head before dropping it in my hands and rub my face as I brace my elbows against my knees.

That's not me, though. No matter what the truth is, I've never been, nor will I ever be, a foolish, oblivious person. I can't live in the belly of the beast without knowing its breed. I need to find out what I have gotten us into, and how to leave.

I jump when a knock sounds at the door, but it opens before I can react. Jay walks in, followed by a tall, dark shadow.

"Maddox," I say on a sharp exhale, my back relaxing the moment the man comes into view.

He nods his hello, looking awkward as he walks into the apartment and shoves his hands in his pockets. I'm not sure if he's uncomfortable being here, or in those jeans that seem a little too stiff on him. Are they new?

"Is everything okay?" I ask when he doesn't say anything.

This might be the best opportunity for me to get answers to all those questions I've been having. Although, I've noticed that he's quite guarded and doesn't like to speak much. It's not like I can ask anyone else, besides Katya. I don't know the others.

Yes, you do—the golden-haired man who slipped into your dream once you fell back asleep last night.

I shut down that ridiculous train of thought before it has time to settle.

"Everything's fine. Just wanted to see how you're doing," Maddox finally answers, and I'm so freaking thankful he did, because my mind needs to stay occupied. And distracted.

Definitely distracted.

"Actually, I remembered something, a name." I pause, but Maddox doesn't say a thing, just waits. "Vassallo. That guy with a lisp called him boss."

Maddox nods and pulls out his phone that looks comical in his huge hands.

"Katya mentioned you haven't left the apartment yet," he says as he slides the phone back in his pocket.

"Not yet, no. We just"—we don't have money to go anywhere—"didn't know where to go."

Maddox tilts his head, fixing me with his gaze.

"I thought Katya told you to use Jay or Brinn. They know Queenscove like the back of their hands, they can show you everything. You must need something. Clothes or... whatever cosmetics you women use."

Women. The choice to use that word instead of girl feels good enough that I'm tempted to confess why I haven't been doing any of the above. I despise being called a girl.

"She did, but I didn't want to bother anyone."

I don't realize I'm chewing on my lip until a coppery taste touches my tongue.

"You're not bothering anyone. No matter. Incidentally, I came here to take you and your sister out."

Did he really? Or does he know how pathetic I am? Who am I kidding, of course he does. Where would I have money from?

He's perfectly aware.

My lips part, but I'm unsure of the answer I want to give him.

"Can we go for ice cream, please?" Maya rushes into the room, skipping the entire way to Maddox and me with a great big grin on her face.

I need to have a talk with her. She's too... open. Too eager. Too trusting with these people she's barely just met. It scares me.

"Of course. If your sister agrees, we can," Maddox answers.

"I can't, umm… I don't—"

"It would be my treat," he interrupts, his gaze flickering to mine for a moment. It's stern enough to show he knows exactly what I'm thinking and that I can't argue with him.

"Can we, Evie? Please, can we?" Maya tugs at my sleeve.

"Yes." I cave, knowing full well there's no getting out of this. "Go brush your hair and put your shoes on."

"Yaaay!" She jumps and sprints out of the living area before I speak the entire sentence.

There was no way I was going to say no. Not because I can't deny her, but because I need to see if this outing will scratch this incessant itch and ease the ache beneath my flesh. I'm praying even to the gods I don't believe in that it will work.

I know what would, but I'm afraid to do to myself what was done to me.

Twenty minutes later, Maya, Maddox, and I are walking through the clean, bright streets of Queenscove. Katya's apartment overlooks a large natural park, and I didn't realize how close she actually is to the center of the city.

Or town?

I'm not entirely sure what this place is. I think it's big, yet there are no modern skyscrapers or cold architecture made of nothing but metal and glass. There's not enough concrete to make it feel like a metropolis. The building Katya lives in is one of the tallest, and I only counted seven stories.

The streets are lined with period buildings, grass and flower bed verges, and mature palms amongst beautiful birches. And the smell… It's intoxicating. Honey and sea. Sweet and salty weaving through the humidity that's just at the edge of too much.

Maddox insisted on walking. Now I understand why.

We're quite close to everything. Dozens of both luxurious and charming storefronts, cafés and cocktail bars with tables outside, and people walking about everywhere. Yet, they all have a strange calmness in their step. Like they have no care in the world, no worries, nowhere to rush off to.

They seem happy.

Such a contrast to the place I call home. Fleeton always looks gray, like a cloud covers it permanently. The streets are nowhere near this clean, there's barely any patches of grass, let alone trees. And the only people who smile are the ones who can afford to.

Maddox leads us to the right onto a cobblestoned side street, and my breath catches at the view at the end of it— the ocean. Sun sizzles the calm surface and that ache that has settled beneath my skin quiets.

Beautiful.

I had no idea it was going to be like this. I barely register Maya's excitement as she pulls at my hand.

We near the beach, catching a glimpse of people sunbathing on the soft sand as Maddox leads us to a charming, small building right at the edge of it. Big, bold letters signal that we're about to have Ice Cream and Coffee, and the corner of my lips twitch at the sight of this place. It's simple. No pompous luxury or fancy branding. Stepping inside is like stepping back in the 1960s. An old-time, classic ice cream parlor with all its signs of aging.

But the decor blurs behind the patron's reactions to us. There are probably a dozen people in here, half of them got a glimpse and averted their gazes in an instant, the tenseness evident in their shoulders. The other half are staring with a fervent mixture of sentiments etched on their faces. Everything from fear, to awe, and lust.

None are directed at my sister and me. They look at

Maddox like they want to flee, yet I get the feeling that they're deepest desire is to throw themselves at his feet.

Who did I come here with?

I narrow my eyes on the man who walks a step in front of me completely ignoring everyone around him, apart from the old shopkeeper who gives him a warm smile. He nods as he leads us out on the other side of the establishment and onto a small wooden deck set on the beach.

I want to ask what's happening, but more sets of eyes fall on us. This time around they notice me too and stare in confusion. I don't blame them. I feel utterly out of place in my too-big worn out jeans and ripped Converse—I didn't want to wear Katya's hand-me-downs out, so I'm dressed in the same clothes I was kidnapped in. Albeit washed way too many times to drown some of those memories. Maddox is wearing jeans too, but not only are they perfectly fitted on him, they look brand new.

Yes, clothes haven't been my priority in the last couple of years, yet I've never felt so inadequate.

"Sit, Evelyn."

I rip my gaze off my poor shoes and let go of Maya's hand. She already took a seat and is dangling her legs excitedly as she reaches for the menu. I awkwardly sit, my gaze drifting to the eyes fixed on us.

"You get used to it," Maddox mutters.

He shifts enough to swipe his gaze over the curious ones, and in unison, they all go back to their drinks.

"Why are they staring at us?"

He turns, sighing, and looks over to the soft waves of the calm sea. "Nothing better to do," he grumbles.

No other explanation then. Maybe I should push and ask about them.

"I appreciate all Katya and you have done for us. Offering

us a temporary place to stay and feeding us. I just..." The words fail me. Courage too. I'll sound ungrateful, not just nosy.

"No worries. You've been through enough, you deserve it. Plus, your... situation." He skirts around that particular area, pushing a menu toward me.

"I'm okay. I don't need anything." I slide it away without opening it.

"Nobody needs our gelato, little lady." The man from the counter startles me as he shows up at my side, a notepad in hand. "Everyone wants it, though. All you need is a taste, and you'll be hooked."

His smile is infectious, a single gold tooth gleaming in the sunlight as he scribbles something on the paper.

"Usual for me, Genaro," Maddox says, pushing the menu my way yet again.

His gaze tells me he's not going to take my crap. He's onto me, and I hate it. It's not only embarrassing, but down right humiliating not having money of my own to buy my sister an ice cream. Having strangers do these things for us is uncomfortable. Wrong, even.

"Can I have the salted caramel millionaire's Sunday, please? And lemonade?" my sister orders, grinning from ear to ear, oblivious to my struggle.

Christ, she's glowing. Thriving, even, here in Queenscove, with Maddox's attention and Katya's books. I'm heartbroken that I haven't been able to put a smile like that on her face in... actually, I don't know in how long.

Have I ever?

"And you, gorgeous?" Genaro turns his attention back to me.

"Oh, I'm sorry, I didn't read the menu. Um—"

"Tell you what, I'll surprise you." He interrupts, and the prospect seems to excite him. Like I gave him an interesting challenge. Although, technically he gave it to himself. "What don't you like?"

"Mint. I hate mint."

"Finally! I swear everyone loves mint, and I can't stand it. They all ask for it when they come into my shop, but I refuse to make it. Even the smell puts me off. You're my kind of gal!" He squeezes my shoulder and shakes me a little.

The old man is filled with such energy, for a few moments I forget that I was feeling miserable.

"I'll trust you then," I say, giving him a gentle smile, and he seems to brighten even more. "And a cappuccino, please?" My gaze moves to Maddox involuntarily, seeking some sort of approval.

He doesn't react, he only listens.

"Coming right up." Genaro leaves and I'm left with Maddox's gaze on me.

"What?" I ask.

He shakes his head once.

"Evelyn?" Maya pulls my attention. "Can I go there until the ice cream comes?" She points to a half built sandcastle at the edge of the wood decking, a small plastic bucket and little tools forgotten next to it.

"Sure. But you can't move any further than that without me." She's only a few feet away, yet here, out in the open, it makes me tense.

When they took her from me, I was still holding onto her. Nothing could stop them now. Well, this giant of a man could.

"Take Jay shopping this afternoon, or tomorrow," Maddox says out of the blue, his palm sliding on the table toward me. When he lifts it, a shiny black card remains.

"No." I almost rasp, offended by the piece of plastic.

"You need clothes. Something of your own. Maya—"

"We're fine." I push the card back to him.

"Are you?" the question is rhetorical. "You're in limbo,

and refusing to leave this state is pointless. You have to get comfortable, and I know Katya's clothes don't fit you properly. Plus, wearing the same clothes as that night," he nods toward my outfit, "is probably not doing you any good."

"My clothes are none of your concern. We. Are. Fine."

My tone seems to attract some looks around us, and I lower it immediately. Not because of the attention, but because I'm too embarrassed for people to hear we're arguing over my crappy clothes.

"And it's not forever," I add, "I'm looking to get a job, then we will go back to our home."

He raises an eyebrow at that last word.

"Home, Evelyn?"

"Do not dare—"

"You are stubborn. We both know you need this." Once again, he slides the card my way. "Why are you refusing the help?"

"Why are you giving it?"

My question lands with a thud, and he narrows his eyes on me.

"Because it's the right thing to do."

"Forgive me, Maddox, but you and your... friends... don't seem like the type of people to help someone off the street for free. Not only that but let them into your homes. Why us?"

"You didn't come off the street, Evelyn." He emphasizes my name with a hint of condescension.

"It's not good enough. For days I've been trying to wrap my head around what we've been offered. Yes, I did tell you my sister and I can't go back to Fleeton yet, but I was expecting to be put up in a motel. Not in Katya's home. And judging from what I've seen so far, her work gravitates around yours. This is... it's too much." I breathe in deeply and prop my forearms on the glass table. "Why me, Maddox?"

"Like I said, it's the right thing to do."

Once again, I inhale deeply, focusing on that breath rather than the growing tension in my temples.

"What did you do for the other kids? Did you place them with people that work for you?" I ask, pushing the subject.

"Most are back with their families, but they have gone under the radar for their protection. Others have been placed in... a home, let's say, as we track down their families."

Wait, they actually care?

"Any of them with you guys? Anyone but us?" I press.

He doesn't answer right away. I already know what he's going to say.

"No."

There it is.

"It makes no sense to me, Maddox. Why are you and Katya doing this? Why us?"

"We don't want anything from you, if that's what you're trying to ask," he answers, yet I'm not freaking satisfied with it.

I don't think he's hiding something important from me. More like he would rather keep the reason to himself. Is it more personal? Surely, it's not because he likes me or something. That would be ridiculous.

"You don't like me, do you?" I slap my hand over my mouth the moment the sentence spills out.

The man's eyes bulge, and I swear he slid his chair back a few inches.

"No!" he answers quickly. "Christ, Evie, it's not like that. Not with me. I mean I do like you, but definitely not like that."

Thank God. I think I kind of like him too. As a friend, a protector, and without a doubt in no other way.

Wait, did he say not with me? God, none of my business.

"You helped us. If it wasn't for you and your... sacrifice." His words trigger the itch in my veins and flashbacks threaten to sneak through. "We wouldn't have saved all those kids. A hotel was out of the question."

Okay, when he puts it that way, it kind of makes sense. It doesn't mean it's easier to accept, but it does make sense.

"Fine. But tell me one more thing…"

He cocks his head, waiting.

"Who are you people?"

CHAPTER 4
Finnigan

I SPRING FROM ONE FOOT TO the other, jumping back before Madd's jab connects to my ribs.

"You're too slow, Hennessey."

"Fuck you, Severin. I dodged it, didn't I?" I spit back.

Only, he wasn't wrong. I'm distracted.

He shakes his head and in two steps I barely acknowledge, he's facing my side and punches me straight in the middle of my back. I land chest first on the rope of the ring, my breath snapped out of my lungs. The asshole doesn't even bother to rub it in—he proved his point.

"I saw her yesterday," he says as I push away, back into position.

"*Her* who?" The question doesn't come out as nonchalant as I hoped.

"Evelyn Shaw."

I miss his jaw when I take a swing, distracted by those two words. He whips around like he's not just shy of seven feet tall and built like a mountain, and I turn, narrowing my eyes on him.

"What you do on your own time, Severin, is not my concern."

How was she doing? I don't dare ask out loud, pushing the curiosity away.

"I took her and her sister out for ice cream," he continues, disregarding my words.

I swing at him again, catching his jaw, but not hard enough to make him shut up about her.

Was she happy to go, or did she fight you?

"Ice cream? Really? What the hell is your goal there?" I ask.

What flavor did she get?

"You tell me," he counters, swinging his leg in a turning kick that catches me in the hip.

"I'm minding my own business. You should too." I haven't seen the girl since I went to Katya's a few days ago.

He scoffs and I spurt toward him, side-kicking him in the stomach before swinging for his jaw again. But my fist doesn't connect. He swats my hand away, kicks my feet from under me, and slams me back against the floor.

"And what is your business, Hennessey? Does it have to do with the shiny black card Katya gave me this morning?" He presses his forearm into my chest, his amber gaze pinning me in place.

My eyes widen, and I lift my leg, attempting to push him off. Why did Katya give my goddamn bank card to him? She was supposed to use it on Evelyn herself.

"Or maybe it has to do with the two people who were told to keep an eye on her, help her, follow her around, even if they are assigned to Katya and the building?" he continues, pressing just a bit harder into my chest before he snaps back and rises.

He offers me his hand to help me up, but the pulse in my temples rages. I grab his hand and use all my force to swing my legs around, hook them around his ankles and pull him down, throwing him over my head. The floor of the ring shakes like a goddamn earthquake, but I'm even more furious when I rise and find Madds snickering to himself as he lies there.

I draw a deep breath, trying to steady myself, because he's reading too much into this. There is no ulterior motive. "I was simply trying to help Katya, since she took on this situation, and it's unfair to leave her on her own. We need her to be focused on the escort service."

"Situation..." he repeats as he rises back to his full height. "So, are you going to go see the *situation* again?"

Yes.

"No. I have no reason to," I answer.

"She's a smart woman, you know," he says, and I lunge at him just to shut him the fuck up.

I don't want to hear any more about the silver and gold eyes that have haunted me since the moment she came out of that godforsaken container. I don't want to be reminded of the glow of her olive skin. Her wheat-colored hair that grazes her too-slim waist. Nor of the look of disdain she shot me the last time I saw her.

The girl can't occupy any space in my mind.

I'm a sick bastard for allowing any of these thoughts.

"She's been taking care of her sister for the best part of two years." Madds deflects my attack, but I block his back.

Why has she been doing this?

"Working to support her through school, while dodging the authorities. She's resourceful. She fooled the system."

Then she got herself kidnapped by the scum of the fucking earth. The same type of bastards who took—no!

"She asked about us," Madds continues, distracting me from that dangerous train of thought.

"What did she ask?" I stop, scowling at him.

"Who we are. *What* we are." He throws a combination of jabs and crosses that I just about manage to block.

Why the hell would Evelyn ask these things? She doesn't need to know who we are, and she doesn't need to know what we do.

"And you didn't find that strange, Severin?"

"No."

Fucking idiot!

"What did you tell her?"

I swing a few punches at him, barely managing to catch him with an uppercut. He's fast. And good. Too good. It's why he's the one in charge of training our men. But our sessions are not about beating the shit out of each other. Over the last eight years or so I discovered that this is my way of coping. It's masochism in its purest form. And fuck knows I need the punishment.

"I kept it vague," he answers, "Told her we're businessmen. We have a few ventures around town."

It's not a lie. We do. We have this space here—The Fightclub—which is exactly what it says on the tin. Only, we organize high-stake matches with a select audience, bare knuckle boxing, and some brutal sessions that end close to death. Over the years, a few have ended up that way. Maddox is the one who handles all the affairs here. He's also the reigning champion.

This place is also a front for money laundering. But that's the back of house business. Carter Pierce, our resident, brutal genius started that hustle, but I took over a few years back. I don't regret not finishing university, but for years I felt like I couldn't match the talents of the rest of the Sanctum. However, it turns out I have a knack for numbers and strategies.

Above this expansive basement we have our speakeasy, Midnight, which is our most legit business. It's another one of Carter's ideas, and his true baby. It only caters to a select clientele, and even those on our list need to request a password for every visit in order to enter. No one can simply show up, and it's not open to the public.

However, our primary business, for years now, has been gaining and using information. And no one is better at extracting it than Vincent *The Serpent* Sinclair. We make it our business to know as much as possible about everything moving in our city and beyond, and we control it all, too. Some call it blackmail, we call it good business. Information is power, and in our underworld, we are kings. Even normal folk whisper about us, but in their ears, our ventures are mere rumors. Legends. They fear us, yet respect us. Likely scared that we know their biggest secrets.

We do.

This side of our business is where Katya and her girls are involved. The escort service is a front, and the women working for us have bigger goals and stunning skills much more important than accompanying someone to a restaurant or fucking them. They know how to get information out of people, they know how to steal it, too, and they're highly trained. Katya oversees them all, and I'm also involved there, supporting her.

I'm glad Madds had the sense not to get into all these details with Evelyn.

"She was fine with that vague answer?"

"No," Madds answers.

I stiffen, exasperated that I keep having to pry the answers out of him. "And?"

"She's not an idiot, Hennessey, she knows we're not legit. Especially considering how we found her, and then... rescued her. Though, I'm not sure she remembers anything of her rescue."

"But that doesn't mean we have to give her a goddamn introduction course to our business," I snap.

"I didn't. But I had to give her something since it was impossible to hide how everyone was looking at me. I told her our organization is called The Sanctum, and our business means people know us around town." Madds drops his arms to his sides, his head cocked. "Why are you so tightly wound when it involves her?"

"What the hell are you talking about?" I am not tightly wound. He's being fucking ridiculous. "She's an outsider, Severin. I don't want her living at Katya's biting us in the ass. She's a stranger."

The man grunts, and I scowl.

"Whatever makes you feel better, man. Don't fucking expect her to stay blind to our world, not when she's living in it now."

"Not for long," I mutter.

"What's that supposed to mean?"

"Did she say when she plans on leaving?" I deflect.

"And go where? Who's gonna protect her since we're still finding the rest of the trafficking ring? And where is she getting money from? Not to mention that we already know she can't go back until she becomes her sister's legal guardian."

A man can dream.

"I'll give her money."

"Yeah." He scoffs like it's the most idiotic thing I could have said. "Good luck with that."

What's that supposed to mean?

"She did ask something else."

I already know I'm going to regret his next words. Though, what bothers me more is her features materializing in my mind the more we talk about her. I'm about to beg him to slam his fist into my temple, in the off-chance it will make them disappear.

"Spit it out already," I rasp.

"Why are we helping them. Why her."

My scowl softens, my stomach drops. I wipe a gloved hand over my face and wonder just how fucked I am.

Yeah... good question—why her?

"I gave her my answer," Madds continues. "Someday maybe you'll give her yours."

I right hook him in the cheek before his last word finishes its short echo.

Evelyn

I DON'T RECOGNIZE THE PERSON looking back at me from this gold framed bathroom mirror. She doesn't belong in this beautiful, expensive room. Even if her wheat-colored hair matches the theme of this apartment she's been living in for a few weeks now.

I rake my fingers through my long strands, hating how even my own touch makes me feel so vulnerable. I used to love my hair. My only pride, even when my fading body stopped feeling like mine as my meals became more scattered. The sweet memories of my mother brushing it when I was a child are now tainted.

We have to go back. There's no way we can stay here amongst these strangers. Maddox told me what they allegedly do—businessmen. I scoff at the thought. Sure... because businessmen rescue little girls from containers. Organize operations to destroy sex trafficking rings. And have 24/7 security.

They may be businessmen, but they are definitely on the wrong side of the law.

Just as the men who took us.

Burning flares over my scalp, and I find myself clutching my hair, pulling at it. There's a few too many hairs tangled between my fingers when I release it, and bile rises in the back of my throat. *Even by my own hands I can't handle it...*

God, I need to pull myself together.

It's too early for me to leave. I need money. A bit of time. And a plan on becoming Maya's legal guardian. When we're returning to Fleeton, it will be in a place of our own, not on the streets again.

Which means I need a job.

I flinch when a knock sounds at the door, startling me out of my thoughts.

"It's me," Katya says. "I wanted to let you know I'm home and that we've been invited somewhere."

"I'll be out in a second."

Invited somewhere?

I rush to wash my hands, running them through my hair to fix the mess I made, and walk out. Katya's in her bedroom, door open as she takes off her blouse.

I whip around, cringing. "I'm so sorry."

"It's okay, don't worry. I'm only changing."

I've never been part of a family or group of friends where undressing in front of each other was normal. Nudity has always been something rather private in my life. I always found it peculiar when girls from school casually mentioned going into their bathrooms when their moms took a bath or something.

When I turn, I find her pulling on a T-shirt and switching her skirt to a pair of loose jeans. I can deal with that, but something about nudity makes me feel like they're going to think I'm gawking at all their private parts.

"Where were you invited?"

"Not just me, all three of us," she answers.

"I don't understand."

"One of the guys is having a little get-together at his house. Just our... *group*."

Did she want to say *The Sanctum*? Maddox said that's how they're known in Queenscove. Like that isn't another indication that they are more than just a *business*.

"They suggested it would be good for you and Maya to join," Katya says. "Socialize in a comfortable, safe environment."

"Who's *they*?"

"Maddox and the others." I hate that I was hoping she would name a certain blue-eyed, striking man. "He lives in a secluded house in the middle of Queen's Woods. It's safe and private. I'm not forcing you, but Maddox and I think it would be nice for you to meet a few more people."

My gut tightens with unease, but intrigue too. Diving deeper into their world is something I really want to avoid, especially when it's in their home. But this might be the only opportunity I have to see just how safe Maya and I are. I don't trust them, even with Katya I have reservations, and I need to find out if I'm making the right choice by staying here, or if we should take our chances out there on our own.

"I promise, you'll be perfectly safe. Brinn is driving us, and he's staying too. So, if at any point you are uncomfortable, he will bring you right back."

That doesn't sound too bad.

"I guess it would be okay."

"Great. Now, I stopped by a shop and got you and Maya some new clothes since I heard you're choosing to be stubborn." She walks out before I have a chance to voice my protest.

I follow and find her pulling some garments from an expensive-looking bag. "Nothing crazy, a few T-shirts, some joggers, leggings, underwear, sports bras, and jeans. Basic colors. I have the receipt if the sizes are too big." She forces the clothes into my hands. "Now, go try them on and pick something comfy to wear. We're leaving in twenty minutes."

I want to protest yet again, but it's beginning to sound not only repetitive, but silly. Are new clothes really so bad? I'm not signing my soul away or anything. I can force myself to accept them and repay them when I can to make sure there are no strings attached.

"Oh, um okay. I'll go get Maya."

"Don't worry, I'll sort her out."

"Katya." My voice holds too much urgency, and she whips around instantly. "Can I see what you bought for her?"

The brief confusion softens, and she nods, pulling out more clothes than she bought for me. It pulls at my heartstrings just a bit seeing this, and I'm thankful she's not insulted by my need to be aware of what she got for Maya. There are leggings, T-shirts, underwear, a couple of skirts and dresses in an array of colors. I can't help the meek smile, and she takes it as a seal of approval and walks back out.

I'm stuck in place, watching the door and debating if I should go be with Maya while she picks clothes... when she gets dressed. I have no reason not to trust Katya, but getting used to letting someone else alone in a room with her has been more difficult than I thought it would be. I'm not sure if I'll ever get used to it, but I know deep down I hope I will. Having constant eyes on my sister will be impossible, especially if I get a job.

I'll try harder tomorrow, but for now, I leave the door cracked so I can hear her voice in the other room as she squeals and giggles.

Ten minutes later, dressed in a simple, black T-shirt, mom-style jeans rolled up at the bottom, and brand-new Converse, I'm back at staring in the gold-rimmed mirror, debating using some of Katya's make up. It's been so long since I've used any. Before our life went to shit, I was just starting to dabble in it, and I knew exactly the style I loved. Dark, moody, edgy, just like the rock music my dad was playing when he tinkered in the garage. I was terrible at it though; no one taught me how to draw a proper wing with the liquid eye liner. At the end of most of my experiments and practice runs, I looked like a panda. By the time I started getting better at makeup, I couldn't afford it anymore.

Maybe I should just settle for some concealer today. Cover the dark circles.

Katya's reflection pops up in the mirror as she stands in the open doorway. "Do you need any help?"

"I'm not sure. I don't think I want to wear any makeup, but..." I trail off because I don't actually know where I'm going with this.

"There's more stuff in that drawer." She points to the right, in the tall, corner cabinet.

"Thank you." I cast a quick glance, but stay in place.

"You're beautiful no matter what, Evelyn. And where we're going you don't need to worry about make up. Only if you want to make yourself feel better."

I didn't realize I was tense, but with her words, my spine relaxes instantly. She puts a smile on my lips, too.

Yes, makeup does make me feel better.

I pick up the concealer and dab a bit under my eyes. It's a bit too light for my complexion, but it will do. I decide to add some mascara, the silver and gold of my eyes popping when my dark blonde lashes turn black, and finish with a little peach blush.

"Here." Katya hands me a lipstick. "It's new. Sheer and natural."

It's a pinkish-peachy color that instantly puts me off. But Katya's nodding to me to use it, so I reluctantly open it and swipe it over my lips.

"Oh, it's sheer." This is more a balm than lipstick. "Thank you."

I love a bold lip, but I don't feel bold at all right now. This is perfect.

"Don't mention it. All done?"

I nod, glancing in the mirror one final time, before I walk out to find Maya in the living room, twirling in her new dress.

"She chose it herself," Katya says, "I suggested some leggings and a blouse, but she saw the dress and I think I stopped existing for her after that."

I smirk, knowing full well that girl adores dresses. As girly as possible, too. She's not that fussed about colors, although she seems to love this dusty-pink. This one is casual, long enough to cover her knees and slightly pinched at the waist. When I shift my gaze lower, I realize Katya bought us matching Converse, and Maya is wearing hers, too. This might be the cutest thing.

She's adorable.

"Come on, little girl, let's go." I grab her hand and follow Brinn and Katya out the door.

* * *

When Katya mentioned woods, this stunning house was not what I expected to find in the middle of it. Dark wood and enormous windows blend seamlessly between the trees of the forest. But that's not what's been making me gawk like an idiot—it's the people. The atmosphere.

"Welcome! Come in, come in." A stunning woman with wild, red curls waves us inside.

The enticing smells of grilled meat and something deliciously sweet make my mouth water, but the laughter from the background distracts me. This house is *alive*.

"Hello!" my sister says with a teeth-showing grin, but she doesn't leave my hold.

"Hi! You must be Maya," the redhead says. "I'm Morrigan. You can call me Morri."

"Hello, Morri!" My sister waves with enthusiasm, a great big smile on her face.

She switches her attention to me, and her red-lipped smile and striking green eyes pull me in. "And you must be Evelyn."

Christ, she's gorgeous.

"I am. Hi. Thank you for inviting us."

"Well, I heard the trip to Genaro's went well, so I thought we could take it a step further."

"It did. His ice cream was delicious," I say with a smile.

Morrigan shakes her head and pats her full hips. "And utterly addictive."

"Good," a deep voice sounds behind her as a tall, broad man approaches, wrapping her in his arms. "I should ask him for a daily supply."

He gives her a sweet, yet suggestive smile before turning his attention to Maya and me.

"Hi Evelyn. Maya." He nods at us, but that smile is already gone. "I see you met my wife."

He's not rude, though. It's like his smiles are only reserved for her.

I know him—he's Vincent, the owner of this house. He helped rescue us, Maya specifically. When Maddox returned the next day to ask me some questions about the warehouse, Vincent came too, and I was instantly apprehensive. The man looked cut from stone. Stern and hard with his pitch-black eyes.

"Thank you for inviting us," I tell him.

"No need to thank me."

I doubt that. We're in their home. Their actual home. I really don't think any outsiders ever step foot in here, and I'm definitely one.

We're led into the open space kitchen and living area, and there's a view to die for at the back of the house. Floor-to-ceiling windows overlook a cozy deck, and the forest surrounds the whole thing. It's so beautiful, I want to scream. If it weren't for the people sitting on the outdoor sofas and chairs, talking and laughing, there would probably be no sound out there beyond the rustling of leaves and bird song.

"Hello there!" A sweet voice pulls my attention to the kitchen, and an older woman with an apron dusted with flower, comes toward us. "Come in, come in. Food will be ready in a bit, the boys are grilling out there too, but come get a drink. I'm Mamaw June."

Okay, this is getting more surreal by the second. "Hi, nice to meet you." I stumble over those words as my brain struggles to compute what I'm seeing. "This is Maya, and I'm Evelyn."

"I heard, yes. I'm so happy to finally meet you both." She grabs my hand in hers, her warm smile bringing a uniquely warm sensation. What is that?

"She's my mother-in-law," Morrigan says as she heads over to the kitchen island and grabs a wooden spoon to mix something in a large bowl, and Mamaw June joins her.

"Come, I'll get you both something to drink." Vincent signals us to follow toward a bar area that's next to the kitchen.

My mind is spinning, and I follow him without question, stealing another glance outside. It takes a ridiculous amount of effort not to trip over my own feet at the sight—Finnigan Hennessey is staring right at me. Only, unlike everyone else here, he does not smile. That sharp gaze does something to me. Good or bad, I don't know. I haven't figured that part out yet.

"We have everything. Juice, fizzy drinks, lots of alcohol."

"Do you have apple juice?" Maya asks, pulling her hand from mine.

I rip my gaze from the blonde man and place my hand on my sister's shoulder, turning to Vincent.

"I do. Evelyn, what would you like?"

"I'm not sure. Um... beer?"

He raises an eyebrow but straightens it immediately.

"Do you like Corona?"

Did I think he was going to question my age?

"I do, thank you," I answer.

He pulls one out of a glass door fridge, pops the cap, and points to a glass and lime, but I shake my head to both.

"Feel free to come here and grab whatever you want. Including the stronger stuff."

Ah, that's why he raised his brow. He was surprised I didn't go for spirits.

"Come, meet the others." I hear Morrigan before she appears next to me.

We walk out onto the patio, and I stiffen when all focus turns to us. They're not scrutinizing, but all this attention is daunting.

"You already know them." Vincent waves a hand toward Maddox, Finnigan, and a man who's name I didn't catch that day in the container. He brought me the tracker. "And this is Cillian, Morrigan's brother." He points to a bearded, redheaded man who belongs on a magazine cover. "That's Tina and Beau."

Two people sharing an armchair nod and smile—definitely a couple.

"And this is Raven." Morrigan points at one of the most beautiful, black-haired women I've ever seen in my life. "And my lovely Loreley. Or Lulu."

I was wrong, Loreley might be the most beautiful, with her long, icy blonde hair and golden eyes. Jesus, they're all beautiful. Not even a normal amount of beautiful, crazy stunning and handsome. Maddox's jagged scar sweeping from his forehead down his cheek just adds to the charm. Even dressed in joggers, leggings, and casual T-shirts, they could just jump on the catwalk right now and no one would bat an eyelid.

"It's nice to meet you," Maya says, leaning into me a bit more.

I stifle a laugh. Wow, she finally found her shyness.

CHAPTER 5
Evelyn

THERE WAS NO WAY I wouldn't doubt if it would be appropriate for Maya to be in this environment, but my worries have been squashed. Everyone so far has been... oddly perfect. No one is bothered by Maya's presence, even as I thought a kid might become annoying. She's making sure to pull everyone up if they swear in front of her, which has made most of them laugh and comply with her demands. Some of the guys retired inside or walked farther away whenever it looked like a conversation was turning a bit too serious.

The whole evening is... strange.

Not bad. Definitely not bad.

It's homey.

Such a contrast to what I thought this experience would be. Mamaw June is infectious in her attitude. These brutal men are menacing even when they smile, yet they'd probably kneel at her feet. They might even be a little afraid of her.

Their whole dynamic is peculiar. I didn't ask, but it looks like they've known each other for a long time. It sounds like Mamaw June helped raise at least one more of these guys besides her own son. And she's so warm.

She's the only thing that made me sad this evening. I saw it in Maya's eyes too. Passing memories from our once happy life... the woman who gave us more love than we could ever ask for. Something about Vincent's mother reminds us of ours.

Even that sadness brings a strange sense of comfort.

One thing has distracted me from it this evening—the icy stares of the blue-eyed man sitting across from me. Though, I think his stare only flickered into ice when mine landed on his.

I'm lounging in a comfy outdoor armchair, watching the sun bleed in dark shades of orange just above the tree line, and wonder if I'm getting too comfortable. Not in this chair, not with their support, but with them. With who they are. So far this evening I've heard things in passing—something about a fight, meeting a hotelier who has some interesting information for the guys, and there was something about money. But I must have heard that one wrong because the number mentioned didn't sound real with all those zeros at the end.

"You need to put some meat on your bones, little lady. It will help with the chills."

I shudder as Morrigan drops a soft throw on my lap. Some meat on my bones would be great indeed, but it hasn't been in the cards for me. I did, however, notice a slight difference since staying at Katya's. Folding my legs under me, I wrap the blanket around my shoulders. It smells divine, like pine needles and sugar.

"How are you doing?" she asks as she sits on her husband's

lap at the dining table to my left.

"We're doing well, thanks to Katya. And all of you." I haven't been told who's actually contributing to helping us, yet one can assume. "But my sister and I will have to move on soon; we can't take advantage of your hospitality for so long."

A brief, throaty sound pulls my attention to the armchair across from me. Finnigan has a bottle of Corona stuck to his lips, and his eyes fixed on me. Did he just mockingly clear his throat?

What is his problem?

I've been trying to ignore him all evening, but this time I hold his gaze, challenging him.

"Don't worry," I hear Maddox say, but don't turn to him. "All in good time. There's no reason to rush this. No one is kicking you out."

Finnigan raises an eyebrow, and I narrow both of mine. I bet he wants to kick me out. I just can't quite figure out why.

"You're uncomfortable with us."

I turn without sparing a breath, the gorgeous, blonde woman with mile-high legs pulling my attention to her. The others look like they want to argue with her for her daring, yet they bite their tongues. Finnigan rests the bottle on his knee and straightens.

What am I supposed to say? It wasn't a question, and it's not an untrue statement.

This evening has been peculiarly comfortable. The complete opposite of what I was expecting from, what I'm further inclined to believe is, a criminal organization. This is what I'm uncomfortable with. It took me by surprise.

"It's okay," Loreley says, continuing without my answer. "We're a bit desensitized to it all. But I want you to understand that no one here is going to put a mask on for your sake."

Excuse me, what? My eyebrows shoot up, but I refrain

from saying anything.

"Lulu!" Morrigan says with slight shock in her tone.

"What I mean to say, Evelyn, is that what you've seen so far is exactly who we are. We're not putting a pretty face on just for you, and we don't have any pretenses for this evening. I understand how you came to be here with us, and I just want to make sure you know that you're not being deceived into seeing something we want you to believe."

"You're telling me that you really are this... *family*." The word tastes strange on my tongue.

"The guys are a family. I'm Morri's friend, and my involvement in this little group of theirs has been reluctant at best."

I don't miss the scoff from Maddox. Loreley doesn't either and shoots him a piercing gaze with eyes that almost match his in color.

"But I didn't want you to think that anyone was putting on a show for you. Maybe you'll find some comfort in that."

Oddly, I do.

I nod, but my gaze drifts toward the inside of the house, to Mamaw June and Maya fiddling with something on the kitchen island. My sister has a great big smile on her face, and Vincent's mom is beaming, fully focused on her, clearly enjoying the young company. Even if I know Maya has been happy and content all evening, what bothers me is the fact that I felt in my gut that we've been safe all this time. I wasn't uneasy, I wasn't on edge, and after an hour or so, I stopped looking over to her every minute to make sure she was okay.

I relaxed. And I'm terrified of this feeling. Truly and utterly terrified.

Back in Fleeton, when those scum tried to take her away from me, I was relaxed as well. I was comfortable in our situation, and it caused our downfall.

I cannot be guilty of that all over again.

Yet... Maya looks so happy. I haven't seen her like this in so long. No matter how hard I tried to protect her, to shelter her, we were still living in motels or our car. I could never offer her... this.

There's no way I can wipe that happiness off of her sweet soul. Not yet anyway.

I have to do better for her.

"Evelyn?"

I turn at the sound of my name, but I don't know who spoke it.

My gaze involuntarily falls on the wavy-haired blonde man who seems to glow in these burnt orange hues of the sun. The dying light sharpens his almost square jaw, the wide bridge of his nose, and perfectly sculpted cupid's bow. I hate the ethereal light Finnigan's painted in. Especially as he sits in that armchair like it's his throne, one leg crossed over the knee of the other, back straight, and head cocked, slightly leaned back. He could make any chair look like his own, personal throne.

Christ, Evelyn, get it together.

I turn to Loreley with an apologetic smile. "Sorry, I got distracted by Maya. Yes, I understand where you're coming from, and I appreciate it."

"Just don't expect us to suddenly start sharing all our fucking secrets." Finnigan snarls, addressing me directly for the first time tonight. The unnecessary harshness startles me.

"Finn!" Morri snaps.

I don't dignify him with a response, turning to Vincent and the others instead.

"Do you have any news on the two men who seemed to lead that operation when you found me?" I ignore Finnigan altogether, asking a question that defies his whole speech about their secrets. Though, this shouldn't really be a secret. Not from me.

I swear I practically hear him sneer at me, and I bite the inside of my cheek to keep the grin off my face.

"Not yet," The man whose name I was reminded earlier is Carter replies. "There's little to go on, but we will. Let us know if you remember anything else."

"I will."

It was a true stroke of luck that the men who... did things to me, Frankie B, as I recalled his name, and the one they called Vassallo, left before The Sanctum arrived. From the snippets I caught through the haze, they were meeting someone. They weren't tipped off; they simply left for their meeting probably mere minutes before. Though I was so out of it, minutes or hours felt the same to me.

It was pure, dumb luck.

"Have you? Remembered anything else, I mean," Morrigan asks.

Very little, and nothing I wish to share with the group. There are still wide gaps in my memory, and considering the little I do remember, I'm thankful for those holes.

"Nothing relevant that could trace to them."

"Everything is relevant, Evelyn. Not to this, but to you... your healing. If you ever need to talk..."

"I'm okay. Thank you."

She nods but clearly doesn't believe me.

"Just know you're safe here. We didn't leave a trail, so it's unlikely anyone's going to come knocking on our door. Or yours," Maddox says.

His rough features, devoid of a smile, are comforting.

They all fall into comfortable chatter, and I catch brief mentions about a club Morrigan and Loreley apparently own. Something about renovations after a fire, playrooms, and... a stage?

I haven't asked what exactly this club is, but my curiosity is piqued. I've never actually experienced any clubs to be fair, no matter what type theirs is, it's going to be a novelty for me.

A few minutes later, I walk back into the house to check on my sister. She's getting tired, but she's engrossed in a fairytale Vincent's mom is reciting. Maya doesn't care much that I'm here, too engrossed in the storytelling, and I step away to the bathroom at the opposite end of the house.

I spend a minute longer here than I need to, enjoying the silence on this side of the house. I'm not used to being surrounded by so many people, so many conversations. It's overwhelming at times.

Turning the light off, I take a deep breath in the comfort of the darkness and walk out onto the short corridor that leads back into the living room. Only, without light, I smash straight into a hard chest, failing to see that I'm not alone.

"I'm so sorry." I pull away, but someone grips my shoulders, holding me in place.

"It's my fault."

Finnigan.

I can't help the gasp, drawing in the scent of sea salt and something... sweet and rich, like dark chocolate. *Sweet Mary Mother of God.* It's intoxicating. I can almost taste him.

"I want to apologize." His words startle me.

"For?"

"I was rude... out there," he answers.

I stay silent because I have nothing to add. He was, indeed, rude.

"You're not saying anything?"

"No. You said you want to apologize. I didn't want to interrupt you." I shrug in his grip.

"I just did." His scowl taints even his tone.

"You didn't. You said you *want* to apologize. You didn't actually do it."

The harsh exhale brushes against my forehead and the hands that still hold me tighten against my shoulders. "I'm sorry."

"What do you have against me?" the question drops from my mouth before I have a chance to stop it.

"I don't have anything against you."

"Don't lie. You'll have something else to apologize for again."

Maybe my eyes haven't adjusted fully to the low light, and I imagined the corner of his lips quirking.

"I think you should go back to the patio, Evelyn." God... the way he says my name. He adds an old world twang to it, like a strange caress.

I don't move. I can't.

"You're the one holding me here," I say.

He doesn't let go.

Silence falls. More dark chocolate whirls around me. A peculiar electric quiver brushes over my spine, wrapping around my neck and my belly simultaneously, and I think I moved closer to him. Or did I lean in? I don't know, but my front turns warmer. My mouth drier. The air weighs heavy between us. Even if the hairs on my arms stand up.

"Finnigan..." I whisper.

His hands fall like his name on my lips burned him, and he steps around me, stopping shoulder to shoulder, albeit his is quite a bit higher.

"Go, Evelyn."

I sigh, disappointed, but with what... I'm not sure.

Finngan

I TRULY AM AN IDIOT.

Why did I follow her here?

What did I hope to achieve?

All I got is confirmation that I'm a sick fuck.

I hoped that when it was just us two, when she was that close to me, when I could touch her, that I would see I've been imagining everything. Over-thinking the horrible thoughts I've been having about her.

There are many reasons why someone like me should not dare even think of someone like her, but to add our age difference on top of it all... it's disgusting.

What the fuck is wrong with me?

I was wrong. I was so goddamn wrong. What I felt was worse than what I imagined. Even my name on her lips sounded a thousand times better than in my dreams.

I slam my hands on the vanity, barely able to gaze at myself in the mirror.

How could I? I fucked my way through every pussy in Queenscove. I'm all kinds of disgusting and dirty. But having

Evelyn Shaw haunt me, is even fucking worse.

Turning the faucet on, I let it run cold for a minute before I splash some of the water on my face.

Okay. I can do this. I can stop.

There are ways to distract myself.

After all, she's just a random girl we're helping. I've had more women than I can count, and I barely remember their names or faces. Yet I've had them in so many memorable ways.

I've only ever looked at Evelyn. She's not going to linger in my mind for long.

That's it. I'll focus only on helping her. She did say she doesn't want to impose for too long. I'll give her an incentive to leave quicker than planned.

She's not going to refuse me. Not if she was serious about what she said.

I'll offer her more if that will help convince her. I'll fucking give her everything to get her out of Queenscove. Out of my goddamn sight.

I take a few extra minutes in the bathroom, and when I finally walk out, self-assured and with a brand new plan, I find the house completely empty. Shifting my gaze past the floor to ceiling windows, I notice Mamaw June outside, but there's no little human with her. And no Evelyn either.

They left.

That's what you wanted, you asshole. You wanted her gone.

Yeah... I did.

Movement stirs from the patio, and I curse the disappointment when Carter walks in, stepping toward me.

"What?" I ask when he doesn't say anything.

His silence pisses me off sometimes.

"I'm asking The Ghost to come to Midnight tomorrow. I need to find out if he's heard anything after that whole unsavory business with O'Rourke, Holt, and Boseman.

Enough time has passed, and things might start to stir again."

"Sounds good," I agree.

Jonathan Reese, aka The Ghost, controls half of the docks and a very lucrative on-ground transport route. A few months ago, Liam O'Rourke, Morrigan's father, and Holt, her ex-boyfriend, went into business together. They needed what only Jonathan could offer, and that's where we came in. The man is a recluse, doesn't do business with just anyone, and we put them in contact. For our own benefit, of course. Morrigan's hand in marriage was also sold in this partnership between father and boyfriend. She's Vincent's first love, and The Serpent wanted her back. A lot of shit went down there. Plus, the containers they needed to shift were supposed to carry ammo and drugs. Some did, but then the children came... and along with them, Evelyn.

In their quest for power, the two men along with Boseman, thought they had what it takes to take down The Sanctum. It was rather funny. They didn't even make a fucking dent. However, considering what Evelyn shared with us, we've concluded that the operation the trio started was part of a much larger partnership. They weren't doing it alone.

"I think you should get in contact with someone else. Just in case word has spread," Carter says.

"Who?"

"Your cousin."

I grit my teeth at the mention. My distant cousin is not the reason why, but the old memories I sometimes associate with him. Haunting memories...

"You think word of this has reached Venator?" I ask, disbelief clear in my tone.

"I think we must be smart and use all of our resources. Sloan Buchanan is a good, reliable resource that we can trust."

"It's not the only source we have in Venator. You know

that woman from school. What was her name? Pandora?"

"It's not the same thing," Carter replies. "With Pandora, it's an exchange, and I have no desire to trade anything. Talk to Sloan."

Sighing, I roll my eyes and walk toward the patio door. "Fine."

I have nothing against Buchanan. Carter's right, we can trust him with our lives. Eight years ago, he helped us come out of a small war. Only, I came home with a dead body in my arms instead of a future. It's why mentions of him, or anything to do with that time, makes me irrationally angry.

It's not like I haven't kept in touch with my cousin. But I try not to overdo it. The man's empire in the city of three hills where he rules one of them, has grown stronger than ever. More dangerous than ever. It's the rumors of the brewing conflicts with the other two hills that make me reluctant to get too involved with him. We have enough on our plates in Queenscove and beyond, we don't have time for someone else's battles.

However, there's nothing I hate more than scumbags who traffic humans. The proximity of these ones to Queenscove disgusts me. So, if there's even the smallest chance Sloan heard something, I'll talk to him.

I say my goodbyes to everyone and get in my car. I've only had two Corona's. The moment I heard Evelyn was invited, I knew I couldn't drink more in case I needed to escape.

But now... I could smash a whole ass bottle of vodka on my own. I'm gonna drop the car off at home, then go to a bar to do just that.

Any bar... as long as there are women there who can make me forget.

CHAPTER 6
Evelyn

THE NIGHTMARES CAME BACK IN full force, and I wake up with a chilling shudder. Cold sweats shatter my body, the dreams and memories mixing into a debilitating concoction, venom seeping beneath my skin.

A feverish itch blooms, turning relentless through my flesh. I scratch at my forearms, determined to bleed the poison out of my skin. Tears I didn't realize I was shedding blur my vision and the pain... the pain becomes unbearable.

I thought it was hidden, but it's not—it's entombed. Burrowing deeper and deeper, sinking its claws so it can find a permanent home in the fabrics of my being. I can't reach; I can't rip it out.

So, I dig my fingernails deeper, breaking the skin on a tearful wince, hoping I can bleed it out. Only, it itches more.

It hurts more.

I need more!

Tears of frustration stain my cheeks, and I swallow in a bellow at the shame plaguing me. Only one thing will fulfill this need, scratch the relentless itch and dilute these nightmares. And I cry harder because that one thing I crave is exactly what those bastards injected me with.

But... it kind of helped then. Maybe now, it could keep the nightmares out of my living world.

Maybe it will help.

Make me forget.

The shame. The feel of him. The loss of control. The disappointment I am. How I failed her.

I have to forget. Even if for a few hours. I want to be back in that place where my body isn't mine, where I am... free.

Reality sets in, and the inner pain quiets in favor of the outside one, and in the faint morning light, I see what I've done.

"Oh my god."

I jump to my feet, realizing that I fell asleep on the sofa, and run to the bathroom. My inner forearms are scratched badly enough that I'm bleeding, stinging when I run them under the cold water.

At least I wasn't in bed with Maya.

My muscles still when I catch the first glimpse of myself in the mirror. I look exactly like I feel—a failure. Maya's smile and laughter filters through my mind, emotions I didn't give her, but these people we now live with. I'm not taking care of her—they are. I have done nothing to contribute to her happiness.

Did I really deserve to leave that warehouse alive? Is there a point for my presence here?

Looking down at my forearms, blood seeps out of the jagged scratches; their ugliness sure does fit on my skin. I shake my head on a sharp exhale and start rummaging through the cupboards for some gauze or anything to cover the evidence of my nightmares. Or better yet, of that searing need begging from inside my veins. I find a small basket stocked up with all sorts of first aid stuff and skip the antiseptic and whatever else I should do to tend to my skin, going straight for the roll of gauze. I make quick work of wrapping it around my forearms and hurry to go throw a long-sleeve on before Maya and Katya wake up and see me.

Living here for free makes me feel like a leech, so I've been trying to pull my weight as much as I can. Washing, cleaning, cooking, whatever needs doing, even if Katya keeps telling me off. Now, I'm about to pull some oats out of the cupboard for some oatmeal, but my phone pings on the counter. I twitch at the unfamiliar noise.

"What the...? Who has this number?"

Reluctant, I grab it and a new text flashes on the screen.

> Hey! It's Loreley. Katya gave me your number. Morri and I are going out for breakfast. Come join us. Pick you up in fifteen?

I look around the quiet space, bewildered as I scratch the back of my head.

This is wrong, I can't just leave my sister here... alone. Since we've been brought here, I've always been around, even passed out in the other room, I was around. No, I can't go. I have to be here with Maya.

But the pacing continues. As does the scratching.

What if I go, though? Is this something I can do? Just... go out for breakfast? On my own, without Maya?

God, this is strange.

I'm on my eighth tour around the kitchen island, and the idea sounds better and better with each one.

"You okay?"

"Ah!" I jump, pressing a palm to my heaving chest.

"Sorry, sorry." Katya puts her hands up in apology.

"My fault, I was distracted."

"Did something happen?"

"No, it's just..." I sigh, realizing I'm worrying her with my reaction. "Loreley texted me. I guess you gave her the number. She invited me for breakfast."

"Go," she says before I even finished the last syllable.

"I can't just—Maya is—"

"She's fine. I'll stay with her here. I have nothing planned today anyway." She cuts me off.

"Katya, I know I shouldn't have any reasons to be uncomfortable with this, any rational ones anyway, but... Look, after everything her and I have been through, the only time we've spent apart in the last two years was when she went to school and when we got separated in that container. That's it. Leaving her..."

"I understand. I'm not going to force trust on you. I can't do that. But sometimes you have to listen to your gut. If yours tells you to keep your guard up around us, around me, then fair enough. Just make sure that's the reason you're doing it. All I can tell you is that none of us are here to hurt you."

I know. Rationally I know all they've done has been more than generous. Selfless too. Maybe they're keeping me around in the hopes that I'll remember something useful about the men who took us, which is fair enough. But if that was the only reason, we wouldn't be sleeping in Katya's soft bed and expensive sheets every night.

I have to try this. Let go, if only for a bit.

Perhaps later on I will be able to go out on my own and seek something more.

It's my birthday today, after all.

I look at the phone and my fingers fly over the letters.

I'll be downstairs. Thank you.

* * *

"This one would work so well on you." Loreley holds up against my front a blouse with a deep V neckline. It's in a goldish color that would, indeed, look great with my skin tone.

Morrigan cocks her head as she looks in our direction, but she seems more focused on my face rather than the blouse.

"I don't think it's a winner, Lu," she says.

"Why not? It looks lovely." Loreley pauses and looks up from the blouse to me. "Oh, my bad, I think you're right."

I stifle a laugh because the interaction between these two has been both hilarious and sweet all morning. They fit together like they share DNA, not just a close friendship.

They took me out for breakfast at the cutest café in the center of Queenscove. A narrow little building nestled in-between two large, elegant facades, and it didn't really look like much. Only, as we passed through the small, cozy space, I quickly found that the attraction of the place wasn't inside, but at the back. We passed through the back door and found ourselves in a stunning enclosed courtyard where every inch of the walls were covered in trailing plants and two large trees shaded the space.

Maybe I was imagining it, but that café, the atmosphere, really helped me be more comfortable with the situation. The fact that Katya has been sending me photos of her and Maya might have also had something to do with it.

We had a surprisingly enjoyable time. They didn't push me to talk but involved me in every conversation. They didn't ask intrusive questions or urged me to open up about what happened to Maya and me. They did ask a bit about my family and how we ended up on the streets, however they were fine when I decided to keep it vague, and simply tell them that we were staying with our mom, and she died.

Telling them the whole story would pose too many questions and reveal more than I'm comfortable with right now. My aversion to what and who they are as well.

Either way, they didn't push, even as they could clearly tell there was more to everything, and I appreciated that.

Afterward, they dragged me around town, showing me all sorts of interesting places, including a quirky little bookstore that seemed to have been there for at least a hundred years. I went inside to find a couple of books for Maya, and that's when I caught sight of that shiny little black bank card again. Same one that Maddox tried to give me, only now it was in Morrigan's hand as she paid for the books.

She gave me a look that told me not to dare protest, and I kept my mouth shut. I think that if I do decide to buy anything from the department store we're currently in, I'll see that card again.

Will she try to slip it in my pocket when we leave?

Will I protest?

Loreley puts the blouse back on its rack and turns, stopping to look at me. "This is not you, is it?"

"What do you mean?"

"All of this"—she waves around the clothing racks and shelves—"is not your style, is it?"

I don't want to sound ungrateful. I can't afford to be picky. "I'm not really fussy. I'm okay with what I have."

"That was not the question, Evie."

Evie... that sounded rather sweet.

Morrigan hooks her arm around mine and gently drags me away from the pastel-themed shelves.

"Come on, dare to dream a little. If you could have anything, what would it be?" she asks.

If I could have anything, I would buy it for Maya. Not me. There's no guarantee for how long I would have *everything*, because just like our mom, it could be taken away in the blink of an eye.

"Anything." Loreley joins in and grabs my other arm.

I sigh, finding that there's no escaping this. Yet, I don't actually want to. Maybe I could dream a little.

"Black," I say.

"Black?" Morrigan asks.

"And really dark greens, teal, and purple."

"Oh." Her eyes sparkle.

"Fishnets and platform Doc Martens."

"Hmm." Loreley says with a cheeky smile, and I swear I can hear cogs spinning in that beautiful head of hers.

"Leather, velvet, and oversized sweaters."

"Now we're talking." Morrigan tightens her hold.

"We can definitely do leather." Loreley joins in, that cheeky grin turning down-right devious.

"You should see our collection. Though it's probably a different vibe," Morrigan says, laughing.

"I've never actually worn anything like that. Never had the opportunity, but it's the style I've always admired. Dark, rock on the side of gothic, moody," I explain.

"I love that. I can honestly see it on you," Loreley says.

"I think we should," Morrigan adds. "Come on, I know where to take you."

"Honestly, you don't have to. I can't buy anything anyway, but I also don't need to, it's all good. Really," I argue, tugging them back uselessly.

"It's only a few doors down from here, and you don't have to buy anything," she continues as we exit the department store and turn right. "And if it's money you're worrying about—don't. Seriously, you have to stop that. None of us are going to allow you to struggle or feel bad because you can't buy your sister two books or some clothes for yourself. I get it, it feels like shit, but it's not your fault you were kidnapped, or that you're like two thousand miles away from home, or that you can't pull money out of your ass. You're here because The Sanctum wants to help you, just like they helped all the others."

"Hey," Loreley argues.

"I know, I know, you're not part of The Sanctum. That's not the point here. The point is that we are the ones offering to help you, you are not taking advantage of us. Okay?" Morrigan finishes just as we turn another right into a side street with smaller, quainter shops.

"I appreciate it. I really do."

I'm prepared to argue against it again, but I realize that it just means that I will be having the same debate later. I know what's stopping me, and it's not just my ego, but the provenance of this money I'm being offered and the fact that I'm still not convinced that it comes with no strings attached.

"I'm used to taking care of my sister and I on my own. This is difficult to adjust to. Harder to accept."

"We can start small, right about now." Morrigan halts us in front of a small storefront, black baroque style woodwork framing the window and the glass-paneled door.

The window display looks like it might just be the store of my dreams. Platform boots, combat boots, lace-ups, leather skirts and thick, dark lace and velvet, cozy knitted sweaters, and some sexier things I would never dare to buy. Maybe.

Damn...

They don't have to drag me into this one, I walk in willingly.

"I understand it's hard. Lulu had to beg me to accept the apartment she gave me in her building when I had no money of my own to move out of my parents' house, after university," Morrigan says.

Loreley has an entire apartment building? If she's not part of The Sanctum, what exactly does she do for work?

"I thought you live with Vincent in the woods."

"Our situation is a little different. Our marriage is quite new and let's just say it was not planned. But the apartment happened before this, and it's still mine." She starts looking through the clothing racks, pulling a myriad of items out as we move through the store and showing them to me for approval.

"Sorry, I didn't mean to pry," I apologize.

"No, don't worry. It's no secret. But I just wanted to tell you that in a small way, since our situations are different, I do understand that accepting help is hard on the soul. God knows I had to make a deal with the devil just to justify accepting help."

Loreley snickers at that, and I narrow my brows.

"She's referring to her *hubby*. He's The Serpent... and he calls her his *Little Eve*. Get it?" the blonde woman shakes her head in mock disapproval. "They did make an actual deal... crossroads and all."

Well, someday I will pry a little more to find out the whole intriguing story.

"I want to do this for myself," I say.

"You will. But you can't expect it to happen right away. You have some serious healing to do." Morrigan hands me the clothes I nodded to in approval. "Try them on."

"I'm not buying all of these." I hold the items like they burn me.

"You don't have to. Just try them on. At least now you know where the store is," she says, shrugging.

Before I close the dressing room door, I turn to her and Lulu. "It's not stubbornness, by the way. Getting back on my feet is more about Maya and my responsibilities back in Fleeton than it is for myself. I will search for a job and start saving as soon as I figure out the logistics about my sister."

I close the changing room door before either of them can continue this conversation. There's no debating this plan. Pulling my clothes off, I'm happy when I notice the gauze is still neatly in place and there's no blood seeping through from the shallow wounds. The first thing I try on is a pair of tight black jeans and a thin, oversized knitted sweater.

"Childcare for Maya can be arranged." Morrigan raises her voice behind the door and says, "I believe that a certain mother of the group would be happy to help. But you can also enroll her in school here."

I know she's referring to Mamaw June and I don't disagree.

"I want to enroll her, but I can't." I crack the door and peek through so I can whisper, "She was enrolled in Fleeton under a slight misspelled name. Intentionally, of course. But that doesn't mean that CPS, and probably the police if the school alerted them of a missing child, couldn't make the connection. More importantly, I don't have custody of her yet, and I won't risk going on the radar until then."

"I think all that can be sorted. I'm sure The Sanctum has some *resources* at their disposal," Loreley says in a lowered tone.

I'm not sure what she means by that, and as intriguing as it sounds, accepting more help from them is off the table. At least until I'm convinced it doesn't come at a cost. No matter what, it has to start with custody, and I can't even begin to fathom how incredibly difficult that will be.

"A job can be arranged too. I could always use the extra help," Loreley adds.

"Maddox and Finnigan will kill us if we bring her in Metamorphosis," Morrigan counters, as I close the door back up, to try on more clothes.

I scowl at the sound of that. What does Finnigan have to do with this decision? I can do whatever I want to do. But, what's Metamorphosis and why shouldn't I be there?

"Christ, babe, no. I meant the café," Loreley says, laughing.

"Aaah. Okay, yeah, that makes more sense."

"That's kind of you, but it's okay. I'm sure I will find something," I say.

"It's up to you. The offer is there."

Loreley basically offered me a job. Just like that. Though accepting it wouldn't be any different from taking their money.

Or maybe I'm overthinking this too. After all, Loreley isn't part of The Sanctum, is she?

CHAPTER 7
Evelyn

I T'S LUNCHTIME WHEN I GET back to Katya's place with three large bags and a shiny new black card that Morrigan threw in one of them. She gave me a warning glare that told me she was gonna bite me if I dared return it, then said it's not hers, anyway. I haven't touched it. It's Maddox's for sure. It looks exactly the same as the one he tried to give me at the ice cream place.

Jay helps me with the bags as I walk in, opening the door for me, but I stagger when the living room comes into view. It's not Katya I find sitting on the couch with Maya.

What the hell is Finnigan doing here with my sister?

My steps toward them quicken, but falter when I see Katya in the kitchen, calm as she potters about. Feigning a relaxed wave to her takes effort, but it's the strained smile she puts on in response that confuses me. I don't stop to ask her about it, because I'm curious about the intense conversation my seven-year-old sister is engaged in with a man twenty years her senior. The back of the sofa faces me, and they don't appear to see me coming.

"Evie told me that some of the other books are for older kids, but I still want to read them." I hear Maya's little voice.

"I may be in favor of breaking the rules once in a while, but she's right with this one, sugar. I read them when I was older than you." His gaze drifts to me. He knew I was here all along.

I'm sorry, what? Finnigan Hennessey is talking books with my sister?

My sister turns too and jumps and squeaks when she sees me, rushing toward me with yet another great big smile on her face that I didn't put there.

"You're not going to believe it, Evie! Finnigan likes Jules Verne, too. We've been talking about the one I'm reading now, and he said there's another one I will love when I finish this one—*Treasure Island*. Can you get it for me, Evie? Please? It has pirates!"

My eyes widen, lips parting as I creep back to the entryway on uneasy steps, pulling out of one of the bags I came with exactly that—Treasure Island—a second-hand copy I bought from that little bookstore.

I'm still wrapped tight in disbelief as I return to her and hand her the paperback. Her eyes bulge when the title sinks in, then with an ear-piercing shriek, she throws her arms around me. It only lasts a second before she whips around and jumps back on the sofa, showing the man who looks like he just came from a beach photo shoot. He looks just as stunned as I am.

"Look, look!" She jumps on the sofa next to him. "It's the same one. It's like you talked!"

He only manages a nod before he straightens his surprise and gives her a quick smile before rising.

I want to ask him what he's doing here, but it's not my house. He probably comes here for Katya all the time.

It doesn't explain why he's watching me like that, though. His focus heats my skin and the hairs on the back of my neck rise. It was the same at Vincent's house—every time he looked at me, I felt exposed down to my soul.

Tiny electric shocks flourish down my back, wrapping around my waist, and I move before they can reach the area that threatens deeply inappropriate thoughts.

"Could we talk for a moment?"

His voice stops me dead in my tracks. On a slow inhale, I turn, breathing in through the tightness gripping my chest. Katya walks over, a cold annoyance in her gaze directed straight at him. She obviously knows what this is about, and I'm not loving her expression.

"Evelyn, you—" she begins.

"Katya," Finnigan warns, and her nostrils flare in response.

She wants to but doesn't argue. I cross my arms against my chest, tightening them ever so slightly, as I cock my head.

"Maya, could you come with me for a moment?" Katya shifts toward my sister, and a moment later they are both out of the room.

This is only the second time Finnigan and I have been alone, and the first one did not go well at all. I suspect this one won't be any different.

"You can't tell me to leave again." I begin because I can't stand this silence, not when that prickle is back on my spine, "I live here. You'll have to be the one to go."

He drops his gaze for a second and my heart follows the moment realization strikes. That's exactly what he's about to do. I take a step back, eyes widening as I force my composure.

"I'm going to give you money so you can go back home. I know this is the only reason you're not going back yet, and I want to make it happen. I will provide transport or a car, a place to stay when you get there, and enough money for you and your sister to be comfortable for a long while."

Excuse me?

"You're messing with me, right?" My arms drop, fists tightening as I force my anger into them rather than my tone.

"I'm happy to do it this week. I have a number in mind, you tell me if it's enough or if this is gonna cost more."

"Cost?" I choke on the word. "You're actually being serious?"

This is not help, this is borderline bribery. The fact that my voice stayed at an almost calm level is nothing short of a miracle.

"Yes, I am." His tone is cool, so matter-of-fact something tightens in my chest in response. "You need money to leave, and I have money to make it happen."

Taking an involuntary step toward him as heat fills my chest, I let his words sink in along with their implication. Conflict flickered in his eyes for a split second, but I don't care to unpack that right now. We're two steps away from each other, too close, yet not close enough for me to slap him. And God, how my palm twitches to slap his handsome face.

"How dare you?!" The disdain bleeds through my voice, but I'm keeping my tone low since Maya's in the other room.

"Excuse me?" he says with a scowl.

"You heard me. How dare you pay me off to leave Queenscove? Do you really think I'm that type of person?"

"It's not any different from us helping to return all those kids to their parents or to whomever they were taken from." He shrugs, the gesture irritating me further.

"Is that what you tell yourself to justify this? It definitely doesn't have anything to do with the other night?" I take another step toward him, flexing my hands at my sides as the itch intensifies.

The man sneers. "I don't know what you're talking about."

The conflict is way clearer in his eyes now. The ire too.

"Prove it, then. Because I've been trying to make sense of your attitude toward me, Finnigan."

His eyes flicker at the sound of his name and nostrils flare.

"From the first moment I saw you, when you found me in that container, you looked at me like I broke something of yours I didn't know existed. And you had such... revulsion for me. I understood it then—I'm a poor, dirty, uneducated homeless girl who screwed up and got herself in trouble. But you still have not stopped watching me. You're doing a better job at hiding the revulsion, but now it's like you're demanding I fix whatever you think it is I broke." Where did I get the guts to call this man out on his attitude?

This is going to bite me right in the ass, judging by his darkening expression.

"You're crossing a line, girl." His tone turns to a low rumble, and my palm whips against his cheek on a loud crack.

"Do not call me *girl!*"

I freeze, eyes widening as if what I did only just sinks in. His eyes widen in shock, his lips are pursed in annoyance, but the man is too stunned to speak. Or act.

Nope, I was wrong. So, so wrong. On rushed steps, my back is pressed against the wall, the hand I slapped him with pinned by the wrist above my head, as his other slams against the wall next my head. I'm caged in. His chest rises and falls on strained, heavy breaths that sizzle against my skin. He's so... so close, yet his hand around my wrist is the only part of him touching me.

I have to crane my neck to look him in the eyes, but

the intensity in them presses against my soul. My breath is trapped somewhere in my lungs as I await the impending punishment. All the courage I had a moment ago has stalled, simmering beyond this painful anticipation.

But something else seeps in through it all. Through the closeness of our bodies, in the heat radiating between us, amongst the heavy breaths and the touch of his powerful grip, invisible threads sizzle. They start over my lips, sliding down and wrapping around my throat, turning to goosebumps as they fall over my chest. They graze my breasts before they drop to my belly and my gaze widens on a slight gasp when I realize I can't stop where the sizzling sensation is heading to.

This is so wrong. The man just insulted me down to my bones, and yet my body has no reservations. I expected punishment, but he looks at me like he's the one being punished. I may be seeing things, but I swear he looks just as I feel—charged with a heated tension we can't control.

"Evelyn," he whispers my name like it's too heavy on his tongue. "I need you to go."

"Why?" It comes out like something between a breath and a whimper.

"Leave Queenscove." He ignores my question.

"No."

"Goddamn it, woman!" His hand flexes around my wrist and my free hand shoots up before me instinctively.

His muscles tense when I grab onto his side yet he doesn't let go. Doesn't even move an inch. But his bright blue eyes darken, and a few curly strands I itch to wrap around my finger fall around his face as he leans in further.

Christ, no man should ever be allowed to look this good.

"You can't do it, can you?" I whisper, my gaze straining to stay on his eyes and not move further down. "You can't prove that you're not chasing me away because of the other night.

What are you afraid of, Finnigan? Why do you want to get rid of me so badly?"

"You're reading too much into it."

"Am I reading too much into this too?" I look between us, at the closeness of our bodies, before returning to his azure eyes.

His nostrils flare again, and his gaze drops to my lips for a heavy moment before it comes back to my eyes. A raging fire burns through the blue.

"Yes. You're just a—"

"Don't you dare say it again." I seethe. God, the way I despise being called a girl.

"Too young. Far, far too young."

"For what?" I challenge.

He sighs, too many seconds passing without an answer.

"Stop being fucking stubborn. I'm offering you money with no strings attached. An easy way out," he deflects again, but this time I'm absolutely done with it.

"No strings attached?" I scoff. "I don't believe that for a second. Your kind doesn't operate like that, and we both know it. There's always a price to pay with the *mafia*,"—I throw the word to see how it lands, if he's going to deny it—"and I've had enough taken away by your world. I will never, ever accept your blood money."

That, he did not like.

He releases me in a split second and takes a step back.

"Blood money?" he says, raising his voice. "We saved you, Evelyn. When the hell did you get up on your high horse and forget about that fact? This fucking *blood money* made it possible!"

He doesn't deny the name I called them by. Anger seeps through my veins like liquid fire, throbbing in my temples.

No. I refuse to entertain this. I had no choice in any of this.

His world took everything from mine. Even if he didn't wield the hand who did it.

"I'm not taking your money, and I refuse to be chased away. You know very well why I can't return to Fleeton yet. But don't worry, I will gladly leave *you* and this place once I earn my way back."

"Looking forward to it!" he spits back with a sneer.

And with those harsh words, he spins on his heels and walks out.

CHAPTER 8
Finnigan

"TWO OF THE SAME?" the bartender asks.

"Yes!" I raise my voice over the loud music.

"The fact that you called me was a shock, but this mood you're in tonight is an even better surprise, baby!" Clara, the blonde I probably made a mistake inviting out again tonight, says in my ear.

The need to wipe her breath off of it gnaws at me, but I refrain, turning to her with a reluctant, cold smile. This might not have been a good idea, and it's gonna bite me in the ass, because I rarely invite a girl out more than twice. It creates an expectation I'm never going to meet. I refuse to. Relationships are not my thing. Dating is not my thing. Fucking is. And I make it clear to all the women I do it with.

But this is the third time I asked Clara out, and she's perfectly aware it's out of character. I know I have a reputation.

Even if I'm not the only bachelor in The Sanctum, I'm the only one who sees women on a regular and fairly public basis. I think I inadvertently made it into a challenge for women to try to get me past that second interaction. Many have tried, but I shot them down without remorse.

I'm not a dick, at least I don't think I come across as that, but I have my boundaries and I make sure whoever I go out with is perfectly aware of them too.

Clara, here, might be getting the wrong impression, and it's my own fucking fault. However, after the day I had, after that stubborn gir—*woman*—decided to screw over my plan of getting rid of her, I had to get out, wipe my memory of her, and replace her with someone else. I was livid and impatient. There was no time to find someone else, and I picked the first woman I knew is everything Evelyn Shaw isn't.

Though, I must admit I felt something strangely close to pride at her attitude toward me. Weeks prior, she could hardly make eye contact with others.

The four vodka sours, six Jager shots, and loud music help ease the worries about Clara.

What they don't do is drown Evelyn out.

When I look at Clara's brown eyes, I see bright gray seeping into gold. When I look at her dark brown hair, I see blonde like wheat on a cloudy day. When I look at Clara's voluptuous body, I see slender. And instead of her porcelain skin, I see soft, olive tones, sun-kissed even if Queenscove's sun hasn't touched her.

Another shot, along with a fifth vodka sour is slid in front of me, and Clara's wide smile fills my vision.

"Here, baby!" she shouts, handing me the drinks.

That pet name rakes through my eardrums.

I take the shot, cheer quickly, and down it in the hopes that the spirit will make it sound better.

It doesn't.

"Another one!" I holler at the bartender who just turned away from us.

He narrows his eyes on me for a moment, but when I cock my head and give him a look Carter would be proud of, he quickly straightens and jumps into gear without question.

"You're on a mission tonight. Bad day?"

"I just want to have some fun," I answer.

"That's what I like to hear. Let's dance!"

I glance between her and the dance floor, debating it. I would normally say yes, but tonight I need at least one more drink in me.

"Later."

"No problem, *baby*, we could just sit here and..." she trails off and so does her hand, sliding up my thigh as her eyes spell something even more suggestive.

Another shot appears in front of me, and I down it before she can say something else, then step off the bar stool, grabbing her hand. I guide her to the dance floor in the middle of this bar that's both seedy and kind of nice at the same time and pull her to me once we're in the middle of all the bodies swaying on a hip-hop song I don't recognize.

Clara wraps her whole body around mine, clutching my nape and pressing her breasts against my chest, her hips against my own, rubbing against my cock. It responds to the friction, but in this hypnotic flickering low light, her face morphs into the one I'm fighting to fucking forget. The whole reason I'm drinking my weight in alcohol and rubbing against a woman I don't actually want.

I flip Clara around, her back against my front, shutting down the image of the forbidden woman.

It works.

Gripping her hips as she rolls them against me, we sway

to the rhythm of the music, and I fall deeper into the alcohol haze. *Christ, I really overdid it.* My feet move on their own accord, my body weightless, yet something is off. Closing my eyes, I tighten my grip like it could push Clara deeper into my mind, and I run through the filthy things I'll do to her once we're out of here. Only, I'm finding myself forcing my way through those thoughts, because somehow... not sure how... each and every one of them feels wrong.

This whole situation is—the body in my arms, the sensation against me—it's all wrong. Even her scent.

Until it's not...

Drawing in a deep, hypnotizing breath, spicy ginger sneaks through my senses. It's on the verge of faint, catching my attention without overpowering. A moment later the sweet smell of rich brown sugar hits me with mind-bending force and my steps falter.

I'm at a precipice, but I can't quite make the leap to rationalize, or accept its implication. It's delicious, decadent, and disturbingly familiar.

My eyes pop open when I pinpoint the familiarity of the combination, and who it belongs to.

Goddamn it! She was finally out of my mind.

Okay, not completely out, but I was so fucking close.

Someone bumps into my back, probably another dancer.

"Sorry, man." A deep voice follows, teetering on slurring. "How about I get you a drink, baby?" I know that's not aimed at me.

I lazily turn my head—the man who spoke wasn't the one who bumped into me, and *her* fucking scent wasn't in my head. Our eyes meet, hers as glassy as mine probably are, and the shock at my sight quickly gets replaced by anger.

"A drink sounds great!" she raises her voice over the music and walks away, some random guy on her tail.

What the actual fuck just happened?
Evelyn-motherfucking-Shaw is in this bar right now.
With a random guy hitting on her.
Drunk.
Oh, hell no!
"Come on, baby, come back to me." Clara's voice is just another thing about her that's wrong.

I turn my gaze from the spot where Evelyn stood, back to the dark-haired woman. Two options run in a loop through my dizzy head: put Clara in a taxi and send her away... or do that to Evelyn and go home with Clara.

Fuck!
"What is it, baby?" she asks.
Did I say that out loud?

She wraps her arms around my neck, running her fingers through my hair, and I have an urge to shove her as far away as possible. What is happening with me?

"Let's get another drink," I tell her, prying her hands off my neck.

"Um, yeah, sure... okay." She doesn't sound all that sure.

I force my gaze on our seats, refusing to stray and search for Evelyn. I don't understand what she's doing here. She's not even old enough to be in this bar, goddamn it!

On clenched teeth I take a deep inhale, trying to rationalize it. Nah, I must be overthinking. She must be with Morrigan, Lulu, or Katya.

She's fine.

I reach the bar, my untouched vodka sour waiting patiently. I throw back half of it, then sit.

She's fine.

But I'm not. My only choice is to use Clara as goddamn bleach and drown myself in her to forget about the woman who threatens the wall I built in the last eight years. All the work I've done to be able to survive as I have, is now at risk. My goddamn integrity too since she's... fuck! Way too young!

I turn to the right, and just on cue, Clare steps between my legs, wrapping an arm around my back, the other palm laid over my chest. She leans in, her hot breath on my ear, before she wraps her lips around my lobe.

"Maybe we should head to my place before the alcohol does more damage. It would be such a shame not to... consummate this night," she whispers sensually in my ear.

I'm just about to open my mouth to answer when I catch sight of something that boils the blood from my veins in one second flat—Evelyn dancing far too close for comfort with that same douche. He's behind her, his hands on her hips, and looking down at her like he wants way more than a dance.

Then I notice she's dressed differently. All black. Tight high-waisted jeans, intentionally ripped in too many places showing far too much skin, combat boots, a loose leather crop top that doesn't touch her waist, and a thin, oversized cardigan that's fallen off one shoulder, exposing her soft skin and thin straps of her top. She looks... at home.

She looks goddamn perfect.

I'm fucked.

But so is the guy currently lowering his hands dangerously.

"Excuse me."

I calmly push Clara back before I get off the stool, and head straight to the wretched woman and the asshole who plans to fuck her.

"You!" I point at him as I near. "Leave," I order him.

"Get your own, man. This one's mine," he says with amusement in his tone, not sparing me a glance.

"*This?*" I sneer. She's not a fucking object. And she's definitely not his.

He also doesn't sound like he's drunk, which pisses me off

further because now I know he plans on taking advantage of Evelyn. I step as close as I can get, caging her between us, and I wrap my hand around the guy's throat without hesitation. Evelyn gasps but doesn't move. He lets go of her and goes to grab onto my arm, but his eyes land on mine before his touch does, and I don't miss the moment recognition hits through the haze of the dim lights.

"My bad. She's all yours." He quickly throws his hands up in surrender, but with his throat in my hand, he can't move.

I give it one last squeeze before I let go, but don't step away from her.

She turns toward the asshole. "Hey, no. You don't have to go. I am *not* his!" Evelyn argues, but her words come together a little slow.

"Um, yes, I really do. So... yeah, thanks for a good night. Bye." And with that, he disappears into the crowd.

I sense eyes on us from the other patrons, but I couldn't give a shit about the attention we're attracting.

"You need to go home," I say to her, but it comes out like an order.

She narrows her eyes, slowly cocking her head, and uneasiness scrapes its way up my spine. It leaves goosebumps in its wake. I feel horribly seen. Logic whispers to me that I'm imagining it, but the way her gaze seeps into my veins makes me wonder if she's discovering all my secrets right about now.

My fear eases when her gaze softens, but dread replaces it when she slowly, so fucking slowly, bites one side of her luscious bottom lip. I'm transfixed. It's impossible to rip my gaze away.

Then the woman does the unthinkable—she laughs.

She motherfucking laughs!

And it sounds ridiculously good. Dangerously so.

Brown sugar and ginger intensifies through my senses,

contributing to the haze that already took over my brain. Only, now I'm drunk on her.

I'm sick... so goddamn sick.

"I was dancing. You interrupted me," she complains, yet her eyes spell mischief in multiple languages.

I was expecting more protest, fighting back, but it's clear as day—she really is drunk. How did they serve her here? The legal age is eighteen.

"Who are you here with? Katya? Morrigan?" I ask.

She shakes her head slowly and smiles. "I am all on my own. Can you believe it? On my own." She's giddy as she says those words, oddly proud too.

There aren't enough curses and swear words in the English language for me to express how I feel about this piece of information.

"What the hell were you thinking?" I swipe a hand over my face at the stupidity of what she's done. After all that happened to her, being alone is the last thing she should do.

She shrugs and starts looking around, seemingly uninterested in the direction of this conversation.

"I was thinking that I deserve this... especially today."

"You need to go home, where you are safe, and sleep it off," I tell her, my tone grave.

She laughs again and moves along to the music. To my dismay, a slow, R&B tune fills the barroom, and her hips sway torturously from side to side. We're lost in the crowd as more people join on the dance floor, and in a strange paradox, it's turning more intimate. Like we're alone.

"You, mister, need to go back to your girlfriend," she says.

"She's not my girlfriend."

She purses her lips, but then shrugs and straightens.

"Home. Now!" I insist.

"You don't get to tell me what to do, Finnigan Hennessey.

Remember?" She pokes me in the middle of the chest as her steps falter, and I quickly grab her bicep to steady her.

She takes it as a cue and wraps her hand around my nape, gripping my side with the other, so warm on my ribs. She starts moving against me without warning, swaying her whole body as she pulls me to follow her rhythm.

All night I felt wrong with Clara around me. But now, with Evelyn's body lined against mine, her scent wrapped around every inch of me, her incredible eyes holding mine in their invisible tether, it feels disturbingly right.

I can't tell if it's the alcohol guiding my feet or my will, but they move with her. As if hypnotized, they follow her flow, our eyes locked onto each other as we lose ourselves in a world that's only ours. It feels both right and wrong. It's perfect and forbidden. It's meant to be and doomed to fail.

This makes no sense.

She makes no sense.

But us... we make all the sense in the world.

It's been too many years, and not one woman has managed to stick to me. But Evelyn has crawled right under my skin, and she's slowly bleeding her soul into my veins. My muscles tense when her warm touch leaves slithering electric current in its wake as she draws down to my clenched fist. I didn't register the ache from the strain until she guided me to relax my hand, then pulled it to her waist.

My touch meets bare skin, the softness so electrifying that it seems as if she's the one caressing me. I can't help but squeeze her delicate flesh. Just once. That's all I allow myself.

But the minx pulls herself closer, pressing against me and making me far too aware of the hard on that I'm failing to control. She's not acknowledging it, and I'm not sure if I'm relieved or slightly disappointed. Before I can think better of it, I reach up and brush the back of my fingers against her cheek, down the soft line of her jaw, and under her delicate chin, guiding it up. Liquid gold sparkles where it meets the gray in her mesmerizing irises, and I don't know if it's her gaze or the touch, but whatever it is ignites a heat that floods my chest like it's seeping out of my very soul. And there's nothing foreign about it. It's a slotted piece of a puzzle I decided long ago I will not try to solve. It's been begging to be let out, to slot into place in the fabric of my being and wrap around the one thing inside my chest I have to protect.

Keeping it at bay has been easy. Until now. After all these years, all it took was one look at *her*.

My fingers trace her bare flesh mindlessly and my feet are still guided by her. I should stop this. It's not right, none of this is right. This must be a sickness.

She's too young, she's not for me. I've never done anything this stupid in my entire life. I'm better than this, and she deserves to find someone better than me.

A man she can trust. A man who can take care of her. Who can protect her. Who *deserves* her.

I am not that man now, nor will I ever be.

Before I can change my mind, I grab her hand, spin on my heels and move away from the dance floor, pulling her with me. She follows willingly as we head toward the exit.

"Wait!" She tugs at my hand. "My bag."

"Where is it?" I stop and turn to her.

She points toward the bar, and I gesture to her to take the lead. There's a joyful sprint in her step. It's new, and it looks peculiar. Not wrong. Not right either. Just... out of character.

You don't know her character, asshole.

When we reach the bar, she gets the attention of the bartender who nods before turning and heading out of sight.

"Oh, my drink!" she exclaims and reaches over to a glass of some pink liquid.

She grabs it quickly, and in a split second, I smack my hand over it, pushing it back on the bar top.

"What the hell do you think you're doing?!" I raise my tone, unapologetically.

"It's—um... my drink."

"That you left unattended for God knows for how fucking long. Literally anyone could have spiked it. Do you understand how much danger you could be in? Jesus Christ, Evelyn! Anyone could take advantage of you!"

She opens her mouth probably to protest, but I can see the exact moment she acknowledges my words, and as her gaze softens, I feel a tinge of guilt at my outburst.

"I didn't think. I've never... this is my first time." Her brows draw together as her eyes lower.

"No, you didn't think. Wait. First time out?"

She nods.

"Well, you shouldn't have been. I should kick the bartender's teeth in for even serving you."

She frowns for a few moments, and then her expression shifts to a realization she doesn't share with me. Just on cue the bartender shows up, sliding a small bag toward her. Before I can grab the guy by the collar, she swipes the bag from him and pushes me away from the bar until we're too far away for me to do anything.

"Where are you going to take me?" she asks, an expectant expression on her face, but her hand doesn't leave my chest.

"I'm putting you in a car and sending you home."

"What? You're joking, right? After all of... that?!" She gestures wildly to the dance floor.

The glassiness over her eyes seems to dissipate, replaced by pure annoyance.

"Goddamn it, you're doing it again. There's nothing here, there can't be anything between us. Do you understand?

You're fucking jail-bait, Evelyn!"

She throws her head back, laughing hard enough that she attracts attention.

"That's what bothers you? My age? You can stop feeling so guilty because I'm officially eighteen today. Well, according to that clock on the wall it's past midnight, so technically it happened yesterday."

Oh, fuck...

My mind is spinning with the flurry of thoughts assaulting me. Too many voices argue inside my head, throwing arguments that shouldn't matter right now. I strain to focus and the first emotion I grasp is sadness. This creature has had so much taken away from her, and now this pivotal moment in her life might have passed without proper celebration. We should have known. We should have tried to make her feel special.

Am I overthinking it? She was out with Morri and Lulu today, after all. She probably celebrated.

Then why didn't Katya mention anything? I shake the subject away and grasp one other voice screaming inside my mind. It's the loudest one and the one I want to squash the most—*she's legal now*. I would punch myself in the face if there weren't so many people around me, because that thought eases the sickening guilt. It shouldn't. It will not, because her age makes no difference at all. One year added onto it is still too many away from mine. This is still wrong.

But it could feel so fucking right.

Goddamn it, no!

"It's your birthday? Did anyone know?" I strain to pull myself out of the cesspit of dangerous thoughts.

"Nope. But don't change the subject. There's nothing stopping you now," she says, a smug expression on her pretty face.

I shake my head and snort. "It doesn't change anything."

Before she can further protest, and before I can convince myself that it does, indeed, change something, I grab her hand and pull her toward the exit. This time she does fight me, but I don't give her any leeway as we pass through the door and into the crisp night air.

"Are you serious right now?" Even now, in her drunken state, she still doesn't yell.

Her tone is filled with annoyance and a hint of embarrassment, but no raised voice. I ignore her as I catch sight of one of my guys who's my designated driver tonight and gesture him over.

"Are you even listening to me?" She pulls on me to grab my attention.

The hurt in her eyes takes me aback, but I can't fucking falter.

"Listen to me, Evelyn. You and I are never going to happen. I don't do relationships, and I certainly don't do quick fucks with *girls* like you."

Her nostrils flare at my choice of words and tears pool in her eyes, but there's much more fury than upset shining in her gaze. She's livid. The rejection seeps through her just as fast as the regret does through me. But it had to be done.

My driver pulls the car next to us, and I yank the back door open. When my eyes drift back to her, the drunk Evelyn is gone. The one I see now could cut me into a million pieces and not even bother burying me. Her back is straight, her gaze stern, and I almost... almost cave and go back on my words. Even if they are for her own protection.

I can't stand the way she looks at me. Fear seeps down to my bones, the kind I never wanted to suffer. Because now, I'm scared she'll never again look at me like she did mere moments ago.

What have I done?

CHAPTER 9
Evelyn

I WAKE UP WITH WRONGNESS IN my veins. It burns all the way up my throat, and the flood of emotions and pain from all those weeks ago when I was taken, fills me with a raging vengeance. I flip the cover off my body and run to the bathroom, sliding to my knees and hugging the toilet.

Not much comes out as I wretch—apart from the alcohol I drank last night that burns all through my throat. Though I'm surprised I didn't just absorb it all into my system, because it certainly appears that way.

Only, that's not what's making me sick right now. This sickness is different, raw and needy, emptying my veins and leaving me desperate. The itch beneath my skin, the need in my blood vessels, the craving for escape, is back. I should be used to it by now. It comes every morning, and even as it eases through the day, it returns at night. It haunts my dreams and calls for me in my nightmares.

I want to rationalize it, I try to anyway, but I haven't managed yet. I can't wrap my head around the fact that I was only drugged on one occasion. Yes, it was multiple times in a short amount of time, but that was it—one night. I can't justify why this need is chasing me still... it was just one time. It's a terrifying desire to poison my blood, and I'm not sure for how long I can resist this call.

I don't know if I want to anymore.

Images from last night flash through my treacherous memory, and I slide all the way down to the floor, my back hitting the cold tiles as the blue-eyed bane appears in my mind.

"God, what have I done?"

I completely threw myself at him, stupidly thinking he was dragging me out of the bar with such possessiveness because he wanted me. All day at Vincent's house he pushed me away, until we were alone, and suddenly, he seemed lost. It twisted my perception of us.

"You and I are never going to happen."

The stare he pinned me with was just as cold as those words. Then he threw the final blow.

"I don't do relationships, and I certainly don't do quick fucks with girls like you."

How could I have been so stupid as to think that this man wanted something to do with me? He's right—I read far too much into it.

Didn't I...?

I must have imagined the conflict that tightened his eyebrows and darkened his gaze as he threw his rejection in my face. More than once.

I probably read too much in his possessiveness last night, when he found me dancing with that guy who touched me a bit too insistently. Though, even as I protested, I was secretly thankful he got rid of him in that over-the-top display of power.

No, I didn't read too much into that.

This man holds a power over me I don't understand. He stirs something that has been growing deep within the fabric of my soul for a long time. A longing for selfishness and hedonism. A heated look, a lingering touch, even his harsh rejection makes that unfulfilled creature inside of me think it could reach the surface and be free. But it can't.

Especially as I'm slowly seeing the staggering truth—I didn't imagine the way he touched me, how he fought to hold himself back, or his stare as we lost ourselves to the rhythm of the music.

It was real. All of it was real.

"And I was an idiot to think that it could mean something." I slam my palm against the tile, and a knock on the door sends a tremor through me.

Christ.

"Evie, are you in there?"

"Yes, Maya." I jump to my feet, and I catch myself on the door frame as dizziness sweeps through me.

I swallow, forcing back the nausea, and open the door.

"Oh, you look bad. You got so much beauty sleep today, you should be all perfect and glowing," she says, giggling with that cheeky amusement.

"Beauty sleep?" I ask, ignoring the childish insult she doesn't notice.

"Yes. I asked Katya why you weren't having lunch with us, and she said you were having your beauty sleep. I didn't know what that meant, so she said that it's so it helps you be healthy, beautiful, and glowing."

Glowing? I snort, knowing full well sweat is the only thing that could make me glow right now. It sounds like Katya got uncomfortable and had no idea what to say to her. Wait, lunch? What time is it?

"I'm sorry I didn't wake up, sweet girl. I was very tired."

"That's okay. Katya said to tell you that Mamaw June is coming over later to see me, if that's okay with you. So... you can continue that beauty sleep."

At this point I would like it to turn into a coma. No sleep is going to help with what I'm feeling.

"Are you comfortable with her, Maya? Is this something you want to do?"

"Yes. Mamaw June tells me stories, all sorts of fairy tales and legends. And her food is delicious. She said she's gonna teach me to make crêpes. You know, like the ones you used to make all the time. And the cakes too. And—"

"Okay," I interrupt her before she walks further down memory lane and pushes me deeper in this despicable feeling that's making me sick right now. Though, I don't understand how she could possibly remember me baking; she was so young. "If you want to spend time with her, as long as you are comfortable, I'm okay with it. But you tell me if this changes. Yes?"

"I promise."

"Good. Now, let me brush my teeth."

She turns on her heels, skipping out of view, and I close the door, locking it behind me. All I can do right now is allow her to spend time with people who can offer her what I can't. A life, food on the table, safety. People who bring happiness in her life. Who enriches it in some way and puts a smile on her face and laughter in her voice.

I can't offer her any of that.

I haven't been able to in so long. She deserves better, so much better, and all these people... Katya, June, the bloody Sanctum, are giving her just that.

Once again, I slide down until my ass hits the cold tiles, and gather my knees to my chest, clutching my temples in my palms. I know what I need—a plan. A job, money, a roof over our heads, and... to go back to Fleeton.

The idea of returning to that wretched place turns the itch under my skin into molten lava, searing me from the inside out. It's my home. I was born there. Lived there my whole life. Everything left of me, of us, is there. But the pain and sorrow have replaced the good memories I have of that city.

Whether I like it or not, we have to go back. There's no other choice. No matter how much it will hurt to return to the place that took so much away from me—I must.

That thought brings another wave of nausea, and only when the pain becomes too much do I realize I'm digging my nails so hard in my skin, I'm piercing it.

I just need a little help. Just this once. A little help to quiet the rush of dread, to find a happy place, to escape, even if just for a few hours, or minutes. Only once, so after I can come back to the real world ready to tackle it, to make a plan that gives my sister the best life, maybe build one for myself too. A little escape, that's all I need.

I wasn't dancing with that guy last night by pure chance. I chose him because I caught him wiping a certain white powder off his nose and knew he could help. He didn't have what I'm looking for, but told me about someone who sells all sorts of substances and where to go to find him. I saved the information on my phone. It would be so easy. *It will be.* I have no idea how much it costs, but there's enough on Finnigan's card to take out at an ATM along the way. Yeah... Finnigan's card.

I found out that tidbit of information in the bar last night. Because it was either Maddox or Morrigan who used it for me, I didn't pay attention to the name written in gold. I just assumed it belonged to Maddox and didn't bother to look. When I tapped it on the card machine, the name caught my eyes and I swear I bought more alcohol just to spite the man.

Buying something harder than alcohol to quench this need is fitting, after all... he's the one who turned me into this. With his empty promise of saving me before something happened to me. Him who makes me think I could feel alive. Who rejects the possibility of us.

"Oh my god, what am I doing?"

My sister's laugh sounds farther away on the other side of this door, and it wakes me up from this self-destructive trance.

I can't do this to myself, chase the need for this high, I have to be strong for her. If not for me, definitely for her.

I peel myself off the floor and jump straight into the shower, washing off the stickiness from my skin, the stench of alcohol, and hopefully this disgusting craving with it, too.

* * *

For two hours I sat in an armchair listening to or watching Maya smile, laugh, and overall, fully enjoy her time with Mamaw June. Two hours of stories, of June teaching her how to beat eggs, how to mix in flour so it doesn't clump, two hours of twitching. On my part. My legs have been so jittery, I had to gather them both under me on the seat, because both my sister and Mamaw June started looking at me a little funny.

I thought staying here with them would help take my mind off of things. But it did nothing. I'm still a failure. The man with the lisp and his touch on me still haunt. And Finnigan's blue eyes are still here... rejection shining like a lighthouse in the recesses of my mind.

And after the sun went down, night began to fall, and I was feeling even worse, I left. Not before I put Maya to bed and kissed her goodnight. Not before I told her just how much I love her. But before I told her more... like how I wish I didn't fail her, that I didn't bring us to this point where strangers are taking better care of her than I ever could, how I wished she wasn't exposed to the ugly things she still doesn't talk about.

I left before I spilled it all into a confession her little ears didn't deserve to be burdened with. The buzzing in my ears and the sharp prickle in my veins got worse as I told Katya I was going for a walk. She was apprehensive, but I assured her I'll stay close; I just needed to be alone and clear my head. She told me I have to take someone with me, otherwise Finnigan or Maddox are going to kill her, and I mumbled something that sounded like approval before walking out. It was hard to sneak by the security they have in this building, and I thought I was successful until I got downstairs. I lied through my teeth when the guy downstairs asked me if I was going out alone. I told him Maddox was waiting for me outside. He wanted to check himself, but I told him we're in a rush and walked out before he could argue, and disappeared around the corner out of view.

My lies will probably bite me in the ass later, but I can't worry about that now. It's been about twenty minutes and no one has tried to find me, so I must be good. The ride I booked dropped me off a couple of streets away from my destination, since I thought it would be weird to show up right on the dealer's doorstep. Now, I'm walking wherever the navigation app on my phone tells me to. It's following the directions the guy from the bar gave me. I still don't remember his name. I'm not even sure I asked, or if he even offered it to me. Did I tell him mine? Christ, last night was a mess.

However,... tonight will be an even bigger one.

I take another left out onto a main street, crossing toward a road that takes me further toward the edge of Queenscove. It doesn't look quite as elegant as the main street. Not bad, just not as well maintained. There are a few bars dotted around, and what look like tourists walking about the street making a mess of themselves, clearly drunk on this Saturday night.

Maybe I should abandon this *mission* and take the safer way out. Alcohol will be safer. More controlled. Less, much less damaging.

Only, alcohol won't take me to that place where happiness comes in waves of purity and filth. Where it hurts and exhilarates at the same time. Where I forget how to feel and just… exist. Not live—exist. I don't want to live right now.

I turn onto a darker side street, a little quieter too, and the app says I'll be there in one minute. My nerves quiver with anxiety as I near the destination, and I mentally go through each step of my plan to settle them. I already stopped at an ATM and took out enough money to be able to afford a motel for the night. Considering my last experience, I'll probably wake up in a few hours. Though, if I dose wrong I might not wake up. It wouldn't be much of a loss… not when Maya is so well taken care of.

"This is it," I whisper to myself when the app signals I reached my destination.

I look around at the mundane-looking street like I was expecting a giant neon sign saying 'Drugs Here' with an arrow pointing at some guy. But there's nothing out of the ordinary here. A few townhouses, a couple of shops that are closed now, a tattoo shop that still seems to have some people inside, and a bar.

"What the hell am I looking for?"

"Me."

I whip around so fast, I stagger, and five feet away from me stands the guy from last night. At least I think it's him. My memory's a little hazy, but he looks familiar enough.

"You came," he says when he sees I wasn't going to initiate.

"Was I supposed to?" I'm confused.

"After last night's conversation I had a feeling you would show up. You looked a little... impatient."

Sounds about right. Though, his presence fills me with a different anxiety. It's the reality check I needed, but it's not sinking in the way it should, shadowed by the need inside my veins screaming over the recklessness of my predicament.

He grins, obviously reading me like an open book, and takes a step closer.

"You're going to go in that bar over there"—he points to the only establishment of its kind on this street—"you're going to ask for Carl and say a redheaded chick is looking for him outside, then you're gonna walk out. After a guy walks out, follow him. He usually picks an alleyway or something. Got it?"

I don't move a muscle.

"I'm not coming with you." He turns his head toward a storefront a few buildings back. "I own that barber shop, and I was cleaning up when I saw you walk by. My kid's in there waiting for me."

"Okay," I finally say. Kid or not, I just want to get away from him and be on my way. "Did you tell *Carl* I was coming?"

"No. But he's used to strangers asking for his... merchandise."

I nod and take a step backward. "Right. Thanks."

"Sure."

I turn before he can say anything more and speed my pace as I head to the bar. One deep breath later, I stop staring at the door handle and walk inside. A few people turn to look at me, but there's a game on TV they're more interested in. I wait far too long for the bartender to be free, even though probably not even half a minute has passed.

"What can I get you?"

I repeat in my head the words I was told to say, making sure I don't mess it up somehow. I'm sure the *code*, if I can call it that, only works if it's said in the right order.

"Umm... Is Carl around? A redheaded chick is looking for him outside."

The bartender cocks his head, scrutinizing me for a few too many stressful moments, allowing me too much time to remember what a ridiculously reckless situation this is.

Finally, he nods. "I'll let him know."

With a brief thanks, I turn on my heels, wiping my now sweaty palms against my jeans as I walk out of the bar. I stand awkwardly a few steps away from the door, questioning my life choices, when the same door opens, and a man comes out. He barely even glances at me as he turns right and walks away, and I'm debating if this is the right guy that I'm supposed to follow. I look back into the bar, but everything looks normal. No other people are walking about. I turn to the man walking away and he doesn't stop or turn to give me a sign.

I run a hand through my hair, gripping tighter the further back I reach, and just as I'm about to give myself a bald spot, the man turns toward an alley and for a brief, charged moment, he looks at me with a knowing look.

That's him.

All my anxiety toward this situation seeps somewhere in the back of my mind where ignorance sits as well, and I finally follow him.

"What do you need?" he asks the moment I'm a few paces away from him in the alley.

He's maybe mid-forties, with a receding hairline and the most inconspicuous outfit ever. He looks so normal, I wonder why I expected him to scream *drug dealer*.

"I'm not quite sure. I think—"

"You came seriously unprepared, didn't you?" he interrupts. "Look, I'm not some mall shop where you can just browse for hours. What are you looking to achieve?" He raises his eyebrows in a slight exasperation.

"Escape," I say before he barely finished the sentence.

"You want... the hard stuff?" He's rather reluctant.

"Yes."

"Vein, smoke, or nose?"

"Vein," I answer.

He cocks his head yet again and for a few moments, I really thought he was going to tell me off and send me on my way.

"Oh, screw it. Who am I to judge? H, right?" he asks for confirmation.

According to my research, the effects of heroin—H—are the closest to what I experienced when Frankie B injected me.

"Yes," I answer.

"I'll give you enough to make you escape, but not enough to go for good." I should admire his business skills. He's trying to keep his clients alive.

"Okay.

"Sixty, please."

I scramble to get the money out of my pocket and clumsily pull out three bills. I hand them over to him at the same time he pulls out a couple of little baggies from his pocket.

The air shifts behind me just as the tips of my fingers touch the clear plastic.

"What the fuck do you think you're doing?!"

The blood freezes in my veins all at once at the sound of *that* voice.

Shit, I'm screwed.

CHAPTER 10
Evelyn

I THINK I TURNED TO STONE, because even my lungs have stopped working. I'm not even sure my heart is beating anymore.

"Answer the fucking question."

A shiver explodes beneath my sternum, and it shakes me out of my stupor as I fully register just who stands behind me.

The dealer's hand snaps back into his pocket and something past apprehension strains his features as he takes in Finnigan.

"Move along, man," the dealer answers, yet it seems like the wrong thing for him to say.

A shadow looms over me, and that shiver that was running rabid through my nerves, now reaches my feet. I start to move when his stern voice stops me dead in my tracks.

"I'm not talking to you, asshole," Finnigan warns as he

steps to my right. "You're not doing what I think you are. Right, Evelyn? You're not buying drugs, because that would be fucking ridiculous. Even stupid."

"Did you follow me here? That's seriously screwed up, Finnigan. Am I under surveillance?"

Or is he *stalking* me? How long has this been going?

"Answer me." His tone lowers just as his head does, the blue of his eyes turning to ice, "Are you buying drugs?"

"It's none of your business," I answer, but my voice comes out much shakier than it sounded in my head.

"Everything to do with you is my goddamn business!" he roars, and I flinch.

It's not the tone drawing the reaction, but the underlying implication of his words. In the slight widening of his eyes that lasted less than a blink I can see that his words surprise him too.

From my periphery I notice the dealer attempts a step away from us.

"I didn't say you could leave, motherfucker." In one swift move, Finnigan's arm is extended and at the end of it, right in my eyesight, a gun with a silencer attached is aimed at the man.

I take a step back, but don't dare another when those icy eyes pin me in place. This is a different Finnigan Hennessey than the one who brought me flowers. Different from the one who pinned me against the wall after I slapped him. This Finnigan is made of malice and rage. Even with the soft curls of his hair brushing over his ears, his preppy, pretty boy look has dissipated into an abyss brimming with dangerous power.

Yet, this display is not what shocks me the most—the tingles blooming out of nowhere deep into my lower belly do. They're running wild, chasing a thrill straight to parts of my body that should not react to this aggression. But they do... and I'm forced even stiller, because there is no way I will cross my arms over my breasts or move my legs closer together. I fear I'll give myself away. Though I fear rubbing against those sensitive parts more.

"What did she buy from you?" Finnigan asks the dealer.

"Like the lady said, it's none of your business," he answers.

My breath hitches a moment after the snapping cock of the gun, and the guy's hands shoot up in surrender.

"Heroin."

"Are you fucking kidding me, Evelyn?! Heroin?! Is this it? You're a junkie?" He's truly appalled. And most of all, furious.

Though, it's the look in his eyes that affects me more than his words or tone. It squeezes at my heart because the disappointment is painfully vivid.

"Stop it. No, I am not." There must be another explanation for why my body bellows for it. "You don't understand. You will never understand what it all feels like."

"Make me." He utters those two words like he asked me for a glass of water, not to share my entire story and how I ended up here.

"Excuse me? Yesterday you tried to pay me off to leave. Hours later you shipped me off back to your friend's home because you wanted nothing to do with me. Now all of a sudden you want to pretend that you wish to understand me?" I scoff as I shake my head. "Seriously, go away, and leave the man alone."

The itch beneath my skin grows, and on instinct, I go to scratch my forearms but wince when at the first run on it, Finnigan notices. I drop my hands in the calmest way possible, hoping he doesn't want to investigate the reaction.

"Last night has *nothing* to do with this. You expect me to stand by, watch you destroy yourself for a cheap thrill? Damn

it, Evelyn. I thought you were way smarter than this. This is..."
But he only shakes his head, emphasizing his disappointment.
Then he focuses on the man whose arms are still in the air.
"You're seriously protecting the guy who was contributing to
your self-destruction?"

I shake my head, scoffing. "A thrill? I may have kept you
all at arm's length, but you don't need to get too close to know
thrills are not what I want in life. You're perched too high on
your gilded throne, and you're failing to see what the world
looks like for the rest of us. I may be wrong, but if I'm not, then
you're a hypocrite. Here's a hard lesson for you: when the
horrors of this world put their hands on you, they sear through
your flesh until they reach your very soul and brandish you.
But that mark never scars, it sizzles. Constantly. An ember
that catches fire once in a while and brings you down to your
knees all over again. I'm not chasing a thrill, Finnigan. I'm
chasing anything else but... this."

I'm heaving when the words finally die on my tongue, and
though he only glances at me as he keeps an eye on the drug
dealer who looks more horrified by the second. I can still see
the shift in his expression. I can't make sense of the feelings
breaking through his icy gaze. There's hatred, pain, too, and I
wonder if he also bears a sizzling scar that never heals.

"Evelyn," he begins through gritted teeth, "you need to
get in the fucking car."

"No. What I do is none of your business, you yourself set
that boundary. If anyone's going to leave, it's you."

"So you can continue the *transaction?*" He doesn't disguise
the disgust in his tone.

"If I want to do drugs, Finnigan, it's nothing to do with
you. Go home and leave us to it," I yell and it actually startles
him. At this point, I don't want to continue the transaction
anyway, and I'm pretty sure I can pay this dealer all the money

in the world, and he won't sell to me, but I'm standing up for the bloody principle of it.

"Oh, is that how it is?! Okay."

Finnigan whips his head back at the dealer and the gun jerks before me with a muffled pop. The noises that follow are ones I'm not sure I understand—a short gasp, a strange thump, a soft crack, a gargle. I follow the direction the gun is pointed at, but there's nothing there. The man is no longer in its aim.

I gasp when I look at the ground, covering my mouth with my hands as my vision remains stuck to the small hole in his forehead and the blood that starts to pool underneath his head.

"There. No drugs for you tonight." he says calmly as he turns his attention back to me.

"Yo—you..." But the words get stuck somewhere in my throat.

"I solved a problem, yes."

There's a dead man here... at our feet. There's panic skirting at the edge of my senses, but outrage is what comes forth instead.

"You're insane. A murderer."

He cocks an eyebrow, looking increasingly bored at my words, slightly confused as to why I'm pointing out the obvious.

"This means nothing to you..." I add.

"It does, but not in the way you think. I refuse to have any remorse for taking his miserable life. Men like him shouldn't be tainting our city."

"Men like him? You just put a bullet in his skull, what makes you so much better than him? Is your perception of the world so twisted?" I lose my cool because for the life of me I can't understand why he thinks what he's doing is better.

"Did I say I'm better? What I do, what *we* do, is fucking different! There are rules, limits that we draw, and they aren't made of chalk or smoke. They are clear as fucking day. Like... human trafficking, in case you forgot, Evie darling."

Oh, he's using that?! No, he's not winning this. But it looks like tonight I'm not winning anything either. Though, the itch I came here to scratch seems to have eased with our heated interaction, and that is downright terrible. He cannot be the one this craving depends on.

"There must be many others in this city. I will find someone else," I blurt out, like that's what matters right now. Christ, I'm an idiot.

"Go ahead, sugar, I dare you. Find ten. Find a hundred. Do me a fucking favor so I can get to them all and clean these streets of filth."

"You wouldn't," I say in disbelief.

"Try me. Fucking try me. I will kill each and every one of them until there are none left for you to seek." There's a feral look in his icy eyes as he speaks those words, two menacing veins pulsing in his temples, and I swear he got taller... wider, all of a sudden. Not that he doesn't tower over me already.

"Christ, Finnigan! You don't want anything to do with me, you made that abundantly clear. Why can't you apply that to this too?"

"I didn't save you out of that container so you can disgrace yourself like this. You fought for your sister! For what?! So you can stick a motherfucking needle in your arm and abandon her? Just so you can feel something other than pain?"

"You don't know anything," I shake my head, holding back a sob as the pain strips me bare. "You don't know what your world did to mine. Even if you did, I doubt you would understand."

He frowns, but I rip my gaze away from his because I can't

stand the scrutiny anymore. He looks at me like I'm a circus animal. With disappointment and anger, intrigue and pity, and I can't take it anymore. But when my eyes land on the dead man on the ground once more, I whip around and walk away before I take the blame for his death too.

Silly girl, you are already to blame. It is your fault... whether you run away from the thought or not. You may not have pulled the trigger, but it was your finger on it.

I make it a few steps before my wrist is caught in a strong grip and I'm halted.

"Where do you think you're going?"

"Home. Let go of me." I try to wrench my hand out of his just as his other hand grips my waist and pulls me toward him.

"Get in the car, Evelyn." He points toward the black, boxy SUV a few feet away.

"I'm not going anywhere with you."

"Why? Do you still think it's a good idea to walk alone, in the dark, in an unfamiliar neighborhood? You really have no self-preservation instincts?"

"Why do you care?" I whip around stepping right in his face.

His chest rises and falls with deep, controlled breaths that look too slow to be calm. No words come, but his gaze on me is so intense, focused to the point that it seems to burrow into me. It digs further and further until I'm afraid it's going to find a home inside of me. My eyes widen and my chest bursts in uncomfortable prickles.

"Fine." I roll my eyes and turn toward his car when no answer comes.

Ever the gentleman, he opens the door for me, and before we leave, he pulls his phone out, typing furiously as his gaze snaps between me and his screen.

"Feels like an inappropriate time to text your *girlfriends*," I snap, crossing my arms against my chest, hating the tinge of jealousy that slipped through.

Finnigan cocks an eyebrow and I expect a pinch of amusement at the corner of his lips, but it never comes. I can't tell if I was right or just very wrong.

"Clean-up crew," he mutters under his breath.

I'm confused for a brief moment until my gaze drifts to the dark alley where the dealers body lays in the shadows.

"Oh." I leave it at that since I have no idea what else to add. I don't feel bad for assuming it was one of his women.

My phone vibrates in my pocket, and I jerk at the sensation, pulling it out in confusion. *Maddox Severin* lights up the screen, and I stare at it until Finnigan huffs next to me. I shoot him an angry look as I swipe over the screen and answer.

"Are you safe?!"

Maddox sounds anxious. Almost breathless.

"Umm yes."

"Then what the hell are you doing on Lloyd's Street?"

"Wait, you know where I am too? Are you guys tracking me?" I turn to Finnigan, but he just cocks an eyebrow like I just asked a ridiculous question.

"Yes. Katya called to tell us she was worried and found out you didn't take security with you, just left alone. You could still be in danger, Evelyn." His tone is right on the cusp of guttural, his protective instinct bleeding through. *"Why are you there?"*

"It's my own business," I answer with a clear edge to my voice.

"To buy fucking heroin!" Finnigan raises his voice over me, and I shoot him a piercing look, seething. "What? Embarrassed?" he taunts.

"I did not just fucking hear that," Maddox seethes.

"I'm done with this conversation. Thanks for the worry. Finnigan is taking me home." I end the call before the man who's making me feel two inches tall can show anymore disappointment in what I was about to do. I can't stand it.

This car feels too small, even if it's one of the biggest SUVs I've seen, I'm too close to him and the air is too heavy. I pull at the collar of my T-shirt, I fiddle with the sleeves, I do anything and everything to calm me down, but it doesn't work.

I'm heaving. "Can we go already?"

"Once the crew arrives. A few more minutes."

I run my fingers through the length of my hair, urging time to pass by faster.

"What the fuck is that?" Finnigan exclaims, and I quickly swipe my gaze out the windows, looking for whatever triggered him.

But tightness bounds my wrist, and he extends my arm toward him. My blood turns cold and before I turn to look, I know exactly where I'll find his gaze. He lifts the sleeve of my cardigan, looking at the gauze wrapped around my forearm and no matter how hard I try to wrench it out of his grip, it's futile.

"It's just one more thing that's none of your business," I snap at him.

"Did someone hurt you, Evelyn?" His eyes shine and darken all at once, malice seeping through. He looks too affected by the thought that someone might have.

"No one hurt me."

"Please tell me you're not—"

"No." I cut off his train of thought, knowing where it was going.

I managed to rip my wrist out of his grip, but in the process, he reached over and grabbed the other one, exposing yet another gauze. His gaze shoots to mine and pierces right through my very soul, demanding and ruthless.

"For fuck's sake, Evelyn. Explain what's happening."

"Stop it. Let go of me. I told you it's none of your business." I pull the sleeves down, fisting them in my palm, and wrap my arms around my middle, turning to the side window.

I watch as a van drives down the street toward us, but stops in front of the alley, blocking the access and our view. Finnigan starts our car at the same moment, flashes his headlights twice and drives off.

Freaking finally!

"I need to know you're okay. Safe... even from yourself." He drops his tone, pulling a sense of calmness in it.

My chest rises with a deep, strained breath, and I drop my head against the headrest on a long exhale.

"Sometimes the nightmares seep into reality and it's hard to tell the difference." I let the answer flow out of me without turning, without offering further explanation.

He can do with this what he wishes, because I'm never going to say more of it. But Finnigan doesn't ask anything else. Silence falls inside the car, and he takes me on one of the most uncomfortable rides of my entire life. Our tension is a palpable, living thing mixing together.

But underneath it all, not as deep as I would like it, there's something else. A sizzling sensation made of heat and unquenchable thirst.

Even as the car slides to a stop in front of Katya's building, my breaths aren't lighter. The tension still there.

"Remember, Evelyn"—Finnigan says as I open the door, and step out—"find another and I'll fucking kill them too."

His words crash straight in my gut. He knows what he's doing, that I'll be reluctant to try again in case he speaks the truth, and I'll end up with more blood on my hands. Even if I'm not the one pulling the trigger.

"I'll kill them all before you ever get your chance to poison your soul," he adds as I whip around, slamming the door behind me.

Jokes on him... the poison is already in. Though, I'm not sure why the state of my soul is on his mind.

* * *

This time around I actually woke up in the morning. Not that I slept much after the events of last night.

As much as I hate to admit it, my interaction with Finnigan did something to me I didn't expect. It calmed the itch, and I think I hate him more for it.

What bothers me more, though, is the fact that I am not more affected by the murder I witnessed. Until I drifted off to sleep, I replayed it in my head. I woke up expecting to be completely torn up, traumatized. None of that happened.

You know why, Evelyn, but admitting it means swallowing your pride and accepting more than you're ready to.

That incessant voice speaks in my head yet again. The dark side of my consciousness.

You don't care...

I care. I do!

You didn't care back then either...

I'm losing my damn mind!

I pull a cardigan over the tank top and jeans, and walk out of the bedroom, straight to where Maya is sitting at the dining room table, eating her breakfast.

I need coffee. I need to get out.

"Maya, want to go for a walk?" I ask her as she pushes the empty bowl away from her.

"Umm... yeah, sure. Can we go to the park?"

"We can. Are you okay? You don't seem that keen," I ask.

She nods. "It's just that... not sleeping in the same bed has been strange," she says in her sweet little voice, and it pulls at my heartstrings.

My lovely, sweet girl. I thought she would enjoy having a bed all to herself, finally. Although that's not the reason why I did it. I'm terrified that I'll become even more vocal during my nightmares, and she'll hear something she shouldn't. I don't want to traumatize her, especially if I say something about what happened to me after we were separated in that warehouse. So, I make it up like I'm going to bed later, wait until she falls asleep, and then settle for the night on the sofa. It's safer.

"Don't worry, you'll get used to it. But I can keep you company until you fall asleep, how about that?"

"Yes, please!" Her eyes light up and that little bit of happiness I gave her warms me.

I did that. I put that smile on her face. There may be some hope for me after all.

"Katya came last night when you were gone. I like her. She came and kissed my forehead, Evie. Can you believe that?!"

I almost can't, no. Yet, from the way she looked at me when I came back last night, I can understand it. She stood in the middle of the open space living area, arms crossed tight against her chest, and no word at all fell out of her mouth. Her stern eyes and tightly pursed lips were making me feel horrible enough, even a bit afraid, but the disappointment was the one tearing through my soul. Yet another person I disappointed, all in one night.

"That was very nice of her. Now, go on, get your shoes on and we'll leave," I urge my sister.

She climbs off the chair and rushes to the hallway as I follow, pulling my own shoes on. When Jay shows up in the corridor outside the apartment, he insists on coming with us.

I assure him we're only going to the park next door, but he's having none of it. Only after I text Maddox and tell him I'm going out with Maya, alone, does he finally relent. I'm not a prisoner. I know they're doing this for my safety, I'm sort of happy someone cares, but it's annoying, nonetheless.

"Oh, wait." Maya tugs her hand out of mine as we walk through the ground floor lobby of the apartment building toward the exit. "Need to retie my laces."

I turn to her but pull my phone out to look on the maps for a coffee stand in the park. I'm engrossed in the search, when the elevator dings and only moments later a chill runs down my spine.

"Finnigan!" Maya calls out excitedly, and I swear, the blood freezes in my veins.

I turn, ready to berate the man for daring to follow me yet again, but what I find instead leaves me speechless, mouth slightly agape. The doors of the private elevator I've never been on close behind him, and attached to him is a gorgeous, tall, platinum-haired woman with enviable curves she sways as she walks in my direction. No, not my direction, the exit.

The woman is all over him. He doesn't react to her touch, his gaze fixed on me, but he doesn't push her away either. I'm nervously scratching the edge of the phone case, acknowledging silently that it's ten in the morning. There's only one reason why he would be leaving her place at this time in the morning—he's sleeping with her.

Here... in the same damn building I live in.

The nerve! Did he pick her up in front of the building or something after he dropped me off? Did he already know her? Couldn't he have picked a woman who doesn't live *here*?!

And this is a completely different woman than the one he was with at the bar. Fleeting comments I caught from his friends cross my mind, like the one that Finnigan doesn't settle, always a different woman. The man is a playboy. According to Maddox he's making his way through all of Queenscove and its tourists.

But he could do that anywhere but here.

That pang of irrational jealousy pulls at me again, and I curse it back down. I have no claim on this man, he doesn't owe me anything, and he certainly wants nothing to do with me. If we don't count the following. And wanting to keep me safe. And the heated dance in the bar.

Something brushes against the edges of that wretched muscle pumping blood in my chest, but I refuse to acknowledge what blooms at the touch.

"Good morning, Evelyn," he says calmly, yet his gaze flickers away from me.

Is that discomfort? No, it can't be.

"Here, Finnigan? Really?" The words spill before I can stop them, but the man infuriates me. "You couldn't go do *this* at your place?" I wanted to say *her*, not *this*.

Lifting an eyebrow, he cocks his head and amusement replaces the slight confusion. "This *is* my place. This entire building, actually, and I live in the penthouse."

Excuse me, what?! I finally know how it feels for your soul to leave your body—this is it. Mortification isn't quite a strong enough word to describe the horrifying embarrassment, shock, and emptiness plaguing me. He owns the building I currently live in. He lives here. This whole time.

I don't understand how this has never come up before. All this security makes much more sense.

"Right." That's all I manage to say.

It doesn't erase the amused expression pulling at all the painfully handsome lines of his face. The chances I will bump into him now that I go out of the house more, just like this, with another model-looking *date* on his arm, late at night or too early in the morning, will grow exponentially.

That's the cherry on top, because his presence alone is enough to drive my anxiety off the wall. He lives here... in the same building as me, and I'm somehow supposed to find the strength and peace of mind to sleep soundly at night with the knowledge he's just above me. Doing *things*.

The thought makes me mildly nauseous.

No. I can't do it. I won't.

"Maya, come on. We're going."

She looks between us, her little brows scrunching as she tries to understand what's happening, but fails. She's still staring as she moves to grab my open hand.

I don't even say goodbye as I walk out in the mildly humid, warm air of Queenscove and breathe in the slight salty scent.

"The park is that way." Maya pulls on me, trying to sway me in the opposite direction.

"Change of plans, honey. We're going to go see Loreley."

"What for?"

"I think it's time we move out of Katya's and into our own place."

CHAPTER 11
Finnigan

*Y*OU DON'T KNOW WHAT YOUR *world did to mine.*

Evelyn's soft voice wraps around the threads of my mind for the hundredth time.

After a few days of wondering what had been done to her, I went to barge into Katya's and demand she tell me what she knows. I managed to turn around just in time. A little horrible voice in my head had to repeat to me over and over that Evelyn Shaw was trouble, and getting close, knowing more about her, will destroy me.

All over again.

I barely stopped myself when, after over a week of being haunted by those words, I wanted to call Carter and ask him to find out every single aspect of her life. It was a horrible invasion of privacy and trust, but I couldn't bear those words anymore. Everything in me was demanding to know what she meant. That horrible voice I know to be mine, raged at me to back away from her. Far, far away, where the feelings taking root inside of me could rot and die before the tendrils could reach too deep. I stopped myself, nonetheless.

Weeks have passed now, and I'm just as clueless about the meaning of those words as I was when she all but spit them in my face. I haven't laid eyes on Evelyn in just as much time.

Their meaning is a mystery, but they offend me too. What did she mean about *my world?* What did I, or us, ever do to her? We saved her, damn it! We helped her. Offered her shelter, food, money, even a one-way ticket back to where she came from.

Yet, as the tip of the stiletto knife draws the slowest drop of blood from under the chin of the long-haired bastard currently strapped to a chair before me, and his condescending beady eyes attempt to stare me down, I understand Evelyn's words just a little more.

My world is this one. Where men like him roam the streets freely, kill families, rape little children, sell boys and girls, and use people like they're worth less than cattle. *My world* ripped her and her little sister out of theirs and tried to take their innocence away.

Though, I can't help but be angry and downright offended that she thinks I fit in the same category as him. What she thinks of me shouldn't affect me like this, and I hate her because it does. I hate myself more for allowing it.

There's no worth in me for a woman like her. *My world* will ruin her... I'll find her naked body, broken gruesomely, dead in a pool of her own blood, before I can reach her. I won't save her. I will only damn her. Just like I did *Hanna.*

There is no other outcome.

It doesn't matter that Roberto Bartiste was the one who wielded the blade that cut the soul out of her; I might as well have handed it to him.

My brother, Ronan, and Vincent are idiots for bringing women they love into this world. My brother left for this reason, but I don't think he can ever be truly out. *Crime* is not our job, this is not a goddamn profession. It's a force that lives in our blood and the fibers that form our being, programming our brain from its early development. Eventually, this life will find my brother, his wife, their son, and drag them back into it. For their sake, I hope they can skirt at the edge of it rather than submerge themselves back in its enticing clutches.

Because it is enticing. I could never live a different life devoid of this power, adrenaline, and blood. This is where I belong, and no woman should be here with me.

"Who is your boss?" I ask the man tied to the chair in the middle of the warehouse we found him in.

I don't wait for words to fall out of his mouth and sink the tip of the knife deeper into the hollow part under his chin. If I go deep enough, I'll impale the tendons first, then his tongue.

Not yet though, I need to know who he works for. All we have are two untraceable names that are leading us in circles. And the only men who could have given us the information are dead—Morrigan's father, Liam O'Rourke, her ex, Ryan Holt, and Vincent's father, Lester Boseman. Now we know they were just a connection to the docks of Queenscove and the trading routes, and the operation is bigger, run by a whole other organization.

Right now, we're almost two hundred miles away from Queenscove, on the tip Dietrich, Loreley's father gave us. We're finally face to face with someone higher up in the organization we're trying to find. Higher, but not fucking high enough.

"You're pathetic. All of you," the guy says, laughing maniacally like he has a leg to stand on. "You came all this way, and you don't even know who you're looking for. Who are you people?"

I ignore the question about who we are. It's not like he'll be alive long enough for the answer to matter.

"You think that we would have found you if we didn't know something? We need *real* names!" I say, watching his blood drip down the shiny silver, quicker after I push the blade deeper holding the back of his head steady at the same time.

A mangled cry escapes his exposed throat and satisfaction blooms. No words do, though.

Carter stands behind the man, and need sparks in his hazel eyes as he looks down at him. He's *The Carver* after all, a nickname he has thoroughly earned in the last two, three years. Carving is not my thing, but torturing for information, pouring emotions into an instrument that draws blood, I do thoroughly enjoy sometimes. But Carter... he needs this. I'm not sure if blood is what he sees when he peels the skin off his victims. I don't think it's emotions he draws on either. It always looks more like punishment. Of his victims or him, I don't know.

Carter is twitching now as I interrogate this man, but this one is mine.

"Give me a name. You think that there's no point in talking since we're gonna kill you anyway, right?" I wait and he just stares at me, afraid to breathe so my knife doesn't sink deeper in his flesh. "But keep in mind that you're not alone in this world. You seem to have made some commendable efforts to hide your family, but..."

His eyes widen with fear as I pause for a reaction, and what I'm seeing is what I need.

"It wasn't enough to hide them from us," I continue.

"Your wife is pretty..." Vincent appears on my right, phone in hand, showing our prisoner a photo of his betrothed in front of their lavish house in a secure, gated community.

"How did you get in?" The man dares to speak and hisses in pain as the knife sinks a little deeper with the movement of his jaw.

"You can get in anywhere as long as you know the right information about the right people. Everyone has a weak spot to exploit, and information is always the key," I explain.

"For example," Vincent continues, "I know that this photo of your wife will make you twitch, but it's the next one that will loosen your tongue and make you spill your secrets."

He swipes once on the screen and the man all but jumps off the chair when he sees his dear mother on it. I pull the knife down to avoid this idiot slicing his own throat on it.

Finding out he's a mama's boy was easy, finding out that the sick bastard has had an inappropriate relationship with her for years was a bit harder. But we did. Anyone who *loves* their mother that much will sacrifice their wife for her.

"Leave her the fuck alone! Where is she?!" he bellows.

"Give. Me. A. Name!" I scream right in his face, and his ass hits the chair with a thud.

"I don't know it!" he cries.

He actually fucking cries, and I exchange looks with Carter and Vincent. Carter looks bored and Vincent shrugs.

"He told us to call him Vassallo, but only some of us know it's not his real name. None of us know what it is though. The only one who might, is Frankie B," he says.

Frankie B. What a stupid fucking name.

But we already know these names, we need the real fucking ones. However, it is interesting to find out that not only do people in their organization not know Vassallo's real name, but most don't even know it isn't. So, we'll need to go straight to the top.

"Who is the guy for the organization?" I ask.

"He comes across like an idiot, but he's Vassallo's right-hand man. Young, half his age maybe. He's not the sharpest tool in the shed, but even that blunt edge could do some damage."

I know for a fact it does. Evelyn's memory from that night is patchy, she has more gaps than information. When Maddox found her, he said she was out of her fucking mind, in a trance from how heavily she was drugged. She refused to tell us if she remembers what happened to her after she was separated from her sister. I noticed a few winces, some straining when she moved or sat down, so I know the motherfucker hurt her, she doesn't need to spell it out for me. I'll crucify Frankie either way, slice him from throat to dick, and deliver his guts to her.

I owe her that much.

Goddammit... why is this just dawning on me? Was she seeking drugs that night because she's starting to remember more?

I take one deep breath, looking at the man panicking before me, and wonder if there's any more I can get out of him.

"Where is their headquarters?" I ask.

"Not with the rest of us. There are multiple centers of operations. He visits, but he has his Sergeants who handle each one. Vassallo prefers to meet in random locations for briefings, missions, and others. He only comes when an important shipment arrives. I don't know where the other centers are, he keeps his operation fragmented so if something happens, we don't all go down. My center is in Eastling, North of the city in an old asylum. It's big, but I don't even know if it's the biggest one. Now, is my mother going to be okay?"

The man spilled the information like it was nothing, all loyalties and fears gone when it came to his dear mother.

"Vassallo only comes when big shipments arrive?" I ask.

"He used to, but rumor has it one of them got raided a month or so ago by someone, and if they would have come half an hour earlier or something, they would have found him there. He hasn't intercepted shipments since," he answers.

"The only chance is to catch him if he meets with his Sergeants or visits a center?" Vincent asks.

"Most likely. What about my mother?!" he asks impatiently.

"Give me the name of the Sergeants." I ignore his plea.

"Is my mother safe?" he rages, fear reddening his eyes.

"The names, motherfucker!" I slam my knife right under his balls, scratching his suite trousers, his mouth gaping as he attempts to move backward in the chair. Carter is truly bored now, and he already walks toward the exit. Vincent moves away, ready to follow.

"We don't have knowledge of the others." He shakes as I push the blade up just enough to make him sweat, and breathes out loudly when I decide to retreat and pack it in my rib holster. "Mine, the one who's supposed to come here today to make sure this warehouse is ready for the next shipment, is called Leopold Gr—"

The word sticks in his throat as his head whips backward with a bullet lodged in the middle of his forehead. I jump to the left, ducking and rolling onto the dirty, concrete floor, just as gunfire and grunts erupt all at once.

We weren't stupid enough to come here alone. A whole team is outside, and from the sounds of it, they're all fighting. I catch a faint flashing light at the other end of the warehouse, between some old, rusty equipment forgotten here, and I draw my gun as I duck behind a concrete column. I'm strung so goddamn tight, a buzzing grows in my ears, and my hands twitch to squeeze the trigger and release this pressure.

A moment later a bullet lodges itself at the edge of the pillar, and I lower myself, taking aim toward its source. Three more shots, a loud thud, and the gunshots aimed at me stop.

"I think it was a stray. Clear!" I hear Vin somewhere behind me.

He was caught close to the exit, but ducked behind some rusty machinery. That was quick. Yet, the pressure in my head hasn't eased, and the buzzing is still there.

Slowly, the commotion dies down outside, and we move toward the exit. The door creaks open, and both Vin and I take aim. Carter steps through, a thick streak of blood running from the base of his throat, down to his crotch, stray splatters everywhere.

"Yours?" I ask quickly.

"No." He turns and exits, leaving Vin and I with no further explanation.

"Okay, I guess." I gesture at The Serpent to walk out, and I follow.

"I'll call the clean-up crew," one of our men say.

And boy are we gonna need them. In this thirty-second massacre, at least twenty bodies dropped. I spot a couple more around the corner as we head to our car, and one more in the bushes. I'll have to give Madds a pat on the back, because he's damn good at training our men.

"I need a driver, the rest of you stay here and wait for the clean-up crew. Leave the bodies where they are, but hide and guard the outside perimeter in case more come," Vincent orders our men.

"I'm staying. I think a shipment is coming. If it is, I want to coordinate the rescue." Carter steps away from us.

"Okay. What's the plan if it is?" I ask.

"Kill all the bad guys, clean it up, and give an anonymous tip to the local police to deal with the shipment. They'll interview the victims, and I'll get all the info from their system after," he answers.

I nod, liking the idea. As much as it would be nice of us to deal with this *shipment*, we don't have the capacity to accommodate more people. The last rescue operation was so complex mainly because we had to figure out who all those kids belonged to. It was fucking expensive to protect their families after we returned them, and it ate a lot of our time, leaving us uncomfortably vulnerable. We really weren't, but it felt like it.

"Let's go then." I gesture to Vin, turning and heading toward our car.

I climb in the back seat, rubbing a hand over my face and wondering just how I'm gonna burn out through this gnawing pressure that's making me twitch. My usual method, getting pinned under a woman bouncing away on my cock, isn't going to work. It hasn't worked for weeks... no matter how much I tried. I'm not even excited over a blow job anymore. When lips wrapped around me, it was like slugs sliming their way up my length.

Twice I managed to fuck to completion... and both times I left their place like I was being chased away. I couldn't bear looking them in the eyes and holding a conversation, not when they were a cheap version of the one woman who haunts my dreams and fills every conscious thought when I'm awake.

"Take me home," I say to the driver who climbs in after Vin.

Though I plan on going a few floors below mine.

Maybe this time she'll actually be there.

CHAPTER 12
Finnigan

"YOU'RE NOT HERE FOR ME," Katya states bluntly when I show up in her apartment.

I narrow my eyes on Katya, that gnawing pressure turning hot at her knowing gaze. I don't need her to tell me why I'm here, and I certainly don't want her to act like she knows me so fucking well that she can predict what I'm thinking.

It's my own fault for allowing it. No matter if she's basically family.

"Evelyn doesn't live here anymore." She continues.

That much I gathered, but I can no longer track her phone, so I couldn't be sure. I know Carter can track her in a different way, easily, but I couldn't fucking ask without arousing suspicion or a long line of questioning. Despite this, more than once I had to stop myself from asking him or Maddox about her. Maddox, especially, since I know he's been training her. At what times, I have no idea, because no matter when I go to the Fightclub, I never cross paths with her.

"I'm here to talk about a mission." I say, crossing my arms against my chest.

It's difficult, but I ignore her cocked eyebrow and suggestive look. It's even harder to keep my eyes from wandering about the space in search of *her*.

"And the *mission needs* to be executed tonight?"

"No."

"Then why did you drag me out of bed?" She crosses her arms over her chest, dressed in her silk pajamas.

"We need to try a different angle." I ignore her question. "We found out that their operation is fractured intentionally, so the different centers don't know where the others are or who works there. It's why no matter who we find, we can't get any fucking useful information out of them. The guy from tonight said their center is North of Eastling, just a bit further West than we were, in an old asylum."

She narrows her brows, pursing her lips like she always does when she's mulling over the information.

"And?"

"Think of who you know out West, around Eastling, if you have any connections there. Someone over there would have heard something. These people aren't fucking perfect. Just like the ones in Queenscove, they'll talk when they think no one important is listening. I want to avoid sending girls, but if you sniff something that tells you we should, then go for it. And here, focus on people who knew O'Rourke and Holt, not necessarily professionally, with some sort of connection out West."

Thank fuck for thinking on my feet, because leaving Katya's apartment without saying anything, after her implication about Evelyn, would have proved her right.

Is Evelyn here, though? I pace casually, my gaze sweeping around the spots she might appear from. Like the door leading to the pantry, where I once found her checking out some small jars of colorful sprinkles, before she put them down as if I caught her doing something she shouldn't have. Or out on the terrace, where I saw her several times from outside, quietly watching the world beyond her with heartbreaking hope in her eyes. Like the world could be hers... in another time, another life, breeding a disturbing need inside of me to prove to her it could happen in this one. Or maybe she'll come out from the corridor that led to the room that was briefly hers.

"Yeah, I know a couple in the general area. One is luxury, the other more... common. I might have to go, but I'll put feelers out first. How many girls do you want me to send out in Queenscove?" Katya's voice pulls me back in the moment.

I can't think of the girl who's now technically a woman. The issue of her legality doesn't change how screwed up this is for me to think of how she felt against me when we danced.

What the fuck am I doing here?

"Maximum five, we don't want to attract attention when they all start sniffing around about the same subject," I answer Katya, continuing to pace, my steps heavier now, following my increasing pulse.

"I'll do three and start tomorrow."

We'll soon have to stop calling them *our girls*, because we've recruited a few men too recently, since some targets swing that way and we had a gap in our service. But the men aren't fully trained yet and we value safety and skill above all else. Katya's been hard at work, as always, coordinating, training, and everything in-between. Though Raven has taken on part of the responsibilities too since she's our most skilled employee in that department.

This is not your run-of-the-mill luxury escort service. Their training is not only about sex, but spying and extracting information. They are taught various methods of manipulation, but they also handle the installation of trackers and listening devices. Most of them started off as escorts and wanted more, or even attempted more on their own as they had better skills and inclinations. Some don't even get to the sex part since they deal in particular kinks and sexual desires. They are all brilliant at what they do. We also train them hard in self-defense and combat, though they are never alone at a job. But the brilliant part about all of this is that no one outside of our organization knows the escort service is ours.

We only interact with Katya publicly if she has an employee with her and it looks like we're assessing or hiring, but even that happens very, very rarely. Our interactions are always in private to ensure that whoever hires the girls doesn't suspect that whatever information they spill gets to us. Some of these pompous cunts treat them like the help, and it doesn't cross their minds that they pose a threat.

It's done now, Katya has all the information she needs, and I have mine—she's not here. And I can't be in here anymore either, in this space that was never Evelyn's, yet she haunts incessantly. Even if it's my memories and wishful thinking doing the haunting. I say goodbye and head out the door, but before it closes, I hear Katya's voice behind me.

"She doesn't live here anymore, Finnigan. I don't know what happened between you two, but she told me not to tell you where she went. If you asked."

I slam my hand against the door, stopping it before it shuts. "I didn't fucking ask."

"And I didn't tell you. When you go looking for her, keep in mind that sometimes, in order to escape the past, you have to let yourself experience the future. You don't have to let what Bartiste did to you take everything away."

Why the hell does she think I'm going after Evelyn?

"You're crossing a line, Ekaterina. Don't fucking dare analyze me or assume what I want." My tone is low, but hard enough that the security guy closest to the apartment stiffens.

I turn once again and leave.

"You deserve it, Finnigan! It's time!"

The door slams over Katya's raised voice, and I stifle a laugh. She has no idea what the fuck she's talking about.

Deserve…

No, I don't. And I won't fool myself into thinking there's a goddamn chance.

Evelyn

"WHY ARE YOU HERE?"

The words don't linger in the air. This room gives off the impression of a padded box with large, period windows and classy decor. The words melt when they touch the wallpapered walls. It's my fourth session here and every time I hold back from appeasing my curiosity about this structure.

"Evelyn, why are you here?"

Same thing—the sounds dissipate in the softest way.

The Dr. clears her throat in that polite gesture women of her caliber tend to make. My vision focuses on her once again just as she tilts her head and narrows her eyes for only a split second. The analysis has begun.

Who am I kidding? It began the moment I walked through that solid, paneled wooden door.

"Is this room soundproof?" I finally ask that burning question I've kept in since the first time I stepped foot in here.

Or am I just stalling?

She straightens her head, and her eyes soften.

"It is. I believe in my patient's privacy."

"It's quite extreme, don't you think? Are we expecting people on the other side of this wall to press their drinking glasses against it to hear the confessions of depressed housewives and men who fantasize about their mommies?"

Her gaze narrows on me once more, only, this time it doesn't shift back. Either she's finally losing her patience with me, or my words gave her new and brighter ideas for the next lines of questioning.

"Wait. You are," I continue, slightly shocked. "This is not just for privacy, is it?"

She draws in a deep breath and relaxes back into her thickly padded, high-back armchair.

"It is, Evelyn. For protection as well."

"Victims…"

"And criminals," she adds. "I take private patients, referrals from hospitals, and also from the police. I work as a forensic psychologist too, which means that I took precautions to keep these conversations as private as possible, before court appearances."

She's honest. Interesting.

"What most surprises me is that people actually end up in court in this city."

She leans forward in the dark brown armchair. "What do you mean?"

She places the tip of her shiny black pen against the paper notebook she holds on the armrest, ready to add to what is probably her conclusion of me. It's distracting, and it takes me a few seconds longer than necessary to answer.

"Look around you; crime is everywhere. Walking on the same streets, eating in the same restaurants, waiting in the same lines as everyone else before they return to their underworld." I scoff. "Underworld… Like it's not all out in the open. Yet, no one seems to care around here."

"Is this *underworld* the reason why you are here?" the Dr. asks.

Nothing makes me angrier than the answer to this question. It's a battle between good and evil—not just in my brain, but my morals too. My heart screams at me every day to deal with it, but the rest of me can't obey. Not when the flashbacks come... when the ghosts of my scars remind me that they're still there even if they no longer mark the skin of my forearms, and the ridiculous need to poison my veins flares up.

"Yes," I answer, but even I don't miss the slight tremble in my voice.

"Yes?"

"Umm... no." I look down to my tightly clenched hands, then back up at her, hating how little self-control I have over my feelings and body language.

"No. Okay." She cocks her eyebrow, and I itch to push it back down with the tip of my finger.

"Look, it's complicated."

"How?" the Dr. asks.

My gaze fixes on hers and she holds it. Doesn't blink, doesn't move. I'm not even sure she's breathing. She's like a soft, dark-skinned statue, glowing in the sunlight streaming through the window.

"Why is it complicated, Evelyn? Were they the ones who hurt you?"

I sigh and turn my attention to the view, the thick, sharp leaves of an old palm tree just about touching the glass with every breeze. Every time it gets real close and I think it's going to make contact, I open my mouth to answer her question. But it never does, so I don't either.

"It's funny, isn't it? How this concept gets ingrained in us as children—good and evil—like it could ever be so black and white. Like good doesn't depend on evil for the universe to consider it good, and evil doesn't depend on it to become despicable. In reality, there's no such thing." I turn back to her. "Is there, Dr. Moss?"

"It is one way of looking at it all," she answers, seemingly accepting the slight change in the subject.

"It's all gray. We're all morally corrupt in some way. Most of us are willing to do the unimaginable for the ones we love, but the ones more inclined are willing to do it just because. Evil isn't just evil." A soft thud pulls my attention to the window—the palm leaf. It's time to answer the previous question then. "Evil has many shades, and I was both hurt and saved by it."

"Which one makes you angrier?" she asks. "The evil who hurt you, or the one who saved you?"

My lips part as that question takes me aback.

Both... right?

"Or is it you who actually makes you angry? Do you belong on the same color spectrum, Evelyn?"

My gaze whips to hers, eyes wide as the words crash into my bones. It doesn't take me more than a couple of seconds to realize that the question was rhetorical in her eyes. She only asked it so I can answer it for myself. So I can admit it to myself.

"*They* make me angry. The ones who hurt me, who took me away from my home, and the one who promised to save me before it was too late, yet failed." This is the only thing I'm admitting today.

I don't share a color palette with *them*.

I definitely do not, no matter my vicious crimson dreams, once the nightmares end.

* * *

I left Dr. Moss's office with a new need inside of me. One that took me straight to Maddox and The Fightclub. He brought me here a few weeks ago, after I had a particularly bad reaction to a man walking behind us on the street. It wasn't exactly a panic attack, but I freaked out.

It reinforced how powerless I truly feel. The vulnerability was slowly killing me, and Madds acknowledged that I needed to gain control. Not back, but more than I had before. Because mine and my sister's kidnapping happened while I was technically in control.

I wasn't.

I glance down at my strapped hands for a moment, rejoicing in the ache in my knuckles. After that therapy session, I needed a different type of treatment for that frustration.

"Duck," Maddox orders, and I follow, narrowly avoiding his heavy fist. "Sidestep left. Good. Now right, duck, and jab to the sternum."

He grunts slightly, as I follow each of his commands and strike him as ordered. Only, he doesn't stop there. He ducks quicker than a man his size should, and swipes at my feet. He manages to catch one, but I jump before he can catch the other.

"Good. And after a move like this, your opponent might have their guard down while they get their balance back or rise to their feet. So, you strike the vulnerable spot closest to you. Throat, nose, in the hollow spot under the sternum, or anything else close to you," he instructs.

He's already up but, for some reason, I decide to strike anyway. I lunge, but my back hits the springy floor before my fist hits him.

"Wrong timing, Evie," he scolds and reaches over to help me up.

"I know, I just..." I trail off, thankful that the Fightclub is almost empty tonight, save for three guys sparing in the ring.

"Burning anger?" Madds asks.

I pause for a moment on my way up, wondering just how transparent I am. Because neither the therapist, nor him, have had any trouble reading me today.

He doesn't press when I don't answer right away, instead turns to put away the equipment we used in my training. I'm not sure what he thinks of my progress, but I believe it's been going quite well. I feel it in my muscles, my reflexes, and in my confidence too. I'm weary about it too, because confidence can be deceiving, and I don't want to get too cocky. That will definitely get me hurt. I can't deny the increased strength though. And not only the physical one.

"There's nothing wrong about it," Madds says from somewhere behind me, and I stop mid unwrapping my hands.

"About what?"

"Burning anger, frustration, or... other emotions." His last two words are loaded, but I don't dare pry.

Maddox is an interesting character. Usually quiet. The type of person who can happily sit in a comfortable silence and doesn't feel the need to talk just for the sake of it. He's been better since we got closer, not that we've had any deep conversations, but I swear sometimes I see these sparks. Like he wants to ask a slightly more personal question or give an insight that allows a tinge of vulnerability, but then he stops himself, using words like *other emotions*.

Sometimes I even think that it's the right time to push, ask about the scars I've seen etched into his skin when he was training shirtless. So many of them. Long, short, thin, thick, round... most of them over his torso. Apart from the one sweeping from the middle of his forehead down to his cheek, luckily missing his amber eye.

I never ask though. Just as he doesn't ask me. If I'm not

ready, I can't expect him to be. His mostly silent support is enough, and he's given so much of it. Even Maya is slowly starting to see him as a big brother. It scares me, this platonic emotional attachment to him, to Lulu, Morri, June... it's growing roots that will bleed when finally cut. And they'll have to be cut, because my sister and I will have to go back to Fleeton.

I realize I haven't moved, midway through unwrapping my hand, the answer to his statement resting at the border of my mind.

"Is that why you fight?" all those thoughts about never prying, and here I am... crossing that invisible threshold.

He doesn't answer for a long while, and I wonder if he's still there.

"Sometimes. More so in the past. Nowadays things are somehow calmer."

I turn around to face him, as it seems the polite thing to do when the man answered my first remotely personal question.

"Baby girl, here you are!" Lulu's melodic voice fills the expansive space of The Fightclub, but it's followed by a peculiar grunt from the giant before me.

I fight a curious frown as I take in his expression. The calmness he spoke of has evaporated.

"Lulu, what are you doing here?" I ask.

"And how did you get in?" Maddox's voice is an octave or two lower, a deep frown thickening the scar on his face.

The woman raises an almost frustrated eyebrow, giving him a quick once over pausing for only a moment. A very curious moment. But she quickly turns her attention to me.

"Your security knows me, obviously," she answers, but her gaze is on me.

"Knowing you and being authorized to waltz in here are not the same thing."

Wow! There's nothing calm about the man now. I've never seen him like this. As a matter of fact, I've never seen Lulu like this either.

"Train them better, then," she bites back.

Maddox grunts and turns to leave.

"You're coming tomorrow, yes?" she shouts after him, but all she gets in response is a louder grunt. I don't realize my eyebrows are raised in shocked surprise until Lulu gives me a stern look, and I quickly straighten.

"Do you need to change out of your training clothes?" she asks.

"Umm, maybe. Why?"

"I've been trying to find you. Did you forget you asked me to take you with me to the supermarket, to get the red paint thing?"

"Red food coloring, crap. Yes. I'm sorry. I just... time got away from me," I apologize, quickly running to my bag.

I desperately need the food coloring for Morrigan's birthday cake.

"It's fine. I know you had a therapy session today. I figured you would be here afterward."

I exhale sharply, frustration seeping through my tone. "Am I really that obvious?"

"What do you mean?" she asks as I whip around, clutching my bag to my chest.

"My therapist, Maddox, you... all of you seem to read me like a book. My thoughts, my emotions, my—hell, everything."

She chews on her lips for a few moments, weighing her next words.

"The therapist is trained to read you, honey. But us... we tend to recognize our *symptoms* in others."

Oh.

That stops me dead in my tracks.

"I didn't—"

"Don't get me wrong, I'm not saying any of us went through the same thing as you did, but perhaps experienced the same or similar emotions. Some had it easier, some so much worse. Recognition comes from experience."

"I'm not sure I like the sound of that, of Maddox and... you, recognizing from experience."

"I'm just good at observing your behavioral patterns whenever you go to a session."

Which means Maddox has the experience.

"I'll give you that." I shake my head, wondering if I should try harder in the future to mask my emotions. And patterns.

"When's Maya next in with Dr. Moss?" she asks.

"Tomorrow."

"I presume before the party?" Lulu asks.

"Yes, at one o'clock. I spoke with Mamaw June, and she's coming over after we return. She'll watch her for the evening."

"Sounds good. You deserve to let your hair down a little."

I'm not sure if Morrigan's surprise birthday party will be the best place for me to let my hair down. Not with the knowledge that I may be seeing a certain blue-eyed man.

Every time I walk in here I wonder if he's going to be around. Even if I go to Morrigan's apartment, I still wonder if he's going to drop by without warning. But it's been weeks now without setting eyes on him. Weeks since I found out I was living in his building while he screwed other women there.

The way I feel in my skin now... it might as well have been years.

And I still don't know if I'm ready to see Finnigan.

CHAPTER 13
Finnigan

I'M STILL PISSED. THOUGH THE chill, fluttering inside my chest is different from any anger I've experienced in the past. I get it—it's Morrigan's surprise birthday party, and it's for family and close friends only, but I'm desperate for the distraction tonight. One girl is all I asked for, a date to hold my attention.

Though, it seems I may be in luck. I've been here, at Morrigan's apartment, for about an hour now. We've already surprised the birthday girl, though her reaction to our enthusiastic screams showed a tinge of knowledge. And I have been watching her accept wishes and hugs from everyone.

Cillian, her red-haired pain in the ass of a brother, wrapped her in his arms and spun her a few times, and put quite a smile on her face. The man is actually quite decent, but I just like to give him a hard time. He helped us save his sister a few months ago from a really shitty situation.

A bunch of our people are here too, Katya, Raven, Beau, and Tina, since Morrigan has become friends with them. Her bartender from Metamorphosis is here as well. And of course, Maddox and Carter. But no Evelyn... thank fuck.

Though Carter has been watching me peculiarly since I got here. The man is peculiar all around, so it shouldn't flag as strange, yet there's something in his weird hazel eyes. I can't put my finger on it, but it's like he knows something I don't, and it's making me uneasy as fuck.

Come to think of it, Katya has been giving me some strange looks tonight, too. I want to ask about it, but I'm more focused on the fact that the wheat-haired woman is absent. Maybe she's gone. I want to smile about it, I want to rejoice, but... for some reason that thought fills me with something that doesn't evoke relief. The chill in my chest seems more like icicles stabbing into me. I think I need to cut this party short. I'm nearing Morrigan when Lulu sweeps in and wraps her into a tight hug.

She has been running around like crazy to make sure the party is perfectly planned for her best friend. Though, I've gotten to know Morrigan pretty well in the last few months, and I'm certain she won't care if all this turns into a clusterfuck. She only cares that we're together. That's something that surprised me about her. My expectations were set a few years back by my brother and his wife, and I waited for the moment Morrigan took Vincent away from our Sanctum. Only, the opposite happened with the wild redheaded vixen. She fits right in. Lulu too, even as she rejects it.

The two women burst out laughing and as I approach, I catch snippets of their conversation.

"You knew, didn't you? Did Vincent spill? Or did that brute?" Lulu's smile falls ever so slightly as she looks beyond

Morrigan, straight at Madds.

And he scowls right back at her.

I have a sound theory about these two, but I've been told by Vincent to keep it to myself if I don't want the wrath of both Dietrich and Severin upon me. Loreley's family is old money crime syndicate. The Dietrich mafia legacy is one built on blood, bullets, and a fortune bigger than my family's. Even though Lulu pulled out of the family business, her blood is theirs, and I see that ruthless spark in her eyes. I won't dare step on her toes.

I wait patiently until the two women finish talking, then swoop in. I don't want to prolong this night more than necessary. Evelyn might have left town, but why risk it if she didn't?

"I have a confession to make," I say to the woman.

"Go on..." She eyes me wearily.

"I didn't like you at first."

She dramatically presses her hand to her heart as her mouth drops. "Oh my! I had no idea!"

I can't help but roll my eyes at the theatrics, but the need to smile prevails. She's taking it much better than I thought she would.

"Alright, alright. Christ, you wouldn't win any acting prizes," I tease.

"Fuck you, Finnigan."

"You wish." I flash her another wicked smile.

"Do not let Vincent hear that. He'll fucking scalp you," she jokes, yet there's truth in that. "What did you have against me?"

Here goes nothing. "Everything. I don't think it was you, specifically. Although I was quite skeptical. I didn't like what you represented... to Vincent."

"I'm not taking him away from you, Finnigan." She reaches over and rubs my arm.

My breath hitches at the unexpected, soothing gesture,

but her words are heavy enough to make me think she knows exactly what, or better yet, who she is talking about.

"No. I think that's when those feelings started going away. When I realized you weren't going to change a thing. Well, obviously, some things have changed."

"They will, of course. For all of you, eventually," she says.

"Nah, not for me, darlin'. I'm happy as I am."

"Fucking everything in sight and never getting attached to anyone?" she insists.

"I have standards, Morrigan. I don't fuck *everything*."

"You're avoiding the attachment thing, though," she cocks her head slightly, her green eyes fixed on me.

I swear she stole the look out of Vincent's book, because I think she's peering straight into my goddamn soul.

"Avoiding would entail a prospect. I simply make sure there is no prospect. Ever."

"Whatever works for you, buddy." She flashes a smirk, and I decide to shut her up, pulling her into a hug.

"Happy Birthday, Morrigan."

She finally accepts my explanation and smiles warmly. It broadens into an excited one as her gaze flashes past me, and the next word that comes out of her mouth makes the hairs on the back of my neck stand still.

"Evie!" she exclaims before pulling out of my arms and waving.

"Who?" My god, could I have asked a more stupid question?

"Evelyn Shaw. You know her, the girl you rescued."

Yeah, unfortunately I know exactly who she is. As I slowly turn around, trying to think through the booming pulse getting louder in my head, I vaguely hear Morrigan mumble something about me seeing Evie at her house a few months back. I don't bother acknowledging the comment, my temples starting to throb as a scowl settles deep between my brows. It dawns on me that Evelyn hasn't talked about me to Morrigan, since she thinks she has to explain to me who she is. Katya clearly hasn't said what Evelyn asked of her, not to tell me where she lives now. How very interesting. And somehow fucking annoying too.

"What exactly is she doing here?" I didn't even bother covering my disdain at her presence.

Though shock weaved through it too. Not the bad kind, unfortunately. Those icicles stabbing through my chest have turned into something else, hot and sharp, and yet so soothing, it feels dangerously close to excitement. I can't help but look over my shoulder.

Christ, she's stunning.

She's walking over, looking like a different woman. Her features are somehow more settled, fuller, still skinny, yet no longer gaunt, and more mature than last time I saw her. Only weeks have passed, and though it's still Evelyn, she somehow looks different. Comfortable. There's a confidence in her step that was not there before, and in those 'fuck me' leather leggings, she could be walking all over me, and I'd fucking thank her.

I'm so screwed.

"She's my friend. She also lives in the apartment underneath with her little sister, and works downstairs."

"In Metamorphosis?!" I whip around so fast, I have to brush away the hair from my eyes.

"No. In the café. Finn, what—"

"What do you mean she lives here? Since when?"

This is where she went after she left Katya's? Not out of town? Goddamn it, I have so many questions, but judging from the look in Morrigan's eyes, I'm already arousing suspicion.

"About a month ago. We took her in to help her out while she's saving some money. How do you not know this?"

Yup—suspicion. I'm part of The Sanctum. If Evelyn and her sister were offered a home in the same building as Vincent's wife, I should have technically been aware. Maddox should have said something. Though, Carter is the one I'm most disappointed in. He knows everything that moves, and yet this particular piece of information didn't slip his tight lips.

You didn't ask, you asshole.

"I guess... I tuned out," I finally answer, avoiding the curious look in her eyes.

"Morrigan! Happy Birthday! Sorry, I'm late, I was adding the finishing touches," Evelyn exclaims enthusiastically as she pulls the birthday girl into a tight hug.

My feet turn to lead and pin me in place. Though I'm not sure I would move even if I could. Her perfume whips by me, and once again I'm being buried in her wicked world filled with forbidden temptation. I'm back in the bar on her birthday, swaying against her body, my hand on her bare waist, hers on me, and all the thoughts I've been burying deep since the last time I saw her, hit me like a ton of bricks.

Fuck. If just her scent does this to me, what will her touch do?

I can't take my eyes off of her. Her soft, olive skin seems to glow in this light, and I curse that oversized cardigan for covering so much of her. I curse the T-shirt she's wearing even more, because she would look so much fucking better if she were wearing mine.

Oh my god, stop it!

"You remember Finnigan Hennessey?"

My gaze whips to Morrigan when I hear my name.

"Hi," Evelyn says with such bite in that word, the teeth scrape against a part of my soul I thought didn't exist anymore.

I'm confused. My breathing turns to short heaves, my heart begins to pound erratically in my chest. What is happening?

"Hello," I manage to say before prying my feet away from this spot I've been stuck in, and get the fuck away from this witch.

I don't dare turn to check their reactions—or their possible shock at my strange one. All I know is that I need to be as far away as possible from Evelyn. My steps follow every second beat of my heart, the heaviness of them seemingly crushing any intention I had but a second ago.

I stop at the far wall by the kitchen counter and look toward the door that could take me to my freedom. Away from the woman who wrapped a goddamn noose around the hollowness left in my soul years ago. Yet, I don't move any farther. I can't.

Turning around slowly, I catch the exact moment she shifts away from Morrigan and heads toward Maddox who carries a huge, tall box. Probably a present. As if she can sense my eyes on her, she turns and hers land straight on mine. They don't stop on any other person, or object—but straight on me. I would fall on my ass if this counter wasn't holding me steady, because what I see in her gaze is made of pure silver flames, cold and searing at the same time—a challenge.

Yup... I'm fucked.

CHAPTER 14
Evelyn

"YOU ARE GOING TO BE the death of my hips. And belly. And... mmm damn." Morrigan groans as she takes another bite of the coffee and walnut cake I finished baking with Mamaw June. She loved the birthday cake I made for her a few days ago, so I'm not surprised.

"I'm not complaining." Vincent walks into the kitchen, giving his wife a once over, and pausing suggestively over her ass.

"You know I'm here, right?" his mom asks rhetorically, even as her focus is on the dishes she's currently washing.

"We need to find her a man to focus on so she can stop judging us," he whispers to Morrigan, and I choke on the sip of iced tea.

"For god's sake, I'm too old for that."

"Old?!" her daughter-in-law exclaims. "You're not even sixty yet. I'm sure we can find you a good man to keep you busy."

"I have Maya keeping me exactly as busy as I want to be. And she's more worth it than any man. No offense, son." June shrugs at Vincent currently scowling at her.

But his gaze softens when he turns to his wife, as if he's reminded of why there's truth in his mother's words.

"Aren't you supposed to be leaving in a few minutes?" Morrigan asks her husband.

"Change of plans. They're coming here." Vincent presses a quick kiss on her lips, but my mind is spiraling.

They? Who's they? Carter, Maddox... Finnigan?!

The echo of his name inside my mind awakens the visceral urge that's been making a home inside of me. A beast growing hungrier each day, but it's a picky bitch. I've already decided that my life will not stop just because of what happened to me. I may not give into the hunger wholly, but I need something to sustain me. The problem is, I can only bear the thought of one person feeding it. But he sees me as unripe, forbidden fruit.

My thighs squeeze together at the thought of making him change his mind, and I have a ridiculous need to go check my new hair in the mirror. I've seen the women he takes out... none of them look like me.

"I have no idea, but he did sound... strange." Vincent's words pull me back into the room, and I'm kicking myself for missing part of the conversation.

"Somehow, I'm not surprised. Did you notice something three days ago?" Morrigan asks.

"When? The day before your birthday?"

"Yeah. Because at the party I noticed he was a bit different. I don't know, I just noticed some passing looks."

"Hmm…" Vincent looks away, pondering the question. "No, I don't think so. But he was quiet yesterday."

Morrigan shrugs. "But then again, none of this is out of character for him, right?"

"Right. I'm sure everything's fine, and even if it isn't, I'll handle it."

Morrigan's face lights up, and she wraps her arms around Vincent's waist, looking up at him. There's so much love in her gaze, it almost hurts. Yet, it's the adoration in his that hits the hardest. The dark pits of his eyes sparkle with the stars she put there. He may have hung the moon for her, but she filled the sky with stars for him. In the last six weeks or so, I've been spending enough time with Morrigan to grow to understand that my view of her world—*their world*—was very inaccurate.

I was in Morrigan's apartment once when her husband returned from a *job*. Only, the person who passed through the door wasn't Vincent, but The Serpent. There was a look in his eyes that could stop the flow of my blood, cold and vengeful, ready to rip the world apart so he could punish whoever filled him with that simmering rage. But then his pitch black eyes landed on Morrigan… and his gaze flipped, but did not change. Now he looked at her like he would rip the world apart at her signal, only because she desired it.

Their paradox is what made me question my judgment. My preconceptions.

I've known evil. Felt it on my skin. But them… they're a whole other brand. I understand this world much better now. It's not black and white as I thought. Not all villains are the same shade, and these… they scare me.

Downright terrify me at times. Because more and more they make me feel like I belong.

And the more I think of the man who took me, the one who haunts my nightmares and ruins my dreams, the more I start to believe that I do belong with The Sanctum. Because the things I would like to do to Frankie certainly do not fit in the brand of person I thought I was. It's all a moot point, because I can't stay in Queenscove, not when I have a responsibility in Fleeton.

"Evie..." My sister comes in from the patio.

I know that voice. It's her *I'm gonna play cute and put on a sweet voice so I can get something I'm not supposed to have* voice.

"Yes, Maya?" I turn to her, crossing my arms over my chest, ready to be stern, but I burst out laughing instead when I see her sweet little face. "Did you just smash your face into that cake and forget about the spoon?"

Her eyes go wide, and she quickly goes to both lick and wipe the cream and crumbs stuck to her face. She did something similar with her own birthday cake a few weeks back, when she turned eight.

"Maybe?" she says innocently. "Look, it was delicious."

"And let me guess, you want another piece."

Her little dimples make an appearance as she looks between me and Mamaw June in the hopes that at least one of us will say yes. I can't help it, the happiness I put on her face makes me give in. I'm already turning to the cake platter when she continues.

"It's been so long since you baked. I don't know if you'll stop again, so I have to take advantage."

I cut a small piece, pop it on her plate, and she all but runs back on the patio. Like I'll take it back from her if she doesn't move fast enough.

"What did she mean by that?" Morrigan asks.

"I protected her as much as I could, so it seems she believes that I chose to stop baking."

"And that's not the case?"

"My car or the motels we managed to stay in didn't

exactly offer the facilities. And the few times we managed to underhandedly rent studios with kitchens, my priorities didn't allow it."

Morrigan nods at my explanation.

But it's not the whole truth, is it?

I sigh at that voice inside my head. It *is* the truth. There were other priorities. More important things to spend our money on than this *hobby*.

Though, I did miss the chemistry of it all. The anticipation of the oven timer going off after experimenting with new flavor combinations or recipes, the excitement of that first taste, and then there's the decorating part of it. That is my true ecstasy. Before I was taken, I kept a tattered old notebook where I drew—in pencil—all the designs I hoped one day I would get to do. It was the only thing I owned that I cared about. It's gone now. I thought I forgot those designs, but just like the baking techniques, they're all coming back to me like I've been doing it all this time. After moving out of Katya's and into Loreley's downstairs apartment, I fell right back into it. Well, not straight away, because I pushed back at first. Harder than I probably needed to. I had a point to prove, though I already forgot what it was. And I'm not fond of the reasoning my therapist suggested.

I'm not saying she's wrong, or right, I'm just not fond of it. I still don't have an answer to her question, and I'm unsure why it stumped me so hard.

Do you think you matter, Evelyn?

"You could make money out of this." Morrigan catches my attention again, punctuating that sentence with a deep moan as she takes another bite of cake.

I could.

"Sure." I laugh awkwardly instead.

The monitor next to the TV signals that the motion

sensors have detected movement on the long drive to Vincent's forest house.

"It looks like Madds," he says as he watches the car drive down.

"Hide the cake!" Morrigan yelps and jumps off the bar stool.

We all burst into laughter, and I can't resist imagining that if I were ever to do this for money, she would be my most loyal customer.

Stop wasting your time on silly dreams, Evelyn.

I sigh internally, wondering if my therapist was right.

Finnigan

"HE REALLY DIDN'T SAY ANYTHING to you?" I ask Madds for the second time since we got into his car.

"He didn't. But I think he found something big."

It better be. Too much time has passed since we've been trying to find Vassallo. It's never taken us this long to track down a person or group and it's getting downright embarrassing. I can't keep track anymore of all the people we blackmailed, tortured, or killed for this goddamn information. It kills me that this asshole, whoever the fuck he is, bested us. Not only when we rescued the children, though, according to Evelyn, it was dumb luck that they left just before we arrived, but he's besting us now too.

Carter is even more frustrated. Even if Vin tried to calm him by reasoning that we have absolutely nothing to go on, apart from an alias, he was not satisfied. The man allows only success in his portfolio, and this frustration is bringing The Carver out... and he demands satisfaction in pounds of flesh.

The motherfucker is scary. But fuck me if he's not effective. And it sounds like the blood paid off because he's finally got something.

"He's not here yet," Madds says when we pull into Vin's driveway.

I push the car door open and draw in a deep breath that makes me feel more at home than my penthouse. Damp moss, faint sea salt, and tree bark drown me, but there's a tension in the air I can't quite put my finger on.

Foreboding.

It prickles my skin and turns my head, watching for something, anything, to come out of the shadows of the forest trees.

But nothing does. It's just us here.

"Coming?" Maddox calls for me, a few steps in front.

"Yeah..." I trail off, following him to the front door, just as he pushes it open.

The smell hits me so hard, I stop dead in my tracks.

"Oh wow!" I can practically hear the drool pooling in Madds' mouth.

Can I blame him? Food is nothing more than sustenance to me, no matter what it tastes like, it's all the same to me, because it serves only one purpose. But this smell... Christ, what is that?

We advance and head straight to the kitchen, the aroma drawing us in like hypnosis, and we're powerless to its charms.

"Hey guys!" Morrigan spins in the barstool to face us.

We both wave, but Madds goes straight for the cake sitting on the kitchen island. *What is that flavor?* It smells divine.

Divine?

What the fuck is wrong with me?

It's just cake.

Mamaw June comes out of the pantry, and my fellow giant only has time for another quick wave before he cuts a piece of the dessert, slaps it on his plate, and digs in. The moan that follows raises some brows in the room and a chuckle from Morrigan.

"I can die happy now," Madds mumbles through bites.

"Eat like that and you'll definitely die."

"Shut up, prude. Go back to your plain oatmeal like a damn heathen. Who eats plain oatmeal?" He shakes his head.

"It's just food. It does the job it was meant for." I shrug.

Yet, I can't take my eyes off that cake. It looks so good, but the smell it infused this house with is downright decadent.

I'm exaggerating. It's just cake. It will taste like cake. Nothing special.

Okay, maybe just one bite?

"Go on, Finnigan. I know you're not a sweet person, but it won't hurt to try it," Morrigan coaxes me.

"Fine." I pretend to agree reluctantly, because honestly, when I actually see the cake up close, I couldn't stop myself even if I tried.

Mamaw June cuts a slice and slides it over on the kitchen island. I take a seat and dig the dessert spoon into the sponge, bringing it to my mouth still thinking it likely smells better than it tastes. But the moment it touches my tongue, I'm seeing fucking stars. Walnut, coffee, and something I can't quite pinpoint fills my mouth with something so akin to ecstasy, I burst into goosebumps.

Jesus Christ, this is incredible. The soft and light coffee cream, the walnut sponge, the crunchiness of the actual walnuts... it's unreal.

Is rum the mystery flavor?

I take three more bites, one bigger than the last, and confirm in triumph. *Definitely rum.*

"I have never, ever, seen you enjoy dessert quite this way." I hear Morrigan's remark next to me, just as I swallow another bite and repress an embarrassing moan.

"Mamaw June." I look up at the woman across the island,

wiping the top. "You have outdone yourself. I've never eaten anything as good as this cake."

The woman laughs and shakes her head. "I can't take the credit, son, it's all Evie."

I must have been chewing too loudly and not heard right, because I think the woman said *Evie* baked this cake.

But then she turns her attention to her left, somewhere beyond me, with an all-knowing look in her eyes.

No, this is not happening.

"Hey Evelyn," Madds greets her.

I'm too stunned to move. Or chew. The only shift in me is the blood rushing in all the wrong places, like my damn head because I'm getting a headache. But then there's my chest, and the sudden hollowness in my stomach... the anticipation, the curiosity.

The cake seems to melt in my mouth, and the spoon clanks on the porcelain plate as I drop it.

Finally, when eyes burn into me from all directions, I turn my head, and I instantly wish I didn't. It shouldn't, but the vision before me fills me with such visceral emotions, I swear the seat shakes beneath me.

Who am I kidding?! I'm the one shaking, and the chair is holding on for dear fucking life, because I have no idea how to physically react to what I'm seeing.

Plum-colored hair, shining a deep red where the sun rays hit it, barely grazes that treacherous spot where the neck meets the shoulder. High-waisted, black, flared jeans hug gentle curves I never noticed on her, cinching a narrow waist I could wrap my hands around, with an oversized distressed T-shirt tucked in, but ripped in a V-neck shape to reveal just enough cleavage to make me wanna rip it further. Then there's the makeup—black winged eyeliner that makes her gray and gold eyes shine like fucking stars even on the day sky, sculpted brows, and the same color lipstick on her lips as her hair.

I can't look away. I can't stop taking in the details of the woman standing before me. She's... different. Yet she looks more like herself than ever. Gone is the natural wheat-colored blonde, gone is the long hair she frequently wore tucked away, gone is the innocence she exhumed.

Now, Evelyn looks... dangerous.

Unlike any woman I ever looked at before, yet I can't seem to stop.

Her olive skin shines in the contrast with the purple that, on her, looks like it belongs. Like she should have been born with the unnatural color. And that bob-length haircut, parted in the middle and framing her delicate features, is not anything I would have imagined her with.

Stunning.

And I get angrier. More at myself than her, because she looks like the dessert I want to taste, the flavor I want to discover, one layer at a time, until I get to know all her notes.

She watches me with a mixture of curiosity and embarrassment, and the sudden flush in her cheeks fills me with a warm, thrilling emotion.

I open my mouth to speak, to say something, anything. Either about the cake she apparently baked like she's been doing this her whole life, or maybe about her new look. Does she look stronger? I swear there's more meat on her bones, more muscle too. But the sound of the front door distracts me before any sound spills from my lips.

As I turn and my eyes land on it, I wish I wouldn't have turned at all. Or came here. My lungs strain with the pain of a suppressed gasp at the sight of him, but that ache goes way beyond the physical, through my very soul, and stabs me straight in the fucking heart.

"Hello, little brother."

CHAPTER 15
Finnigan

blink once, twice, but the third time it's clear that the image before me isn't going away.

He's here.

No—they are.

Annika, an older but somehow more beautiful version of her, walks in holding the little hand of a child hiding somewhere behind his *father*. Christ, that word tastes bitter even when it doesn't touch my tongue.

"Hello, Finnigan," my *darling* brother's wife greets me, and her tone throws me far in the past, because she sounds just as shy as she was eight years ago. "Aaro, come here." She looks down at her son—my nephew—and the little boy finally steps out from his father's shadow.

I hear a small gasp somewhere behind me, and as my eyes find the little boy's, I share the sentiment in its entirety.

I know that kids often take traits from their uncles or aunts, but this is too much. That head of wild, sun-kissed curls is mine, not my brother's, and that bright-blue of his eyes is much more like mine than Ronan's.

I wonder if it kills him, looking at his son every day and constantly being reminded of me. Of what he left behind. Who he abandoned.

"Hello." Aaro's little voice comes out. There's a forced confidence in it, yet it compels me, nevertheless.

"Hi," I answer. To him only, not my brother, nor his wife.

"Are you Uncle Finn?"

I swallow a lump caught in my throat, because the anger that's seeping through me, searing one vein at a time, is forced to hold back. This kid hasn't done anything to me. But his father's eyes burn through me, and my god do I wanna pummel him back through that goddamn door.

"I suppose I am, yes," I answer reluctantly.

I'm an uncle.

I knew the theory of it all, I knew I was an uncle. After all, Annika's pregnancy was one of two driving forces in my brother's decision to quit this life and leave. But I was never faced with the prospect of it. Never faced with my... nephew. The moment Ronan left us—left *me*—he was all but dead to me. Eight years have passed, and still I haven't spoken a word to him. Yet here I am, talking to his son... my blood.

"You don't seem too happy about it," the boy states bluntly, in such a matter-of-fact, casual way, that I twitch in my chair, close to losing my balance, and I swear I hear someone snort to my left.

When I turn my head in that direction, Evelyn's lips are curled inward and she averts her eyes instantly.

"Aaro!" Annika warns her son. "Sorry, Finnigan. He is... umm... very straightforward."

I turn back to face them but realize that none of the words I have for them are good. What the actual fuck are they doing here of all places? Then I see Carter stand to their left—he brought them here. Is this why he called the meeting?

My fists clench repeatedly, pushing back a need to drive them into something, anything, until it crumbles beneath them. My temples pulse violently, and my lungs sting at the brink of heaving. I can't fucking do this, not with them here.

"Annika..." It's not a greeting, but a request, and she catches onto it right away.

"Aaro, didn't you say you needed the bathroom?"

"I'll take you there." Mamaw June passes by me and ushers them out of earshot.

I turn to Evelyn who's firmly planted in place, but I really need her to get out of here. As far away as fucking possible, because I can tell by that look in her eyes that she knows she's getting an insight into me. And she's staying for it. But this is not fucking happening. I'm barely containing these wretched emotions, but I force them down because I can't give them the satisfaction. I refuse to let my brother see how he affects me, and I most certainly can't let the purple-haired vixen any closer. She cannot know me any better. Not now. Not when she looks like she found sin and decided to douse herself in it, pulling me to the brink of deviancy.

Morrigan still sits next to me, watching this interaction, or lack thereof, with a mixture of apprehension and curiosity.

"You must be Morrigan," my brother says, and when I hear his footsteps, my head whips to him.

He stops halfway between us, his gaze flashing to my angry one, and the redhead jumps off the stool to go greet him, reading the room.

"I am, yes. Hi..."

"Ronan. I'm Finnigan's older brother."

I scoff. Yes, technically it's true, but blood is the only thing tying us together. That doesn't make him a brother, just a fucking sibling.

"Yes, I've heard. Welcome back," Morrigan greets him.

"Thanks. Sorry I didn't get a chance to introduce you to my wife, Annika and our son."

"It's okay." She takes a look around the room then meets my brother's eyes once more. "I think I'll go find them and introduce myself."

He nods and Morrigan moves past him.

"Evelyn, how about you introduce yourself too," I say, turning my head slightly in her direction, my gaze still pinned on my brother.

I don't hear any movement or agreement and when I finally meet her eyes, I swear the silver in them turned to steel, like she's forging a dagger she's about to stab me with. She holds my stare with such intensity, it weighs down in the pit of my stomach. There's a challenge in there I crave to unpack, but shouldn't.

"Hi, Ronan," she says at the same time she breaks my gaze and turns to my brother. "I'm Evelyn. Excuse me, I'm gonna go check on my sister."

She whirls around and walks out the patio shutting the door behind her before my brother can reply. The annoyance in her step is unmissable, though.

"So, she's—"

"Morrigan's friend," I interrupt Ronan before he dares to insinuate anything.

He doesn't respond to that, but his cocked eyebrow spells too many words I want to shove down his throat.

"Why did you bring them here?" I ask the burning question lingering like ash in the air.

Only, I direct it at Carter, not my brother. He cocks his head and waits a few seconds before he finally decides he's replying.

"There was no other way. Something changed, and it was with Ronan's help that I uncovered it all."

"Excuse me? Are you telling me that you're involving him in *our* business? He's an outsider!" I snap, dropping to my feet off the chair.

"Easy, brother."

"You shut the fuck up! I told you if you leave, you're out. You gave up the right to be my goddamn brother eight years ago." My tone lowers, my voice vibrating through my chest.

Christ, I thought those memories were forgotten. Seeing him now, his sleek blonde hair a shade or two darker than mine, his deeper blues, and features that resemble mine so much, that night comes back to me like a goddamn truck slamming through my chest. That phone call in the car as we were rushing to save Annika and Hanna before they were taken, the moment we reached the empty island and witnessed the aftermath of their abduction, all these moments crash down on me like no time has passed at all. And the blood... so much blood. The anger finally breaks the surface too.

"I came because—"

"You made your goddamn choice!" my voice cracks to the precipice of shouting, interrupting him. "You decided to leave us. And you agreed that you can't. Fucking. Come back. Now Carter tells me that he's involving you in *our* business? Our motherfucking Sanctum? No. Either you leave or I do."

The man only sighs, standing here in all his glory, his stance rigid and proud, but his eyes... his eyes are the ones threatening to break me. There's pity, sadness, and regret all balled into one in there, and I fucking hate each one of those sentiments.

"Fine. I'll go."

But I only manage two steps.

"No." Carter stops me. "We have work to do."

"You don't understand, Pierce. You're different and I get it, but—"

"I don't have to," he interrupts. "This is important. Ronan is here for a reason. He's—*your* family, too. I'm gonna go set up in the office. Follow me." Carter whirls around and heads toward the room in question, leaving me all riled up.

"I'll come with you," my brother says, his tone wearier this time.

"I need air." I turn and walk toward the terrace, and rush over the threshold, shutting the door behind me.

"Who exactly do you dare think you are?" There's a chilling quality to her voice, her tone filled with an eerie calmness, but I can practically taste the anger beneath it.

"Excuse me?" I turn to face the purple-haired woman, realizing the grave mistake I made.

I knew she was out here. Why the hell didn't I go literally anywhere else in this huge house?

"I must have done something wrong if I gave you the impression that you can boss me around as you see fit. And in front of other people, nonetheless. How dare you?" There it is again, that low, calm tone.

Somehow it fills me with even more frustration, fueling the unnatural anger my brother's arrival instilled in me.

And the dam cracks.

"This is none of your business, goddamn it! All of this!" I wave my hands around. "This is not your world, and whatever the fuck just happened in there has nothing to do with you! You are not part of it!"

She all but sneers at me, her eyes darkening with the type of malice I never thought could mar her features.

"You have no idea what I'm part of. You're not here to witness it. You haven't been for a while. You made it very clear that I have no place in your life, not to mention the impression you have of me—"

"Impression? How would you know what I think of you?" I ask, seeping anger through the seams.

She wouldn't talk to me like this if she knew exactly what I thought of her. If she knew how she filled my dreams. What nightmares she bred. If she found out how depraved my mind truly is. The things I want to do to her, force on her, take from her. And the things I'd beg her to do to me.

She wouldn't talk to me like this if she truly knew my sickness.

"Because you told me." She seethes, the only break in her calm tone of voice. "You thought you could pay me off to get me out of here. You thought I would take it, just like that. You think I'm some worthless homeless woman, who can be bought. Though, that's not exactly what you were doing, was it? You were buying yourself distance—escape."

She pauses, not for effect, but to give me a chance to intervene. Only, I'm stuck. Not stunned, but actually stuck on her words. *Escape.*

No. I was buying *her* escape from Queenscove. A chance to go back to where she was taken from, and I can't believe she's still pissy about that. Then again, it wasn't quite the best idea on my part, and I knew the moment I left the apartment that day. I knew Vassallo and his men were still out there and even though we have no confirmation of this, he could be looking for her. Plus, she doesn't have custody of Maya yet, so of course it was a bad fucking idea for me to tell her to go back to Fleeton.

But I couldn't think straight. I never can when it comes to her.

"You're a coward, Finnigan Hennessey. A coward. You can't face what's staring you right in the face. Because you fear it."

"Yeah? And what exactly is staring me right in the fucking

face, Evelyn?" In two strides I'm right in front of her, our bodies close to touching, her neck craned to look up at me.

Up close like this there's no missing it—the fire might be absent from her voice, but it burns feverishly in the gold of her eyes.

"Go on," I coax her. "What's stari—"

"Me."

The bluntness of her answer jolts something inside my chest. It spreads a chill through my body, and my skin sizzles, finally realizing just how close it is to the woman who makes my soul burn. Only, I want to feel the sting, the ache, the pain... the pleasure. I can't move.

Christ, there are so many appropriate and smart things I want to say to her right now. But what comes out of my mouth is neither appropriate, nor smart. It's retaliation in its most immature form, and I can't stop myself.

"Is that why you got a makeover? To grab my attention? Trying to turn dark and mysterious, dressing skimpy and tight? Is that how it works? You learn to do make up and get dolled up? You're eighteen now and you're coming out to play, trying to attract all this attention of men to you?"

Her mouth falls open wider and wider with every idiotic sentence that falls out of mine.

She takes a long, deep breath. "This is how you're fighting this fear? By trying to hurt me?"

"I have no fear!"

"Yet you still hurt me."

"Goddamn it, woman! What do you want from me?"

"For you to admit it." She moves closer, our fronts touching now, our breaths feeding off each other. "Admit that you don't see me as a girl at all. You're hiding. Fighting it." Her delicate hands go to rest on my chest, and her touch turns to electric fire, and I crave to douse myself in that feeling.

"Evelyn," I warn.

"You wanted more when you touched me, pressed me against you and danced with me. Admit it, Finnigan. It was not enough. We both know it. It's been months now."

Her scent of ginger and brown sugar wraps around me like the finest, lightest of silks, yet there's an odd heaviness in it, pulling me down to her. A peculiar spell I'm trapped in. I did, I wanted more. More than she could give, and definitely more than I should take.

"Admit that you wanted your hands to go lower, to press harder, to sink further. Admit you like the feel of me, the thought that when I do all those things to myself, it's you I'm thinking of."

She's hypnotizing me, and I can't help being pulled deep into those words, imagining every move she speaks of. This is so goddamn wrong, it almost feels right.

"Stay away, Evelyn. Do not dare cross this line," I warn with venom in my voice. "Even by yourself, do not fucking think of me when you..."

She raises an eyebrow at that addition.

"Tell me, then." Her chest rises and falls on erratic breaths, yet she again reins in her anger, and I'm kind of disappointed. "Tell me you don't want me, and I'll never speak a word of it ever again. Like it never happened."

I have to squash this.

"I'm going to say it one last time—do not cross the line. You're leaning too hard into this rebellious, childish phase that you girls go through. But I'm not your target!"

"You—"

"We're done here." And on that note, I turn and walk away.

The door doesn't move after I walk through and close it behind me. She's not following. What a great mood to go into this fucked up meeting with.

I didn't tell her though. I couldn't tell her I don't want her.

That was close. Too close. I wanted, no, I *needed* to touch her. To feel her. But there is a line, and I have to be on the other side of it.

"Finally."

I give Maddox a grave look in response to his exasperation, as I step into Vin's office and close the door behind me.

"Let's start," Carter orders, turning to the two large screens on the wall behind the desk.

"Not yet," I interrupt, ignoring The Carver's sigh.

"Why come now after all these years?" I turn to my brother who was already watching me. "And for how long?"

He exhales a heavy sigh, and replies, "It's not permanent. But in order to protect my family, while doing what we will need to do, this was the best place for us."

"Protect them... what are you talking about? There is no *we*, Ronan. Why are you here?"

"Because, brother, I'm not the only one who came back."

What?

A picture pops up on the screens, and all at once my heart stops, blood stills, and air leaves my lungs.

It's not possible.

My past is staring me right in the face, brought back to the present in what looks like a very recent photo, and it crashes down on me with enough force that the assault of memories breaks me.

Roberto-motherfucking-Bartiste was supposed to be fucking dead!

A shocked, delicate gasp pulls me back. I whip around at the same time everyone turns to find Evelyn standing in the doorway. Her eyes are wide, not with shock, but terror, her lips parted in a silent cry that seems to split open a dead part of my soul, and the revelation hits me at the same time she utters the name.

"Vassallo."

CHAPTER 16
Evelyn

THOUSANDS OF NEEDLES PIERCE MY body all at once. Each and every one of them is a figment of my imagination, bred of fear and grueling nightmares. They hurt, nonetheless. They paralyze me anyway.

Though, my muscles ache like I'm shaking.

Maybe I am... I don't know.

The world around me disappears. All but the face of the man who was pleased to see that I wasn't broken beyond use, and joined my destruction. Because he wanted a piece of me too.

This memory was vague until now, lost in the drug haze they put me through. I remember him, his limp as he walked closer to where I laid flat on my stomach, his fat hand squeezing my jaw as he lifted my head to inspect me, and now... his weight on top of me.

I had a feeling, but I hoped the memories of him wouldn't come. Vassallo, the one whose face faded from my nightmares. He was lost in the darkness I was taken in. But now, in the brightness of this room... I see nothing else but him.

He's staring at me.

Frozen eyes bore into me, gouging to the surface more of the pain buried beneath the drug-induced memory loss.

My ears pick up on activity around me, but the stinging in my veins and the incessant buzzing in my head mixed with Vassallo's voice, pull me further away from reality and throw me in a pit filled with all I've been avoiding. No, that's the wrong way of putting this, because I haven't been avoiding what happened to me. I came to terms with it. But only because I could barely remember it.

What I have been avoiding is remembering.

A frigid ghostly touch grips my nape, my spine tingles with beads of sweat running down it, and my hands hurt, like caught in a crushing vice.

Burning sears my muscles, the pain contracting them around my bones and crushing me from the inside out. Only, the pain holds direction, like he's yanking on them, controlling the fibers and forcing them to bind me until I can't escape. Until I return to that dark room where he will come for me again. The other one, Frankie B, too. The one who vowed to keep me.

No, no, no!

They can't have me! They can't!

Warm, comfortable pressure tightens around my upper arm, but soft velvet engulfs my cheek.

"Evelyn! Evelyn, please!"

With a painful jolt in my soul, I'm wrenched back to reality. My hand flies to my chest when the shock of the agony growing there hits me. I'm heaving, hard, and aches burst all over my body. Turning my palm over, I find indentations from my fingernails. They pierced the skin well enough that blood trickles out. I hiss when it hits me that the pain in my other hand comes from the doorknob I've been squeezing so tight, it imprinted on my palm.

"That's it, come back, Evelyn. You're okay."

That voice... that touch... the odd softness.

As if only now I realize he's here, my gaze shoots up, and I'm met with piercing, bright-blue eyes the color of the sunlit sky on the coolest of summer days. His soft touch stroking against my cheek is warm, comforting. For a moment, one cruel moment, I lose myself in that blue, flying through the atmosphere he always pulls me in. And this time, he allows me to.

The ache in my muscles melts away, my lungs find a focus, a calmer rhythm within the chaos, and Vassallo is no longer in my line of sight. Finnigan is.

"Good. That's it. You're here, safe, with me." He clears his throat. "With *us*."

My gaze drifts away and, holy mother, mortification hits me like a ton of bricks.

"I am so sorry, I didn't realize you were all in here. I thought this was—I don't—I'm sorry. I'm going to—"

"Evelyn," Finnigan interrupts my erratic speech, as he drops his hand from my cheek.

Without his touch, I'm exposed. Like the contact shielded me from the outside world.

"You didn't know we were here," Maddox says, and I realize he's standing right next to Finnigan.

Was he always there? All the eyes in the room are aimed at me, each in various states of either concern or curiosity.

"Are you okay?" Finnigan asks.

"Yes. Sorry, I was just coming to..." *Shout at you,* I want to say, but it feels inappropriate now. I thought he was going to be alone, I think. I don't know. I was so angry, I didn't think straight.

"Seriously, don't worry. I think we can all agree the timing was… perfect."

Maddox turns away. "Did you know that Vassallo is Bartiste? That he's the one O'Rourke, Holt, and Boseman worked with?"

"No." *Carter.*

His tone is sharper than I've ever heard him. Not that Carter tends to speak too much. I rarely ever see the man, to be fair, but now he sounds downright annoyed.

"So, this meeting was to tell us that Roberto Bartiste is back, but you had no clue—"

"No," Carter interrupts Maddox, the bluntness chilling.

"Evelyn, I know this is tough, but we need to talk about what happened when you were taken. Knowing who Vassallo is changes everything." Maddox turns to me.

I open my mouth to speak, but I'm lost for words.

"No!" Finnigan answers for me. "Look at her, she's shaking like a leaf after seeing that bastard's face on the screen. We can't put her through that!"

"There may not be any other choice." Carter argues the logic. "It's been eight years, and we all thought he was dead. Not only he fucking isn't, but he's been trying to get back into Queenscove right under our noses."

"You think I don't fucking know that?!" The bite in Finnigan's voice pales against the emotions bleeding through the cracks in what I'm starting to believe is a carefully constructed mask.

Because what I see now on his cruelly beautiful face is the same thing I saw the moment I came out of that container months ago—anguish. He's broken…

Just like I am.

Only now I realize that the eyes in this room are no longer aimed at me, but at him. And they hold a hesitant, all knowing expression that makes no sense to me. I can also tell it's making Finnigan uncomfortable. *Why?* Who is Vassallo? Or, what did they call him, Bartiste? Who is he to them? Who is he to Finnigan?

His brother's expression is the worst of them all. It may be that he hasn't been part of this world for a while from what I can tell, but he doesn't mask his feelings like the others. Or at all. His eyes are strained with sadness and something that looks a lot like shame.

"Who is he?" I blurt out and want to slap my hand over my mouth instantly.

The attention returns to me, but no one says a word.

"An old enemy," Finnigan finally replies.

"And a new one?" I ask.

His gaze fixes on mine, the intensity of it pins me in place and stuns my breath. For some reason I start counting the unspoken moments. I reach to five when the charge in the air seems to ease, and the clarity in his eyes takes me aback.

"Yes."

One word was enough to turn my world on its axis.

One word that seems to carry a weight I'm not prepared for. Because his answer had nothing to do with the fact that Carter announced this man's return into their lives. He is a new enemy for a whole new reason... a whole new crime. And this one is against me.

"Come, let's go somewhere quiet." Finnigan's hand wrapped around my upper arm attempts to guide me away.

"Finn, man, I think it would be better for me—"

"No." He cuts Maddox off without sparing him a glance.

"I just think we're closer, and you..." Maddox trails off

while everyone else stays deathly silent.

"*I* will be the one to talk to Evelyn." Finnigan's hand tightens around my arm, and I don't get a chance to argue as he guides me out of the room.

Why is he insisting for him to be the one to speak to me? Or better yet, why isn't he allowing anyone else to? I have so many freaking questions.

There's a peculiar possessiveness in his words, his eyes, even his touch, and I can't fully make sense of it. I'm not even sure if it's about me, or their past.

What happened to Finnigan Hennessey?

Finnigan

THE PRESSURE RIPPING THROUGH MY chest bleeds doom into my soul. If that makes any fucking sense at all. It hurts like it, it terrifies me. Something snapped the moment her gasp split the horrifying scream that filled my head when that photo appeared on the screen. It tore through this old wound, and when she spoke that alias with such horror in her voice, a new wound marked my soul.

But purpose followed it.

Certainty.

"You were rude to Maddox," I hear her say as I all but drag her behind me, and the visceral possessiveness I have over this woman right now, makes those words land heavier than they should.

"He'll survive," I spit out.

"He just wants to protect me," Evelyn insists.

I want to answer, *I'll be the one to protect you. No one else gets the privilege,* but the words don't form. They could, but I don't allow them. It's the least good sense I can have when I've been acting like a goddamn caveman since I saw motherfucking

Roberto Bartiste on that screen.

Alive and well. Sipping on a goddamn espresso on the terrace of a coffee shop.

He took her...

I guide Evelyn into a guest bedroom, shutting the door behind me. I hoped I could breathe easier in here, but the air is just as heavy. And I'm staring at the reason why.

Christ, she's beautiful.

She's standing three paces away, watching me with pain stricken doe eyes, and I'm trapped within that thick dark ring surrounding the bright gray that seeps into gold. I could stare at her eyes for the rest of my life, they're that unique and mesmerizing.

We don't speak a word. Both breathing harshly, trying to find a centering point that could bring us down from the shock we just experienced. For different reasons, one more tragic than the other. Yet, as I sink further in her broken gaze, I know my pain doesn't compare. All I have is old loss, but Evelyn... she has fresh wounds, unhealed and seeping their tragedy like a dark shadow looming over her.

I know she hasn't attempted to drown her pain in drugs again. I told Maddox to ensure there are eyes on her. I couldn't do it myself. I couldn't let myself be in her proximity or know where she was... it was too hard. Too tempting.

That resistance broke into a million pieces the moment I realized that Bartiste is the man responsible for her abduction. The possessiveness I feel over her tears through my restraints as I'm finally realizing that the asshole could've taken her from me before I even made her mine.

He can't have her.

Not her as well.

I won't allow it.

I can't fail her too.

"I'm sorry," I blurt out.

Confusion breaks through the pain in her eyes, and she cocks her head as she attempts to understand what I'm apologizing for.

"Okay... why did you insist that you would be the one to speak with me?"

Oh. That's not why I was apologizing, but it's a good enough reason. The dam may have broken but admitting it to her is a whole different thing. Admitting it to myself out loud is even harder.

"Sit down. Please," I add that final word after a brief pause, trying to deter from the blatant order.

She narrows her eyes for a split moment, then shakes her head ever so slightly, before she looks around herself, and walks to the edge of the bed, but doesn't sit.

"You're wasting your time if you want to talk about *that* night. I have no more useful info to give you," she says before I can ask the question.

"Knowing what we know now, any detail, even the ones you already told us, might mean something else entirely. We know Bartiste. Or at least we knew him... we're looking at what happened to you, to the children, with fresh eyes now."

She sighs, averting her eyes. I can tell her mind is wandering, falling into a memory she doesn't want to be in. I fucking hate myself for pushing her in it, but if anyone's going to do it, it has to be me. I hope Madds isn't going to ask me for justification as to why exactly that is. The only answer I have is not one I want to share with him, or the others. Not yet anyway. I must be the one to comfort her, to protect her... to take on her pain.

"Will you tell me?" She lets the incomplete question flow in the heavy atmosphere before she turns her attention to me. "Will you tell me what he did to you?"

Three rapid blinks it took to fully register what she's asking. Why does it sound like she knows something already?

"Did that bastard, Severin, fucking tell you?" I snap, unable to rein in my temper. The anxiety and adrenaline are a nasty combination.

She frowns and her lips part for a moment before she presses them into a hard line, debating something. Maybe a lie. Maybe a secret.

"He didn't."

I'm not sure I believe her.

"What do you know?"

"That he's the reason why you've learned that pain deals more damage on the inside than out. There's a reason why they say eyes are the mirror to the soul... yours have that broken quality I'm all too familiar with."

I say nothing to that. There are no words that could deter her from this conclusion. There's no hiding. No point in it.

"Will you tell me?" she asks again, her voice softer.

I flinch when she takes a step my way.

We're in here because I wanted to soothe her, protect her, and get her to talk to me about what happened to her. She flipped the coin, and I'm dreading this side of it.

It's not how this is supposed to go.

"Perhaps someday," I finally answer, though I don't understand why I'm giving her hope.

She stops moving, cocking her head and pulling my gaze to hers.

"You want me to talk, Finnigan." She speaks my name like an ethereal chant. "You want me to be vulnerable. Meet me on even ground then."

I take one slow, deep breath, and I don't release it until it tightens my lungs and pressure grows in my temples. Evelyn doesn't push. She waits patiently for me to reach the decision she desires.

She's not giving me a choice.

"Eight years ago, Bartiste came here chasing people who conned him in a black-market deal. Annika, my brother's wife, was involved. A lot happened, it was violent, and Bartiste kidnapped her moments after she told my brother she was pregnant. We tried really fucking hard, but we couldn't get to the—*her* in time." I correct myself before I get too vulnerable with the plum-haired woman. "He had her for a few days, tortured her, and we couldn't find him. When we finally did, a whole-ass battle erupted. We know Bartiste was shot. More than once. But in the whole commotion and after all was said and done, we couldn't find him. We assumed one of his men took his body, because the last we saw of him he was all but crawling. Even his men came to us days later, thinking we had him, and months after we were still finding men who used to work for him who swore they thought he was dead. After Ronan got Annika back, he decided to leave The Sanctum, Queenscove, and start a new *crime-free* life somewhere else."

There, I said it. Kind of.

Evelyn narrows her eyes on me.

"That's terrible." She offers, but there's uncertainty in her tone. "And you were so broken up about your brother's wife being taken?"

Wait, I don't think that came out the way I thought it did.

"The whole situation was intense. We were almost too late," I add.

She's not convinced, her darkening eyes tell me as much. But she takes a deep breath, her shoulders drop, and I think she relents.

"I've already told you all I remember that's relevant to you," Evelyn says.

"You can't make that decision. We don't see things the

same way, and every detail could help us."

She turns away, shaking her head slowly, and even though she tries to hide them, I can see the emotions she blinks away. They're raw, and the brutality of them awakens something in me I thought died with Hanna all those years ago.

"I'm sorry."

She whips her head around at my quiet words. Her eyes are narrowed, the question lingering without spoken words.

"For doing this. For asking this of you. I know reliving this must be... hard," I clarify.

"It's fine." But her tone says otherwise. She sits at the edge of the bed, and I join her.

"Have you started remembering more?"

She hesitates and I already don't like this. "Bits and pieces. Nothing that could help you."

"Walk me through it from the beginning," I insist.

"Nothing has changed about when they took us. They were swift, violent, and they only wanted my sister. They grabbed me by the hair and hindered me useless. I fought them as much as I could and jumped in the nondescript van myself. Only, I failed to get us out. I failed to save her. All they said were curses that they couldn't get rid of me and deemed it safer to take me with them. I didn't even really see their faces. I didn't get the chance to."

"Did you notice anything about the van? Like a smell? Or the way it looked on the inside? Did it feel new or well used? How did it sound?"

My questions took her by surprise. Because she squints and her gaze drifts somewhere in the distance as she ponders.

"Actually, it was pretty quiet. It didn't have the new car smell, but there were some scratches and dents inside, like it transported things in the past. It was used, but barely. There were some food wrappers around, actually."

"So, it's possible it wasn't a rental. What color?"

"Black."

"Did you hear any names? Did they talk at all?" I ask.

"Barely. We were maybe an hour away from the docks, and all they mentioned was that taking me too would cause some trouble. After that we were sedated, and I woke up in the darkness of the container."

They didn't even speak of directions to the docks, so they are familiar with the city and the area in general. We already know they took a few children from Fleeton and neighboring ones, but not needing even one direction is a bit peculiar.

"Nothing else happened during the time we traveled. Then we met you, and half an hour after all that, I met *him*."

"Him?" I ask.

"Frankie B, the one who..." she trails off, swallowing nervously. "The one who separated me from my sister."

There's so much more to this that she's not sharing.

"He seemed in charge. He was young, not as young as me, but not as old as you. He instructed for everyone to be taken to an assessment room... everyone but me. I don't know," she trails off, and I notice a slight tremor in her flesh, "I don't know what they did there. My sister has not given many details."

"What about you? What happened after they separated you?" I ask knowing full well I only have part of the story. I wasn't the one to find her—Maddox was. The bastard is just as quiet as she is, keeps so much to himself.

She gives up looking into my eyes but finds a spot somewhere on the wall, and she's focused on it like it's about to morph into something else.

"The kids' cries still echo in my mind some nights. The fear in their screams when I was grabbed and taken away is alive inside of me. But they hit some of them to silence them, and that... I don't think I'll recover from my failure to protect them."

"It's not your failure, Evelyn."

"I begged to let me go with them, with my sister," she continues, ignoring my words, "but Frankie said I needed to go with him. To find out what I'm worth."

My pulse shudders beneath my skin, and I'm not sure I manage to control my features. Because those words fill me with such rage, I don't know if I should blame that asshole or myself.

"What else did he say?" I ask through gritted teeth. I'm failing to control my reaction.

"Umm... that he might keep me to himself."

Motherfucker!

Evelyn is not his to keep! She is goddamn mi—

"Then he grabbed me by the hair, someone hit me, maybe it was him, and I passed out." She takes a breath that was meant to be deep, but staggers its way down her lungs instead. "After that it's fuzzy. They drugged me, but this time it wasn't a sedative. I've never done drugs before, but I know now it was heroin."

And here I basically accused her of being a junky when I caught her buying drugs.

"I was put in a cold room alone, without any children. There was just this flickering, faint overhead bulb there that went out frequently. That's where Vassallo came and questioned Frankie as to why I was still alive, because I was too old. He told him he wanted to keep me, and I took the fact that they didn't share any incriminating information around me as a good sign... Perhaps I was naive, but you don't usually censor yourself if you plan to kill the person who hears you."

I don't think it would have mattered, but I don't tell her that.

"Do you remember why they drugged you?"

Now her gaze shoots straight to mine, her brows

furrowing in both annoyance and confusion.

"You already know why," she spits back at me.

My brows draw together, tension pulling at my temples along with the confusion.

"I don't..." I shake my head, forced ignorance burning through my chest.

Her features morph to fury, eyes turn glassy as she frowns. But the truth stares me right in the face, it spills from her eyes in wordless whispers, telling me what I've been refusing to accept since the moment Maddox found her.

No... fuck! No, they didn't! Did they...?

"Evelyn..."

"Don't make me say it, Finnigan. You already know why."

"I don't. I wasn't there," I say quickly, the strain too noticeable in my voice.

Her eyes widen, and she flinches back. "But Maddox said—"

"I was part of the rescue mission, but I was with some of the kids... Maddox alone found you."

"And he didn't tell you?"

"Evelyn!" I raise my voice involuntarily, raking a hand through my hair as I force down my own anguish. "What happened?"

Small tears pool in her eyes, and a shuddering crack inside my chest sends shock-waves through my soul. Before I realize what I'm doing, I'm on one knee in front of her, my hands covering hers as she clutches the bedspread. She doesn't pull away, not that it would matter. I wouldn't let her.

"What did he do to you?" I whisper, unable to ignore the reality any longer. If she's suffering, then I should be too.

"They pinned me down, on my front..." She pauses as a light tear grazes down her cheek, and the pain exploding inside my chest makes my ears ring. "I was a virgin before *them*."

They hurt my Evelyn. They took her fucking innocence away!

I don't need to hear more. The echo of unspoken words carry enough pain for me to taste it for myself.

Bartiste fucking touched her. And Maddox didn't tell me!

"Evelyn, I'm so, so—"

"Don't." She stops me. "I don't need your pity."

"It's not pity, I'm just sorry that—"

"You broke your word?" She interrupts me again. "That your failure got me in that situation? Is that what you're sorry for? I sacrificed myself and you, Finnigan, you failed me."

I all but fall on my ass. I... I didn't... she's right.

"You promised me. You promised you would get me out before anything happened to me. You failed." On those last words, she pushes me back and gets off the bed, leaving me on one knee, mouth agape and a big fucking hole in my soul. She didn't even yell. Her tone held a calm disappointment in it.

I wish she would have yelled.

She's right. I failed her.

"Evelyn, stop!" I jump to my feet and slam shut the door she was just opening.

Her back is to my front, her scent filling me with more heat, more guilt, more longing. *I failed her.*

"We'll find them. I promise you on everything I am, we will find them, and I will kill them. I will kill them all for what they did to you." My tone lowers with each of those words because this promise is thick, heavy, and unbreakable.

I will not fail her again.

There will be blood, and I will bring her their heads.

"Forgive me if I have trouble trusting in your promise," she spits as she turns, pressing a hand on my chest to push me away.

I let her, and just as she opens her mouth again, a ringing

stops her. She's so pissed, she doesn't even look at the screen as she pulls the phone out and answers it.

"Yes?" she rasps.

But a moment later she lets out a hiss as she briefly glances at the screen, then at me. I skip around, placing myself between her and the door before she can seek her escape, and I Christ almighty, if eyes could shoot daggers, I would be dead on the floor.

"No, it's fine. Did something happen?" she asks on the phone. "Really? For how long?" Her gaze turns to earth-moving sparkles.

Happiness shines in her eyes and she turns to the door, but when she sees I'm not moving, she rushes to the opposite end of the room, standing by the window. She wants to hide something, though it feels more like a secret she's been holding for a long time. The happiness shining in her eyes plagues my soul more than the secret, and it feels a lot like wretched jealousy.

Yet another emotion I didn't think I could feel anymore.

"Oh, yes! Yes, please!" Her enthusiasm brightens her voice, and I find myself stepping toward that light.

Then the next two words stop me dead in my tracks.

"Hi, Daddy."

CHAPTER 17
Evelyn

I WAS DESPERATE TO LEAVE THIS room, to keep this private, but I don't have time to fight Finnigan. Not when my father is experiencing a rare moment of lucidity.

"Hi, Daddy." I barely suppress the emotions shaking my voice.

"Hi, my sweet Evie." His voice turns my legs to jelly, and I feel around me until I find the edge of the bed again.

"I miss you, Daddy. So much."

"Come see me. It's been so long…"

It has. Months. Maya and I used to go see him every week. More often if the nurses told us over the phone that he was having a good week, when he was actually remembering us. We tried to avoid the weeks when he remembered that the love of his life, our mom, is dead. I wanted to be there to hold him through it, even if he didn't know who I was, but I couldn't put Maya through it.

She didn't understand why Daddy was angry, why he didn't know who she was. Especially since his Alzheimer's has been getting progressively worse in the last year. I had to protect her, no matter how much it hurt not to be able to see my only living parent.

"I can't right now, but I promise I'll come soon."

"Why not, sweet Evie? Today feels perfect. The sun seems to be shining for the first time in weeks. Maybe longer." He trails off and I wander with him, my gaze going out the window, toward the back of the house where Maya is playing outside with her new friend—Aaro.

"Maya and I had to leave town for a bit, Daddy. But we're doing well."

"Why? Where are you?"

"On the South coast. We're safe, I promise. We're staying with—" I turn my head until Finnigan hits my line of sight, and my breath hitches when I catch the unfamiliar worry in his eyes. "Friends. We're safe. Maya's happy." I turn back to look out the window at my sister playing with the curly-haired little boy.

"Is she? You're so good with her, she's so lucky to have you. I'm so sorry I'm not there to take care of you... I'm so sorry, my sweet Evie."

I choke up, swallowing unshed tears. He hasn't been this lucid in so long, and I'm not there to experience it in person. To hug him. Hold him. For him to hold me. Like he used to. Rubbing a big hand down my hair, kissing the top of my head. He made me feel so safe. Even as his memories of me were drifting away.

"You're the best dad ever, you're always with us. No matter the distance."

"Oh, I love you, honey."

"Love you too, Daddy."

"But, why are you there, sweet Evie? It's thousands of miles away."

"I found better work here with the help of friends, and a good school for Maya." Technically the first part is true—my job at Lulu's Café is great, and higher paid for sure.

I hate lying to my father, even if he's likely to forget this conversation by the end of the week. Maybe even the day. It feels disrespectful.

"Okay honey. I trust you. If you thought that was the best for your sister and you. When are you coming back?"

"We'll come home soon, Daddy."

At those words I hear shuffling behind me, and I tense.

"Once we finish here, we'll be back, and we'll come straight to see you."

"I can't wait. It's been too long."

I don't miss the change in his voice. I've heard it enough to recognize it and I wonder if I have any time left.

"Do you want to speak to Maya?" I ask, a hint of hope lifting my tone.

"Yes. But, umm... can I, can I talk to your mom first?"

Sometimes I think there aren't any pieces left of my heart to break. Yet, every time he says something like this, his words find a stray shard big enough to shatter.

He's going away again...

"She's not here, Daddy."

"Where is she?" there's a slight tremble in his voice.

"She's... out." I can't do it. I've broken his heart so many times now, I must have reached a hundred.

"Oh..."

"Is nurse Jackie taking good care of you?" I attempt to distract him.

"She cheats at chess."

I burst out in a short laugh, because only he could have said something so random.

"Let me talk to her, I'll give her a piece of my mind."

"You can try, but she won't admit it. Call me soon, sweet Evie, yes?"

"Of course, Daddy. We'll speak soon. I love you, and Maya loves you so much."

"Um... Maya... oh yes. I love you too."

He's losing her again.

"Thank you, Jackie. I appreciate the call." I tell the woman when her voice comes back on the other line.

"Always, sweetheart. I waited to make sure he was truly there. Did he speak with Maya?" she asks.

"No. He asked about Mom."

"I heard. Don't worry. He's in good hands."

"I know. Thank you, Jackie."

"Are you safe? Last time we talked you said you're down South."

"Yes, I'm safe. I have a good job now, nice place to stay, I'll be back soon," I answer her.

"Okay honey, you take good care of the little firecracker, okay?"

I'm reluctant to say goodbye to the woman, knowing that I will have to turn around and face the man who has listened to this entire conversation. At least my side of it. But I do. I say goodbye and hang up, though the sadness doesn't leave me as I watch my sister out there, oblivious to the fact that I had two good minutes with our father, and she missed out on this sense of utter joy.

Only, that's not quite the case for her. I shake my head as I drop the phone on the bed.

My sister doesn't perceive our father in the same way that

I do. She was too young to form the same attachment as me, the same relationship. He's been in the care home for half her short life. She's always been excited to see him, she loves him, but she's young... she thankfully doesn't hurt like I do.

It's probably why he forgets her quicker than he forgets me.

It hurts so much when he forgets. When his safety is ripped away from me.

I can't help the tears pooling in my eyes now, nor the one sliding down my cheeks, mourning the father I used to have.

"Does anyone else know?" I flinch at Finnigan's soft voice, clutching the bedspread in my fists.

"Only Lulu," I whisper.

"Why didn't you tell us? We can help him... you." His steps are closing in.

Do I have the heart to tell him I did this to protect my father from them?

"I don't need it. He's perfect where he is. It's a specialized home for people with dementia. They have all the facilities, and great staff," I answer.

"But they don't have you..." Finnigan trails off and the kindness in his words takes my breath away. "I'm sorry I stopped you from leaving the room, then. Maya didn't get to talk to him."

I sigh because I wish I could blame him, but in truth, it was too late.

"It's okay. She wouldn't have managed to. He was already slipping away. It's probably better this way."

His shadow looms over me for a moment before the bed dips, my body involuntarily leaning toward him, and I quickly gather my hands in my lap. I don't turn, don't pay him any attention as my focus stays on my sister beyond the window.

"Why didn't you tell us about him? We thought you were homeless because he... passed away."

I take in a shallow breath and realize I don't have the energy to invent a different reason that might not hurt his feelings.

"Because I didn't know anything about you. All of you. Not that I know that much now." I rub my thumbs nervously on my lap. "There was no reason to trust you, and I will protect my family at all costs. I could never risk him being used in any way because of my screw up."

A slow, deep inhale coming from him tenses me up. I wait for the retaliation, for the snappy remark.

"Okay, fair."

My brows pull together, but I hold myself from turning to him.

"Has your opinion of us changed?" he asks.

"Yes," I answer without hesitation, surprising myself.

I know my instincts spoke before me because it's true. They treat my sister and I with nothing but kindness. From shelter, to food, to a decent job, and... friendship. As terrifying as that is, since I cannot stay in this city, they give me friendship. Unconditionally.

"For the better?" he asks.

"You're not what I expected. All of you, I mean." I quickly correct myself. "People whisper about you in town, about the *ruthless* Sanctum, the crime, the sex, the power. They fear you. I'm not saying you're not to be feared, you probably are, but what I've seen so far... it's exponentially different from their perception of you."

The exhale I hear coming from him warms me. There's relief in that whiff of air, and a tinge of hope blossoms beneath my flesh.

"Tell me about your parents." He speaks those words in such a calm, soothing tone, I feel compelled to share.

"They were normal people. Not rich, not poor, normal jobs. We lived in one of those suburban neighborhoods that's almost in the countryside, with plenty of space between houses. It was just the four of us. My mother came from the foster system and didn't know her parents, my father's mom died when I was two, and my grandpa when I was six. No siblings on either side, no great aunts or uncles. It was just us... we were happy." I inhale slowly, defeated. "Until we weren't."

I watch as Maya comes back into the garden, shyly handing Aaro a little plate with a piece of my cake. They both blush and there's something so endearing about this sweet moment.

Finn doesn't say a word. He's perfectly still in my periphery, patiently waiting on me to spill my story. Maybe there's hope yet for whatever this is between us. Though he seems reluctant to even admit it.

"About five years ago, our lives changed. Dad started having strange symptoms that didn't quite add up. At first, they kind of ignored them and passed them off as stress. But then the forgetfulness came, and from then on, he deteriorated. He has early-onset Alzheimer's, and it's aggressive enough that the decision was made for him to go to a care home that specializes in dementia. He insisted himself on one of his good days. Mom fought him so hard, I thought she would win. She didn't, Dad wouldn't let her."

I remember that period like it was yesterday. There was no yelling, no actual fighting, but begging. So much begging from both sides.

"Dad couldn't work anymore, of course, and mom not only had to work harder, but take care of a three-year-old, a thirteen-year-old, and my father. It got to the point where she couldn't leave him alone with us. I had to go find him after school on more than one occasion, because he got lost in the neighborhood. Once he almost burnt down the kitchen. Dad couldn't do this to mom, he loved her and us too much to make us suffer. So he went to the home. A good one."

"Evelyn... I'm so sorry." The sincerity in his tone splits open a little part of me I haven't been allowing to get too close.

"It's okay. I got used to it."

"But who's paying for him now? Who has been paying since you've been on your own?"

"Their savings. Mom put it in a sort of trust and a direct debit runs out of there monthly. She wanted to make sure that money is secure. But... it's running out. No one could have anticipated she—" I have to take a deep breath, swallowing through the emotions the memory of her brings. "That she wouldn't be here now."

"What happened?" Finnigan asks.

"Dad was already in the care home by this point. For quite some time. Mom went to the grocery store, came out to head to her car and... got caught in the middle of a gang war. She was shot in the parking lot. Police called her collateral damage, wrong place at the wrong time and all that. She stood no chance and died on scene."

I think we both stopped breathing, because you could hear a needle drop in this heavy silence.

"Some time ago you told me something—*you don't know what your world did to mine*—is this what you meant?"

I flinch at Finnigan's question. How does he even remember that? I blamed him and his world, and it's hard not to feel a little guilty about it now. A little right, too.

"It's easy to put all crime in one pot. Gangs are still criminal organizations, seeing the commonalities isn't that hard." I answer sincerely. Then there's what happened after... what their world turned me into, but I barely admit that to myself, so I'm not going to tell him. "And after all that, Maya and I fell into the clutches of another side of this dangerous world."

"I understand. I'm sorry about your mom, Evie." He

moves on from the subject. Though, he doesn't deny it.

"Thank you. It's been long enough that I've gotten used to the entire situation."

"You shouldn't have to get used to something like this. You're supposed to have support, people around you to help you through it all. How did you end up on the streets?"

"We had nowhere to go." I shrug. "We couldn't stay home, not as two minors. The only solution was placement, but in different foster families. And under no circumstances was I going to allow Maya to be separated from me."

"How did you escape the system?"

"I never went in it," I answer bluntly. "After the police came to the door to tell us about mom, I gathered everything I could hold in two backpacks, and ran. I knew what the system meant, and I wasn't going to allow it to swallow us whole. I was inspired enough to grab all photos of us as well, though they're all lost now. I wanted the memories, but it was mainly for Maya's benefit. I knew the police would put our faces on the side of a milk carton, especially Maya since she was so young. She's probably on the *missing children* list with no photo, just a name and birthplace."

"How did you manage to get her enrolled in school?"

"Fake documents and a person pretending to be our mom. It helped that Maya was never in school before, it was her first year. And we changed her name from Shaw to Shawn. Thought it would be easy to brush it off as a typo whenever I did manage to get custody and enroll her properly under her real name."

"Jesus..." He sighs, rubbing a hand over his face. He takes a deep breath, and I know he's pondering his next question. I bet he has a lot of them. "I just don't understand how you managed all of this on your own. This... fuck, it's so much, Evelyn. You were what, sixteen? Christ."

"I didn't have a choice. It was between this or losing my sister in the system. Imagine if she ended up in a closed adoption or something. It was not an option in my book. Though, I do wonder sometimes"—more often than I want to admit—"if Maya would have had a better life. If she would have found an amazing family. One who didn't live in shady motels or in their car. Who didn't get kidnapped in a trafficking ring."

Warmth and softness wrap around both my hands on my lap and I'm speechless when I look down—his large hand holds mine. Squeezing. Soothing. Comforting.

"You made the best choice."

I have no idea what to say to that, because his touch is a welcome distraction from all the sorrow I shared. His hand over both of mine drives me down a path of forbidden touch and untapped desire. If only he would move it higher, run it all up my arm, drag this electric current over my shoulders, my throat, my cheek... down my back, over my ass, and—

"How were you able to visit your dad?" He interrupts my dangerous thoughts. "Didn't the staff report you?"

"No. I knew one of the nurses. She wanted to call CPS at first, but I convinced her eventually. When her boyfriend was away on business, she used to take us in for the night. She's the one who called—Jackie. The rest of the staff I came in contact with didn't really ask, but Jackie told them we were in foster care. No one has time to question that." I'm still looking at our hands. "Where are your parents?" I ask.

"This month, on a yacht somewhere off the East coast. I think. They travel a lot." He shrugs.

How peculiar. He's not even bothered by it. His thumb has started moving, rubbing slowly, mindlessly over my knuckles, distracting me.

"You're not close?"

"As close as I can be to two parents who filled their time with work their whole life, and when they retired, they left."

"I'm sorry. That must be rough."

"Not at all," he says, his thumb still stroking over my hand. "It's what I've always known from them. I did have Mamaw June though."

"Vincent's mom, really? How long have you all known each other?" I didn't expect that. I thought they were close because they were business partners.

"Since we were kids. We were in school together. Madds and Vin were already friends, then we came along not long after. June was like a surrogate mother for all of us. She always had enough love in her for all of us."

God, I want to hug him. I may not have my parents anymore, or at least my mom, but the memories I have of them... of my mom teaching me to bake cookies, making pink meringues with my dad, our little adventures through the woods collecting pinecones, or at the beach gathering all the pretty pebbles, and so many more. I would be lost without those memories. Especially now that our photos no longer exist. Well, technically they do, in my old car that's probably in a dump somewhere.

"Mamaw June truly is incredible."

"She's good with Maya," he agrees.

"She's good with me too," I admit.

At my words he tightens his hold around my hands. This means something to both of us. A strange common ground born out of two different situations, different needs, different wants.

"With everything you went through, you fucking prevailed. Look at you now. You're surrounded by people who care."

"Do you?" I turn, my gaze pinned onto the azure of his.

"Do you care about me, Finnigan?"

He flinches, his lips parting, but only unspoken words pass through that slight gap.

Damn it! We've opened up. I've opened up! I thought this was going somewhere, that he was finally going to acknowledge... this. Whatever this is. I'm such a fool.

"I'm not good for you, Evelyn. This"—he points between us, releasing my hands,—"can't go anywhere. We can't cross this line."

"Jesus, Finnigan. You're the one with the chalk in hand drawing lines only you care about." I rise, clenching my fists, trying to rein in my anger, but for the first time in a long time, I fail. "Just... just *fucking* stop it!"

CHAPTER 18
Finnigan

I'M FLABBERGASTED. EVELYN SHAW NOT only got angry, which is something she hasn't done even when I was pissing the hell out of her, but she raised her voice. And she swore. She actually swore.

She's the calmest person I've ever met. I don't know if it's because she's been putting up a front for Maya, or she just got used to it for her benefit, but seeing her like this... close to disheveled, wakes up a primal urge within me.

"You and your goddamn line! I'm done with this." She turns on her heels and storms out of the room, leaving me all alone with her words lingering in the air.

This is for the best. She has to be done with this. As I rake my fingers through my already messy hair, I can't help but wonder if I'm done with this at all.

I'm not. Not even fucking close.

On the contrary. Knowing that Bartiste was responsible for her kidnapping as well, changed the game for me. I refuse to let that asshole take another person from me. Evelyn might not be mine the way Hanna was, but she is... something else.

Don't make me say it, Finnigan... Her words echo through my thoughts. The bastard touched her. He raped her. He raped my Evelyn when he didn't even have the right to fucking gaze upon her.

Did I just call her...? Yeah, I did—I called her *my Evelyn*. Christ, I'm so screwed. It's not even the first time I thought of her as mine, yet I tell her she can't cross the line. Hypocrisy looks like shit on me.

But she really is something else, something to cherish. To admire. I know she's been going to therapy, Katya mentioned it, but living every day with all that sorrow and pain is unfathomable. Her life is a series of tragic events, and no sane person would have come out on the other side the way she did. She's a force of nature.

Evelyn appears in my line of sight out in the garden, squatting to speak with Aaro. My nephew. I might just have to punch Carter in the face for doing this to me.

A knock startles me and I turn to the door.

"Can we talk?"

No.

I'm not prepared for this. I doubt I ever will be.

Ronan takes my silence as a *yes* and walks toward me, taking a seat where Evelyn sat before him.

"I didn't want to blindside you. I told Carter and Katya, and they convinced me to keep quiet."

"I'm sorry, Katya knows too?" My brows pull together, a tension drawing a headache through my temples.

"I brought her in the business. Her and I never stopped being friends."

"But we did." I end that sentence for him.

"That was not my choice, brother."

I can't help but scoff, keeping my gaze toward the garden, on her. "It was. You left."

"But you banished me."

"I was in pain, goddamn it! I was fucking broken, and you abandoned me!" I slam my hands on the bed, turning to him. "What did you expect me to do? I never loved before, Ronan. I didn't know how it felt to have it be ripped away from you... in such a literal sense of the word. I needed you!"

"I know... I'm sorry. You know this. I just couldn't keep Annika and Aaro in that situation. I couldn't keep myself. I know I was selfish, believe me, it fucking hurt me too, but I couldn't see any other choice."

I say nothing because he's not wrong, and goddamn it, I hate that.

"You had The Sanctum, Annika had no one who could understand. Her best friend was brutally murdered and died in her arms... I couldn't just abandon her. Not when she was pregnant with my child—our blood. But don't ever think my choice was easy. I missed you so goddamn much, Finn."

Sighing, I clench my fists around the comforter. So many years have passed, and this explanation makes more sense now. It shouldn't. It should sound the same, mean the same thing, and feel the same. Yet, it doesn't. If I was in his shoes, I wouldn't have left. But do I really not understand why he made that choice?

I think the reason I've been so angry and hurt over these years is exactly the opposite—I do understand. At least I've grown to understand. But I have no one else to blame, no one else to be angry at. I'm not admitting that to him, though. Turning, I look at my brother, really look at him. Lines have appeared across his features, smile lines under his cheekbones, crow's feet around his eyes, faint creases on his forehead. But his eyes are the same. Calm, hopeful, caring.

I want to punch him harder.

Why couldn't he just be an asshole?

"Come on," I finally say. "Your wife and son are probably waiting for you." I rise and walk away before he answers.

I can't bear to be in this room with him anymore.

"He asks about you, you know," Ronan says behind me.

I stop, but don't turn.

"We show him photos." he continues when I don't answer, "We tell him about you, but he's never satisfied."

"He doesn't even know me, why isn't he satisfied?" I ask.

"Because for the first few years he couldn't understand *why* he didn't know you. Why you didn't want to meet him. We told him your job keeps you away."

"Thanks, I guess." I walk away this time, and he follows, passing with me through the hall, then back in the living area.

"He loved the books."

My steps falter.

"He's read them all. Several times. They're his favorites and he keeps them away from all the others."

I never sent anything to Ronan or Annika. Never spoken with them since they left. Didn't even text. But... I felt bad that I had a nephew out there who would never know me. I wanted a connection, even a faint one. Every once in a while, when Katya sent them a package or met with them, I gave her a book. I told her not to mention they were from me, and she promised she wouldn't. It's possible that she lied... or perhaps Ronan simply knew. Hearing that Aaro loves them makes me feel a certain way.

"There you are." Annika walks in through the patio door, heading straight to her husband, and wrapping her arms around his middle. "The munchkin might need sleep soon.

He's wired and smitten, it seems."

Both Ronan and I turn to the patio at the same time. Annika's right. The way the kid looks at Maya is funny and endearing at the same time—he is indeed smitten. Though, he's trying to play it cool. Stealing glances when she's not looking.

"Evelyn said she's leaving, though, so it would be a good idea for us to head out as well," Annika continues.

"Actually, Vincent offered us to stay here. It's safe, there's security patrolling the woods, and it would be better for you and Aaro," my brother answers her.

I could offer his old room in the penthouse, but it feels like a step too far. Too quick. I would rather get him in the ring and smash his face in first. It wouldn't achieve much, but it would certainly make me feel better.

"That's really nice of him. Okay, sounds good to me. I'll ask Katya to bring our stuff from her place."

Katya... I might have to have a word with the woman. I'm not enjoying this secrecy. The fact that she and Carter hid the arrival of my brother doesn't sit right with me. Actually, thinking about it, both of them have been looking at me funny for a few days now. Particularly at Morrigan's birthday party.

"When did you decide you were coming back to Queenscove?" I ask.

"A few weeks ago," Ronan answers.

Huh, okay. "When did you tell Carter about it?"

My brother and his wife exchange brief glances before he answers. "Maybe four days ago."

Oh yes, that timeline fits perfectly. Goddamn it. Though, I do feel better knowing that Carter and Katya haven't been keeping this from me for too long.

"I'm sorry we didn't tell you too. I didn't want to risk it," my brother says.

"Risk what?" I ask.

"Not seeing you, of course."

I'm not sure how to respond to that. Would I have gone away knowing that he was coming specifically to talk to the Sanctum? Maybe. The few times he visited in the past few years, he would go to our parents place and I would make myself busy on missions or going out of town. Any excuse not to be in the same postcode as him.

This was an ambush, and it was the only way for him to see me. I'm bothered that I'm weirdly becoming okay with it.

I nod to my brother. "I understand."

He gives me a faint smile, like he's handling a skittish animal, making sure I don't run away. Christ, have I acted that childish in the last years?

"Excuse me. Nature calls." I didn't need to over-share, but I also didn't want him to think that I'm leaving to end this conversation. Well, I do feel the need to take a break from it, but nature does call.

I walk past the stairs on the narrow corridor to the bathroom, and gentle voices filter through the high, open window—Morrigan and Evelyn.

"It feels... wrong. Dirty."

Those words stop me dead in my tracks, because Evelyn speaks them and my curiosity doesn't just peak. It soars. I'm not proud of it, but I stop walking, hoping there's more to that sentence.

"Have you talked about this with your therapist?" Morrigan asks.

"Not really."

"Why?"

There is a pause. A long one, before Evelyn answers.

"Because I think something's wrong with me. How can someone who went through what I went through still have these thoughts? What if she judges me?"

"Do you think you would be more comfortable talking to me about it?" Morrigan gently speaks the question, making sure there is no demand or expectation.

What the hell are they talking about?

"Oh god. What if you think I'm... wrong?" Evelyn's voice is filled with embarrassment and something that sounds a lot like unease.

"I own a fetish club, Evie. I can assure you, you can share anything."

Wait a damn minute?! What exactly is this conversation about? Evelyn doesn't want to go there. Does she? A burning sense of possessiveness singes through me, and it takes a minute for my brain to catch up. Of course not, the club hasn't been reopened yet after the fire Morrigan's ex started there.

"I guess you're right," Evelyn relents. "If I could talk to anyone about this, it's you and Lulu."

"Exactly! I would never judge, and no matter what it is, I hope I can make you feel more comfortable." Morrigan attempts to soothe her.

There is a brief pause, and my breath is caught in my chest waiting for the intimate confession I should definitely not be listening in on. But I can't help myself, so fuck it. I'm already an asshole.

"After what they did to me, what I feel seems wrong. Inappropriate. Sick. Have you ever felt like you want your partner to just... take? Be at their mercy, sort of? I don't even know how to explain this. Almost like the only consent you give is how turned on you are, but he's already *there* when he discovers this."

"Yes, Evie, I have. There's nothing wrong about that. About giving up control with a person you want, a person you're attracted and connected to."

"But I was raped, Morri. I was forced and they…" she trails off and a burning lump rises up of my throat. "Someone in my situation should not have these kinds of fantasies. It feels sick. What is wrong with me?"

Christ, I want to gather her up in my arms and hold her there. She's not sick. She's so far from that. But it drives me mad thinking that she might end up exploring that kink with someone *else*. Someone who could take advantage of her and not treat her right.

"Many of us who once had the choice stripped away, find solace in the loss of control with a person we trust. A person we want. It's like a different type of therapy. I don't know if it's because the decision to lose control over our body is ours, or maybe it just feels fucking good. Because, let me tell you, it feels so damn good. Fortunately, as you said, your memories of your attack are sparse, and maybe your need for control over it all is even deeper. However, you shouldn't let your fantasies revolve around what happened to you. Let them be. Sometimes a need is just that—a need."

"I never thought of it in this way. Yes, I feel wrong for having these cravings, but they aren't my only ones, nor are they new. I'm questioning them now, their morality, my… mental health, only because of what happened to me."

I am stunned at this conversation. I couldn't move even if someone caught me listening. This insight makes me feel all kinds of wrong. It's utterly intimate and Evelyn would lose her shit knowing that I stole her secret. The worst part of this is that this fantasy of hers is being stored in my mind, like I'm building a list of what would make sweet Evelyn whimper. Should I also add this on the list of all that is wrong about me? Like craving a woman who's barely eighteen?

Yes, I should add it.

"So, it's something you wanted before all of this

happened?" Morrigan asks.

There is no answer, but her next words make me think Evelyn probably agreed in a wordless way.

"Then you think it's bad that it hasn't gone away because of the attack."

"It would be the normal expectation, right? And it's not just that, but before it all happened, those types of cravings already felt disturbing. I never had sex before, but all my wet dreams were forceful, raw. I can't believe I just said that." Evelyn's tone raises a few octaves.

I can't either! Jesus, why did she have to say the words *wet dream* and *raw* in the same sentence? I know what I'm dreaming of tonight.

"It's not necessarily the expectation, no. It goes back to the need for control. Fantasizing, living that fantasy in a safe environment gives you your control back. And trust me, Evie, never having sex has nothing to do with what you crave. There are plenty of forty-year-old virgins out there who fantasize about much kinkier things than some dubious consent." Morrigan explains.

"I guess you're right. Thanks Morri, this really helped."

"Do you have someone in mind you would want these fantasies to come to life with?" Morrigan asks her, and I stiffen, eagerly waiting for Evelyn's response.

"I thought I did, but I think I'm going to be seeking someone else."

Oh, hell no! She wants to seek someone else?! Over my dead fucking body! And even then, I'll take the motherfucker down with me.

"Maybe we should do something about it then." Morrigan giggles and I'm ready to burst through that damn window and give her a piece of my mind.

"Shush, Maya's coming," Evelyn alerts her friend, and I

take it as my cue to detach myself from this wall.

Through my veins my pulse is rushing so hard, I think my heart's gonna burst out of my fucking chest. It takes more than a few minutes in the bathroom to compose myself finally before coming back into the living area. Ronan gives me a bit of a look when I return, probably wondering why it took me so long to go to the toilet, but I ignore it.

"Say goodbye, Maya." Evelyn's soft, melodic tone, mixed with that sweet brown sugar scent weaves around me just as Aaro darts past and sticks himself against his mom.

"Goodbye…" Maya's little voice sounds shier than usual.

"It was very nice to meet you all. I hope we'll see each other soon," Evelyn says.

"We certainly will. Plus, it was such a nice surprise to have someone in his age range here, it couldn't have worked any better if I planned it."

"It was getting boring with all these adults around." Maya gathers more courage and I stifle a laugh.

"Shush. You love us." Evelyn pats her sister on the top of the head, shaking hers. "We'll see you later then." She moves, now only a few steps away from the front door.

"Wait, who's taking you?" I ask hastily.

She stops but doesn't turn. Not before she takes a few agonizingly slow, deep breaths. The silence is so awkward, Annika took a few quiet steps backwards to remove herself from this. Before I can say something, Evelyn's eyes land on me over her shoulder, and I try to swallow through the sudden dryness in my throat, but it doesn't work. A lump forms, and I swear I can hear her screaming in her mind at me, telling me to mind my own fucking business. Maybe I'm paranoid, maybe I'm just creating fake scenarios in my head, but the annoyance is painted in her furrowed eyebrows.

I deserve this, don't I? I pushed her away yet again and

threw the rejection in her face even though my actions don't match my words. I craved opening up to her, craved to share, craved to know more of her, know *everything*, but I don't deserve to know anything at all. I shouldn't. Even if her confession to Morrigan weaves like tendrils of fire through my mind.

She opens her mouth to answer, but another voice pops into the room.

"Okay, I'm done. Let's go." Morrigan wheezes past me and heads straight for the door.

Evelyn says goodbye to everyone, but refuses to acknowledge me anymore. She leaves without a word.

I have a bad feeling about this.

The sparkle in her eyes looked a lot like revenge.

CHAPTER 19

Finnigan

TWO MORE AGONIZING HOURS PASSED before I could leave Vin's house. I thought planning and plotting our revenge would do something sweet to my insides, but the opposite happened. All this talk about the man who viciously took the first woman I ever loved away from me stirred a brutal discomfort. It wasn't pain. Not because it didn't hurt, but because the actual pain was reserved for the other reason these hours were agony—Evelyn.

She left in a strange mood, a look of vengeance in her eyes, but resolve too. Resignation. Like she gave up on something and the idea doesn't sit right with me. I don't know why.

Oh, fuck it, of course I know why.

Because it might be me she gave up on, and that makes me all sorts of uncomfortable. Why, I don't know, because I want her to give up. I was the one who chased her away, but not because I didn't want her.

I want her so much I can't breathe properly unless she's around. And when she is, she sucks it out of me, turning into want, need, and something so visceral my heart beats violently in my chest. I crave her starving silver and gold eyes, their invisible touch, the hunger beneath their surface, the demand to live and indulge. To ask for more and feed on the life she never had.

I want *her*.

Knowing she might go out there to seek her desires from someone else fills me with both rage and unfounded jealousy. I might not deserve her, but neither does any other asshole.

Now, I'm standing under the spray of the shower in my penthouse, trying to wash away these conflicting feelings. But I think I'm asking for far too much from mere water. I give it five minutes before I walk out, striding out onto the terrace that overlooks the sea, with nothing but a towel wrapped around my waist. I'm looking for some answers from the calm waves that look too small from this height, but the conflict seems to have the only reply.

The moon has risen, its light brushing over the water, and the calmness unsettles me. It's a sheer contrast to my inner turmoil, because I haven't gone over today's revelation that Bartiste not only is responsible for Evelyn's abduction, but he also *touched* her.

I can't even bring myself to say the true word of what the dead man did to her. I'm a fucking coward. Yet, no matter the word, the reality is the same. I could have lost her to him.

She could have been gone before I had a chance to know her, to witness the woman she's becoming. Admire the strength of her character, of her beautiful mind, experience her transformation, coming into her own. The chance to feel her against me, taste her, and ruin her in the best way possible.

My cock tents against the towel, a soft breeze brushing against it, and I shake my head at the reaction. It's not as involuntary as I would like to believe. Not when it happens every single fucking time I think of Evelyn. It's been going on for weeks, maybe months. Like some teenage goddamn crush or something.

I swipe a hand over my face when I fully acknowledge the word I spoke in my mind—crush.

I'm a twenty-nine year old man... with a crush.

God save me because I'm fucked.

* * *

I didn't make a decision by the time I reached Evelyn's apartment building. But the look in her eyes when she left Vin's house kept resurfacing in my mind, and the nagging sensation that I could be right was agonizing.

Time to find out.

The Sanctum's security is stationed in and around this building too, at Vin's insistence of course, since Morrigan spends a lot of time at her apartment here. I think Madds might have had a say in this too, as he seems oddly focused on the owner of the building—Loreley—though he would never admit it.

One of the guys lets me in and I head straight up to the first floor, my knuckles against the door before my feet halt. Too many moments pass, and just when I'm about to knock again, the door opens.

"Well, hello there."

"Mamaw June," I exclaim, surprised. "Hello."

She chuckles softly and moves to let me in.

"I must admit, I'm not used to you being so disappointed

to see me."

"Shit, I'm sorry." I don't even bother to deny it. One does not lie to Mamaw June. The woman has a sixth sense about it.

"It's okay." Her tone is light, amused. "But Evelyn's not here, dear."

I'm too late.

"Do you know where she is?"

"Out. She asked me to look after Maya tonight." She shrugs as she moves toward the living room.

I've never been in this place, but Morrigan's apartment on the floor above has a similar layout. This one has a different personality though, as in it almost lacks it. It looks like it was just about finished, some of the light switches still have the protective film over them. But this old building has so much character with its tall ceilings and intricate coving, that not much needs to be done to it to make it look inviting.

"Finnigan!" A little screech makes me swallow my next question, and a small body slams into me from the side, arms wrapped around my waist.

"Maya. Hello." I greet the cheeky girl. I wonder if she reacts like this to everyone she sees. "You seem cheerful. Aren't you supposed to be in bed?"

She pulls back and steals guilty looks at Mamaw June. "I'm a big girl. I can stay up late."

"It's eight thirty now, I'll give you half an hour and then you're off to bed."

"An hour. Finnigan's here. He can read something to me." She grabs my hand and flashes her doe eyes, clear expectation in them.

"Oh honey, I actually have somewhere—" The words get caught in my throat at the shift in her eyes, sadness slowly seeping into them. "Sure, I'll stay." I can't bring myself to deny her.

She squeals and skips cheerfully to a small bookcase, sliding to her knees and rummages through it.

"Did you have somewhere you needed to be? Because I don't think you're escaping this." The woman chuckles.

I did, but I can't bear the thought of disappointing the little one. Plus, I don't know where I should go.

"Did Evelyn say where she was going?" I ask as I follow toward the sofa.

"She did not, no. And you know me, it's not like I know the *hip* places in town anyway, so it wouldn't matter."

"How about this one?" Maya exclaims and rushes to me, a tattered book in hand.

I sit down on the comfy sofa and grab it from her. *Percy Jackson and the Lighting Thief.* Okay, this is not a bad choice at all. Though this book clearly has seen better times.

"Where did you find this?" I ask Maya as she plops next to me, snuggling against my arm with absolutely no shyness or reservations. Her sister doesn't share the same forward attitude, though... she's the one who came on to me every time. Okay, maybe I am wrong, and she does have the same drive, I'm simply the one to squash it every time.

God, I truly am an asshole.

"One of those cool thrift shops. They have a lot of pretty old things there."

I wonder if Evelyn takes her there out of need or actual pleasure for the cheap, secondhand items. I resign myself to pushing back my plan of finding Evelyn, because there is no way I'm going to break the little girl's heart.

"Can you do something for me, though" I ask her.

"Of course! Anything." She wraps her tiny hands around my bicep and looks at me like I'm about to give her the most important mission in the world.

"Could I have a glass of water, please?"

"Coming right up!" She jumps off the sofa and disappears somewhere behind me.

I chuckle at her enthusiasm, and pull my phone out of my pocket. Before I pop it on the table, I shoot a text to Maddox.

Have you seen Evelyn? She's not home. Worried about drugs. Can you find out where she is?

He's the only one of us who knows about her previous *adventure* and has been keeping an eye on her. I feel like a dick for using the drugs as an excuse to find out where she is, but the alternative is to tell Maddox that I rejected her attraction to me yet again. Obviously, I can't tell him that.

On it. I'll text when I find her.

Thanks.

"Here you go." Maya hands me the glass of water like it's liquid gold, and plops back next to me as I down half of it.

Placing my phone on the wood coffee table before me, I settle in for a reading session. I guess I have to brush off my intonation skills, because I think the little one will demand full immersion in the story.

Yet, even as I start reading, my mind still drifts to one question.

Where the hell is Evelyn?

Evelyn

"GIRL, YOU KNOW YOU'RE NOT gonna find what you're looking for here. Right?" Morrigan's words filter through the loud music as I move my hips on the dance floor of the bar.

It's a busy night, and the man I'm currently swaying my backside against is not the first one this evening. At least this one isn't already drunk, and he seems less handsy than the last one.

"I know. But I can practice." I laugh.

"You sure can. I'm gonna go get a drink. Don't go anywhere." I think that last sentence is for the guy behind me more than for me.

I catch a glimpse of Lulu rolling her hips slowly in the arms of a man who looks ready to kneel at her feet and kiss them. He's a handsome one. Tall and broad enough that you know he's fit underneath his clean-cut clothes, with the face of a clean-shaved lawyer who hikes and goes to the gym in his free time.

Yet, he looks totally wrong for her. But she seems to be enjoying herself.

The guy behind me tightens his hands against my hips and pulls me a little closer. I don't miss the half-mast rubbing against my ass, and for a moment I want to pull away, run in the opposite direction. But I swallow through the sensation and allow him to hold me, to lead me on the song that everyone on this dance floor seems to enjoy.

"So, what are you doing for the rest of this lovely night?" he asks.

"Exactly this. Dancing. Enjoying myself."

"Here?"

I debate the answer for a moment.

"Oh, yes."

I know I've been dancing with him for quite a few songs. Maybe it was a mistake. It created expectations I didn't foresee. Maybe being as sexually inexperienced as I am, made me more naive than I thought I was.

"I came with my friends, and I'm leaving with them as well," I add. I don't want to hurt the guy.

"Surely they wouldn't mind if you decide you want to *dance* with me at my place." The insinuation is clear in the way he accentuates that word.

"They are very protective of me, so I'm afraid dancing will be limited to this bar." Okay, he's getting a little insistent.

"Well, I'm sure we can find a spot that's a bit more... private."

He attempts to turn me to him, and I resist, attempting to move away instead. But I'm a little unsteady on my feet after four shots and three vodka sours, and the guy isn't even attempting to catch my delicate rejection.

"Actually, I think I'm going to go check on my friend now." I pull away again, but he holds me tighter.

Oh hell, what do I do? I don't want to cause a scene.

"That would be such a shame. Give me one more dance,

one more song." He begs and I wonder if that will be the end of it.

I'm a bit too tipsy to protest delicately, so I look for the girls to bail me out instead. I catch Morrigan's flaming red hair, but she's talking to the barman. Turning to Lulu, I see she's preoccupied with the *lawyer* guy, hanging around his neck as he guides her hips against his own. I can't just scream for her, that will cause a scene. But her body stills, bones frozen in place as her gaze fixes on a spot in the distance, and she slowly releases the guy she's with. I follow the direction of her stern gaze, and I'm both annoyed and relieved at what I find there—Maddox. I know why I'm annoyed, but I'm not sure why Lulu reacts like this to the big guy.

"Hey, I think it would be best if we stop dancing now." I warn the man behind me in the most delicate way I can muster right now.

I've grown to view Madds like an older brother, and if he feels the same for me, then I know why he showed up here, and the guy behind me should disappear before he sees him. Madds scans the room, and it takes him three seconds to spot all three of us, his gaze darkening with each one. As he stalks over, I expect him to come straight to me and drag me away, but instead, he stops next to Lulu. Shoulder to shoulder, looking down at her as she scowls up at him. No words are exchanged, only glowers, one more intense than the other. One more possessive than the other. *Holy hell, what is happening over there?*

I'm downright curious and I make a mental note to ask Lulu about it. Or at least Morri, since I think Lulu will dismiss me. Madds turns his focus on me, and I feel like I got caught doing something I'm not supposed to. Okay, he definitely has big brother attitude.

The guy behind me jerks me against him, and I only blink

once and Madds is only two steps away from me.

"Having fun?" he asks, but there's no cheerfulness in his tone.

"Umm, yup." *Yup?* What kind of answer is that?

"Who's this," the guy behind me asks.

"You're done now, right?" Madds asks me, ignoring the guy.

I debate being a brat for a few moments, chewing on the inside of my cheek, but self-preservation wins. Plus, I wanna get rid of this dude.

"I think I want a drink," I answer, because I'm not necessarily done with the night, but I'm done with this guy.

"I'll get you one," he says from behind me, his hands possessive against my hips.

"No. You're good, buddy. I suggest you find someone else."

I laugh at Maddox's words, and I bite my lip to stifle it. He notices but isn't amused as he reaches a hand for me. I grab it, but the guy behind me doesn't let go. Madds notices and steps forward, his six foot and too many inches frame towering over the man.

"Maybe the music is too loud, and you didn't hear me. I said find. Someone. Else." He punctuates each word with another small step until he's crowding us.

With a jerk, the guy releases me, and my back cools—he stepped away. I release a sigh of relief and let Maddox pull me away.

"Have a good evening," I say on a raised tone, turning my head slightly.

There's sarcasm in my voice, but I didn't want to be mean and leave without a word.

When we reach the bar, I slap a hand on Maddox's bicep. "What are you doing here?"

"Rescuing you, clearly."

"Oh, stop it. Seriously, what's with the ambush and the attitude?"

He doesn't answer, just rolls his eyes and ignores me as he pulls his phone out and starts tapping.

"Hey! I'm talking to you." I push the phone down and glimpse at the screen, annoyed that he's ignoring me for it.

> Found her. Dancing in Terry's bar with Morrigan and Lulu.

I gasp at the text, clearly about me, but when I catch the first letter of the name at the top of the screen before Madds pulls the phone away, I turn furious.

"Finnigan?! Are you reporting back to him? Did he send you?" Oh, I'm mad. Really mad. The alcohol might have something to do with it too, because I don't usually get so heated.

"He was worried about you."

Those words don't make me feel better in the slightest.

"What right does he have to worry about me? He clearly does not care about me at all. He said that much." I spit back at him, though my words are more directed at Finnigan, even if he's not here.

"Okay, I've kept my questions to myself because prying is not my thing. But what the hell is happening between you and Hennessey?!" Madds crosses his arms against his broad chest, and for a moment there he looks more like a father than a brother.

"I wouldn't mind the answer to that question either." Morri pops up at my side, then joins the scarred man before me.

I roll my eyes at both of them. "Absolutely nothing. Clearly." I want to slap my hand over my mouth because I'm giving far too freaking much away.

They exchange a curious look, and it feels like a silent

conversation about me.

"Nothing at all?" the redhead insists.

I'm not quick enough to answer and her brows shoot up, and yet again she exchanges a look with Maddox.

"Hey! Stop that!"

She chuckles at my outburst and shakes her head.

"I knew it. Christ, it's about time. Isn't it?" She looks to Madds for the answer.

He nods and leans against the bar, a thoughtful look in his eyes, like he's drifting somewhere in the past. But then he shakes his head.

"He's a player, Evie. He fucks a new girl every week, sometimes every night. He doesn't date. He's not for you."

"You cannot decide what is and isn't for me," I push back. "If I decide I wish to sleep around with Finnigan Hennessey, I'll do however I please. But just so you know, no, there's nothing going on between the two of us. Nothing at all." *No matter how much I tried.*

Madds is about to argue, but Morri sets a hand over his forearm stopping him. "I hate to tell you, big guy, but Finnigan hasn't fucked around in a while..."

"What?" Both Maddox and I exclaim at the same time, and he scowls.

"It's just an observation. Though, it is coming from me, Vin, and Carter. Finn lacking a woman on his arm every other night is something noticeable." She shrugs. "And I believe the reason he hasn't is standing right in front of me."

"Come to think of it..." Madds trails off. "Oh, for fucks sakes! I'm gonna kill him!" he bursts.

"Oh, settle down. Christ, you really do take your *big brother* duties seriously." Morri laughs.

I feel all fuzzy with affection for the man, but I catch a hint of sadness in his eyes too. It's gone just as fast as it appeared.

He mentioned a sister once, but the subject was shut down before it barely started. Maybe one day I'll pry.

"Madds, seriously. There's nothing going on with him and I, he just... pisses me off. Kind of like what you're doing right now." I fold my arms over my chest, cocking my head at him.

Is my act working?

Yet, my mind drifts to their words—Finnigan hasn't been seen with a woman in a long while, which they find abnormal. Something swells inside my chest at the thought that I could be the reason why. Not only that, but there's a hot tingle deep between my legs that revels in the idea of it.

He can reject me all he wants, but the man is lying to himself. And I would smile from ear to freaking ear if it wasn't for these two watching me.

"Should we go home?" I ask, eager to end the night now.

"Great idea," Morri says, downing her drink and setting her glass on the bar.

"Well, I don't know how you feel about this"—Maddox speaks as he looks at his phone, then at me—"but he's there, at your apartment. Waiting for you."

"Excuse me?" I exclaim.

My belly flutters at the sound of it, and I sneak a peek at his screen, then fall back, wobbling a little. I think the alcohol is messing with my head, because the words I read make both annoyance and excitement resonate through me.

WHO THE FUCK WAS SHE DANCING WITH?!

Maybe I'm an idiot for flinging myself at this guy, but I can't explain the pull I have to him. I crave to unravel him, even when his rejections are constant, and his words bite harsher than necessary. After today, I was sure I was ready to give up and move on with my life, but I think all I wanted was a bit of revenge. Rouse him up like a petulant child just to get a reaction.

Well... technically *I* didn't get a reaction. Madds did. But I'll take it, nonetheless.

"Let's get Lulu then," Morri speaks and my attention goes to her.

A rumbling growl mixes with the base of the music, and I narrow my eyes at the sound. *What a strange song.* But then my eyes fall on Madds, and his gaze fixed on the stunning, blonde woman. He watches her with a mix of exasperation, anger, and something that looks a lot like yearning.

Yup, alcohol has certainly affected my perception of reality.

A few minutes later and lots of protest from Lulu, mainly aimed at Madds, and we're out at the front of the bar. He's on the phone telling someone, probably Finnigan, that we're heading home now. I have a gnawing suspicion that he's the reason why Madds came to find us. *No.* Find me. Otherwise, how come Finnigan is at my apartment?

We're in the small parking lot next to the bar, less than twenty feet away from Maddox's SUV, and it takes me too many seconds to realize what an idiot I am.

Once again, I ignore the ominous prickles marring the back of my neck, I don't pay attention to my surroundings, to the faint screech of tires as they stop not far behind me, to the car doors opening, or to the steps nearing us.

I don't pay attention until...

"I've been looking everywhere for you."

That voice seeps out of my nightmares, shattering the silence along with my soul, and I don't know if I'll be able to pick up the pieces this time around.

"Frankie..."

CHAPTER 20
Evelyn

GAINST MY BETTER JUDGMENT, I freeze in place, his voice snaking around my body and holding me pinned. I should run. I have to run. But my mind and body are not in sync, and no matter my internal screams, my legs can't move. My lungs are blocked with ice and no breath seems to penetrate.

"Evelyn!" Someone's bellow pushes through the terror and yanks at me. My instincts kick in and I start fighting against the hold, blinded by the memories.

"It's me, it's Morri! Run, Evelyn, run!"

I faintly register the words and my vision clears enough to see her flaming locks, and air starts to fill my lungs again, pushing through the frost that stalled it. My feet feel like my own again and I push against the asphalt, letting Morri pull me away. The sound of the world explodes around me, and I hear Maddox's rage, the violent commotion, grunts of pain and cracking bones.

Maddox!

I falter for a split moment, turning to see if he's safe, and my nightmares come to life all at once.

"Hello, gorgeous. I like your new hair." Frankie's sleazy face is too close to mine, and his bruising grip circles around my middle.

"Nooo!" The scream rips from the bottom of my lungs as I thrash against him.

"That's it. You know I like it when you fight me."

His lisp makes the memories too real, and thorned vines wrap around my spine, spreading around every bone of my body on a violent tremble, until they reach my fingertips.

But somewhere through the bone-choking panic, Maddox's training comes back to me.

"Get the fuck away from me!" I can hardly believe those words left my mouth, but I'm proud of the confidence in them.

Grabbing one of his fingers splayed over my belly, I twist back until the crunch tears a scream out of the man who raped me. I don't let him dwell on it, whipping my head back until it makes contact. I have no idea what I hit, but the pain in my skull and his curses are enough to tell me my aim was good. His grip falters enough for me to pull out of it, and I swing my elbow back, slamming into his middle, before I whirl and swing my foot at his dick.

I smirk when he doubles over in pain, proud that my actions took him by surprise. I take advantage of the distraction, and uppercut him under his chin while he's bent over his precious balls, then sidekick him to the chest. He lands against one of his men who staggers on his feet, a limp look in his bloody eye, and they both fall to the ground.

My training is still fresh, my body only starting to become

stronger, and without the element of surprise, I don't think my moves would have worked this well. Though, a kick in the balls will always work.

I don't dwell. Madds screams at me to get in the car, and I run before he finishes the sentence. Morri shoves me in the back, and we watch as he fights six, crap, no—eight guys. Including Frankie now, who got his bearings and rose. Only, he turns his attention to our car, distracting Madds from the men he's fighting off. Some go down, but—

"Behind you!" I yell, but he can't hear me from the car, and I bang my fists against the window, hoping it will work.

Madds catches Frankie in a headlock, and I take momentary pleasure from his bulging eyes, the pressure in his head likely growing. But in this moment of distraction, another guy punches Madds on the side of his head and Lulu's fear-stricken wail makes me flinch as I suck in a breath.

"I have to help him!" I shout and grab the door handle.

"Evelyn, they could take you again!" Morri holds me in place as we watch Madds grab Frankie and throw him ten feet away like he's nothing but a sack of potatoes, taking two other guys down.

Maddox has blood coming from the back of his head, but ignores it, the look in his eyes feral. In the next moment one of the guys who jumps him is nothing but a crumpled mess on the ground, his head facing the wrong direction, his eyes empty of life.

He expertly beats the shit out of the rest of the men, moving swifter than a man his size should, and just when I think it's all under control, one of the men who was unconscious gets his bearings and rises a few feet behind Madds. He doesn't see him, though, too focused on fighting two of the, surprisingly well trained, men who still stand.

Lulu gasps at the same time I notice the man behind

Madds pulling something from his hip as he staggers toward my friend. The scene runs in slow-motion and my stomach drops.

Oh, God, it's a gun!

"Fuck this! Go, go, go!" Morri yells, and I rip open the car door, jumping out as the adrenaline surges through my nerves.

I run as fast as I can toward the man who's about to shoot Madds, my throat aching from a scream I didn't realize is ripping through my throat. He turns to me, an annoyed and confused look in his eyes, but before he can act, I tackle him to the ground.

One single gunshot is fired into the air as his back slams against the concrete on a pain-filled grunt. He grabs me to push me away, but I smash my fist into his face, and he falters.

Then I punch him again. Harder, faster, the crunch of bones cracking the armor I so carefully constructed around myself, holding at bay the person I pretend not to be.

Over and over, I slam my fists in his face.

There is no skill in my hits, only volatile frenzy. My knuckles ache, but adrenaline surges with each strike, urging me on.

Tires screech in the distance, someone curses, but I don't turn. I certainly don't stop. On the contrary, I try to hit harder, wrapping my fist in my other palm and smashing the sides in his face until he goes limp beneath me.

Something grips my shoulders attempting to tug me away, but I resist. I don't stop. I can't. I won't. The grip lowers, sliding under my armpits to lift me off the limp man, but I fight back.

"Evelyn!"

My fists pause midair when the warmth and urgency in that sweet, sweet voice penetrate the frenzy. It's not his touch around my middle though, I would recognize it.

I turn just as Finnigan slams the car door behind him. Strong hands lift me and settle me back on my feet, but I don't move as I watch his curly hair, as wild as the look in his eyes, bounce as he rushes to me.

"Evelyn." He says my name again, but this time there is longing in his voice too, and I want to sink in the warmth of it.

He reaches me with panic in his wide eyes, breaking through my frenzied state completely, his breathing quick and shallow as he pats all over my body.

"Are you hurt?" he asks in a desperate tone as he continues the rapid inspection.

I shake my head, because I don't think I can open my mouth without sobs breaking out.

"Evie, does anything hurt? There's too much blood, I can't tell." The desperation grows in his tone, meeting my eyes, and I realize he didn't see my previous, silent response.

There's blood?

Of course... the man on the ground.

I shake my head again, but my lips quiver.

Something breaks in him then and there, clutching the sides of my head in his warm hands, as he steps even closer, his body lining up with mine. I seize his forearms, holding onto him, this intensity, his fierce gaze with its longing and pain, to his hidden need and demand, like he might run away from me once he realizes what he's doing. What he's revealing.

"Never again." He growls.

I don't know what he means by that, but I feed on each syllable like it gives me life.

"I'm not letting you out of my sight, Evelyn. Ever."

I don't get a chance to agree or protest, because he crushes me against his warm, hard chest, his arms circling my body and wrapping himself around me. The weight I was holding onto, the panic and fear, leave my body in this tight, comforting hold.

"Madds, is Madds okay?"

He doesn't answer, but he tenses against me.

"That guy was about to shoot me from behind. She..." Madds trails off as he explains to Finnigan, and his hold relaxes once more. "I'm okay, Evie."

The safety of him draws my shock to the surface and every bit of my body shakes all at once. I don't realize my fingers are digging into his skin until I feel his touch on my back, rubbing soothingly.

"It's okay, Evie darling, you're safe."

Then the tears come, the damn just at the edge of breaking, but only a few slip through the cracks. I can't allow myself to break, not this hard. I can't be this weak.

"You're safe. I'm here."

He holds me to him, ignoring the pain I'm probably causing with my sharp nails as I force myself to unload the adrenaline without bursting completely.

I'm okay. I'm okay.

It registers in my subconscious that the man I was hitting stopped moving at one point. Yet, I can't bring myself to care that I might have killed him. I should. Right? There's a strong chance I took a life, and it should feel a certain way.

It doesn't.

It never has before.

Not the first time, only months after I became homeless, when a seedy guy accosted me on the street after my dinner shift was over. I lived and worked in the wrong side of town, I knew it was going to happen eventually. He wanted what I was not offering or willing to give. I was easy prey. But he didn't expect the random slat of wood I found on the ground to be smashed in his guts. And I didn't expect the smile that creeped on my lips at the satisfaction I got when he cursed in pain. I hit him until he gave up on me and ran away.

If only I could have done that when Frankie B took my sister.

Wait.

I pull my face away from the comfort of Finnigan's chest and look around. "Where is he?! Where's Frankie?"

"He's gone," Maddox grunts somewhere behind me. "He slid in his car and drove away when the last of his men was going down. I couldn't stop him. I'm sorry."

He's still out there, and he wants me. The thought brings a shudder back into my bones and Finnigan tightens his hold around me once again.

"We're going home. Now." His tone is sharp and low, pulling back to look at me, one hand possessive on the small of my back.

Then he confuses the pants out of me when he pulls his shirt out of his trousers, and brings the bottom of it to my face, wiping it.

"What the... what are you doing?!" If that doesn't wake me out of my stupor, I don't know what would do the job.

"Maya is in the car. I don't want her to see you like this."

"She's here?" I try to break away, but his hold on my back keeps me grounded as he keeps swiping at my face.

"You don't think I would have left her alone with June, do you? She needs to be kept safe, with us."

Delicious warmth spills through my soul at his words, and I feel it deep in my belly. I can't believe he would think of her, of us, like that. When he stops rubbing at my face, his action finally registers as I see his now dirty shirt—blood. A lot of it. Then I dare look down at the man I pummeled as I straddled him, and I fail to recognize any features on his face under all the blood.

Christ, what have I done?

"We'll wash the rest of it at home. You're sure you're not hurt?" he asks, and I give him a quick nod.

Once again, he tugs me against his chest, pressing me against him, like he wants me embedded in his soul. But that warmth leaves me too soon as he steps away and takes my hand instead.

Morri, Lulu, and Madds stand close by, curious looks on all their faces. Maddox raises an eyebrow, but Finnigan warns him off with a growl as he pulls me toward his car.

"Not a fucking word."

His friend doesn't respond, but Morri's features look lighter, amused in a knowing kind of way, and a flush heats my cheeks. How inappropriate of me, considering I just punched a guy to death.

"Call the cleaning crew," Finnigan tells his friend.

"Done. I'll take Morri and Mamaw to Vin."

Just on cue Mamaw June climbs out of the car we're heading to, giving me a kind, worried smile. I mirror that smile in hopes of providing her with a bit of comfort and confirmation that I'm okay. "Thank you for looking after Maya."

"Anytime, sweetheart. Call me later, okay?" God this woman is an angel.

"Keep Lulu with you!" Finnigan turns to Madds as he puts me in the car and straps me in, refusing to let me do it myself.

"The fuck he will!" I hear Lulu's protests.

"Shush, woman. We're not risking any of you," Madds says, and I would laugh if small hands weren't wrapping around my neck from behind, and the car door shuts.

"Evie!" there's such an innocent enthusiasm in Maya's voice.

"Hi honey! Are you okay?"

I avoid turning to her in case there's still blood on my face. She's not going to see the splatters on my blouse, since it's luckily a dark burgundy.

"Yes! I spent the evening with Finnigan. He read to me!" She sounds calm, unaffected. Mamaw June must have shielded her.

"He did?" My gaze wanders to the man in question, who climbed into the driver's seat and slams the door.

He nods as he turns his attention to the road and drives off.

"Yes. He's so good at reading with... what do you call it? Intonation? Can he read me to sleep tonight? Will you let him, Evie? Pleaaase?"

"Oh, honey, I don't think Finnigan—"

"Of course I will." He cuts me off and answers my demanding sister.

"Thank you!" she squeals, excited.

So, I guess he intends to stay over at my apartment until Maya falls asleep. Right, well, that's going to be interesting. Though, the idea makes me feel a lot safer, especially as Frankie B might know where I live, now that he's made his intentions pretty damn clear. We knew he was pissed about his *shipments* being screwed with, but we didn't know I was even on his radar. There's security in Lulu's building, but I'll stay up tonight just in case. There's no way I can sleep, anyway.

I had hopes that I could fake my way through the system and enroll Maya in school, but that is fully squashed now. Not until Frankie is out of the picture and into a grave.

"So, what happened out there? Mamaw June was hugging me, and I couldn't see a thing," my sister asks.

Oh, thank God. Okay, I need to bake Mamaw June the biggest cake ever. The woman is a saint.

"We just needed a little help to go home. Car trouble,"

I lie to her as I gaze out the window at the pretty streets of Queenscove.

Only, the bar we went to was quite close to our apartment building, and we just drove past it.

"Wait. Finnigan that was—we just passed my street."

He doesn't look at me, his gaze running over all the mirrors, on high alert. It makes me look too, but I don't notice anything out of place. He's probably just checking to make sure we're not being followed.

"We're going to my apartment." He grunts.

"What?" I exclaim but lower my voice so my sister doesn't catch onto my surprise. "Why? We'll be perfectly fine at mine."

"You will be alone," he says with another grunt. "I told you, Evelyn. Never. Again." He punctuates each word with such finality, I'm left with parted lips, unspoken words hanging between them, and a new, burning ache between my legs.

Not again.

Why does this always happen in the most inappropriate moments?

If he notices how I clench my thighs together, or my quickening breaths, he doesn't say a thing. I shut my mouth and settle back in the soft suede seat of his SUV, silently thankful that it's not the normal leather that sticks uncomfortably to my bare skin and wait for this annoying and disturbingly attractive man to take me to his home.

Should I protest more? Probably.

My hands, achy and marked with too much drying blood, tremble, and my legs do the same, for an entirely different reason.

I'm startled when his hand moves from the center console and hovers so close to my thigh. I watch it, silently urging it to drop over my flesh, to clutch it, hold it, anything. Instead, he moves to press a button on the dashboard and warm air blows into the car. I look at him and he steals one short glance at me before occupying himself with the road ahead.

"You looked cold," he explains himself. When I don't answer, he continues, "You're shivering. You should have not worn such a short skirt."

I'm about to say I'm not cold, but I stop myself.

"It's not that short."

Way to make it awkward Evelyn. You could have just said thanks. It's not like you're not silently imagining your sister not being in the car, his hand on your thigh, rubbing down until he finds the seam of your skirt, then runs upward until another seam touches his fingers, and then, without no notice at all, he—

"Are we there yet?"

My sister's excited, high-pitched tone makes me straighten in the seat. This time it doesn't escape Finnigan's notice how I squeeze my thighs together, biting my bottom lip to suppress the need from spilling from my mouth.

Christ, we better be there soon, because this car is starting to feel too small, the air too hot, his proximity too much.

"In a minute."

He takes a familiar turn and there we are, in front of the apartment building where I used to live with Katya. Considering that I was face to face with Frankie B not even an hour ago, it feels like no time has passed at all since I first lived here.

But it has. I'm not the same weak person I was then, and if Frankie B dares to come after me or my sister again, I will be ready.

He will pay.

CHAPTER 21
Evelyn

I WAKE UP WITH A START, drenched in sweat from the grueling dream I just had. There was nothing violent about it. The nightmare part is waking up from it, unable to feel it any longer, because *he* was in it.

I blink several times, acknowledging my surroundings through the darkness—I'm in Finnigan's spare bedroom and it's still the middle of the night. It doesn't smell like him though, and I feel a touch of sadness at that. The moment I got out of the car my adrenaline crash was so bad, I could barely stand. If I was in my apartment, I would have stayed up, alert, but here... with him... I crashed in his safety. He showed me the bathroom so I could clean up while he looked after my sister, then took me straight to bed, promising to read Maya to sleep in the bedroom next to mine.

The tiredness struck me to the bones, and I went with everything he told me to do. He gave me a small bag Mamaw June apparently packed for me in the few seconds she had before leaving our apartment, and I crawled in bed after changing into a comfy, oversized T-shirt I found in a thrift store. Sleep took me fast.

I turn to my side, shoving my hand under the pillow, and force my eyes closed, urging myself back to sleep. But in this position my thighs press together and the ache that follows between them pulls a dirty gasp out of my mouth. They're so slippery, so hot, so unbearable.

Flipping on my belly, I bury my face in the pillow, and close my eyes. I'm back in that dream, filled with ecstasy and decadence, where Finnigan's hand was clutching my breast, his mouth smothering mine, kissing me deeply, and his cock was sheathed so deep inside me, it ached so good.

I can't bear it anymore!

I turn once again on my back, cursing myself for taking this man's word as law. He told me we can't cross that wretched line of his, he warned me not to try, not to even think about him in *that* way, even when I touched myself. I didn't agree with the man, but for some odd reason, I complied with the order.

Christ, I'm an idiot. He would never know if I did it, if I crossed his damn imaginary line, and he has no control over me. It's not his business what I do between my own sheets.

Only, these are his sheets, not mine. Defying his orders here feels perfect, so much dirtier. My skin turns hotter, the T-shirt too constricting, my drenched cotton panties too tight, and I rip them off and throw them across the room, into the darkness. Now the sheets feel slightly cool against my nakedness, and I sigh at the feel of them.

It feels better. But only for a moment, until I close my

eyes and that wretched dream is back, his body over mine, his hands touching me, and I swallow back a moan because now, I'm annoyed. He's so cruel and smug, forbidding me to think of him when I touch myself. He thinks he's doing me a favor, forcing me to distance myself from him and his *line*.

Screw him. There are others out there I can fantasize about as I touch myself, and even if I do choose him, just because he wants to torture himself due to some moral rule he self-imposed, it doesn't mean I have to follow suit.

The fire hums low in my belly, and I press my thighs together once more, hoping to relieve some of that heat. Of course, it burns brighter, my taught nipples grazing against the sheet enhancing the feel of it further.

"Screw this!" I throw the sheet off of me, reveling in the brush of air over my sensitive skin.

I couldn't deny my body any longer even if I tried.

The moment I press my hand over my bare breast, the softest of moans fills the dark bedroom. I splay the other palm on my belly, slowly sliding down, teasing myself with the anticipation that tortures me further. The moment the tips of my fingers reach the hood of my clit, my back arches off the bed and there's nothing soft about the sound escaping from my mouth next.

I rub the bundle of nerves in slow, demanding circles, images of Finnigan flashing through my mind, some out of spite, some because there's no one else I could possibly think of, and the fire begins to rage in my belly.

"Oh... Finnigan," I whisper on a breathless moan as I slide my fingers down, parting myself until I reach that tight opening.

My lips part in a gasp at the flurry of sensations, the ache and emptiness of them all, and I cry out into the darkness.

Then the darkness moves.

I tense, no time to scream or react before it rushes over me and covers my mouth. No time to fight as it rips my hand away from my sleek center, replacing it with his own. I gasp against his hand and the scent of sea salt and dark chocolate melt their way through me. Recognition hits, the scent flowing right out of my dream.

He squeezes my pussy and shame fills me when my back arches involuntarily at the attack. But I still try to fight beneath him, attempting to escape in case my nose betrays me. I try to kick, but he presses harder against me, and I let out a dirty, wanton cry against his palm. Gripping his wrist, I push it away, but it doesn't budge. But I'm not actually that sure if I'm not so much pushing, as I am holding onto him.

I freeze in place as he slides his fingers down the sleek seam of me. It's not panic screaming at me now, it's how wrong I am for getting even wetter.

"I told you..."

All rational thought burns out of my mind when the darkness speaks with the voice from my dream.

"I told you how dangerous it is to cross this line." Finnigan's whisper is heavy, creeping with a decadent darkness.

I can't believe he was in the bedroom. Watching me sleep. Watching me get naked.

"Is this what you were about to do, even when I forbade you to touch yourself with my name on your lips?" One finger pushes inside of me, stretching me too fast. It may actually be more than one.

"So fucking tight." He groans more to himself than me.

But as he pulls out and dives in again even deeper, I release his forearm and grab onto whatever covers his chest, holding on for dear life because I think I'm falling. Falling in this pit of aching need and burning pleasure.

"Is this what you so desperately want, that you can't follow... one. Simple. Order?" He punctuates each word with a hard stroke of his fingers, pulling muffled cries out of me.

"You drive me fucking crazy!"

Thrust.

"So mad that I move through the shadows when I hear your feverish dreams."

Thrust.

"Watching you only to find you moaning my name, not screaming in fear of your nightmares."

Thrust.

He's punishing me with pleasure for his own desires.

"I haven't been able to sleep without knowing you're okay."

Thrust.

"Without knowing you're a good..." *Thrust.* "Fucking..." *Thrust.* "Girl."

I'm losing my mind. Pushed closer to the flaming pit that will change my whole damn life, but not close enough that I feel it's whole destruction.

"Is this why you want to cross the motherfucking line?!"

He curls those digits, touching a part of me I've never been able to find, and my moans turn wild.

"God damn it, Evelyn! How am I ever going to keep my hands away from you now? After feeling how tight, how warm your cunt is? How it responds to me? How fucking ravenous its scent makes me?"

He assaults that spot inside of me with no regard to my cries, my pleas muffled by his palm. He's lost somewhere between my legs like this is his pleasure, not mine.

"What have you done, Evelyn?"

At that same moment he bears down on my clit and pushes me into that flaming pit, burning the world around me. Pleasure sears me from the inside out and I'm sure I would be flying if he didn't hold me down.

What *have I* done?

He releases my mouth and I take shallow, staggered breaths.

How will I go back to how things were? Back to not knowing how his hands truly feel on me?

Was he right all along?

I'm too lost in the aftershock of sensations and burning questions when I realize that he's no longer touching me, because a deep sigh sounds from the shadows, before steps follow, and the door opens. He's in the doorway facing away from me, shoulders dropping as he pulls the door behind himself, uttering the same word I whisper to myself.

"Fuck."

Yes, he was right all along. I can feel it in my gut—there's no going back after crossing this line. I can't help but wonder if he'll try though.

Will he be more successful than I was? I tried to steer myself away from him, my reason not as foolish as his. I don't care that he's eleven or whatever years older than me, though he seems so bothered by it. I thought I needed to get over his promise to me.

We'll get you before anything happens…

He said that before I was returned to that wretched container with the tracker in my mouth. Something did happen, and failing to keep his promise brought so much resentment toward him.

I was blinded. He didn't fail me at all, I simply chose to ignore what I myself asked of him then. The context. I ignored it because it didn't fit my vendetta. The need for a vessel to hone my hate was stronger than the actual truth.

Because the truth is that his promise was a response to my plea. And that plea had nothing to do with me or my safety. I told him I can't fail *her*—my sister—and he answered by telling me that I won't, promising he'll get us out before anything happens. To her. Not to me.

Even now I remember the sorrow in his beautiful azure eyes. He wanted to extend the promise to me too, and the choice of his words told me how much he wished, but he was already unsure if he could even keep the one he made for my sister. It was all out of his control. A sacrifice that was not his to make, but he had to so he could save many. I volunteered for it, knowing the risks.

He gave me exactly what I wanted, what I pleaded for. Madds later told me that it was Finnigan who searched for and carried my sister out. I didn't ask him to save her, I just told him I couldn't bear failing her again. So, he made sure I didn't.

He made sure I kept my own promise to my sister. He made sure I wasn't a liar. That my soul remained intact. Even if my body didn't.

And I responded with disdain and blamed him for the situation I threw myself in.

I was a fool.

It kept me away from seeing him for who he is, from my craving for him. And if Finnigan pushes me away because he thinks our age difference wrong, if he villainizes himself for it, then he is a fool too.

There are other differences between us that worry me, that make me feel so inadequate next to him. And sometimes I do wonder if they are the real reason why he pulls away from me so fiercely.

If he has an issue with the fact that I haven't finished my education because I had to take care of my sister, or that I don't come from the same social standing as him, or have money... or a home, then he should say that. Because I can move on from shallowness easily, but not from the ridiculous notion of age.

He will need a better reason than that.

Though, I can't help but ask myself... am I a fool for pursuing this man?

Especially since I have made no final decision about staying in Queenscove?

* * *

I wake up in the morning with surprising ease. My phone says it's seven o'clock, and my limbs are itching to get out of this bed. Though, my thighs say I need to head into a shower, because I swear I can still feel the dampness he left me with last night.

I dreamed of it, of his hand silencing me, the other between my legs, it was more erotic than I expected. I have similar fantasies, but this... it's surpassed them all.

Before I can get myself wet all over again, I jump out of bed and pull my T-shirt on. This room doesn't have an en-suite bathroom, so I open the door peeking out. Okay, I'm on a small corridor, there's bright light at the end of it, and a few more doors here, but all is quiet. There's bound to be a bathroom here. I try the door across from me, pressing the handle slowly.

Warm sea salt and dark chocolate hits me with such ferociousness my mouth is parched in an instant. Though there's nothing but darkness in here, the blinds closed and curtains drawn, I know I'll find no bathroom if I turn the lights on. And yet, my feet seem to have a mind of their own, because they advance in the dark room, leaving the door ajar. A faint trail of light trickles in, right on the strong form sleeping under a thin sheet. The blonde curly strands of his hair brush against his neck, his strong bare back facing me, and I itch to run my hand through those locks and trace his muscles with the tips of my fingers. As I near him, I see a few faint scars on his skin, and I can't help but wonder what dared mark him. My gaze draws down his muscled back, lean and strong, all the way to where the thin sheet barely covers the curve of his ass. And god dammit, what an ass. If only that sheet would magically slide lower.

I have no idea what I'm thinking, if I'm sane at all, because my fingers are now ghosting against his spine. I can't control the need to find out what he feels like. If he's as warm and soft as I imagine him to be. If his muscles feel as magnificent as I think when they flex beneath my palm.

Then his softness tickles my fingertips, and I could groan if I didn't need to hold in my breath. I slowly run them down his spine, and when I reach the middle he flinches, but not startled, more like his spine rolls into my touch. He doesn't stir though, doesn't wake up, his breathing slightly quicker, but I think he's still sleeping. So, I continue my exploration, sliding down his spine until my prize is just about in sight and I can reveal at least a bit of that stunning ass. He feels so good under my touch, I itch to risk it and splay my palm over him, but that would truly be foolish.

Maybe he's a heavy sleeper, and I can get away with it.

Or maybe I should count my blessings and get the heck out of here before the man wakes up and finds me groping him.

I don't get to make my decision.

Like lightning he moves, grabbing my wrist and hauling me up until he can reach my waist, using it to flip me over and slam my back against his soft bed. I only manage a gasp, too stunned to even register my wrists being trapped above my head, held in one of his hands. Or his thigh pinning my legs to the comfortable mattress. Only when his heaving, strong breaths touch my bare skin do I notice my T-shirt is bunched up above my waist, and I'm bared to him. Since I was *technically* going to the bathroom, that's the only thing I pulled on, thinking it's long enough to cover me.

I tug at his hold, urging him to let me go before he notices my exposed core, though only the short curls I refuse to shave are on display, as the hidden part of me is getting increasingly damp at this proximity. At the constraints.

"What do you think you're doing, Evie darling?"

I melt into the bed at his rough, morning voice, tainted with sleep and needy dreams. It takes me a few moments to remember I was supposed to struggle to break free. And yet, I allow a few more moments because his hot breath against my skin feels like summer sun and beautiful beach days.

"Let me go." I tug at his hand, trying to free my own.

I do the same with my legs, but the moment my thighs tighten, I decide against it, only, now I'm all too conscious of the damp patch I might be leaving on his expensive sheets.

"Answer me." He leans in, his nose dangerously close to my cheek.

When I turn my head in the opposite direction, I realize what a huge mistake it was. His hot breath snakes down my throat, settling in the crook of my neck, and nothing can stop the shudder that rattles my skin and spreads goosebumps on every inch of my body.

"I—I was"—*deep inhale*—"looking for the bathroom."

"And you thought that touching me while I slept was going to lead you there?" His breathy voice is even closer, the heat of him brushing over my skin. I'm squirming, but I tell myself it's because I'm trying to break loose.

"It was leading to something," I mutter sarcastically under my breath, and I genuinely want to slap myself for still thinking of his ass.

Such a good ass, though.

"What was that?"

"Nothing," I quip.

"You're playing with fire, Evie darling."

I turn my attention back to him, and even in this darkness, the blue of his eyes shines and I hold onto every speckle. "Let it burn me then, because I'm sick of this aching cold."

He's on me before the next breath reaches my lungs, bracing himself on the arm that holds my wrists trapped. His weight presses me into the mattress, and the thigh that pinned me is now slid under one of my legs, spreading me open.

"Finnigan..." I all but moan.

"Don't, Evelyn. Don't say my name like it's the air that breathes life into you because I'm tainted down to the bone, and my soul will only scorch yours."

"There is nothing left to scorch, Finnigan. I was corrupted long before your soul touched mine. All I can do is burn. Please Finnigan... please—"

He swallows my next words, crushing his lips to mine in the most brutal, shattering kiss. He breathes me in like my life-force is the only thing that can keep his soul alive, and when he pushes his tongue between my lips, nothing can stop the moan that vibrates through my whole flesh.

With a faint growl rumbling in his chest, he deepens the kiss, pressing me harder in the mattress. Our tongues move against each other, chasing the pleasure only the other can give, our lips molding together like two pieces that were once whole and now found their mate again. The only break he takes is to nip at my tongue, or my lips, plunging back in and stealing every single one of my breaths before he feeds them back to me, enriched with all that is him.

I'm lost in the myriad of sensations until a shock of pure pleasure rips through my core. I gasp into his mouth and my hips roll on instinct, to find the source of that rippling pleasure. A satiny, hard length strokes against me, rubbing that charged bundle of nerves, as it grinds up and down. The insight that he sleeps naked brings a hot flush to my cheeks.

A needy mewl rips out of me, but he swallows that too, feeding on my pleasure and pressing harder into me. God, he's so close to where I really need him. All it would take is for him to grind even lower, so the tip of his cock falls between my legs, and then... one *hard* push.

Would it hurt? Considering what happened that wretched night when we first met, it's pretty clear I'm no longer a virgin. Though, I'm thankful my memories are vague. So, all Finnigan would give me now is nothing but pleasure.

I roll my hips harder, urging his cock to find home, but it keeps slipping away from me. Over me. Stroking my clit into an ecstasy filled oblivion distracting me from the task at hand.

"Stop making me fuck you." He grunts against my mouth, still kissing me.

"Never." I moan back at him.

Then his lips leave mine and we're both breathless as we look into each other's eyes.

"I can't be what you need."

This again? Fine.

"Then let me go and leave me the hell alone, Finnigan"— for a moment his grip on me loosens—"and I'll go back to the bar from where you demanded I be retrieved last night, and I'll find someone who will give me *exactly* what I need."

The rumble deep in his chest is what I hoped for as his hold on me tightens once again.

"You think you can go out dressed in your sinful leather outfits or short skirts, driving everyone mad with lust in those filthy bars, and make them think they can wet their dick inside what is..." he trails off.

"What is yours?" I continue for him.

"You can't be mine, damn it!"

"I already am."

That settles it, because in the next breath his mouth is on my throat, biting like he hates every inch of my skin before he licks the slight pain away and brings a different ache to my flesh. It settles deep in my belly and between my legs, and he grounds against me harder. I roll my hips seeking his cock like it can give me life, and he shushes me when I moan too loud, reminding me that we are not alone in this apartment.

Ignoring my silent pleas for his cock, he releases my wrists, pushing my T-shirt all the way up, exposing my breasts to his greedy gaze. His nips and licks follow a trail over each one of them, sucking my nipples into his mouth like his new mission is to dare me to make a sound. But he does it oh so well, licking gently before he scrapes his teeth over the sensitive bud, and I could come right here just from that delicious assault.

He moves in the valley between them before my core can find out if it can find release just from that, following a trail down my body until his chin brushes against my trimmed curls. I'm embarrassed. I imagine the army of women he usually has sex with are waxed from head to toe, sleek and soft.

"I'm sorry, I'm not—"

"You are goddamn perfect." His fingers rake through those curls, as the pad of his palm grounds down against the bundle of nerves, and the shiver breaking through me feels more like a violent tremble.

Then his mouth is on me, and that insecurity disappears with my loud gasp. Finnigan's tongue parts my lips from the bottom to the very top, groaning so low in his chest, I could cry at the sensation. The second time he does it I whimper as he flattens his tongue like he can't bear not having all his taste buds experiencing me. He presses his hands against my thighs and pushes them apart, his tongue delving deeper, circling my entrance and disappointingly moving away from it. The moment it slides over my clit and laps at it like it could give me life, I realize it really could. Because like this, drunk on pleasure in Finnigan's bed, I feel more alive than I ever have. Biting my forearm to muffle a moan, I roll my back as I grind onto his face, seeking my release, and when he sucks that bundle of nerves between his lush lips, I realize the edge is so much closer than I thought it was.

He grunts harsher, displeased, and I feel a tinge of guilt, wondering if he feels ignored. I brace my elbows on the bed and slowly rise, struggling through the onslaught of sensations.

"Did I say I'm done with you?" he hisses.

I yelp as he sits back on his haunches, grabs my ass, and lifts me up to him, circling my belly with one strong, lean arm. I would be upside down if my head and shoulders weren't still on the bed, and when he buries his face between my legs again, I grab onto his thighs and let him drive me off this magnificent cliff.

He gives special attention to my clit, rolling it between his tongue and lips, nipping at it when my pleasure brings me too close to the roaring flames I'm craving. My sexual experience is mostly fictional, or from random conversations with classmates or co-workers, but I was under the impression that men don't have much patience when it comes to giving head, and want to make it quick. But Finnigan, oh my, Finnigan is dragging it out like he finds more pleasure in this than I do.

That would be impossible though, because every time he sucks at me, every time his tongue drags between my folds, every time he teases the entrance, the pleasure grows more than I thought it could be possible.

"Evie?"

We both freeze on the bed, his mouth still on me, my nails

digging in his strong thighs. Maya's voice sounded distant beyond Finnigan's door. I start moving my legs and scooting back to get off the bed, but Finnigan tightens his hold.

"Finnigan, Maya's coming," I whisper.

"Then you better hurry, darling."

The grin he gives me before his mouth is on my clit again, melts me back into the soft mattress. I'm about to protest, but his eyes gleam with mischief. His hand joins the feverish assault, and two fingers sink deep into me. My ass buckles and ankles cross as my legs tighten around his neck, pushing him deeper into me. Scorching heat burns inside my core, spreading through my belly, then explodes through every single nerve of my body until the loud cry I'm forcing back has no choice but to come out.

The moment it spills from my lips, Finnigan's large hand covers my mouth and nose and I cry out into his palm, riding this blazing pleasure until my legs go limp around his body.

"Evie?" Maya's voice is closer now and I almost jump out of my skin when Finnigan gives my ass a playful slap to urge me to get off the bed.

Now, that was... strangely intimate. Pair that with his panty-melting grin he's giving me, and I might as well hand him my heart on a platter, because this man is going to take it from me whether I want to or not. Regardless of if he wants it.

And isn't that just terrifying?

I push back the harsh thoughts reminding me that this is not my home, not where my father lives, or that all of this is temporary. I'm going to allow myself to bask in this bubble of pleasure and acceptance for a while longer.

Just a little while longer.

IT TOOK ME MUCH LONGER to pry myself out of bed than it usually does. Took me even longer to shower, and especially brush my teeth because I couldn't bear washing away Evelyn's taste from my lips. Jesus Christ, that woman tastes like goddamn rainbows. Does that make any logical sense? No, it most definitely does not, but she has a maddening sweet and musty flavor that threatens to drive me mad.

Addicting. So utterly addicting.

The line is well and truly crossed. Seeing her touching herself with my name on her lips threw me straight over it. But having her tight, little cunt around my fingers, breaking apart for me as I was feeding fantasies she doesn't know I'm aware of, pushed me so far away from that line, I'm not even sure anymore if it ever existed. But then I had to taste her pretty pussy too, see her naked beneath me, and that ensured there is no going back.

Question is, how far am I willing to go?

What would happen if I would get to sink my cock in her sweet pussy? Will I ever want to leave? Will I be the same man after?

Already, her strength, her determination, everything she is as a person has been picking away at my constraints. But watching her slip out of my bed, spent and disheveled from pleasure I gave her, cracked something inside me, shackles holding me back. I'm aware of them, but the crack let out shunned feelings. Pain, fear, I was expecting, but the loneliness tasted bitter. Evelyn changes everything, soothes and turns it all to rich sweetness without even knowing.

Twice, I stroked myself in the shower to settle this growing need for her. I came on the wall of it like a fucking teenager.

Finally, I emerge out of my bedroom and the smell hits me straight in the taste buds, making my mouth water. Blueberry and sweetness, warmth and... home. I inhale deep one more time to make sure I'm not making this shit up.

I know Nora didn't cook, because I told both her and George, my permanent house staff, to take paid time off for the foreseeable future. So, Evelyn must be cooking.

Before I even step into the kitchen, a cheerful mini human slams straight into me, oblivious to the fact that her shoulder connected a bit too violently with my balls. I suck in a grunt and power through, because when I look down, Maya's sweet little face is all sunshine and butterflies, her innocence vividly painted in her green eyes.

"Good morning, Finn!" she says with a wide, toothy smile.

"Morning, sweetheart." I bend over and give her a kiss on the top of the head, my voice strained from the ache in my balls.

I rise and catch Evelyn's gaze, brightened with

amusement, her lips curled between her teeth as she bites down her laughter. Okay, so she noticed my pain, and this is her response.

Noted.

But noting this is bad, because my retaliation plan involves my tongue, fingers, and her begging me for release for hours.

I'm a doomed man.

She turns to open the oven door, and the delicious scent that fills the penthouse distracts me, so much stronger than before, drawing me in like a moth to a flame.

"I hope this is alright. I was... umm... nervous." she says shyly, wiping her hands on the sides of her black jeans. *She changed.*

"Nervous?" I narrow my eyes and take a seat on the other side of the island from her, at the breakfast bar.

"Yes, sorry. I just like to bake when I'm..."

"Nervous," I finish for her.

She avoids my eyes like this is all so wrong and she regrets saying anything.

"I swim or train with Madds." I throw her a bone, because for some reason I hate seeing her so uncomfortable.

It's also peculiar witnessing this side of her. I've seen her nervous and shy before, but this is coming from a totally different place. I fucked her sweet cunt with my mouth and fingers, and I bet she's picturing it even now as she busies herself with the freshly baked muffins, burning her fingers as she tries to pull them out of the muffin tray I had no idea I own.

"Oh, I like training with Madds." She brightens all over, and a pang of jealousy hits me. "He's really helped me. I'm not sure what I would have done without him. Especially last night..." She trails off and even though that jealousy burns harsher, I'm going to talk to Severin and ask him to train her even harder. Might even give her a gun.

Because she's right—if it wasn't for their training, I wouldn't be staring at her right now. I wouldn't have her taste imprinted in my memory. I wouldn't be smelling these delicious muffins I would have never picked for myself to eat.

"Madds called when I got out of the shower and told me everything. Though I hate that you got involved, you did well. Really well."

She beams at my praise and the manacle fixed in my chest cracks a little further.

Hating that she got involved isn't even close to what I'm still feeling. I was on the phone with Madds when they got attacked. I heard his urgent voice, I heard the screams of the women, I heard the punches, the struggle, I heard it all, because he didn't get a chance to end the call.

Maya was snuggled to my side, snoozing softly after I read to her, and I froze in terror. I heard Frankie's words to Evelyn, probably not all of them, but I heard enough for everything I never knew I wanted, to shatter before me. I was losing her. I was losing her fast, before I even accepted that she's mine, before I told her she is, and the déjà vu crept up on me so fast, the blood stilled in my veins.

I was thrown in the back of that car, eight years ago, when Hanna's pleading voice was begging me to come get her. To find her. Save her. When I implored her to be strong and promised her I would find her. No matter where she was, I would come for her, I would hold her in my arms for the rest of our lives and love her forever. I was back in that moment when all I could hear was the roar of the engine because the call cut off and she was ripped away from me on a heartbreaking cry. I was still there after I hung up, and Maya woke and saw the terror on my features. But I forced my features to smooth and told her we're going to go to my place for the night and pick up her sister on the way.

For the entire way to the bar I prayed to all the gods I could name that those last few words weren't a lie. I prayed history wasn't repeating itself, and Evelyn was still in that parking lot when I got there. But a terrified voice asked a different question inside my head... what if I finally tracked her down and just like Hanna, I would only find a soulless, bloodied body? I urged Mamaw June to pack a quick bag. Very fucking quick. And we were out the door in minutes, forcing myself not to show the emotions that ripped me from the inside out, because I couldn't let Maya see any of them. June was a saint. Kept her occupied and distracted, even if fear shone in her kind eyes.

Mine was bubbling like a volcano inside my veins, and the shock of it was becoming too much. For months I kept Evelyn at arm's length, constantly pushing her away and rejecting her, thinking it would ensure I couldn't get attached to her. How she still burrowed into my soul regardless, I don't know. But she creeped just beneath the shackles and pushed hard enough for a crack to form.

Regardless, the bindings are still there, reminding me what I know to be true—too much of me is broken, and none of me deserves her. I can't be what she wants, because she deserves so much more. Someone whole, someone she could lean on, someone who hasn't fucked half of Queenscove and miles beyond. Someone who can love...

As I look at her now, shyly pottering about my penthouse that seems to smell like a home for the first time in years, if not ever, I realize that letting her go will be much harder than I thought.

And I will have to let her go. Because Evelyn already said she might not stay in Queenscove.

Evelyn

I'M NOT SURE WHAT TO make of Finnigan. He looks at me like he found me and lost me all at once. Like I'm here, but just beyond his reach, and I don't know how to take it. Once again that pain I'm becoming so familiar with is back in his bright-blue eyes, and I itch to reach over and smooth his brow over.

I also want to slap my own hand away because I can deal with the sexual side of things, but getting emotional about the man would be such a huge mistake. Well, getting *more* emotional about him. He's a player, screwing everything in sight and never hanging out with someone more than once or twice, according to Lulu and Morri. Top that off with the fact that I technically have to return to Fleeton, and that he clearly told me he can't do this with me, and I need no further proof that I should guard my heart from him.

Though, I'm not sure that bloody organ is listening.

"Do you want one?" I ask him, holding a warm blueberry muffin to him.

He looks at it like I'm offering him the world in a ring box, then nods finally. "Yes, please."

I pop two on a plate and slide them over, then grab two for me and one for Maya on separate plates. He leans over and picks up my sister's plate, directing her to the sofa in the living area to eat, and turns the TV on for her.

"So we can talk freely," he explains as he sits back down, eying the muffins with more hunger.

He grabs one, taking a tentative bite, and when the flavor hits his tongue, I'm instantly wet at his rumble of pleasure.

"Christ, woman, this is delicious!" He takes another, bigger bite before he even swallows the first, and warmth pools low in my belly.

"Thank you. It's nothing though, only muffins."

"Evelyn, I don't eat muffins. Not because they're sugary and I'm careful about my diet, but muffins, or any other food, is all the same for me. I taste the different flavors, but there aren't any that I like more or less. I eat for nutrition, and that's it. But this"—he looks at that muffin like I baked it with gold and diamonds—"is fucking delicious."

He takes another mouthful, and the azure of his eyes brightens, the pain that was there more distant now.

"I don't know what to say." I genuinely don't. Is he appeasing me or is he truly honest?

"Say you'll bake more for me. Different things too. I want to try more!"

I giggle, reaching for my own breakfast, and notice how he stopped, hand mid-air, his hungry gaze fixed on me. But this hunger is not for food.

"And do that again," he says in a much darker, deeper tone.

Heat gathers between my legs, and now I crave to be that muffin he's munching on, so he can spread me wide on this countertop and eat me out like he's starving. But he shakes his head once and breaks the spell, focusing once again on that lucky muffin.

Waking up in this man's penthouse has been a slight shock to the system. Not just because of the mind-blowing orgasm he gave me last night, or the even dirtier one this morning, but because of his home. I already imagined him in a sleek, luxurious place like this one, floor to ceiling windows everywhere, stainless steel appliances, white walls, and a black and deep gray color scheme. Whether it was based on preconceptions about the playboy with blonde curls and cheeky smile, or it felt like it fit his personality, I don't know.

What I didn't expect was the sheer contrast I was faced with. Against those clean, cold walls, antique paintings are slanted. Everything from oil to acrylic, landscapes to portraits, nudes to tragic battle scenes. And around them... there are books. More books than I can count sit in mismatched bookcases of assorted sizes and wood, and on the floor, in messy stacks against the walls and around those paintings. The contrast in styles is staggering. Like this penthouse is but a shell he merely exists in, but those books, those paintings, and the strange little trinkets spread between them, is where he truly lives.

Why doesn't he have matching bookcases? Or neatly stacked books? Why does it look like he's... stuck? Or not settled in yet?

I want to ask him about this discrepancy, but now isn't the right time. There are other questions I have to ask him, and yes, his hands on me were a welcome distraction from what happened last night. He kept me from falling into a panic that wouldn't have helped me. But now, I need to come back down to reality.

Looking around, I make sure Maya's still out of earshot. She's busy with some cartoons on TV, munching happily on her muffin.

"Did they track him down?" I ask Finnigan.

He watches me for a few moments, sighing with disappointment at the change in subject most likely, and shakes his head.

My shoulders slump. "How did he find me, Finnigan? And why? Why did he come for me?"

"I don't know, Evie. What did he tell you last night?"

"How do you know he told me anything?" stupid question. Maddox probably told him.

"I was on the phone with Madds when it all happened. I... heard him." Darkness passes over his eyes, and I can see there's more than just anger there.

Is it unfair that I'm happy he's so affected? That I can see he cares?

"Not much. That he likes my new hair, and... likes it when I fight him." A deep shudder passes through me, turning my blood cold and my spine icy. "And that he's been looking everywhere for me."

That darkness deepens in Finnigan's eyes, his brows narrowed in deep creases. He turned the second muffin into crumbles between his fingers.

"He won't get you, Evelyn. I..." He pauses and shakes his head once. "He won't."

"He might." There is no way he can guarantee my safety. He can't have me by his side at all times.

"I will be with you. He won't get through me. Plus, we are all on high alert now that we know they're bringing the battle here. There will be more security, tightened rules, and eyes everywhere. He will not get to you."

"Security will freak out the customers at the café. Though, I guess you could tell them to act like customers." I think about the table closest to the entrance.

"You're not going back to work. Not now that we know that asshole is after you, determined to get you back."

"Bull—" I shut my mouth and peer around him to make sure Maya is still not listening. "Bullshit," I snap back. "I need to work, Finnigan. Now you know what's at stake for me. I will not risk my father's comfort and health, and you made it pretty clear a while ago that you want me out of Queenscove. So I'm saving money for that, too."

The man inhales so slow and deep, I half expect him to breathe out flames.

"That was then." His answer is short, but heavy with meaning I don't fully grasp.

"Nothing changed. Has it?"

Everything changed. For me at least. But I'm challenging him to face it too.

"I will help you."

"You will do no such thing," I bite back, disappointed at his lack of admission. "I refused your money once, Finnigan, I will do it again. All I need is to work."

He crosses his arms against his expansive chest unfortunately covered by a light-blue T-shirt, and leans back in the bar stool, cocking an eyebrow. "Fine. Call Lulu and see what she says about you going for your next shift."

I frown.

"Please tell me you didn't speak with her. You didn't tell her that I'm not coming back, did you?" I'm braced against the countertop now, leaning in angrily, my tone low and harsh.

He shakes his head. "I didn't, Evie darling, but Lulu loves you, does she not? Do you really think that she would allow you to go out there, in a public place, and work with a target on your head?"

For God's sake. He's right. Lulu wouldn't allow it. She would tell me to hide in the depths of the damn earth with Maya until all this blows over and both Frankie and Vassallo—or Bartiste as they know him—are dead.

"Fuck!" I snap, slapping my hand against my mouth the moment the swear leaves my lips.

Finnigan snickers, his expression lighter. I guess he never hears me swear. Being in Maya's presence constantly, I had to learn to hold back vulgar words and try to be calm all the time.

"Stop laughing," I quip, but even I can't help the smile as I rub my face with both hands and rake my fingers through my hair.

"What's with the hair, Evelyn? Sorry, but I've been dying to ask."

His question surprises me in the middle of this conversation. I shrug. "Needed a change." It's not a lie, but not quite the truth either.

He cocks his head, and I realize something gave me away.

"Very drastic change."

I nod and change the subject. "Were the guys at least able to trace Frankie's car?"

He takes too long to answer, but I don't press. He knows what I'm doing and finally he appeases me.

"They did. It wasn't a rental, which is good. Carter and his team are on it. We'll find him soon. But things will get worse before they get better."

"As long as they get better..."

"They will. Neither of them is gonna touch you ever again."

I nod, even knowing it's not a promise. I wish it was, but that would be very unfair of me.

"How are you feeling after last night? Do you need to talk to someone?" he asks.

I scoff. "Sure, let me go tell my therapist that I bashed someone's head in last night and, probably killed him. I'm sure that won't land me in jail."

"Oh, he's dead." He swipes his hand over his face. "Shit, Evie, I'm sorry. I just... I'm used to—"

"No need to explain. I bet this is just another Tuesday for you."

"It's Sunday, actually."

I glare at him, and the smirk drops off his face.

"It's strange," I finally answer him. "It feels like I was in a trance because I barely remember what happened during. I recall how he raised the gun at Maddox, how I tackled him to the ground, being dragged off of him, and then... you."

"But you saw the aftermath?" I appreciate how he's now trying to be delicate about it.

"Briefly, yes. Though I'm not entirely sure I understood what I was looking at. It didn't feel like I did that, the scene almost looked foreign to me." Though, it's enough to look at my red and bruised knuckles and the sides of my hands to confirm to myself that I was indeed the one who killed that man.

"You can talk to me, you know. What you did, no matter how common it may be for me, it isn't for you. Taking a life is hard, no matter who it is, and it will always take something out of you. I'm here."

I'm not sure what to tell him, because even now I don't know how I feel about it.

"Beyond anything else that's happening between us, I appreciate this. Thank you."

I keep wondering if the ball's going to drop at some point, and then it doesn't. Last night I blamed it on adrenaline and shock, but what excuse do I have now for not reacting like a normal, law-abiding citizen?

I was quick to condemn Finnigan and his Sanctum for their criminal ways, but what does this... and everything from before... make me? Am I at the same level as The Sanctum? Or no better than the people who killed my mother?

CHAPTER 23
Finnigan

"I T'S SETTLED THEN. WE RAID all three locations at once," Vin confirms as he leans back on the couch.

"We might find more kids." I sigh.

"Good. At least something good will come out of it, since there's no guarantee Frankie or Bartiste will be there," Madds says in an exasperated tone.

There's already been a raid today. Madds and Carter stormed Frankie's location they found after tracking him down, but the bastard slipped through our fingers. Not surprising since he knew we would be on his tail. But Carter already tracked down three more locations connected to him. There's a chance neither him nor his boss will be there, but whatever we find will be useful.

We've gathered at my place. Ronan even brought Annika

and Aaro because there was no way he would let them out of his sight. I can't blame him. I feel the same for Evie and Maya, which is why we're all here, even if one isn't my wife and the other not my child. The protectiveness is there though. Mamaw June is entertaining them on the terrace until we finish our conversation.

The plan is clear. We're splitting into three groups and leaving in about an hour or so. Carter has agreed to stay here and keep an eye on cameras, trackers, and whatever else he does. That level of technology baffles me and I'm grateful to have his brain in our ranks. Vin, Madds, and I are taking three teams, and raiding those places. This is not the same as it was all those years before when we went to save Annika and Hanna. We have enough power now that we will demolish them on sight.

We don't need my cousin, Sloan Buchanan, to come from Venator again, like he did last time. However, the moment Ronan mentioned to him that Bartiste is back, the man decided to come and bring an army, regardless. He'll be here in a few days.

There's no escape for Bartiste now. And this time, if he crawls back into whatever hole he went in last time, we will find him. *I* will find him, and he'll eat a whole clip of my gun.

"Are we ready for dinner?" Mamaw June peaks in from the terrace.

We all exchange looks and nod to each other.

"Yeah, we're ready," Vin confirms, and she opens the door fully to let the breeze in and the two kids.

It's been rather interesting seeing Aaro and Maya bond. She's bubbly and bouncy, and Aaro is quiet, broody, yet eager to please. They get along so well. It makes me sad that Ronan and Annika will have to go back to their home once all of this is done and dusted.

Annika has been tense since coming here. Quiet too. She's always been shy, but she hasn't stepped foot in here since they left all those years ago, and her last memories of this penthouse were of tears. So many tears for her lost best friend.

It makes an even bigger bastard out of me, but I'm sort of glad she gets to experience this suffering here, in front of me, because I stayed behind and drowned in it for years. Here, where we brought her and Hanna after we *bonded* on Bovely Island during that terrible storm. We spent our last happy moments in my penthouse, which I used to share with my brother before he left.

I may have lost my first love, but it was a fresh adventure. Annika lost her best friend, her kindred spirit, and she had to watch her be ripped apart by Bartiste's men, then held her as she took her last breath. She's suffered enough.

She looks out past the floor to ceiling windows, her gaze lost somewhere in the horizon, quiet and pensive. I don't miss Evelyn's curious gaze as she studies all of us but pauses just a little longer on my nephew's mom. Everyone rises to go sit at the dinner table, but Annika follows her gaze instead, and walks in the other direction—the terrace. Ronan frowns, a hint of worry shadowing his eyes. He's had his share of sad memories in this penthouse. He never said anything to me. How could he when I was so broken. But I could see it in the way he looked at her through her grief... like he was terrified he would lose her. That she wouldn't come back from the shock she suffered. He takes a step to follow her out on the terrace, but I quickly take two and when he spots me, understanding crosses his features. He nods once, and a hint of a smile dusts over my lips, then I follow his wife outside, closing the door behind me.

It takes two more breaths for me to get the courage to join her where she stands by the railing, her arms wrapped around herself like she's afraid her soul will spill out if she doesn't. She doesn't seem surprised to see me when I finally join her. Setting her gaze on the sunset, she tightens the grip around herself, looking like she wants to talk, but hesitates. Do I make her that uncomfortable?

I take a deep inhale and let out a heavy sigh.

"I'm sorry for how I acted when you left." The words sound awkward, forced, but I hope she can find the genuine feeling underneath all of that.

"I'm sorry we left."

My head whips to her and I suppress the need to press my hand to the spot where my neck just cracked. *She's what?*

"I'm sorry we left *you* when you needed your brother the most," she continues, ignoring my shock.

"I understand why you did it. You needed to protect yourself, your unborn baby, your family."

Then she shakes her head, and I'm even more confused.

"That wasn't the only reason." She turns to me, her eyes glossy, but she fights back the tears. "I had to remove myself from you."

I frown, reigning in what could be a bad reaction.

"Shit, that didn't sound the same as in my head," she says with a sigh and an apologetic look. "I couldn't bear what my presence, my beating heart, was doing to you. I was a constant reminder to you of the cruel unfairness of this world, that two of us were kidnapped that day and only I was lucky enough to return. You deserved to move on, and if I stayed, the pain, the guilt, the anger, would have kept you there... grieving. At least that's what my instinct was telling me. Because every time I looked in a mirror, I saw in my eyes the same guilt, the same anger to this unfairness that looked back at me from yours."

She holds my gaze for a moment longer, then turns back to the burnished sky. So, I do too, leaning my forearms on the railing.

To say I'm surprised is a massive understatement. It was easy to think that they left for themselves, for their baby. It was easy to think that I mattered less. I never allowed myself to think that maybe... just maybe, they did it for me too. I never cared enough to talk to them after that anyway. But many times I wondered if things would have been different if they stayed. I needed comfort, I needed someone to understand my suffering, I needed my brother.

Sighing, I allow myself to accept the acknowledgement waiting in the recesses of my mind—I needed my brother, but I couldn't bear the happiness in his eyes as he looked at his breathing girlfriend. Not then.

Now, I'm holding onto resentment, but beneath that ugly emotion, I find that I'm not bothered by it anymore. Especially not when I catch a glimpse of Aaro, and it dawns on me that the healthy, curious little boy deserved a healthy mother too. Annika was too broken back then.

"You're right," I agree. "I'm not sure how it would have been if I had you here."

"Hard." She answers too quickly, her shoulders falling with the weight of these tough feelings. "I spent many nights on this terrace cursing that I was breathing this pleasantly salty air. Too many times I got close to giving up on myself, and I want to think now that I was so stupid back then for having such thoughts. I want to be embarrassed of myself. But I'm not. There was too much validity in my mindset, in my feelings—and my guilt. Whatever you were thinking about me then, my thoughts were even worse, and that's why I had to leave."

I didn't know her state of mind was so precarious, that she would have gone as far as giving up on life. Fuck, I was never that close. I was grieving, I was sad, but most of all I was angry at my incompetence. I was disappointed in my inability to save Hanna before she was killed. The guilt was eating me from the inside out, but I was never close enough to give up. I'm an even bigger asshole for not noticing how hard Annika was suffering. Though, I'm not sure she would have confessed that to me back then.

I wouldn't have asked anyway, too wrapped up in my own self-loathing. Still am. I am a failure, and it's why I should stay as far away from Evelyn as possible.

What if I fail like that all over again?

What if I lose her too?

Evelyn

THE ATMOSPHERE AT THE DINNER table is calm, peculiar considering that they plotted three violent raids in the last hour or so. One would think it's so light because two kids are present, but that's not it at all. These men are so nonchalantly comfortable with the destruction they're about to rein down on Frankie and his men, that they are at ease now. Even as they're leaving in a few minutes.

All but Carter, who sits quietly next to me, his back straight, movements eerily fluid as he turns his head, observing, or as he cuts into his last slice of roast ham and steamed vegetables. Every single movement he makes, from the glide of his eyes to the rise of his chest as he breathes, is so controlled. It gives me the impression that he's the most skilled of predators, sitting idly at the top of the food chain, waiting for the prey worth his effort. But sometimes, I also have this urge to poke him to make sure he's real. Weirdly enough, I see some of these traits in Aaro too.

Just like Carter now, I've been observing them in silence since late afternoon. Finn told me everyone was coming over because Carter found something, right as I got out of the shower after my grueling training session with Madds. All three of us went to The Fightclub around midday, Maya included, because I was too anxious to sit around any longer. Once I heard they were coming, I was dying to hear what Carter found. I planned on sitting in the shadow of the corridor and listen in, but no one told me to leave.

Annika and Morrigan came too, and I would have stopped feeling privileged for being allowed to listen in as they planned, if I wasn't the outsider. Which I am. Not a girlfriend, not a mother, definitely not a wife. Yet, no one batted an eyelid at my presence. Not even quiet, eerie, Carter. He is the most curious of them all. He both scares and fascinates me because there's a cold emptiness in his peculiar hazel eyes. There were some emotions, sometimes amusement, sometimes a hint of excitement at the prospect of vengeance and murder, yet there was no warmth. Not the type you expect from a person who has been friends with these people for over a decade. From listening to him talk it's clear he cares. He was the first to push back when something sounded like it could put someone in danger or be an unnecessary risk. Then again, that could come from a practical point of view too. I gathered that he's pretty much a genius, applying his wits in his hacking skills, but I heard him more than once being referred to as *The Carver*, and I shudder to think why that is.

Maya happily munches on the rest of her dinner, her eyes wide as she takes in everyone at the table. There's a pang of sadness in my heart as I realize that she's never experienced anything like this, a big *family* dinner, until we came here. I don't think she remembers us and our parents together at the dinner table, and even so, it wasn't like this. So many chatty people engrossed in different conversations, a little boy she can play with, couples loving on each other. And I'm going to take this away from her. I feel like an asshole. How can I rob my sister of this when she looks like this is where she belongs, just to pull her to our miserable existence back in cold Fleeton, living in a subpar place, hopefully never homeless again, while struggling to feed each other and pay for Dad's care? How can I do that to her?

She looks cheerful and content as she observes Morri and Vin, and Ronan and Annika's sweet gestures to each other, giggling to herself whenever one brushes a hand on the cheek of the other or they steal a kiss. I haven't told her yet that our life here isn't permanent, and I can't predict how she will react when I drop the news that we could be going back to Fleeton. To Dad.

My mind drifts away as the conversation dies down around us, everyone probably thinking more about what's coming once they leave the table.

"Evie?" Maya's voice brings my attention back to her, her voice dragging a bit like it does when she's dying of curiosity.

"Yes?"

"Why don't you have a boyfriend?"

I'm so startled by the question, my gaze shoots around the table just for my cheeks to heat when I notice that most of them have heard the question too. Morri chuckles to herself and I want to throw something at her.

"I don't need one, honey," I answer, praying she's satisfied. "Go on, finish your dinner."

She wipes her face quickly with the napkin, too quickly for me to hope that she's satisfied with my answer.

"But I think you should get one. Find someone to love. Then you'll be happier, and maybe you'll smile more. And bake like you used to."

The innocence in her voice breaks something inside of me. I've been trying so hard to make sure that the cruelty and hardship of our life didn't brush off on her, I made sure not to swear around her, not to yell, get angry or upset, I tried to shield her from it all. I didn't even think to pretend to be happy around her. It's only when I realize just how quiet the space got that my cheeks flame with embarrassment and I want to slide down this chair and hide under the table until everyone leaves.

"I have no interest in a boyfriend. I much like spending my time with you." I smile, brushing my hand over her head. "Now stop asking silly questions or you might not get dessert."

"I like it too, but... I can't love you like that, Evie. I can't love you in that pretty way Daddy loved Mommy."

I choke so hard on my food, Carter pats my back to help me. My sister seems set on embarrassing me and making me cry tonight. What is happening right now? Before I manage to catch my breath, to my freaking horror, she continues.

"Like them." She points to the two couples. "They kiss and hug, and they look at each other like Mommy and Daddy used to. Like Finn looks at you sometimes when you're not paying attention. And like you look at h—"

"Maya! How about you go wash your hands? In the bathroom, now." God almighty, bury me now.

My gaze shoots to Finn. I don't want to look, but there's a twisted desire inside of me that needs to see how Maya's words landed. The man in question is stunned, I'm not even sure he's breathing. Everyone's watching us, but I don't turn. I can't bear to face them, yet. Finn's mood shifts and harsh annoyance strains the strong, beautiful lines of his face. Then he rises and leaves.

The bastard actually leaves.

"Come on! We have work to do!" He shouts for the others to follow.

My gaze finally goes to them, and I have no idea what to

think. Madds sighs, annoyed for some reason, Morri looks shocked and amused, Vin shakes his head at her, Carter has this knowing gaze that unsettles me a bit, Mamaw June looks like she's gonna burst from joy, and Ronan and Annika have a mixture of surprise, happiness, and worry on their faces.

"I am going to kill my sister," I mutter to myself, mostly.

Then Morri bursts into laughter, and quickly rises, following the others as they get ready to go out. Only Annika, Mamaw June, Carter, and I remain at the table. Aaro follows after Maya.

"Ignore Morrigan. Her and Vincent drove us mad when they were *courting*." I turn to Carter, checking to make sure that it was he who spoke those words. It was. "Annika even orchestrated a clever riddle and chase to get Ronan. We were all privy to their crazy ways. Some more than others."

Annika chuckles from across the table, but I'm too busy digging through my brain to try to remember if Carter has ever spoken so many words to me before. I'm drawing a blank. The longest conversation we had, which is still one-sided, was when he gave me the tracker before I went back in the container. I think.

"Still, Finnigan and I aren't together. We aren't like that," I counter.

Carter turns his head ever so smoothly toward me and cocks it, his stunning eyes fixed on me. "Are you not?"

There is no missing the slight amusement shining in his eyes. He doesn't want an answer, this question is rhetorical at best. *He knows.*

"Take it from me"—Annika pulls my attention to her—"don't try to pretend, hide, or lie to Carter. The man has a sixth sense."

I would take her words as an eerie warning if it wasn't for the cheeky smile in her eyes, directed at the man next to me. I take it Annika and Ronan tried to downplay their connection then.

"Wait, did you say Annika orchestrated a riddle and a chase?"

"Yes. After she practically conned us of a few million," Carter says in a calm way, like he's telling me about how he went and bought milk this morning.

Annika starts laughing and I turn to her, gob-smacked.

"Hey, I gave it back. Eventually."

Carter chuckles softly and it sounds deeply unnatural. Intriguing, too.

"I'm going to go grab my laptop and things." He rises and leaves the room.

"God, it's so hard to recall good memories from that time." Annika leans back in her chair, crossing her arms against her chest. "The riddle Carter mentioned, brought them to the annual Midsummer party, at the waterfall in the woods, and it was the night that started it all for the two of us. Well, four, really."

Four? I stiffen, pondering the words.

"I was always too withdrawn to do anything out of order. We might have been dealing on the black-market, but Hanna was the salesperson, full of spunk and life. I was just the artist hiding in the background, forging all those paintings. So I wanted to be crazy for once."

I'm sorry, Annika, sweet, kind, shy Annika was a painting forger who sold on the black-market? Oh God, I have so much more to find out about these people.

"When I first saw Ronan, and I realized who we were selling to, I couldn't help myself. I was so drawn to him, like deep down I knew he was *the one*. I know, I know, it sounds insane." She chuckles softly, but then it fades, and her gaze moves somewhere in the distance. "If it wasn't for my obsession, Hanna and I would be retired now. But I stayed, and she insisted on staying with me. Then Bartiste came for us. Sometimes I wonder if we had left after we struck the deal with The Sanctum, would he have found us? Ronan says yes, and the outcome would have been even worse, but it's hard to get over the fact that I lost my best friend, and Finnigan lost his first love."

My mouth falls open, and I fight the gasp too late.

Hanna was his first love?

Annika's eyes widen and she covers her mouth. "You didn't know?"

"Oh, well, I told you, he and I aren't like that. We're not... anything. So, we don't share personal things like this." I try to deflect, but judging by the look in her eyes, I'm not very successful. "I'm sorry for Hanna, losing your best friend must have been terrible."

"It was. The guilt was even worse. I'm almost over mine." She shakes her head, chewing on her lip before she continues. "One day, Finnigan will come to terms with his own guilt too, and when he does, I hope you'll be there next to him."

CHAPTER 24
Evelyn

I'M STARTLED AWAKE BY ANOTHER nightmare. The same memory, the same words spewed by Frankie and Vassallo, or Bartiste, the same slimy sensation lingering. I look around, but Maya is sleeping soundly next to me.

Annika and Aaro took the other bedroom as we waited for the guys to finish the raid. I waited for as long as I could, but in the end, sleep took me. I was hoping, but sleep hasn't settled my anxiety. The guys said that it's likely neither Frankie nor Bartiste will be at the three locations, but I still hope.

More so, I hope Finnigan's okay.

A rumble sounds outside the bedroom, and I hold my breath, listening. It might have been the front door.

Is that him? Is he back?

I slide out of bed, rushing to the door and stepping

out, closing it as soft as I can behind me, so as not to wake Maya. The anxiety rushes through my blood and I rush to the living area.

It is him!

"Oh my god, Finnigan!" I slap my hand over my mouth when he turns, and I get a full view of him.

For such a preppy type, the rich, surfer boy looks a lot like a ruthless warrior right now. Blood streaks his blonde curls, his T-shirt is splattered like a Pollock painting, and his knuckles are red, the skin broken on some of them. I might be sick, because this does something so wonderful and insane to me, warmth pooling between my thighs. He looks... vicious. Deliciously so as he beams at me, as happy to see me as I am to see him.

"Are you okay?" I finally reach him, ignoring both Ronan and Carter's raised eyebrows and faint amusement.

"All good, sugar."

"But..." I take his hands in mine, unable to stop myself. "You're hurt."

He removes one hand from mine and brings it up, pinching my chin between his thumb and forefinger, and lifting my gaze to his. "Nothing but scratches."

I nod slowly but can't breathe easier as I imagine how this must look to the others. Awkwardly, I clear my throat and drop his hand, taking a little step back. I'm rewarded with his cheekiest grin, because I know he sees the flush in my cheeks, no way he doesn't when they feel like they're burning.

God, this man's going to ruin me.

"You didn't find him, did you?" I ask, swiping my gaze over to the others.

"No." Ronan's the one who answers.

"It was still productive. We have leads now." Carter shuts the lid to his laptop and tucks it in a bag along with a lot of other technical gear he brought with him.

"Not long. He'll be ours soon enough," Finn adds.

For some odd reason I feel a bit of jealousy. I want to be there when Frankie is caught. I want to be there when he dies. But most of all, I want to be the one who steals his last breath. The Sanctum might be brushing off on me because none of that sounds remotely wrong.

"I'm gonna go wash and crawl in bed with my family. Night!" Ronan says, a satisfied tone in his voice.

"Good night." We all wish him, and my gaze is finally drawn to the window. It's still night, and now I'm so wired up, not sure I can fall back asleep.

"I'm going to take Ronan's old room. It's too late to drive home and still rest." Carter tucks away his gear, so it's not in the way, and waves us good night.

Then there's just me, and my bloodied warrior.

"You're sure you're okay?" I ask again.

"Yes, but I'm tempted to get hurt just so I can have the privilege of being welcomed home like that all over again, with that worried and hungry look in your eyes."

"Um... hungry?" Here's that damn blush again.

"Oh yes. You're looking at me like you want to rip my clothes off and touch every inch of my body to make sure I'm whole. Every. Single. Hard. Inch."

Sweet Mary Mother of Jesus. He did not just say that. And I should definitely not like the sound of it as much as I do.

"Finnigan, I—"

"You should go to bed, Evie darling." His fingers are on my chin again, but only for a brief second, because in the next one, his hand is on the back of my neck, and I'm pulled into the most brutal, demanding, and hungry kiss.

I fist his bloody T-shirt, holding him to me like I'm scared he'll dare break this kiss, but Finnigan has other ideas. His other hand goes to the small of my back, pulling me flush to his body, before his fingers snake further down, pressing into my ass. I moan into his mouth, following the vibrations with the frantic swipes of my tongue against his, and when his clear hard on presses into my lower belly, the urge to climb him like a tree threatens to make a fool out of me.

His previous rejections still stain my memory, but Christ... this starving kiss might just wipe it clean.

With one last bruising press of his lips against mine, he pulls away, that sly grin once again tugging at his lips.

"I wish this wouldn't feel so right."

I frown and open my mouth to spit back at him, but what would I say? Because I wish for the same thing.

"We can allow ourselves to feel right. We deserve as much. Even if there's a time limit on it."

"Time limit?" he asks.

I nod. "You know of my father. I like it here, but this is not about me."

He doesn't look too pleased with my answer, but doesn't argue. "You may be right, we deserve at least a bit of rightness."

He pulls me back to him, kissing me again, only this time the hunger is different. It begs and demands at the same time, it's soft, warm, and intimate, and I find that I like this kiss even more than the one before.

* * *

Three hours I spent in the gym and training ring today. Madds pushed me so much harder, at my request, and taught me some more moves and techniques. Every muscle in my body aches, but it feels so good. I may not be ready to take on Frankie again, but boy do I feel like I could stand against the asshole.

Madds is still upset I jumped out of the car to get the guy who almost shot him, but he hugged me so hard the other day at dinner, I know he's thankful. He's just not the type to spell it out. And the fact that he's eager to train me harder and show me more fighting moves and techniques says a lot. Moreover, I finally regained control of myself. Of my fate. I no longer feel so useless. Madds, The Sanctum, gave me something I never had before—strength. Not just physical, but mental and emotional. I'm more myself than I ever have been before.

"Is it my turn now?" Maya squeals from her seat on the wooden bench far against the back wall.

"You wanna train too?" Maddox asks, amused.

"Yup!" She drops her book and sprints to us. She tries to climb in the ring, but keeps falling on her ass, much to our amusement. She's determined though, and Maddox chuckles as he goes and pulls her up.

"Alright then. While your sister goes and rests, I'll *train* you."

This man takes his role so serious, and sometimes I just want to cry at how amazing he is with her, with us. I never wished for another sibling, and even if I did, they would have paled in comparison to Madds.

He drops to his knees at her level since he's so damn tall. "Show me how you make a fist."

I chuckle and climb out of the ring, starting to unwrap my hands as I head to my gym bag. I don't bother changing, I just pull a pair of joggers over my shorts and stay in my sports bra since I'm too hot. I'll pull a sweatshirt over when we're on our way to Vincent's house. The guys are so worried about me, they keep an eye on me at all times and avoid keeping me in public places for longer than necessary. It's a bit annoying, but then again, I've never felt so protected in my life. I can't complain, not when all that matters is the fact that Maya is safe. Granted, The Fightclub is not a public place, but even the drive from here to the penthouse or Vincent's forest house could be dangerous.

It's been five days since the three raids, and they've all been the same—Finnigan's, baking, gym, worry, sleep.

I could use a drink.

From what I understand, Carter's been baiting the hell out of Frankie and Bartiste. Screwing up their operations, destroying leads and connections, and making sure those assholes aren't welcomed in the underground of Queenscove. This is Sanctum territory, yet those assholes think they can just swoop in and do business here. They'll soon get angry enough that they'll come out and make a mistake. Bloody cowards.

"Hey, Madds? Is Midnight open now?" I raise my voice over Maya's funny grunts as she hits his open palms.

"No. But Carter and Jian or Tina might be there. A bartender, too."

Jian and Tina are two of the hackers from Carter's team. They've been part of it and The Sanctum for years. Brendan is the other, but I rarely see him. He's a proper recluse.

"I'm going to head up there. I need a drink," I let him know as I head toward the stairs that lead up in the secure corridor.

A few weeks ago, Carter set my fingerprint on the access pads and gave me a code so I can go up whenever I felt like having a drink after workouts. He did make sure to tell me to only go if it's not open, though. I didn't ask why, but one can guess.

I swing my bag over my shoulder, and run my fingers through my sweaty, messy bob to make it look a little more decent as I climb the stairs and pass through all the secure doors.

"Hey Carter, is it okay if I come in?" I ask as I peak through the back door and notice him standing at the bar, a laptop in front of him. As always.

"Hi Evelyn. Yes, of course. Actually, can you tell me if you've seen this guy before?" he gestures toward his laptop and waits.

"Oh!" I don't bother hiding the grimace when I see the picture on the screen—a man slumped on the ground in what seems like a dark street of some kind, with a bullet hole in his forehead, his eyes open, but blank.

I swallow a couple of times and take a step closer.

"Actually, yes. He was one of the ones who ushered us into that warehouse or whatever it was. He didn't strike me as a low-ranking guy, but not as important as Frankie. I never heard his name though."

"This helps. I have his phone and can track all his past whereabouts now, and at least I know that I'm not wasting my time. Thank you, Evelyn."

I smile and nod. Once again Carter speaks with me more than just the polite *hello* or *do you want a drink,* and I find it hard to get used to it. Maybe he's not quite as bad as I thought he was.

"Drink?" he asks, and I chuckle to myself as I drop my bag on a chair.

"Yes, please. A strong one, but sweet if possible."

He nods and goes behind the bar himself.

"Oh, sorry, I thought a bartender might be here. I don't want to bother you when you're busy."

"It's no bother. I'm getting one myself too."

I still feel awkward though, but I nod and smile either way.

"Trust me, he'll eat out of the palm of your hand if you do that."

That sweet voice...

When I turn, Finnigan walks in from the back, Tina next

to him, and when his eyes land on me, I feel naked. I may be wearing loose joggers and a sports bra, but he watches me with startled hunger, drawing his gaze over me so slowly, I want to spread myself wide for him right here, on this wooden floor. No matter who watches.

"Evie…" he says on a breathy voice, his eyes lingering a bit too long on my breasts before they find my eyes.

Tina walks away and gives me a little wave before she takes a seat at the bar, next to Carter's laptop.

"I was just… I trained downstairs."

Oh my god, I'm mumbling. *Keep it together, Evelyn!*

"Yeah… you did."

Hungry, so very, very hungry.

"Carter's making me a drink."

"You should ask Severin to take you back to the penthouse." He takes a step closer, his heated gaze suggesting he doesn't mean those words.

And I don't want to go yet. "I want a drink first."

"There's alcohol at home."

Home. That sounds awfully familiar, like it's not just *his* home. I'm not going straight there anyway. Maya has an overnight play-date since Annika proposed that the kids should spend as much time together as they can before they'll inevitably have to return home when this whole thing ends.

"I'm getting cabin fever. I'm having a drink here."

Before he can give me another comeback, I move to the bar and climb onto one of the stools, my ass sliding back a bit too far in my attempt to be cocky. But I own it and brace my forearms on the bar, watching Carter's curious eyes on us, a cocked eyebrow showing his amusement as he makes the drinks.

Finnigan shows up to my right, facing me instead of sitting on the stool, and his gaze spreads fire over my body. I dare a peak, and he's watching my arched back, my ass, like he's about to tackle me to the floor and feast on it.

Please, please feast on it!

And I realize, utterly horrified, that I'm going to leave a damp patch on this leather barstool. I have no idea how I'm going to hide it from him. Or the others.

There's no going back now.

"One drink," he says on a low rumble, his tone laced with whiskey and fire, "then I'm getting you home."

My gaze shoots to him, drowning in the promise in his voice, and I know he doesn't miss the hitch in my breath, nor the shift in my thighs as I press them together. I have no drink to fiddle with, only my fingers that are getting increasingly damper, and I'm not sure what to do with myself. Not when he doesn't stop looking at me with azure eyes heavy with unspoken promises, his wide, thick shoulders tensing as he holds himself unusually still. A trickle of sweat runs from beneath my sports bra tickling down my spine, and I shiver at the sensation, my back arching slightly in response. His gaze shoots right there, and I think his hand was about to follow too, but he stops himself, flexing his fist as he follows that drop of sweat disappear in the seam of my leggings.

His eyes are still there, unmoving and tense. "Where's Maya?"

"Downstairs with Maddox. She has a sleepover planned with Aaro after," I say it all in one breath. One hot, heavy breath.

"Where?"

"Vincent's."

He only grunts in response, his gaze still fixed on my skin. Or my ass. Whichever it is, I curse the clothes covering the area, and I curse the company even more.

"Here you go, *Evelyn*."

My eyes snap toward Carter who gives me such a suggestive look, there is no mistaking the fact that he wants me to know that he can tell what's going on. My skin prickles yet again, because yes, Finnigan has eaten my pussy with such hunger, the ghost of his tongue is still there when I close my eyes, and he fingered me with enough expertise, I'm ready to beg him for more. But we haven't spoken about it. He hasn't said a word to me about what we have done. He's giving me enough suggestive looks and considering how hung up he's been on the forbidden side of things, I can certainly call this progress. Even without the verbal acknowledgment.

Where is this going?

How far is he going to allow it to go?

And where will I stop?

Because being here, in Queenscove, among people who have done nothing but protect me and root for me, has been gold dust for my growth. I'm a waitress in a café, but on the inside, I feel like I can take over the damn world.

Only, right now it's not the world I'm craving to tackle, but Finnigan Hennessey. The man with a sharp jaw, an even sharper tongue, and forbidden desire painted vividly in his bright blue eyes. I should care about his previous rejections, they should stir me in the opposite direction, and this might make me stupid, but I crave his acceptance more.

Not because I'm a sucker for punishment, not because I'm a doormat, but because the moment he looked into my eyes when I walked out of that container, I saw a soul drowning in the same pain as mine. A person who couldn't bear to scream his loneliness out loud, their mind breaking with the harrowing noise of it. I saw a man with a broken heart and a broken soul who wanted nothing more than kindred company. And I never said it, never even allowed it to touch on my inner monologue, but deep down I knew that person had to be me.

There are shackles around our hearts, binding our souls

in catatonic states of silent despair—and we need each other to break them.

Even if I do leave this beautiful place that gave me my life back, at least I'll leave unshackled. I'll even leave my heart with him if I have to, because at least I'll know that for a moment, I was free. And I'll know that he is too.

I take the glass Carter carefully poured for me, and the first taste warms me with such decadent sweetness, I down three more big sips one after the other, on a groan deep in my throat.

Finnigan's eyes widen, looking at the glass like it offended him somehow. I get only a swift growl in warning as he grabs it and downs it in one go, slamming it back on the bar. One drop glimmers at the corner of his mouth, and when the tip of his tongue reaches to lick it, I'm back in his bedroom, his head between my legs, my cries covered by his hand on my mouth.

God help me...

"Time to go." He grabs my hand in his much larger one and pulls me down from the chair.

"Excuse me?" My protest lands on deaf ears, because he fully ignores me as he drags me back toward the back door.

I barely get to say goodbye as he grabs my hand without even stopping, and ushers me through the corridor I came through. I try to pry myself out of his grip but fail.

"You don't get to say what I do or don't do, Finnigan. If I want to enjoy a drink, I can enjoy a damn—"I run into Finnigan's back as he briefly stops at the top of the stairs.

Warm, wide, strong back I'm dying to rake my nails over. *Christ, what is happening with me?*

"Yo, Severin!" Finnigan calls out for his friend, ignoring me, and then sets off again, walking down the stairs.

"What's up?"

"Are you ready to go now?"

"Yeah, we were just coming up for Evie," he says with a narrowing gaze that drifts to me, then to our joined hands. "Oh, for God's sake."

I force my hand out of Finnigan's hold, furious at his manhandling, because I'm getting tired of his hot and cold behavior. He's reluctant to let go, but I don't give him a choice, then I storm right past him and down the stairs, until I reach Maya quietly lacing one of her shoes.

"Come, sweet girl, let's go see your new friend," I tell her, moving her little hands away and doing up her laces myself so we can get the heck out of here.

"See you later?" Maddox asks, and I know he's addressing Finn.

"Not likely. Busy tonight. See you tomorrow."

He mutters a bye to me, and Maya too, but I let my sister answer, because *busy tonight* for Finnigan Hennessey can only mean one thing—he's going to screw the life out of some random girl tonight.

Something stings behind my eyes, because maybe I was wrong this whole time, maybe I am an idiot, and this man is happy with the manacles binding him. And maybe he doesn't give a shit about me after all.

I twitch when the door slams, and I know he's gone. I thought he was done with his harem of women, even Morri and Madds thought so too, and I wish I wouldn't have read so much into it, because clearly, we were all wrong.

I'm just half a notch on his headboard, the *goth girl* box he probably needed to check off.

I'm just another mark in Finnigan's black book.

CHAPTER 25
Finnigan

I JUMP OUT OF MY OWN skin when the front door slams, and spill the glass of vodka sour all over my T-shirt and shorts.

"For fuck's sakes..." I mutter to myself, putting the glass down and rising quickly to see who the hell that was.

As I cross the terrace and head inside, I'm more pissed about my spilled drink than the prospect of someone breaking into my penthouse. Even if this was my third one already. But as I step over the threshold, I see only a blur of a person as they disappear in the corridor.

Evelyn?

I thought she was at Vincent's for that sleepover. I'm annoyed and confused as I storm after her, because I thought I could have some time to breathe. To think. To cool off. She did a fucking number on me, showing up in Midnight in that tight sports bra that pushed her sinful breasts together, her soft skin on display, begging to be touched. I couldn't stop looking at her arched back, her ass pushed out, and all I wanted was to bend her over that bar, press my hand on her back, and sink my cock in her pussy until she vowed never to be touched—or fucking looked at—by any other man ever again.

My possessiveness over this woman is going beyond protecting. Because I want that more than anything, to keep her in a gilded cage away from this cruel world and give her all she's ever wanted on a gold platter. I want to keep her in furs and silk, and make sure no hair on her head will ever fall again, unless it's with her permission. I'm fucking terrified that something could happen to her. Yet, I want to be the one to break that sweet body of hers, and I want her to give me permission to do it. Even as I know now that she wants to fuck without it.

I can smell the ginger and brown sugar scent of her as I follow the trail through the corridor. It reminds me of her tight pussy and how responsive she was to my touch. Even when I came at her in the darkness—especially then. Groaning, I adjust my cock inside my boxers, squeezing it hard into submission.

It doesn't work.

Not when I hear the shower start and all I can imagine is my Evie darling, naked beneath the spray. She's sin and innocence wrapped into one, she's the threat to my heart and the only thing that could save it. And I'm fucking terrified that she'll decide to walk away from Queenscove and leave with it.

But I open the bathroom door anyway, stripping my clothes on the way to the shower she's standing under with her eyes closed, and before I can think too long about that fear, I'm down on my knees behind her, my face buried between her cheeks seeking that hot, delicious center of her as she yelps and attempts to jump away. My arm circles around her before she can move, but doesn't relax even when she realizes it's me.

"Get off me, Finnigan! Why are you here? Weren't you supposed to be *busy*? Buried in some new pus—"

"I lied." I interrupt her with a growl, sinking my teeth in the flesh of her ass cheek. I expect another yelp, but she hisses instead, pushing against me.

"Why?"

"Because the only *pussy* I can bear to think of anymore is yours. And I felt like punishing you for it. Being alone here was safer."

"And now?" She pauses, her muscles finally melting into me as she stifles a mewl. "Do you still want to punish me?"

"I fear I may never stop."

"Don't stop." Evelyn reaches back, raking a hand through my hair, and tugs me into her.

So hungry and demanding. Placing a hand on her back, I push until she's bent over and fully exposed to me, and now... I'm ready to fucking feast.

And feast I do.

I lick her from front to back, paying special attention to her clit, pressing my tongue over the hooded nerve bundle and circling it over and over until she cries out and her legs shake. She's so sensitive, so beautifully responsive, that she doesn't need much attention there to find that coveted peak. And that's why I move to the center of her instead. I know already that she'll be writhing with pleasure when I fuck her with my tongue, swiping on her inner walls like she's the end to my hunger, the cure to my starvation. I'll only bring her to the edge, drive her crazy with pleasure, but not offer enough to topple her over and light that fire she so desperately wants to burn in. I lick and stroke, push and circle, until every muscle in her body is screaming in strain along with her sweet, throaty voice.

Maya's not here, so Evie can be as loud as she craves.

"I can't... I'm going to fall..."

She moans, but I ignore her, because I'm convinced she won't deny herself this pleasure by crumbling to the floor. So I continue, teasing her clit only enough to edge her beautiful soft body, I'm loving more and more each day. Each pound she's been gaining has added to her beauty, because she looks healthier, happier, safer in her own skin, and never did I think that it would stir my cock quite in this way.

Thrusting my tongue in her tight little cunt may just be my new favorite pastime, especially when she bears down on my face seeking more of it.

"Finnigan!" she yells when once again I attack her clit only enough for the flames to lick her skin, but not enough to set her on fire.

"Beg me, Evie darling."

But I only get a broken whimper in response.

"Tell me what you want," I encourage.

"Please..."

"Please what?"

"Please... please make me come."

Music to my fucking ears.

I rise as she cries in frustration, but before the sound finds its end and she rises too, I press my hand to her mouth, pulling her body flush with mine, her back to my front, and reach over to that sensitive bundle of nerves. She's screaming against my hand as I bear down on her clit, then with small circular motions I bring her closer and closer to the roaring fire. My hand on her mouth is a play into her fantasy, not a restriction of her enticing cries, and as her legs begin to shake, her small arms grabbing onto my forearms frantically, I know she loves it. Then I add just a bit more pressure and the minx explodes, delicious whimpers against my palm as her naked flesh shudders against my own.

I let her ride the waves of pleasure, removing my hand from her core when her legs tighten around it, her nerves crying from the sensitivity, but she holds onto me like I'm her lifeline. And Christ, that feels *really* fucking good.

But I'm not done with the minx. When she twists in my arms and jumps me, forcing me to catch her as she wraps her whole body around mine, and straddles my hips, I know she's not done with me either.

I wanna fuck her in this shower, let her body slide onto my cock and take her until there's nothing but our screams keeping this building standing. But Evelyn deserves better than a quick fuck against the cold tiles. She moans my name into my mouth as she kisses me feverishly, and my resolve threatens to break. But I rein it in, kiss her senseless, taking her breath away and replacing it with mine.

The spray of the shower is starting to get in the way of my enjoyment of her, so I walk us out and attempt to put her back down on her feet. But the minx clings to me, refusing to let go, biting my lip and pulling me back in the maddening spell of her lush lips. We're dripping wet, and since I have a feeling she won't let go enough for us to get dry, I prop her ass on the counter and laugh when she yelps at the cold contact. I reach over for the towel hanging on the side, and bring it up to her hair, soaking up the water running down it. She flinches, breaking the kiss, and I want to ask why, but the moment is gone. I'm already moving on to my own hair and she's already distracted.

"Oh..." She presses her pointer finger to her parted lips, gawking down between us.

I don't need to check to know she's looking at my hard cock

pressed between our bodies. I don't want to either, because she is so much more interesting to stare at—her body language, her reaction, her innocent doe eyes beaming with lust.

"You are..." She trails off. "Can I touch you?" she asks, hesitation quieting her voice.

"I might die if you don't."

I think she's gonna swipe a finger over the head or something, but when her small hand wraps around me, the feel of her is almost too much. Hissing, I press a hand against her ass and pull her so hard into me, her back arches, head falling back, and I know her clit has made the perfect contact, because she hitches her hips up, seeking the burning sensation that drives her in that sweet oblivion.

I can't fucking take this anymore.

Throwing the towel on the floor, I bring her off the counter as she tightens her legs around my hips, and carry her straight to my bedroom. I throw her on the bed, giving her no time to breathe before I jump on top of her, caging her in as I slide my knees under her legs, and crush my lips to hers.

Sweet moans fill my mouth as she reaches for my back, pulling me down to her. I let her, because her tight nipples against my skin are heaven on earth, and I'm growing addicted to the sensation of her bare skin against my own.

But I break the kiss before my cock can start making decisions for me.

"Evie, please stop me from doing thi—"

"No," she says it before I even finish the sentence.

"I don't want to hurt you."

"I've already been hurt, Finnigan. You'll be the one to wipe away those memories from my body."

Fuck.

I can't bear the thought of Bartiste having touched her, broken her, and marred her flesh and mind with his filth.

Evelyn Shaw is mine, and I won't allow the memory of another man to ruin her.

When I press my lips to her now, she sighs and mewls into them, feeling the surrender in my touch.

I can't stop myself. I don't want to anymore.

She wraps her legs around my hips, her pretty cunt pressing against my cock, and I know there's no escape for me. The need to be inside of her prevails over my conscience.

I pull away and reach for my nightstand drawer, finding a condom and ripping the packet with my teeth. I keep waiting for the moment she'll scream me off and tell me she's changed her mind, but it never comes. Even as I sit back on my haunches and roll the rubber over my aching cock, her curious gaze roams over my body, but it's the way she gently bites the side of her bottom lip that turns it lustful.

And yet, she still doesn't change her mind.

When I sink two fingers in her aching, tight cunt, just because I find a twisted comfort in the feel of her, she arches her back and presses into me, seeking more.

And still... she doesn't say *no*.

So I lean over her, braced on one arm as I look into her silver eyes exploding in a gold ray in the center, and drag the tip of my cock down the warm seam of her pussy until I reach the spot that makes her tense the most.

"One last chance, Evie darling."

She grabs me by the sides of my neck, demanding my attention as she holds me into her hypnotic gaze.

"I'll take my chance on you. Fuck me, Finnigan!" And on that sultry, breathy voice, her legs tighten around my hips and with a jolt, she presses me into her, urging me to take what she so willingly offers, stunning the hell out of me.

I let go of my reservations, but my eyes threaten to roll into the back of my head at the vice-like tightness of her. As

I groan at the confusing, ridiculous pleasure skirting at the edge of pain, she squeals and stills, nails digging too hard into my back as her whole body goes rigid.

"Evie..." I whisper, my mouth falling open as my mind plays through the myriad of sensations and thoughts.

What the fuck?

I knew she was tight, but this is too much. She's *too* tight.

Her eyes are wide, her breathing quick and shallow, and her mouth fallen open on a silent scream. The shock turns to confusion, then surprise.

Oh my god! My thoughts are catching up to hers.

"Evie darling, I thought... Are you still a virgin?"

CHAPTER 26
Evelyn

*A*M I STILL A VIRGIN?

My mind is reeling, trying to find the answer. None comes because I don't know what the truth is anymore.

Your body knows, Evelyn.

The sharp pain that tore through me is the answer. The harsh flex of my muscles, my straining lungs, the foreign, aching fullness inside of me, they're all answers. If those aren't enough, Finnigan's gaze, growing increasingly more alarmed, is a definite tell.

"I—I didn't think so. I shouldn't be."

I worked hard to keep the faint memories and flashbacks of the two men on top of me at bay. Now, as my body adjusts to the searing burn and the thick length of Finnigan's cock sheathed deep, I question the little memories I do have.

"I presumed they raped me *here*, too," I whisper, the ache straining my voice.

He cocks one eyebrow, the alarmed expressions shifting to a darker, more possessive direction. *"Here... too?"*

"Well, Frankie B started... umm." Damn, having this conversation now, in this position, is a whole other level of awkward. "You know—*behind*."

Finnigan presses his lips together, swallowing hard. "And you don't remember them touching you... here." He's trying his best to be kind and delicate, but he's not managing to control the horror and anger marring his beautiful features. I could pay for a mirror at this moment, so I can see what look is on mine.

"The memories from after they drugged me are in pieces, so I assumed because of the pain I felt for a while after. Now I presume it was just... general area trauma?" I attempt a shrug but stop myself midway at Finnigan's pained shift in his features. I've adjusted to what happened to me, but I don't think he's processed it.

As the burning between my legs eases, the reality sinks in—*I was still a virgin.* They didn't take this away from me.

Eventually, he nods, expression still unsettled, and shifts slightly. With that simple gesture his whole body moves too, and I gasp at the brief stroke inside of me. I flex my walls too, and he frowns, but the strain in his eyebrows isn't annoyance. It's restraint. What was a burn around my entrance turned into a dull ache, but threads of pleasure are weaving themselves through.

Finnigan is my first. *I'm not completely ruined.*

"Finnigan..."

"Yes?"

"Please move."

And he does. Too fast only the tip of his cock remains inside of me, and I realize as he got there that he misunderstood me. I press my heels into his ass, keeping him from leaving me. "No. Move *inside* of me."

"But you—"

"*I* get a second chance," I interrupt. "I'm not ruined… and there's no way I'm stopping this."

"Ruined? Oh, Evie darling. You are goddamn perfect." He leans in, pressing a bruising kiss to my lips, and I'm not sure if the moan vibrating between us is mine or his.

Then he moves, sliding back inside of me until he finds home, pulling pleasure from my nerves, and I feel like my body is mine again.

"Again…" I beg on a breathy voice, and he responds with a deep rumble in his throat that's much hotter than it should really be.

The man delivers, stroking out of me until I miss the fulness of him, then pushes back in. Only, this time he doesn't wait for me to ask for more. He moves with slow, deliberate thrusts that bring a new flurry of sensations to my core. I'm losing myself in the feverish grinding, but Finnigan brings himself down to earth after each stroke, brows drawn together, as his soft gaze fixes on me. Deep emotions darken his irises, and lips tight like he's holding his breath.

"Let go…" I beg him. "I'm okay, Finnigan. Please, I need more." I wrap my hands around his neck, tugging him to me and clinging desperately until his face is buried in the crook of my neck.

The moment his breath sparks over my skin on his deep groan, and his hand tightens around my thigh, I know his concern is easing.

He settles into a quickening rhythm, driven by my mewls and rolling hips, and my core begins to burn all over again. But, my god, this is a good burn.

No.

An incredible one.

He's touching parts of me that never existed before him, and I'm catching fire with every stroke.

"Jesus Christ, Evie, you feel…" He trails off, rising on one arm braced next to me, gaze heated as it seizes mine.

Sighing, he drives harder into me, yet still holding onto a touch of restraint. I want more. I want it harder, faster, harsher. Yet, his care in these moments makes me trust him with my body more than I trust myself with it. So, I relinquish the control, following his lead, and let him take care of me.

"I feel…?" I urge him to continue.

His hips jerk, and goosebumps spread over my skin at the rush of lightning ripping through my core as a moan fills the air.

"You feel like a dream that should have never come true."

With harsh jerks of his hips, he punctuates the heart-shattering confession, his cock deliciously snug inside of me driving maddening pleasure through my nerves. His movements are more powerful, my body hitching up on the bed, and I brace myself with one hand against the padded headboard.

"Oh god, Finnigan… Yes!" I hold onto the back of his neck with my other hand, anchoring myself as his hips roll in long, hard strokes that threaten to become wilder.

But the threat only lingers, and I'm climbing this mountain of ecstasy, at an excruciatingly steady pace, the pleasure coiling in my core growing stronger.

"More," I demand, choosing to forget about relinquishing that control to him, and slam my hips up to meet his thrust. A hint of discomfort lingers, but I ignore it. I've had my share of pain, and I'm feeding on the control I have over this one. It's finally on my terms.

"You like that, Evie darling?" *Thrust.* "You like my cock filling that sweet"—thrust—"tight pussy of yours?" *Thrust.*

Damn his dirty, dirty mouth.

"I'm not sure *you* do. Do you like filling my pussy, Finnigan? Slick walls strangling your cock? Because you seem... *restrained.*" I tease him, challenging his resolve.

"Jesus fuck, Evelyn!" the man growls my name like he's about to devour me whole, the brightness of his eyes smoldering with darkness, "I don't deserve you, but I'm going to keep you anyway."

And then he breaks.

Walls of restraint crumble to the edges of us and there is nothing more keeping us apart, holding us back.

He pulls back on his haunches, grabs my legs, and pins them on his shoulders, slipping his cock out of me in the process. I never thought this type of loss could make me cry out, but it does. He rewards me with a devastating smirk as he holds my legs with one arm, tight against his chest, and lifts me to slide a pillow under my ass. I'm confused, but then he slides his knees to the sides and just like that, we align perfectly. With the other hand he guides his cock back at my entrance and I bite my lip as my walls constrict, begging to be stretched.

The bastard teases me though, rubbing the smooth head up and down through my folds, and when he presses it against my sensitive clit, my back arches on a soft whimper. He picks that moment to thrust back into me, and I think I finally understand what a religious experience is, because this sure as hell feels like one. I reach up, bracing against the headboard just as this devil of a man presses his free hand on my belly. My gaze flies to him, mouth wide on a silent cry as his cock prods against a part of me that threatens to drive me up the walls.

"Finnigan…" I whisper, though it sounds more like I'm praying to him.

"I got you, Evie darling."

And boy, does he.

He glides into me with long, powerful strokes, punctuating each one with a jerk of his hips as his hand presses on my lower belly. He's molten lava inside my core, a blazing ecstasy pushing me deeper into this world where only pleasure exists. We find a maddening rhythm, the shape of him fitting so perfectly around mine, and my heart hurts that we fit together so well. That we will not experience this beautiful collision if I leave.

Those thoughts are drowned by the song of whimpers, growls, and heavy breaths we compose. We lace it with lust that grows stronger. Quicker. Louder. That song vibrates through my flesh, settling in that aching spot inside my core that Finnigan rubs against with each endearingly punishing stroke.

"I can't hold myself back, Evie. You're so—fuck! You're everything."

I cry out when his words land low in my belly, a quake shattering through my core. Even as his tone bears accusations, blame, but I'm not sure if it's for me or him. His eyes though… his eyes are an explosive blaze of need. A primal desire that demands so much more than my pleasure. It wants my soul.

You're everything…

The hunger in his words scrapes against my heart, leaving me breathless with fear.

I don't get a chance to dwell on the feeling when Finnigan's thumb bears down on the aching bundle of nerves at the apex of my folds. He circles it with such deliberate movements, adding just the right amount of pressure for my back to arch, and my legs squeeze around his head. Or neck.

I may be suffocating the man, but as long as he fucks me like this through the loss of air, I'm okay with it.

"Oh, Finn—my God, Finnigan I think—" I cry out and cover my mouth with my forearm, biting down.

The roaring ecstasy doesn't come out of nowhere. It blooms deep in my belly, spreading like silk threads weaved with electric fire all through my body. It's an omen of pleasure curling my toes and locking my arched back, and that blaze detonates around his thick, rigid length with such viciousness, stars dance in my vision. The waves of euphoria roll me deeper in this trance where nothing but pleasure and Finnigan exist, his hands stroking my body, his cock jerking violently, turning into molten lava inside my own warmth, his enticing grunts of pleasure... my name on his lips like a chant for more. For everything.

This is it. The culmination of all those aching dreams that made the nightmares harder to remember.

I find my voice again, panting like a wanton whore as my shaking legs fall around him just as he drops on top of my body, caging me in under his satisfying weight. I wrap my arms around him, unwilling to let go of this moment, and hold him as close to me as I can, pushing back the need to crawl under his skin and feed my obsession for this man. He doesn't protest one bit, but peppers soft pecks on my forehead, my temples, the apples of my cheeks.

The intimacy of this moment bears promises of all we're not allowing ourselves to hope for.

It doesn't feel like a beginning, but an end. The end of what we were separately, who we were alone, and what our souls were missing.

IN MY TWENTY-NINE years, I've learned a thing or two about sex. Yet, I've learned nothing about what just happened between Evie and me.

How could I? It's not something I've ever experienced before. This was not sex; this was a collision of two smoldering souls begging for each other.

It truly was *everything*.

And I'm utterly terrified.

"Thank you..."

I pull back when those soft, breathless words tickle my shoulder.

"Did you just thank me?" I bite down the chuckle that would probably ruin this moment.

I can't see the shade of her skin in this dim light, but her little nod makes me wonder if her cheeks are reddening.

"For… sex?" I ask, eyes widening in slight bewilderment.

"For not stopping."

Oh, that makes more sense. "I should have…" Sighing, I lower myself, brushing the tip of my nose against hers, before I trace down her cheeks, around the curve of her jaw, then the slope of her neck.

The satisfied, feather of a gasp she exhales threatens to get me hard all over again. Not that my cock is particularly soft right now. I'm also reluctant to pull out when I found home inside of her. God save me if I'll ever have her wrapped around me without a condom. She'll ruin me. I crave the real feel of her without the barrier, though, I should be thankful for it, because I'm sure I would have blown my load in half a minute without the latex separating us.

I shift up to meet her eyes, and she tightens her grip around me. This time around I do chuckle, and when she attempts to protest my reaction, I press my lips to her swollen ones. Her hold eases and I begin to rise again, breaking the kiss.

"No… don't leave me," she pleads, her voice throaty and low, drunk on pleasure.

"I have to take care of you."

"Leaving me defeats that purpose," she argues.

"Hell, it's hard to argue with that. But you need something else right now."

Before she can protest further, I pull out of her and rise, taking care of the condom when I get in the bathroom. I make quick work of cleaning myself, then soak a clean washcloth under the spray.

"Give me a sec." She slides out of bed on shaky legs, and disappears in the bathroom for less than a minute, before she comes back and lays back down.

"It's going to be cold," I warn Evelyn as I lower myself

back onto the bed and give her a few seconds to acknowledge my words before I press the thick cotton onto her. She gasps but doesn't move.

"Alexa, bedroom lights set to soft," I order the speaker, and after she confirms, the two bedside lamps turn on to a very dim, warm light.

"Oh, you can control your lights?" There's such an innocent wonder in her tone as she looks around.

"Yes, it's a voice assistant and speaker. There, on the dresser." I point. "You can ask it all sorts of things."

"I heard of these, but never had the opportunity to try one."

I want to say something to that, but what can I? They've been around for quite a while now, but she's been living in her car or shoddy motels. Not exactly the place for what I now consider basic technology. I turn my attention to her, her swollen pussy looking fucking delectable before me. But now's not the time to feast. I wipe slowly, then fold the cloth to an unused part and press it to her, holding it there as I look up into her eyes.

I fight back a flinch when I'm met with her intense gaze. Jesus fuck, she's beautiful. In this dim light her wild hair in that deep violet looks ethereal, her lips are deliciously swollen, and now I can definitely see a flush on her cheeks.

"Do all men do this to their... umm, after sex."

She corrected herself. To their *what?* Fuck friends? Partners? Girlfriends? What exactly are we?

"I really hope so," I answer, though I feel like an asshole instantly because I haven't done this nearly as often as I should have. But then again, none of the women I've been with were virgins. *Or Evelyn.* "How does it feel?"

She nods and lies back down, making me miss the eye contact. "A bit sore, but good." She says before she lets out a soft sigh. "Really good."

Oh, Christ.

I have to work hard to remind myself that it would be wrong to sink into her again so soon. Even if I only use my tongue or my fingers. I rise and lie next to her before I can convince myself that it would be a good idea, but I make sure to hold the cloth to her.

"No pain?" I ask.

She shakes her head, turning to me, and graces me with those stunning eyes again. Even dark as they are in this dim light, they still work well to shatter my resolve.

"I'm finding it hard to keep my hands off of you right now, Evie darling."

"Then don't." She reaches down, pulls the washcloth from my hand and throws it onto the floor as she turns on her side.

She doesn't hesitate one bit when she throws her leg over my waist, her heel pressing on my ass as she wraps her body around mine. When her small hand brushes the hair from my face, and her breasts press onto my chest, I give in. I grab her ass, loving how my hand covers so much of that plump cheek, and flip onto my back bringing her on top of me.

She yelps then giggles, and I realize that's the sound I want to die hearing. That soft giggle that sounds like birdsong on a lazy autumn day is my death song, and I would slowly drown myself right now so I can hear it on a maddening loop.

Like this, straddling me, she's more sinful than my dominance could ever make her.

She tightens her legs against my hips, and her pussy finds the length of my cock at the same moment her tits brush against my chest, and she crushes her lips against mine. The tips of her bob-cut hair tickle the sides of my face, and I can't help but dig my fingers into her flesh, pushing my ass up so I can press myself against her warm, soft cunt. I drag my other hand up her back, holding her in a possessive grip as she slowly grinds against me, moaning into my mouth as she rolls her tongue around mine.

Her hands are in my hair, tugging at the curls like she's guiding me into the motions she needs me in, and with her soft body rubbing against mine, her pussy getting wetter by the second as it rolls against my cock, I realize that I've never known this type of intimacy. I've done plenty of sexual things, I've explored kinks and even experienced light play in Metamorphosis, Morrigan and Lulu's fetish club. But this feels different. Soft yet intense. Slow yet feverish, and the lack of penetration isn't tainting the moment. Quite the opposite, actually.

She strokes her tongue against mine, pulling away only so she can nip my lips before she dives back in, and my strokes on her back are turning desperate. The feel of her skin is addictive, the warmth, the goosebumps flaring when I touch her waist, it's all so intense. I grab onto the back of her neck, holding her to me as our tongues tangle and the urgency of the kiss grows.

There used to be a line separating Evelyn and I... mere days ago. Now, I can't even distinguish where I end and she begins. I don't want to. Ever again.

Evelyn Shaw is—

"Mine," I growl into her mouth, biting her lower lip before soothing it with my tongue, and dive back into the kiss.

That single word melts her body against mine, and the slickness of her pussy drenching my cock threatens to drive me down a path of madness.

Over and over, we kiss and grind against each other, falling in a beautifully brutal rhythm as we make up a song of mewls and groans. I thrust my hips up as I hold her ass down, and she cries out, throwing her head back. We'll have to do something about that loud mouth of hers when Maya returns, but for now... I want more. I thrust up again, rubbing my length between her wet folds and she meets it with a stroke of her hips, shuddering as she falls back against me. I would call it dry-humping, but there is nothing dry about the drenched seam of Evelyn's pussy.

I run my hand down the length of her spine before returning to the back of her neck, then thread my fingers in her hair, fisting it.

Evelyn yelps, terror breaking that sound as she slaps frantically at my arm and rips her body away from mine. It happens in two seconds flat and I'm too slow and stunned to catch her when she jumps off, cowering as she backs away to the foot of the bed, before she drops off of it.

"Evelyn, darling, I'm sorry I didn't mean to—" The rest of the words catch in my throat when I rise to my knees and see her sitting on the floor.

With knees drawn to her chest, her body shakes uncontrollably as she rakes her fingers through her hair in frantic, trembling motions. Her gaze is unfocused, brows drawn together, and pain weaves with fear on her features.

I drop to my knees on the floor, sliding close to her, careful to not freak her out. "It's okay. It's me, Evie darling, you know I won't hurt you."

She nods with agitated movements, like she knows it to be true, but her body and mind can't fully grasp the truth in the words. She still doesn't look at me, or stop the frenzied combing of her hair.

"You're safe. No one in this life or the next will ever touch you, will ever catch you, will ever hurt you. You belong to yourself and yourself only."

She blinks rapidly, the only indication that those words landed somewhere where she understood them.

I bring myself closer to her, in touching distance, but I don't reach for her.

"Was it the hair?" I ask.

Her movements slow, and I notice the tears brimming her eyes some already streaking down her cheeks. Fury fills me for the men who did this to her, who taught her how to fear, who showed her what pain is. But now is not the time to add to the revenge plot I've been planning for a while. They will pay in blood, and I'll surely make even The Carver himself proud.

Until then... "Can I touch your arm?"

She nods, the gesture still strained with the shuddering of her body. I reach for her upper arm, stroking slowly up and down. She's cold. Like we never even touched for the last hour.

"I'm going to come closer, and hold you to me, okay?"

She takes a few seconds longer to respond now, but then she nods again. I slide closer, but turn my back to the bed, and lean over, wrapping my arms around her. She's stiff even through the shaking but doesn't pull away. So I gather her closer and when she doesn't protest I slide my arm under her knees and lift her to my lap, holding her against my chest as I lean against the bed. With slow, soothing motions I stroke her arm and back, and as her body relaxes, her breathing sounds louder.

I don't speak for a long time because no words should force this situation. I'll be what she needs—warmth, safety, a shoulder to cry on. I'll be anything she wants me to for however long she needs me. I never had the chance the last time I could have been needed like this, when Hanna was dying on that cold concrete floor, and I was there too late. This is it, my second chance. I will not fuck this up.

Her body has softened, her shaking stops, and even her breathing has leveled. But she stays on my lap, sinking just a little deeper into me with every minute that passes.

"I'm sorry…" she whispers.

"Don't you dare apologize for this." I think my tone came through a bit too harsh.

She nods against my shoulder anyway.

"It was the hair," she confirms.

"Can I ask why?"

She breathes in deeply and swallows it before she answers. "It's how they caught me. How they held me, controlled me. It was used against me… viciously. I should have told you I have a thing for…"

"I know now, don't worry. I will never do it again."

She shifts and raises her head to meet my eyes. "Maybe someday," she whispers, sweet hope in her voice.

I smile, because how could I not. She's the strongest person I know, because surviving and moving on with life after what she experienced could break most people.

"Maybe, but only if you do it for yourself, not me. Not anyone else."

She nods, then looks down, a tinge of embarrassment curling her eyebrows.

A thought crosses my mind.

"Is this why you cut your hair?" I ask.

She nods but doesn't meet my eyes this time around. Instead, she lays her head back down on my shoulder, and settles more comfortably into me.

"I would have chopped it all off if I didn't hate short hair on me. This bob haircut felt like a good medium… even if someone caught it, it would be harder to hold it for long, since it can't be wrapped around a fist."

Heat fills my chest and uncomfortable tension pulls at my temples. What a fucked up world we live in where women have to change their bodies to protect themselves. Me and my Sanctum aren't saints, but we understand the sanctity of innocent life.

Which is another reason I shouldn't keep Evelyn. She deserves the simple, calm life, deep in the suburbs with a white picket fence, and cupcakes baking in the oven. Not this, not steeped in crime and constant weariness. We may not deal in human life, but we blackmail, we launder money, we murder. So much murder. We aren't much better, and she deserves better.

"I'm sorry you had to do this to find comfort. Safety."

"It's okay. I love it with this color. I never had the opportunity before, but now... I can finally express myself. Though, the cut was actually Maddox's idea."

Somehow, I'm not surprised it was. After all, he keeps his hair buzz cut for a reason.

"It suits you. Color and all. The clothes too. Of course, you look like a goddamn wet dream in leather trousers, but beyond that, you look like yourself."

She giggles and I swear the sound is music to my fucking ears. She's gonna be okay. I finally breathe easier, I didn't realize how tense my body actually was.

"Thank you," she says. "This has always been the style I've been attracted to. It's quite a privilege to be able to dress like this now. Someday I will have a house lathered in dark walls, maximalist corners drenched in gold frames, plants, and weird art, and a deep-emerald kitchen."

"Really? Is that your dream?"

"Well... actually my dream is to open a bakery."

I pull her away enough for her to see me properly. "That shouldn't be a dream, Evie darling, that should be a plan. You would have Queenscove at your feet with your indulgent cakes."

I catch the soft blush heating her cheeks as she averts her

gaze for a moment.

"Thank you. But I'm not sure anyone would actually want my cakes. You see, sunshine and butterflies are not what I like to make."

Well, now I'm intrigued. "What do you like?"

"For lack of a better term, I'd love to own a Gothic bakery. Deep gemstone colors for frostings and icing, intricate designs, anything from lace-work to anatomical hearts and skulls. Of course they can be cute, but... a different kind of cute."

I smile, having absolutely no trouble imagining what a fantastic job she would do. I saw her cake, she might have kept it classic, but her technique looked flawless. Even for my untrained eye. "Your kind of cute," I agree.

"I guess so."

"How about we get back into bed, and you can tell me more about it?"

She beams then, her smile wide, her eyes filled with excitement. I have never seen this look in her gaze before. Like she finally has permission to think and dream for herself, though the limitation is self-imposed. It's intoxicating and infuriating at the same time. She deserves the fucking world, and she deserves to live all her dreams, not avoid conjuring them.

I pull her up with me, settle ourselves in bed, and nestle her in the crook of my arm, so she can share all her dreams with me.

CHAPTER 28
Finnigan

WAKE UP TO AN EMPTY bed and a sweet, aromatic scent weaving around through the penthouse, pulling a groan out of me and a growl from my stomach.

I wonder what she baked now.

We stayed up too late as we talked about her bakery dream with a dark, gothic twist, her ideas for the interior, the designs she's been conjuring for years, the flavor combinations that intrigued even me. I was bound to wake up hungry. Though I never crave particular foods, yet now I *need* whatever's cooking in my kitchen.

Rising, I head straight to the walk-in closet to grab a pair of boxers, and stumble around as I slide them up on my way to the kitchen. The scent makes my mouth water, but as Evelyn finally comes into view, it seems to turn bone dry. She's on her bare tiptoes as she sways between the counter and the island on a rock song set on low volume, long, lean legs in full view, and I swallow a curse when my gaze is interrupted by the hem of a long T-shirt that covers her ass and everything above. She used to be concernedly skinny when we brought her to us, but now... there's some meat on her bones, and thanks to Maddox's help, some muscle too. She's still skinny, but Christ, health has never looked so good on a woman.

She glides around my kitchen on the rhythm of the hard guitar strings and the flow of the wind-swept curtains of the open terrace doors, and she looks divinely at home as she pours some dark batter in a baking tin I didn't know I had. George buys all sorts of things when he does his chef duties in my kitchen. Maybe I should actually search these cupboards to see what else I have. *What else Evelyn needs, too.*

I lean against the door frame, crossing my arms against my chest, and watch her. Slender, long fingers wipe the rim of the bowl as she moves further down the tray, and I suck in a groan as she sticks that very finger in her mouth, sucking slowly at it while she keeps pouring that batter. It's not a stretch to imagine something else between those pretty pink lips of hers. She can cover my cock in whatever she wants as long as she sucks on it just like that.

Seemingly satisfied, she grabs the tray and taps it a few times against the counter, before she turns to the oven, drops the door and slides it right in. She doesn't even notice me when she turns after closing the door, taps something on her phone, then goes back to the counter, picking up the same bowl. When she dips in again and swipes at the sides, I suck in a breath, because I know what's about to come. That finger slides between her plump lips, but this time she closes her eyes and the softest of sighs turns my cock so rigid, it almost fucking hurts.

Raking a hand over my face I wonder how long until this woman's going to kill me just by being her own, enticing little self. When she's about to suck on that batter-coated finger again, some of it drips on her chest, staining the T-shirt.

Wait, that's my T-shirt.

Just like that, she turned even hotter, if that was even a possibility.

"Oh no!" She drops the bowl and turns frantically to the sink. "Evelyn, what have you done? You klutz!" She rants at herself as she finds the sponge and attempts to clean it.

I'm behind her in fewer strides than I thought I needed, and when I grab onto the hem of the T-shirt, she jumps, yelping, but I give her no time to protest or fight. I pull it up, forcing it over her head, leaving her arms trapped in it, then I turn her around to face me, grabbing onto the sides of her head.

"Finnigan," she says on a breathy tone that sounds more lustful than startled. "I'm sorry, I—"

But my mouth is crushing hers before she can finish the sentence, her intoxicating ginger and brown sugar scent luring me to dive between her soft lips. I'm careful not to thread my fingers through her hair as I tip her head back, holding her just where I want her, deepening the kiss. A rumble of desire shakes my chest and vibrates straight through hers, drawing a soft cry to fall from her lips, and I swallow those muffled sound-waves like they're the life-force keeping me alive. They might as well do, because the life I used to live before her is done and dusted. Even before I felt her against me, tasted her, swallowed her moans, she tainted my existence with her energy.

There is no going back for me, I'm falling deep into her, and I fear that, once again, I'll be abandoned with a heart I can't put back together myself.

I shake those thoughts away because ignorance truly is

bliss, and I release Evelyn so I can pull the T-shirt off of her completely, and bare her naked body to me. Reaching behind her, I turn the tap off, then dip down, and lift her to me. She yelps, but it turns into a giggle as she wraps her legs around my hips, and I walk us to the kitchen island. When her bare behind touches the cold granite, she hisses, I lock my lips onto the crook of her neck, sucking softly at the skin there, and it melts into a feverish cry. Her head falls back, arms settling behind her as she props herself up, and I lick my way down to her breasts, circling one nipple with my tongue, and rewarding it with a soft bite when it hardens to a peak.

Back arching, she pushes her breast against my mouth demanding more attention, and I move to the other one, refusing to leave it waiting for too long. When she moans and sinks her fingers into my hair, all but forcing me where she wants me, I know I'm going to have my hands full. Evelyn might have been a virgin last night, but the way she demands pleasure without speaking a word tells me that she's a greedy little slut in the making, one who has far too many unfulfilled desires that have been piling on for long enough.

But this is my feast, not hers, and I decide what I devour.

A clinking noise sounds as she shifts, and I break away from her enticing skin as it dawns on me that I didn't make sure there aren't any knives sitting on the counter. All I find is a spoon sitting next to a great big bowl. A different one than the one she was licking earlier. Curious, I take a peek.

"Is this icing?"

"Frosting," she corrects on a strained whisper.

"There's a difference?"

She nods, raising an eyebrow as one corner of her lips quirks, her chest rising and falling with heaving breaths, her cheeks deliciously flushed. After the discussion we had last night, I'm intrigued. I swipe my pinkie through the soft, creamy *frosting*, and dip it in my mouth. The dark purple color that matches her hair so well made me think it was going to be sickly sweet, but there's a delicious sourness to it, and I'm compelled to hum in approval. Evelyn's brows furrow with a wanton gaze as she bites into her lower lip.

"What gets you off, Evie darling? Is it me sucking on my finger, or the fact that I'm moaning at the taste of your frosting."

Her brows straighten, as if she only just realized she was lusting over me.

"Come on, don't be shy," I insist.

"Maybe both."

"Maybe? Let's test and find out."

Her doe eyes widen and lips part, but she stays silent. Waiting curiously.

I dip my index finger in the bowl, and suck on it again, this time slower, my eyes fixed on the not-so-innocent-anymore vixen before me. She watches every movement with hawk eyes, and I'm oddly turned on. Not because I'm sucking on my own fucking finger, but because she looks at me like that. Like she could devour me whole, just as I would her. And isn't that just goddamn beautiful?

Returning to the bowl, I pick up more frosting this time, and I go for my mouth slowly, watching how her lips part with the same speed. Only, this time around I drop the cream, letting it fall right on her belly, just above the navel. She gasps and reaches for it, but just as it touches the sweetness, I grab her hand and bring it to my mouth. I lick her finger clean before I place her palm back behind her, then dip down, swiping my tongue over her skin, licking her clean. A soft mewl flexes her belly, and I realize this taste is becoming addictive. Mostly because it pulls those needy sounds out of her.

I grab more frosting, and smear it in a clean line from her navel to the trimmed curls between her legs. Goosebumps spread all over her flesh as she quivers, and there's something addictively beautiful about that. A sort of innocence bread from discovery and I'm going to enjoy helping her find out what makes her wet. I bet she's getting real wet right now. Just as beautiful is the contrast of this dark, violet frosting against her light olive skin. Then again, Evelyn makes everything look beautiful.

When my tongue touches her skin once more, she blatantly moans, her head dropping back as I lick the cream off of her belly, sucking the sensitive flesh.

"I want more." I groan just as I grip her waist, bring her down to her feet, and turn her around, her back to my front.

She doesn't get a chance to lean into me as I press my hand to the middle of her back and bend her over the kitchen island. With a yelp she tries to protest, but I hold her down with one hand and bring the bowl of frosting closer with the other.

"Be a good girl, Evelyn"—I give her right cheek a quick smack, grinning when she yips in shock—"and I might just make you come."

"But I—"

Her protest earns her another slap on the other cheek, and this time her little cry sounds charged. It's not pain twisting on the notes, but something much more carnal. I kick her feet apart, and take half a step back to admire the woman I claimed as mine.

"Fuck me, you have such a pretty cunt." I shake my head, because it should be a crime for that dark-pink slit to look so unbelievably tempting.

Dipping two fingers in the frosting bowl, I scoop a fair amount of it, and she twitches when the cream touches the hood of her clit. When I drag those digits up the seam of her pussy and don't stop when I reach its end, she whips her head around, eyes locking onto mine. I say nothing as I grab the spoon and scoop up more of that cream, holding eye contact with her as I continue spreading it, brushing it over that tight, puckered hole, then up to the top of her ass.

She follows me with her gaze as I dip on one knee, and when I wrap my hands around the tops of her thighs, pulling them apart to better expose her to me, her muscles tense. But then I swipe my tongue over her now even sweeter clit, sucking at that nerve center with newfound fever. Evelyn's head falls against the countertop on a deep sigh, and I lick her slowly, from that sensitive bundle of nerves, through the seam of her delectable pussy, reveling in her shudder and slight yelp as I pass over the tight hole beyond it, and up to the top of her ass.

"This feels... dirty," she says in a throaty voice.

"And yet look how beautifully your flesh trembles when my tongue worships you." Pressing my mouth against her folds, I suck at the sweetness lathered there as she yelps at the contact. "How perfect this frosting looks against your soft skin." I drag my tongue over her ass, insisting on the tight muscle that contracts at the contact. "How responsive even the dirtiest parts of you are to me." I lick between her cheeks, sucking and cleaning every single part of her covered in that tangy sweetness. "I think you like *dirty*. Don't you, Evie darling?"

A soft whimper escapes her throat when I bring my mouth back to her needy clit, rolling the bundle between my tongue and lips as her legs shake ever so gently. I part her with my thumbs, exposing the pink, wet flesh to me and hold her like that for a moment longer, enjoying the magnificent view of her opening gripping on nothing but air. Blowing over the sensitive flesh, I pull a soft groan out of her, but it turns feral when I dive my tongue inside that delicious pussy I made mine mere hours ago. It's only ever been mine, and that thought fills me with a possessiveness I never thought I could feel. I roll my tongue against her walls, fucking her like I'm starving for her essence, and I know just how dirty my sweet Evelyn is when she thrusts into my face, taking what she deserves.

"Oh, Finnigan!"

I want to encourage her, tell her to take everything she needs from me, but she's settling into a rhythm I don't want to disrupt. Not until she comes all over my tongue and face.

So I release one cheek as I keep thrusting into her needy pussy, and bring my other hand to the sensitive bundle of nerves that must be missing the attention. The moment I press the tips of two digits on the hood of it, she cries out and bears down onto my face, rubbing herself against me.

"That's it! Oh my god, Finn, oh my god! I'm going—I'm going to—" But all that comes out next is a lust-tainted scream as her legs shudder, and she gushes her sweet flavor all over my tongue and chin.

She's not exactly a squirter, but feeling how unbelievably wet she gets, I think I could get her there. I hold her up as wave after intense wave of pleasure rolls through her nerves, her pussy spasming around my tongue, and I realize that somehow... I'm still hungry.

I want more.

I *need* more of her.

Something about Evelyn Shaw draws forth addiction.

And I realize that I'll happily turn into a junkie for her.

Evelyn

MY LEGS ARE STILL SHAKING by the time Finnigan rises, and when I attempt to peel myself off the kitchen island, he has to catch me, because apparently I can't stand anymore. I can't believe he spread frosting between my ass cheeks and licked me clean. The thought brings a fresh wave of heat to my cheeks.

"That was definitely in violation of some health codes." I snicker as I turn to him.

He laughs in response, filling the space with such casual joy, and Christ, I don't think I've ever seen anything as beautiful. His smile is devastating, but laughter turns this man into a god.

"We'll be more careful when we'll be in your bakery," he says with a wide grin on his lips, and pulls me into a deep kiss like what he just said didn't just shake my entire world and threw it off its axis.

Not only did he imply a future between us two, but my bakery dream isn't an *if* for him, but a *when*. Yes, I opened up to him last night and talked about my dreams, and yes, he did insist on me not calling it a *dream* any longer, but I don't know… I guess I just thought he was indulging me after my panic attack. Or because we just had sex.

But his casual words now don't sound like he was simply indulging me.

I really want to say something, but I'm just going to ruin this amazing bubble we're in right now. I'm not ready to screw it up just yet.

"Now," he starts as he breaks the kiss. "Are you going to tell me why you're baking at this crazy time?"

"It's almost ten a.m.," I say, snickering.

"Is it?! Shit, I don't remember the last time I slept in." He looks around the kitchen, noticing the finished batch of cupcakes cooling on the side. "I hope one of those is mine."

"Yes. They're for all of us. Annika texted me this morning to tell me that they've decided to celebrate Aaro's birthday early, since everyone is here. Plus it would be a nice distraction before the craziness starts. I'm baking these to take over there because the little guy apparently doesn't want cake, he wants cupcakes."

"Oh, so we're doing this today?" he asks.

I nod. "Around lunchtime or just after. Either way, we're supposed to go there for lunch."

"I guess we need to buy a present."

"We?" This time I don't hold back, because there he goes again, using a word that implies so much more about *us*.

"Yes. I'll happily buy something from the three of us. Though, you better ask Maya what she would like to get for her little *boyfriend*."

"Excuse me?!" I squeal, grabbing onto his strong biceps and hold him at arm's length. "My sister does not have a boyfriend. She's just a kid!"

But the pretty, blonde asshole just laughs, shaking his

head like I'm being silly.

"I'm serious!" I slap at his shoulder.

"Oh, fuck. Evie darling, come on..."

I give him the most menacing look I can muster in this situation, but he just curls his lips inwards, suppressing more of his amusement.

"You can decide for us two. But Aaro is *not* her boyfriend," I say once more. Though, I must admit, even I don't believe it. Doesn't mean I have to like it.

"Okay. I'll send someone to get the gifts." He pulls out his phone and starts typing.

"We're not going?"

"There's no need. I'll send someone now, and by the time we're ready, they'll bring them to us," he explains.

"But I could go buy the presents myself."

"Out of discussion." He protests before I even finish the sentence. "You know very well you're a target now. Until Bartiste and his organization are crushed, we cannot risk you being out of our sight. I know it sucks, but you have to bear it for a little longer."

I really do want to argue, but this is a stupid hill to die on and he has a point—there's a target on me. Even so, I don't trust Frankie not to follow and *claim* me for himself like apparently, he wishes to do. A shudder rips through me and Finn's expression darkens in response.

"They won't get to you, Evelyn. They will all be dead soon enough, and I'll make sure it's not going to be pretty." He grips my chin between his thumb and forefinger and brings me in for a peck that's much sweeter than it should be from a man of his reputation.

He's a playboy, what is he doing making these kinds of promises to a formerly homeless woman?

"You're so unbothered by talks of gruesome murder." Of

course I had nothing smarter to say, Jesus Christ.

Though, I don't seem to be that bothered about it either. I shouldn't be that surprised that my moral compass is so off center. Not after what I've done.

His fingers on my chin tighten, pulling me away from that dark memory.

"You want me to pretend you're some naive bimbo who doesn't understand the world she found herself in? You know what we are, Evelyn, what we do, but I'll sugarcoat it for you in the future if it will make you feel better. However, it doesn't change the fact that for what they've done to you, Bartiste and Frankie will pay in pounds of flesh, and I'll make sure their deaths are slow, excruciating."

CHAPTER 29
Evelyn

AM I REALLY THAT DIFFERENT from the *bimbos* he's usually with? After all, I lusted for him, wore him down until he slept with me. Surely I don't stand out in that sea of faceless, nameless women.

Yet here I am, listening to his violent words and promises of death like the man is making some sweet, grand gesture I should be swooning over. Who am I kidding? I am swooning over them.

"They've done so much more to so many others. Why take revenge for me?" I blurt out without thinking as he releases my chin.

He frowns, cocking his head. "Because it's you here, standing in my kitchen after sleeping in my bed. It's your taste on my tongue, it's the memory of my cock in your pretty pussy."

"There were countless others before me. Here. In this kitchen."

His hand is on my throat in a flash, the tips of his fingers reaching the back of my neck, he uses his thumb to tilt my head up so I can meet his eyes. The touch is gentle, but so possessive.

"The women who have crossed this threshold, in the last few years, haven't stayed past a few hours. Most have never seen this kitchen. None have slept here. You, Evie darling, are the one and only."

He lets those words linger in the air, their soundless echo licking my skin and penetrating my soul with devastating effect.

The one and only...

I want to ask him why. Demand an explanation. Beg him to make sense of this, because... *why?* Why, damn it? Tension builds between my brows, threatening to turn into a headache. Maybe that pain can make sense of this man, because he's certainly not explaining himself. I don't care why other women haven't been here, I want to know why I am.

But, how can I ask him such a question when the answer might influence my decision about Queenscove and my future? I cannot base my decision on this man. Asking him about it could break us both.

That question, though, lingers on the tip of my tongue and makes my lips tremble. Finnigan notices, too. He waits. And waits, watching my parted lips with a soft frown between his dark blonde brows. But those bright blue eyes of his carry so much danger, because I swear there's a tinge of hope sparkling in their depths.

"Ask me."

I gasp at his words, but don't speak.

I can't.

"Ask me, Evelyn," he demands, tone darker.

I press my lips together instead, attempting to shake my head, but his grip allows only slight movement.

Finnigan sighs and drops his hand. "Remember when you accused me of being a coward?"

"It's not the same," I snap back.

"Isn't it?"

"This is not just about me."

"*You* came after me, Evelyn. *You* insisted even as I kept repeating that crossing this line is a mistake. *You* pushed. What the fuck did you think would happen once we got here?"

"I..." I don't know.

Maybe I didn't think this far. Because I had it in my mind that Finnigan was different. The perpetual playboy who doesn't get attached.

You lie, Evelyn.

Maybe I thought that at first, but it's not what kept me here, still interested. It was hope that he was the exact opposite of that beneath his charmingly slutty exterior.

"*You* what? Was this all just a game to you?" he asks with both anger and a tinge of disappointment in his tone, and the sound cracks a part of me, making me feel like a terrible person.

"No, it wasn't a game." There's little confidence in my voice.

"Then? What did you expect to find once we came together? What do you want from me, Evelyn? And don't you dare tell me you just wanted to fuck me, because I refuse to believe *you* are the type."

"Maybe you overestimated me," I fight back because there is no way I can get into this now.

I have no answer for him. There is one, weighing my soul deep down, but I can't even acknowledge it for myself.

"Maybe I did."

His words crash down on me, and I swallow the bitter

emotions they bring, but I can't hide away from the impact. It's right here, staring at me with sharp eyes, challenging me, and what scares me more is the trace of desire to retreat that gazes back. I'm doing this, I'm responsible for pulling him out of his shell, just to push him back down again.

But this is not all on me. It can't be. He wanted me gone not that long ago, so I'm just giving him what he wanted.

"Staying in Queenscove was never a permanent arrangement, I just needed time. You know this. After all, you wanted to *help me* leave." There's a clear bite in my tone. It wasn't help he was offering—he was paying me off.

Finnigan narrows his brows, crossing his arms against his chest, and takes a step back. "So that's it then? You decided?"

I stand by the kitchen island, suppressing the need to wrap my arms around myself. "Not yet. There are still things I need to sort first."

"Well, hopefully you'll decide to share with me when you make a fucking decision."

"Why are you acting like you tell me everything, and I'm the bad one who hides stuff from you, Finnigan?"

"What's that supposed to mean?"

"I know I can't be the only one who spent the night. I know that the revenge on Bartiste is not just about what they've done to me! Annika's *friend*, right? That's all she was…" Though I'm sure of the words, they don't taste as good as I thought they would when I speak them. Now, they feel like a low blow.

His arms drop to the sides, his gaze filling with something akin to dismay.

"Since then, Evelyn. Since then there has been no one else. And even then…" He trails off, but those words turn my stomach into a flutter of wings.

"Even then… what?" I ask in a whisper.

He shakes his head and looks away, sighing. "I'm gonna go dress. Be ready in forty minutes." And just like that, he turns to leave.

"No!" I snap back loud enough that his steps stall.

One by one the thick muscles of his back flex and seem to expand, his stance menacingly stern and somehow wider. I urge myself to continue, because if I don't speak now, I might not be able to once he turns around.

"Maybe I've been insisting exactly because of this! I know you want me, I know you like me. You've constantly pushed me away for no rational reason!" That came out much louder than I thought it would, but damn it, I'm pissed.

"Morality, Evelyn!" he shouts as he whips around, drawing his fingers through his hair, his gaze a stormy inner-battle. "You were—*are* too young, and I still have some fucking morals, you know!"

"Don't give me that self-righteous crap again. I thought we passed it. No matter my age, I am the same person I was a month ago, or three, or bloody six. The same one who had to grow up two years ago and learn to both survive and raise a child. Do not dare insult my maturity again, or my ability to make a decision about a man, or my body for that matter." Taking in a deep inhale, I continue, "There's more to your push-back and you know it! Stop blaming it on our age difference."

"Goddamn it, Evelyn, stop it! You don't know anything."

"I know about *her*."

"You know nothing about Hanna. Nothing!" with clenched fists to the point his knuckles turn white, he storms off, out onto the terrace.

"Then tell me!" I follow him into the humid day, the sun far too cheerful for this conversation.

"What do you want from me? Are you so desperate for me to admit what a fuck up I am? What an utter failure?" The rage in his voice splinters and the pain in it scares me just a little.

"Finn, you're not—"

"But I am! You don't understand." He whips around and startles me when his broken gaze finds mine. "She's dead because of me!"

No, that can't be right.

Annika already told me he's blaming himself for Hanna's death, but this is much more than that.

"That doesn't sound right—"

"No, no, Evie darling, it sounds perfectly right. Because it's true. You wanted to hear it all, so here it fucking is! If my stupid, naive, young ass wouldn't have become infatuated with the older, enticing woman, she would have been far, far away, on the same island my brother and Annika live on. Alive and well even today. She fucking stayed because of me! Bartiste found her here in Queenscove because of me! When he did, I wanted to keep the girls with us, to keep them safe and in our sights, but I let myself be convinced by everyone, including them, that we should separate. Some bullshit about the girls not being a distraction while we went for Bartiste. God, what a fucking stupid mistake that was." He's pacing now, raking his fingers through his hair, his features marred with too much self-hate. "Bartiste was smarter than us back then, he got one of our guys, and found out exactly where the girls were. I had to sit, Evelyn, sit in the back of a car and listen to Hanna's voice pleading with me to get to her in time, unable to do anything about it, as men pounded on her door to get to her. I could hear every single tear fall as shots were fired into that room, and with each word she spoke, I sat there listening to the slithers of hope leaving her. She was strong, but even she couldn't hide the fear from her voice. And I listened to it all."

He stops pacing, gripping the railing and bracing himself

as he looks toward the rumbling sea. My heart is caught in my throat, heat simmering behind my eyes as I wrap my arms around my middle.

"I failed," he continues. "Her, myself, Annika... We got there too late. They were gone, and all that was left was a sea of bodies who died because of the same failure. I should have been the one there, protecting her, not our men. So many souls ripped out of this world because I didn't stand firm in front of Hanna, Annika... my brother. By the time we found them, when Bartiste was done with Hanna... she was an empty, bloody shell. They didn't just break her, they fucking decimated her. So much damage, so much blood, cuts and burns... Bartiste used her to punish Annika. Made her watch her best friend get raped and broken, because he was creative in his torture. He knew emotional pain, guilt, can inflict just as much damage. Annika said she begged and begged to take her instead, even as she was pregnant... I can't imagine being restrained and forced to watch a loved one like that."

Finnigan takes a deep staggering breath, as silent tears slide over my cheeks, adding to the ones that have been flowing since he said his men died because of him too.

"She took her last breath seconds before I found them," he continues. "I didn't even get to say I'm sorry. All I could do was carry her empty body out of there."

So much blame... so much sorrow... he can't see past his guilt, and my tears aren't for Hanna, but for him. He didn't fail, he tried so hard, but—

"You couldn't control everything that happened, Finnigan." My voice is soft as I step toward him. "We blame ourselves for things out of our reach, but there are too many battles to fight, and we can't take them all on. She didn't die because of your decision, because you didn't protect her. She died because of a bastard with no soul."

I stop when he shakes his head.

"That's not even my only shame." He takes a deep inhale and breathes it out like fire, "I don't remember what she looks like anymore."

His hands flex around the railing, the confession heavy. He pauses for a long time, but I don't dare interrupt his process.

"I couldn't bear to look at any photos of her, of us, in the last few years. I thought what I did, or failed to do, would keep her imprinted in my mind, but it didn't. The color of her eyes, her general shape, those are still there, but there are no details... only a blur and shadows. She wasn't the love of my life, but I couldn't even give her the courtesy of my memories. How fucked up is that?"

His head drops and I just want to scream. This is exactly what happens when you refuse to talk about how you feel. You hold onto guilt, pain, and turn it into something so deeply ugly.

"Finn... I'm forgetting too."

His shoulders stiffen, head straightening.

"I have nothing of my mother. No photos, no videos, there's nothing left. It's only been two years and yet... I already forgot the shape of her nose, the sweep of her brows. You've kept it all in, and there was no one here to tell you that what you feel, as valid as it is, is normal. Your guilt..." I shake my head, pushing back the rest of the tears. "Your guilt can be healed."

I don't miss the slight sag in his shoulders now. Did I take a weight off of them with my own guilt? Memories are fickle... and they're just another one of those things out of our control.

He looks over his shoulder for a brief moment, the sunshine behind him turning him into a tragic god with his features marred with sorrow. "If I couldn't protect her, how can I protect you? How can I keep you safe if I couldn't before?"

Oh God, this is what he was afraid of?

I'm rushing to him, even if I wasn't that far, and throw my arms around his waist, clutching him tight.

"You are! You're doing so much. You're enough!" I whisper into his bare back I'm staining with my teary cheeks.

Only when he tries to turn do I loosen my grip, and he wraps me in his arms, pressing his lips to the top of my head. "I'll never be enough."

There's so much trauma carried in this salty breeze, too much pain, and unfathomable guilt.

Denying ourselves is only adding to it all.

CHAPTER 30
Evelyn

FINNIGAN'S CONFESSION CLEARED SOME OF the air, but revealing something like that about yourself, by force too, deals damage. We shared a shower in silence as we processed the heavy words. We dressed in silence, stealing stray touches as we passed each other. I put my makeup on in silence as he dealt with the gifts that were bought for us. And now we've been driving to Vincent's in silence. It allowed me to think, maybe too much. He may be the playboy, but I'm the one playing him and I can't believe I didn't see it until now.

Maybe just as worse is that I'm playing myself too. I want this man. As much as I want a good job, a nice house, a better life for my sister and me. I want him there... to share it all with me. A pipe dream. And I can't believe how stupid I was to pursue this without thinking of consequences, without making a decision about our lives first. I've never been selfish, never done anything just for myself, and this was a really, really stupid place to start.

But as I turn slightly, catching sight of the sharp line of his jaw, those almost boyish messy curls brushing against his ear, tense, full lips, and strong hands gripping the steering wheel and gear stick, I can't help but stare. He is... mouthwatering. I know that beneath the cream shirt open at the collar is a strong, wide chest with the finest dusting of blonde hair, taut abs, and arms that beg for my nails to sink into them when he drives into me. But Finnigan Hennessey is so much more than that—he's the man who always takes the time to talk to my sister, who takes care of us, checks on us, he's the man who came after me when he knew my veins itched for poison, who took us in his home crowded with all the books he reads with fervent passion. He's more than I ever gave him credit for.

And he's pissed at me. Not because of the confession I pried out of him, but because he had to share it with someone who might be leaving him.

"Can I ask you something?" Maybe I am wielding that knife after all.

His hand twitches on the gear stick. "Go on."

"Where are your parents? You've only ever mentioned them once."

He frowns and looks at me as if to check that he heard me right, before he turns his attention back on the road.

"I told you before, on their yacht somewhere."

"And you don't care where?"

He sighs. "My parents are... interesting characters. They owned half of Queenscove, if not more, in real estate and other ventures. One day, about ten years ago, they decided they've done enough, sold off most of their businesses, transferred a few to my brother and I, and left to travel."

"And just left you?" I blurt out without thinking.

Finnigan snorts and shakes his head. "My parents did many things without us throughout our lives. Ronan says they love us in their own way, but even he was surprised when they voluntarily showed up at his wedding." He sighs yet again and continues. "Our parents didn't raise us. They provided for us, yes. We had everything we needed and more, we were given anything we wanted if we asked for it, we went to great schools, and had any opportunity, but it wasn't them who raised us. Even if we went on a holiday, it wasn't them who spent time with us outside of meals at restaurants."

I'm not sure how to take this. His upbringing was deeply different from mine. It wasn't great, but it wasn't bad either.

"I know, it sounds a lot like *poor little rich kid*, but it's not money a kid wants, you know?" he says. "We want lo—memories. Memories with our parents, our family. Our grandparents were gone early, our only uncle lived far away, it was just us. Only, it was actually just me, Ronan, babysitters, and housekeepers."

"I'm sorry..." I can't imagine feeling so unloved. My heart breaks for the little boy who just wanted to spend time with his parents.

"I'm not sharing all this for you to feel sorry for me."

"I didn't mean—"

"You didn't, but you still feel sorry for me. Don't. I'm a grown man, Evelyn. I'm over it. I've been over it for a very long time. Long story short, I have no idea where they are. Last month they were somewhere off the West coast. From time to time they return to their house here, check in, spend a few weeks, then leave again."

"Do you miss them?" I know the answer before I finish asking the question.

"No."

My heart squeezes at the nonchalance of that word that should be loaded. He doesn't even speak it in a cold manner, it's just... blatant. I find it hard to imagine what that feels like when I miss my mother so much. My father even more, knowing he's alive, but not... fully there. I yearn for their touch, their hugs, their sweet kisses. Most of all, I miss their laughter. They were amazing separate, but together they were incredible. I can't imagine how Finnigan would have turned out if he had parents like mine. Would his life be different? Would he still be involved in this *business?*

"Do they know about The Sanctum?" Curiosity gets the better of me.

Once again he turns to me, frowning. "They're on a need to know basis," he answers anyway.

"What does that even mean?"

"My parents are businesspeople who built an incredible fortune and managed to retire before they turned forty-five. Not many people manage that by being upstanding citizens. Most of their business ventures were clean, but some... some were just as stained as what I do is. They aren't even the only ones in Queenscove like that. They're just the ones who rose the highest at that time. I'm sure Morrigan told you about her parents? But yes, they've heard enough about The Sanctum."

I'm still reeling in from the information, and it takes me a minute to answer his question.

"Umm... briefly, I guess. I don't think it's necessarily something she likes talking about much."

"Yeah." He scoffs. "The way it ended might not be the type of story you share over brunch."

"What do you mean? How did it end?"

He glances at me, the narrowing eyebrows spelling concern more than annoyance.

"Let's just say... badly for her parents and ex-fiancée, but great for her."

"Why do I feel like you're sparing me from some gruesome details?"

"Because I am. Evelyn, I'm still unsure how much to share with you. How deep you want to be in this world of ours. Especially when you say you don't know if you want to stay. You know so much already."

"So what, you're going to *off me* if I leave and I know too much?" I scowl as I spit those words at him, a bit too much disdain in my voice covering a tinge of fear.

But the man laughs. A sinful rumble that shakes that strong chest of his, messy curls bouncing against his cheek making me want to sink my fingers between them.

"No, Evie darling. Because I don't want you to end up in trouble because you know too much. What you have seen so far scratches the surface. But we deal with threats to our power and people who think they can swoop in and take it from us, constantly. We are masters of blackmail, but there are many who try it on us too. We're trained to deal with this. Our people are trained too. But you, sugar, you're not. And the last thing I intend to do is share too much, get you in too deep, just for you to run away from me and for someone to catch you and hurt you for what you know."

Well, when he puts it that way. My chest relaxes, and I didn't realize how tense the subject made me until the breath left me with a heavy exhale.

"I'm not *running* away, Finn." Though, I'm not sure I believe my words.

In the last few days I've felt like the only way to leave this place, if I do make a decision to do so, is by running away. Not out of fear for them. I'm scared of myself, of allowing the time for goodbyes that I know will threaten to change my mind about the decision. Because deep down I know leaving will be the last thing I'll truly want to do.

"Are you not?" he whispers, but I'm not sure he intended for me to hear him, his head turned to his side window.

I bite my tongue, because I started this conversation in an attempt to smooth things over after upsetting him with the exact same topic.

"I'm sorry for assuming. Thank you for thinking of my safety, I guess."

"It's all I've been thinking about lately." This time he intended for me to hear his whisper, and it brings a heated flush to my cheeks.

"Thank you." I bite my bottom lip and that's the moment he chooses to look at me again, his attention fixed right there.

"What else do you enjoy doing? Besides reading?" I attempt to distract him further.

"What's with all the questions, Evelyn?"

"Well... you've learned so much about me, but I know almost nothing of you."

He sighs again, but it doesn't feel heavy anymore. "Swimming. Not in a pool, but out in the ocean. It helps me clear my head. I like the extremes... the early morning cool water, and the late at night warmth."

Figures. He has a swimmer's body.

"I never heard you mention going swimming." My tone is dreamy, distracted, my imagination filling with strong naked shoulders... the wide expanse of his chest, all wet.

"I haven't done it as often as I wanted to. I've had other... *things* keeping me busy."

"Things... right."

I imagine him looking like a god as he walks out of the sea, ripped lean muscles all over his arms and powerful, long legs, dripping wet. *So, so wet.* And that's not the only thing long about him. I shake my head, squeezing my thighs together at the mental image.

"Are you okay?" he asks.

We've stopped at some traffic lights and he's watching me, but I've lost myself in the image of him naked. His gaze travels down my body, to my joined thighs still tightly pressed together.

"Yes. Sorry, I was just—"

"Imagining me swimming?" he interrupts and heat flares over my cheeks.

"No, of course not! I was just thinking..."

"Thinking. Right." a devastating dimple appears in his right cheek and my god, I want to lean over and kiss it. No, I want to lick it. All of him. Top to bottom.

Jesus Christ, Evelyn!

This is why I'm in this situation. This didn't happen because of my selfishness, but my damn hormones. I let them take over, and now I'm worried his leather seat is going to have a damp spot on it. I always seem to worry about that. I have a problem.

"What else do you think about, Evie darling?"

My gaze whips to him, the change of tone, filled with innuendos, hitting a nerve deep in my core.

"What do you mean?" my voice staggers.

"When it comes to me, what crosses that dirty little mind of yours?"

"What makes you think it's dirty?" I ask, half confused, half intrigued.

He sighs, chewing on his lip for a moment, then wraps his large hand around my thigh, as he starts driving again. The gesture startles me, but I'm sinking into the warmth either way.

"I have a confession to make." He glances over for a second, before turning his gaze on the road, and continues when I don't say anything. "I overheard—purely accidentally—a conversation you were having with Morrigan."

"Umm... what conversation?"

"At Vin's house. I was going to the bathroom and the window on the corridor was open. You were somewhere on the other side of it." He says, squeezing my thigh, the gesture both reassuring and sensual.

"Okay..." This isn't helping.

"You were confessing your fantasy about... control. Or the loss of. Being taken..."

My jaw drops, eyes widening as I attempt to turn in my seat to look at him, gripping the sides. "Oh my god! Finnigan!"

When the ball drops, I'm both mortified and furious, my nails digging into the leather of the seats, and an ache takes root in my temples. I was talking about my dubious consent fantasies.

"How much did you hear?"

"Enough..." He chews on his bottom lip again, turning his gaze on me.

I hate that my core is responding to the roguish look in his eyes, though my heart does too.

"You stayed through it all, didn't you?" I say in disbelief. "You bastard! That was a private conversation!"

"It was and I am sorry. I walked past just as you said something that caught my attention and... I couldn't help myself."

"Oh my god, I can't believe you—"

"I know, it was wrong of me. I honestly admit it. I admitted it then too. Though..."

"What?!" I snap at him.

"I did learn something."

"What, that I have fantasies about being manhandled?!" I can't believe I just said that.

Finnigan smirks, turning to me with a mischievous grin

on his beautiful lips. "That too, and I found that information very useful, as you remember."

Images flash through my mind of Finnigan moving through the shadows the first time he *touched* me, and it's probably the hottest thing that has and will ever have happened to me.

"But that's not what I was referring to," he continues. "I learned something valuable about how you feel, or felt, about how you view yourself, and what you struggle with. It didn't help much then, but now that the line is well and truly crossed, I will do anything in my power to make you feel... *right.*"

I remember the words I spoke to Morrigan that day. How I felt wrong for wanting to be in a non-consensual situation considering what I went through. That feeling hasn't left me.

"And what if I don't want you to?" I ask.

This time he doesn't turn, but the hand wrapped around my thigh slides up, reaching the warm place between my thighs. The skirt isn't quite in the way, but I still curse it as he cups me beneath it. As he applies more pressure, I realize the thin cotton of my panties is giving away the effect he has on me.

"Finnigan..." In my mind his name was meant as a protest, but as I grip the sides of the seat, a breath caught in my chest, it came out as nothing more than a desperate, whispered mewl.

"Your body says otherwise, Evie darling."

He drives casually through the outskirts of Queenscove toward Vincent's house in the forest, his eyes fixed on the road, but the tips of his fingers scrape against the fabric covering me. I press my back deeper into the seat, squeezing my thighs together, attempting to trap his hand there, though all I end up doing is press him harder against my aching pussy.

"My body could lie." I finally gather my wits. "It responds, but that doesn't mean it's what I want."

"Stop me then," he says as a finger slides against the seam of my panties, goosebumps exploding over my flesh where he barely just brushes against it.

My thighs stay pressed together, though I don't attempt to stop him further.

"If I say *no*, will you stop?"

"Jesus, Evelyn, of course. Though, I think we can work on your acceptance of yourself and desires, differently." His finger slides over my skin, pushing my panties to the side, and finds the wet seam of my pussy.

I moan and roll my hips against the seat, my nipples hardening at the shudder that rips through me.

"How do you mean?" I ask on a breathy voice.

"Use the word *no* to fuel your fantasy. With me, you can enjoy it, play into it." That wandering digit brushes through my core, and as the car swerves onto a bumpier side road, he drives into me, and a wanton cry spills out. "Relinquish the control and let it drive you deeper into pleasure. And for when you really want me to stop, we'll set a safe word."

"S—safe word." I moan as he adds another finger, pushing into me in a maddening rhythm, not bothering at all to take it slow. Or drive the car slower for that matter, adding to the intense pleasure of it all.

"Yes. Keep it simple and use the word *red*, or choose a different one you prefer better. And if your mouth is covered, snap your fingers." This conversation is slightly surreal with his fingers sunk deep inside of me.

But then they curl, and my thighs slide wide open allowing him all the access he wants and I need.

"Red..." I whisper, my hips bucking against the seat as my hands are desperately searching to grab onto something else.

"Red it is, then." His thrusts grow harsher and my head drops against the headrest, eyes closed as I take his long, thick fingers.

Then the man rolls them, brushing against a part of me that makes my ass shoot up from the seat.

"So damn responsive, Evie darling. And so, so wet." That boyish grin makes another appearance, and I swear I would jump him if it wasn't for the whole driving situation.

The road turns darker, the high trees of the forest sheltering it from most of the sun rays, and I wonder who would hear me if I were to scream my ecstasy out there. It makes me want to do it, but Finnigan strokes me to the cusp of exploding, and not an inch past that threshold. I want to bathe in the pleasure of it all. It burns me from the inside, searing my nerves and turning me into a puddle of need and unbearable cravings.

"Jesus fuck, Evelyn. I could just—"

"I'm so close," I interrupt in a breathy whisper, grabbing onto his forearm and squeezing it to me. "Oh, Finnigan, please…"

"You're so beautiful when you beg. I almost don't want to push you over the edge so I can enjoy it for longer."

"Such a cruel man you are." I moan, as the pad of his palm rubs in a brief, torturous motion over the bundle of nerves crying for his touch.

"Not as cruel as you in that sinful skirt and thigh-high stockings. I swear you dress just to drive me crazy. What I could do to you…"

"Then do it, for the love of god, make me—"

"Not sure you deserve it, Evie darling. Only good girls get to come, but you… you're playing with me. With my desire, my emotions…" His words hold a harsh tone, but his fingers deliver the punishment. Such sweet, cruel punishment, holding me at the precipice of explosive pleasure.

A deep need for revenge for this situation grabs hold of me, and my hand shoots between his own thighs, landing on his stiff cock. He groans at the contact, the car swerving for a split second as he mutters a quick series of curses. We could crash for all I care, and I would still have only one thought in mind—earth shattering release.

I rub him over the trousers, reveling in the way he twitches under my touch, but it doesn't seem like torture yet. I need more. My palm itches for this man and my movements grow urgent, alternating between stroking and gripping him tightly until he hisses under his breath. I like the noises he makes. The slight pain laced with longing. I have to have more of it.

Only, he seems even more determined to punish me, kneading the pad of his palm over my clit, as he finger fucks me with harsh, jerked strokes, threatening to drive me to the brink of lust-filled madness, but holding back just before I reach the precipice.

I retaliate, fumbling with his belt, then his zipper, and finally that one button keeping his beautiful cock away from my itching palm. And damn it how I itch for him. Finnigan is a different type of drug, an addiction I'm scared even he can't keep me away from.

The moment I slide under his boxers and touch the bare, soft skin of his throbbing member, he shifts with a jerk backward in the seat, fisting the steering wheel like the object wronged him in some way. But it's my core he takes vengeance on.

"Evelyn, are you trying to fucking kill me?!"

I stroke my palm up and down his shaft in response, satisfied when a few drops of pre-cum help me along the way. He can make of this what he wants, but he better not die on me, because the feel of him pulsing in my hand, his soft, slippery skin, might just be my new favorite thing. Though the man this cock is currently attached to isn't really my favorite at the moment. Not when he strokes into me with demanding fever, bringing me toward the edge of the cliff that promises unbearable ecstasy, then pulls me right back on the ground before I get to plunge.

So I stroke him harder, faster, with erratic movements I can barely control or focus on as his fervid touch threatens to hypnotize me. But he responds all the same, shifting more and more in his seat, his quickening breaths audible over the roar of the engine.

"You're gonna end us both," he all but growls, though he doesn't sound bothered by the prospect.

Then he pushes a third finger into me, and I cry out as I plant my palm on the ceiling of the car, my back arching from the onslaught of deliciously decadent feelings.

"Such a greedy little cunt you have, Evie darling."

"Stop the damn car, Finn!" I demand, slamming my hand against the dashboard.

"Do you need to use the safe word?" he says, his tone leveling.

"I said, stop the car!" I punctuate the order with a tight stroke of his cock, flicking my wrist at the end, and watching his jaw drop on a sharp inhale, followed by inaudible curses.

The car screeches to a halt on the gravel as he turns his attention on me, his eyes deviously dark, pinning me with a passion that makes me tense and squeeze the fingers stretching me. That shifts something inside of him, his brows furrow, gaze turning feral, and I suck in a breath as the danger rolls off of him in waves. On my protesting whimper, he slides his fingers out of me, and in one swift motion unclips both our seat belts.

"Get the fuck out of the car, Evelyn."

The order rips through me like a lightning bolt, and I'm not sure if I'm in control of my body anymore, because I comply in an instant. Our eyes are fixed on each other as we rush to the front of the car, stray sun rays hitting the blonde man like the gods themselves are licking his skin, and before I can throw myself into his arms, he grips my shoulders and turns me around. He presses my back to his front with his arm over my chest, hand under my chin holding my head tilted to him, and reaches between us until he finds the wet fabric of my panties.

"Is this what you want? Turn me into a feral, uncontrollable creature around you?"

I don't answer, too distracted when he presses his fingers back into me, and I shoot up on my tiptoes, seeking the car to steady myself.

"Because you managed it, Evelyn. I'm fucking feral for you, uncontrollable, only, you're the beautiful creature at my mercy."

He releases my jaw, and before I can complete a gasp, I'm bent over the hood of the car, my skirt thrown over my back, ass up in the air. I hear the faint rustling of a plastic wrapper, then a brief tear, before he pushes my panties aside and runs his fingers through my dripping core.

"Beg me to fuck you. Let me hear how beautiful you pray for my cock to stretch your soft, wet cunt."

His crude words pull the dirtiest of moans out of my throat, and they spill off my lips too loudly, but in the middle of this forest, on Vincent's private road, I don't care.

"Finnigan, please fu—"

I cry out the rest of the word when his cock plunges into me on a harsh stretch. He holds my hips to him as I sink into the pleasure the ache brings.

"Oh God, you feel so good." I moan.

"Like I was made for this tight, little pussy of yours."

He pulls out and pushes back in on a powerful thrust, but this is not like our first time. He doesn't pause. He doesn't linger. He doesn't wait to give me time to adjust. He drives into me in punishing strokes, fingers digging into my flesh as he pulls me to meet his hips each time he slams back in. I have nothing to hold onto, the edge of the hood just out of reach, but it doesn't matter. He uses me like a puppet, controlling my movements or lack thereof, holding me just where he wants me as he fucks into me relentlessly, the rhythm quickening, the slap of skin on skin a depraved anthem that echoes through the trees along with our moans and grunts.

I'm quickly turning into a spent mess, unable to function beyond the ability to take all the pleasure he offers, my brain refusing to acknowledge the existence of anything else beyond the man who fucks me like he owes me punishment.

"I would apologize for how quick this is gonna be"—he says in a breathy grunt—"but you're to blame, dirty Evie. You, with your talented hand, mesmerizing pussy, and sinful eyes."

"Then punish me..." I cry out as he slams into me with enough force to drive me higher onto the hood, the grill pressing against the front of my thighs. My front is too hot from the engine, but it adds to the adrenaline, the intensity of the moment.

"I intend to."

He releases me before his palms land on either side of me with a thud that might have dented his car, and fucks me until I my eyes roll back and my legs shake. There's no space for either of us to reach for my clit, but the heat of the hood, the fabric of my skirt, and the intense friction is more than enough, because in the next moment I cry out, my whole body spasming against him. He thrusts through that orgasm, preying on the sensitivity of my core, even when I feel too tender to keep going.

Finnigan doesn't care. He pistons into me over and over, his movements fast, but so precise. Enough that I feel another orgasm inching in, and I'm still in disbelief when he whispers into my ear.

"One more, my Evie. Come for me again."

I don't know if I can, but for him... I'll try.

This time I force my hand between the car and me, and when I press two fingers to my clit, stars explode behind my eyes, and my body bursts into infinite goosebumps. Finnigan's cock throbs inside of me, suddenly so much warmer, twitching and prolonging my orgasm until I'm entirely limp and spent.

As I lie there, waiting for him to rescue me since there's not enough strength in my muscles to get up and drag myself back in the car, I wonder... how am I supposed to go back to my previous life, when this man is beyond my wildest imagination?

Memories of him will never be enough.

I need the real Finnigan Hennessey in my life.

If he'll take me.

CHAPTER 31
Finnigan

I PULL THE CAR IN NEXT to four others parked in front of Vincent's house, and I'm a bit apprehensive at the sleek, black SUV I don't recognize.

"Looks like we're not the first ones here," Evelyn states, looking over to the row of vehicles, after she closes the mirror she just checked herself in.

She had to fix her makeup after what we did, but the sight of her barely disheveled look made me crave to ruin her even more. An image of my sweet Evelyn, with black makeup running down her cheeks as she chokes on my cock has been floating through my mind incessantly, and at this point, I'm praying that it's a premonition.

"Well, I'm glad they got here before our impromptu stop," I answer, cocking an eyebrow with a grin.

She blushes instantly, and I can't possibly miss how she squeezes her thighs together at the fresh memory imprinted between them. Though, I would much rather it would be me between them right now. Again. And a thousand times after.

I've had more women than I could count, and none out of vanity, but need. Only, that need wasn't physical, it was mental... emotional. The only purpose for it was to distract me from what I really craved, but after the way I lost Hanna, I couldn't allow myself those desires. I plugged in the hole with endless women and none of them ever tempted me to want more from them.

Until Evelyn came along.

She drew me in like no other, preyed on vulnerabilities she didn't know I had, and filled gaps she couldn't possibly know existed. And I rejected it all from the start. I was foolish to think I could resist her, that I was strong enough. Maybe I didn't fight it hard enough, or maybe fate really is a thing.

Only, I don't want to leave the rest to fate.

"Evie"—I shift in the seat and catch the silver and gold of her eyes—"give staying in Queenscove serious thought. For me."

Her eyes widen for one fleeting moment, before slight concern saddens them.

"I am."

"Really? Because you speak more of leaving than of staying, and I need you to give this—Queenscove—a real shot. I've been thinking about it all. Maya will have to be enrolled in school once all is said and done with Bartiste, and it's something I can help with. Give it a chance without having one foot out the door."

"You can't ask this of me, Finnigan."

"I don't want to *ask* this of you; don't you get it? I don't even want to demand it, I want to *take it*. I want to tie you in my penthouse and give you no choice. That's what I actually desire. Which is why I'm holding onto the ounce of self-control I have, and I'm asking you to give it a proper shot."

She's speechless, her lips parted in surprise as she takes in my words and underlying threat.

"You wouldn't," she whispers.

Maybe my glare is answer enough, because I swear there's hope weaved through the shock in her gaze.

"Tell me you will do it, you'll give it a chance. A good one. You've already built a life in Queenscove, Evelyn. There's so much more for you here," I add.

"I will give it a chance. I already am," she finally agrees.

But there's a little voice inside my head that mocks me. It knows what a man of my failures deserves, and it's not a woman like Evelyn. I nod, pensive at the inner turmoil, recognizing the tinge of fear that's been growing inside of me at the same pace as the attachment to this woman.

"I'll grab the cake trays and your things. Get the gift bag, please."

We exit the car simultaneously, but a moment later she's by my side, taking one of the trays from me.

"I can handle it," I argue.

"Me too." She walks away with a strut, but not before cocking an eyebrow and giving me a look more sinful than it should be. I should move, but that damn skirt fluttering with her sway, distracts me. It's not even that short, just above the knees, but knowing she wears thigh-high stockings underneath as well, I want to bend her over and sink into her warm, sweet cunt all over again. She looks like a rock goddess and I get all sorts of ideas of things I want to buy her. Latex bodysuit. Fishnet stockings to rip off. Leather harnesses to frame her waist, or her breasts...

"Coming?" she calls after me, and I have to rush to get

to her.

Though, I don't bother pretending to be unaffected by her. I probably should when we get inside. I have a feeling Maddox might demand my head for what I did with the violet-haired woman he's started seeing as a sister. He warned me before to leave her alone, but I think he was thinking more of her emotional state.

She knocks on the door, but I slide in front of her, open it and walk in.

"Vincent has cameras and sensors." I say as I turn her way. "They know we're here."

She shrugs and follows, but once we're in, she's looking somewhere behind me, apprehension in her gaze. I whip around at her slight distress.

"Cousin!" the dark-haired, broad-shouldered man exclaims as he comes toward us.

"Sloan, you've arrived," I greet him, then Morrigan who arrives next to me and helps me with the tray I carry.

I hug my cousin, who left his crime empire for a few days to lend a hand with our Bartiste situation, then step aside to introduce him.

"Evelyn, this is Sloan Buchanan. Our cousin abandoned his hill up in Venator to assist us."

"Your hill?" She looks curious, but a little flustered too. "Sorry, hi, nice to meet you."

"It's great to meet you, too. Though, I feel like I know you already, as I've had the pleasure to meet your sister," Sloan greets her, his stance quite stern, but like always, there's warmth in his eyes and tone. "And yes, my hill. The city of Venator is old. Back in the old days three fortresses were built on its three hills, and it created a bit of a... divide, let's say. One of those hills—Alnit—is my territory."

"Oh, what an interesting name. I know of Venator, but

I never looked into its geography. It sounds… familiar," she answers, curious now.

I know Evelyn hasn't finished school after she had to give it all up to take care of her sister. It's a bit of a sore subject with her, mostly because I think she sees it as a flaw, like she's somehow worth less because of it. But I've also noticed her thirst for knowledge. Her sister may be a big fiction reader despite her fragile age, which I thoroughly enjoy. But my Evie has a curiosity like no other, always sifting through my books, and almost every time she chooses non-fiction. Anything from ancient writings to modern history. She never discusses it, though, and always drops the books when I come in the room. One day she'll get over that insecurity, but I won't rush her.

"It comes from Alnitak, one of the stars in Orion's belt," Sloan explains, a little pride in his voice at the interest Evelyn shows.

"That's fascinating." Her gaze drifts, and if I could crack her head open now, I swear I would see the cogs spinning, filing this information for further research. "I would love to hear more about it, but you'll have to excuse me, I need to finish the cupcakes for the birthday boy." She nods to us, her gaze lingering a few moments longer on me, then walks away.

I don't realize I'm still staring after her until Sloan speaks.

"It's good to see you *interested* again."

I turn to him, mouth open ready to bite back, but I have nothing. I can't deny it, but I feel like I have to say something to clarify.

"We're not… together. I guess."

He quirks an eyebrow, challenging my answer.

"She's not sure if she's staying in Queenscove, and we haven't approached the subject about how *interested* we are."

He smirks and shakes his head. "If only relationships

were simple."

"What about you?" I ask, trying to deflect.

"I'm doing well. There's some shit stirring up in Venator, but hopefully it won't escalate. It's why Duncan couldn't come, he has to hold down the fort."

"I was asking about your love life," I say, laughing. "But how is your son?"

"Honestly, a bit too good at this *job*, but he's young and his mind is a bit distracted. Money, women, you know the drill. And my love life is just fine."

"*Just fine.* Sounds promising. Duncan will be okay, he'll have a wake-up call soon enough and step up, especially if you say he's talented at the family business," I assure my cousin.

"How are you doing with Bartiste's return and all?"

Sloan was there last time. After the girls were taken, he came to our rescue. We probably would have all been dead without him and his men. He even offered some of them the option to join our Sanctum, to replenish the army we were only just building back then. I inhale deeply and start walking with him, toward the voices I hear outside on the patio.

"Fine. We all really thought he was dead. But it seems my brother and Carter never stopped looking, just in case. But yes, it was all unexpected."

I look at Sloan and his narrowing green eyes scrutinize me. Clearly I didn't answer the question he was truly asking, but getting in the emotional side of things about the PTSD Bartiste left me with isn't going to happen. I haven't gotten into it with my Sanctum brothers, so I'm not doing it with the cousin I see a few times a year.

"He'll be dead soon."

"That he most certainly will. Thank you for joining us in the hunt."

"Believe me man, it's my pleasure." He taps my shoulder

and smiles, but it doesn't touch his eyes. They only spell malice.

"Finn," Ronan greets me when we get outside, and Vincent, Carter and Maddox nod toward me, signaling Sloan over.

My brother and I may have started to work through our shit, and I know he really yearns to get closer to me, but I find it somehow difficult. I'm not sure what's holding me back, but I have a feeling it's not to do with him.

"How are you settling back in Queenscove?" I ask as we take a seat next to each other on the outdoor sofa, Sloan moving on to Maddox who looks at me a bit wearily.

"It's... odd. It feels like home, but it also doesn't. I can't explain it. Being on edge doesn't help."

"Are you worried?"

He looks me in the eye like I grew a second head. "Worried? I'm petrified, brother. Bartiste is back. The man who took so much from us." His gaze drifts to his wife who's currently entertaining their son, before returning to me. "I know it's not the same as it was with you; I'm not trying to downplay it in any way. But the fear that it could happen again to Annika, to Aaro, is debilitating."

No, Bartiste didn't take as much from him, but Annika was pregnant when she was kidnapped along with Hanna, and my brother only found out about it over the phone, as she was being taken. There is no way to describe that feeling of helplessness. We couldn't do a thing. It left deep, jagged scars that we share because our trauma is our failure. We failed to protect them.

How can I deserve Evelyn? What if I fail to protect her too? I know Bartiste will be dead at the end of this, I know I will not fail there, but it's her safety I fear up until that point.

"You have a lot to lose now. I understand." I answer finally. "Is this why you came back?"

"Partly. I have hired help at home, but here... I have you

and The Sanctum. I knew Annika and Aaro would be safe now. And no matter what happened between us, how you felt about me, there was no chance I wouldn't come for you after realizing Bartiste is back."

It sounds like he didn't care if I wanted him here or not, he was going to be by our—*my* side anyway, through the asshole's return.

"What's the other reason?" I ask.

"I need to see Bartiste dead. I need to make sure."

I nod. No one from our whole group can understand that better than me. I'll treat him like a fucking vampire if I must, and carve his heart out or cut off his head, just to make sure he'll never come back to fucking life.

"Did you find out how the motherfucker lived?" He had a few holes in him, his men couldn't find him either.

"I found a hospital record that matched some of his injuries. He used a different name, so I can't be hundred percent sure, but it sounded like he was found by a random person, half dead. The records were altered though because that's the only thing there. No evidence of surgery, recovery, death, or anything else. He disappeared," Ronan answers.

"I'll make sure he's dust this time around."

He nods in response. It's a certainty for the both of us. For all of us really. Bartiste has been taunting us for long enough, and The Sanctum does not allow errors, let alone failures. We were young when he disappeared on us, but we aren't the same people now. The wheels are in motion, Bartiste is leaving breadcrumbs, and he'll be ours soon enough. The worst thing to admit is that the guy is a master in disappearing and hiding. If he were anyone else, we would admire the talent, but there's nothing to admire about this man.

"You and the girl—" Ronan changes the subject.

"Evelyn," I correct.

"She's young..." His words strike me.

"And that bothers you?"

He takes a deep breath in, then releases it as he ponders, his gaze turning to Annika, still playing with their son.

"She seems mature enough, don't get me wrong. But pulling her into this life at her age seems unfair," he says as he refocuses back on me.

My fists clench and tightness grips my chest. "I know you're not fucking insinuating that I'm forcing her to stay here. That I'm coercing her in some way."

"I'm not, it's just—"

"Evelyn is free to make her own decisions, brother. But I'm not gonna sit idly by and not show her all her options. And *I am* an option. I fucking deserve this too! Fuck knows I've waited long enough." I rise and storm off before he can say anything else.

I'm rounding the house, needing a damn moment to myself before I end up taking my anger out on someone else. But footsteps crunch on the grass behind me, and I whip around, ready to tell them to fuck off.

"Finnigan, sorry, can I talk to you for a moment?"

Loreley.

My warning stops in my throat and I nod, curious. The blonde woman and I don't interact that much, though we are in each other's presence fairly often.

"I know you and Evelyn are getting... close."

"Oh for God's sake, not you too." I step back shaking my head. "Look—"

"No, listen to me. I'm not here about *that*. I want to talk to you about her and Maya. Has she spoken to you about the custody situation?"

This, I didn't expect.

"I tried to approach it once, but she brushed me off and

changed the subject. Why?" I ask, fully intrigued now.

"You and I both know she cannot get custody of Maya legally without jumping through enormous hoops that girl can't afford. We spoke of it, she's not really doing anything about it because she's terrified she'll lose Maya to the system until the custody is decided by CPS and a judge." She takes a deep breath and looks behind her, probably making sure Evelyn isn't around. "I offered to help, obviously. But she got really defensive. She's a stubborn one."

"What reason did she give you?" I ask, crossing my arms against my chest.

"She's not comfortable with me doing anything about it because I already helped her so much. I hired her in the café, she lives in my apartment, though she insisted on taking rent out of her salary. You can imagine I barely charge her, but anyway, she fought really hard and actually got angry at me. You probably know as well as me that Evelyn does not get angry. Ever. So I had to back off. I want to speak to Morri about it, ask her to get The Sanctum involved, but I thought I would talk to you first. I see how you look at her..." she ends with a suggestive smile that would make me blush if I wasn't distracted by the custody matter.

"Thanks for coming to me. I'm looking into it."

Loreley's eyes widen as she snaps back. "Really?"

I nod, feeling a bit lighter now. She smiles, a great big smile showing all her perfectly straight white teeth.

"Thank you!" Her shoulders drop on a calming exhale. "And... I probably don't need to say this, but if you hurt that girl, I'll chop your balls off myself and feed them to you."

My brows shoot up as she whips around, her long ponytail brushing against my chest, and walks away. *Jesus Christ*. I kind of believe her though. Loreley is a Dietrich, and that family has quite the reputation in the criminal underworld. She may be out of the family business, but who knows what she learned before. This conversation seems to be what I needed, because I'm calm, another goal added to the list of all that concerns Evelyn.

There's no denying that I would like to keep her, make her stay. Such a contrast to just a few weeks back. I'm still not convinced that I shouldn't just force her hand, but I know what the best decision is—give her all the resources to make her own decision.

I'm about to push that limit though, and I can't anticipate if she's going to take it as an amazing gesture, or manipulation. It's pushing the limit for sure, but I guess I'll find out tomorrow.

"Come, they're going to sing happy birthday to your nephew." Katya appears out of nowhere.

I didn't even realize she was here, and she's gesturing for me to join them where they're all gathered inside. I follow her, and they make room for me around the dining table so I can see Aaro. He's giddily staring at a whole tray of cupcakes with impeccable frosting layered on top, and I have to concentrate not to drift to what we did with the leftovers of that cream earlier today.

Instead of putting only enough candles to cover his age, all the cupcakes have one. There's probably over forty of them and the boy looks just about ready to burst with joy.

If only our lives would just be this... how different we would be.

CHAPTER 32
Evelyn

THIS DAY HAS HELD A strange normalcy to it. Everything so far has felt surreal. A big happy family celebrating a kid's birthday. Only, this family is the criminal kind, not that you would be able to tell from the way they behave.

The guys have disappeared into Vincent's office a couple of times, likely discussing their businesses, but they returned like nothing happened. Calm and wholly unaffected, carrying on enjoying their family time.

I caught some glimpses of conversations I probably shouldn't have listened in on, like how Bartiste apparently has been taunting The Sanctum, either by trying to send them on fools errands or get them killed. He failed. The Sanctum didn't take the bait, and they were also not weak enough to be touched by his men. Finn and the others apparently are quite pleased with this, because Bartiste is getting bolder and bolder, probably annoyed that all his attempts are being shot down, which means he'll make a mistake soon. From what I heard, he's already made a couple that luckily led to the discovery of two more locations where children were found. They're free now—safe. And Bartiste is angry.

I couldn't take the smile off my face when I overheard this. That bastard needs to rot, and though I want him dead as soon as possible, I can't be mad at this delay when I know that more innocents are being rescued.

Despite all this, today has still felt peculiar. There's a heaviness lingering in the air, and it doesn't seem to go down with the setting sun. On the contrary, it thickens. It turns me restless, threads of anxiety rustling my nerves, and I'm struggling to settle.

From across the garden, flames from the fire pit dance over Finn's features as he talks to his cousin, only, his gaze settles on me with a quiet intensity. My lungs fill with the lightest of air, the relentless buzzing in my ears easing.

I've been thinking about this, his ability to calm my nerves, cool my blood. When I didn't know how to handle myself, what I've been through, and the strange withdrawal from whatever drugs I was injected with, it was him who fed that need. Our rows didn't distract me, they... helped me. It makes no sense when I think about it, and I'm not even sure he knows he's doing it.

Evelyn, that's such a stupidly ridiculous thought.

Of course he doesn't know. He's not damn psychic. Though, I have heard that certain people have a sort of empathy or they read others so well, they can tell when there's a change in blood pressure, or other physical signs. I'm seriously hoping he's one of them, because I don't feel like feeding his ego by actually telling him he's helped me in these ways. I guess I'm holding onto my own ego.

His gaze is still fixed on me, even as his lips move with words clearly directed at Sloan. The intensity of his stare has shifted with the slight narrowing of his eyes, and sparks bloom in my chest, spreading through my body like lightning bolts. This man does things to me. Wild, wicked things.

I've watched him quietly all day. His interactions with the others, the way he carries himself with the kids, noticing the tension in his shoulders easing more and more with each conversation with his brother. But the most noticeable thing is the way he watches me. We've had little physical interaction, but his gaze has constantly made me feel touched. On every single inch of my body. He's not being very inconspicuous about his attention either, and I would rather everyone not know what's going on between us. Though, I'm not entirely sure what that is, and that's my fault, not his. I also think the others might have an inkling about us, after Finnigan arrived when we were attacked in the parking lot.

I rise from the outdoor sofa, feeling the need to flee before someone asks me what's the deal with his stare, and head back inside the house. It's quiet here since everyone's outside, and I head down the corridor toward the bathroom, loving how the moonlight casts its soft light through the high windows.

My next breath is stolen as a hand circles around me and presses over my mouth. I'm snapped back into a strong, taut body, then rushed to the side, into a dark space. I protest against his palm, grabbing at his arms as I struggle to pull away from his hold after he circles my waist with his other arm. With a loud thud, the door closes behind us and pitch-black darkness swallows us as I fight against him, pointlessly screaming against his palm. He manhandles me around, and I can't tell which way is up or down, or where that damn door is, but I forget all those details when my front is slammed against a wall, my cheek pressed against it. An obvious, hard erection pushes against my ass when he lines up his body against mine, and I shudder at the thought, squirming harder to break away.

"No, no, no!" I protest against his hand.

Can he tell what I'm saying?

Hot breath touches my ear, and I think he's going to say something, but instead slickness runs over the edge of it, from the lobe to the top—*he's licking me.* Involuntary heat pools between my legs, shame too.

Goddamn it, this is wrong!

But it has to be Finnigan, right? There's no one else, none of the other guys would do this. I don't know Sloan, but I don't imagine he is that kind of man. I inhale as hard as I can through the restriction, trying to catch Finnigan's scent, but all I'm getting is burnt wood and smoke. The arm wrapped around my waist releases me, and I'm preparing to push as hard as I can against him to get away, when I hear a snapping sound. Then one more.

Oh, he's snapping his fingers—our silent safe word.

It *is* Finnigan.

The sound of a zipper pulls at my anticipation, before he reaches back down around my waist. This time he doesn't wrap around it, but runs his hand down my body. He pushes underneath my skirt, and presses against my pussy at the same time he releases my mouth and grips my throat in his large palm.

"No! No, please!" I beg as I squirm against him, diving deeper into the feelings of unrest that haven't yet left me.

"Beg me all you want, I'm not sparing your little cunt." He all but growls in a low, rumbling tone.

I whimper as his grip tightens against the sides of my

throat, a shallow breath catching beneath his fingers just as he dives under my panties and into the sleekness of me.

"Let me go!" I cry out, squirming harder as I reach behind and grab onto his sides.

"Scream louder, sugar, and we'll have an audience to our depravity." He grunts into my ear, his hot breath sending shivers down my spine as a finger, or maybe two, press inside of me.

I'm so wet, the sound coming from between my legs is embarrassing. But it only encourages the man *forcing* himself on me.

"Oh god!" I whimper in a shaky voice, as he hooks his fingers inside of me, pulling me with him when he takes a step back.

"Are you sore?" he asks in a whisper, clearly breaking character.

"Yes."

"I'll st—"

"No!" I interrupt him, squeezing my inner muscles around his fingers, trapping him inside my warmth.

He doesn't say another word. Instead, he bends me over, his hand moving from my throat to my nape, and it happens so fast, I barely have time to brace myself against the wall. His fingers come out, the head of his cock nudges my core for only a moment before he jerks forward, burying himself inside of me to the hilt, and through the slight ache of my former virginity, I draw ecstasy.

"Oh god!" I cry out, struggling to keep my tone low when I realize I can feel *all* of him.

No barrier. No condom. God, it's incredible.

"You keep calling for this *god*, darling, but it's me listening to your prayers."

A wanton shudder rips through my whole body at his

sinful words, and since I've never been a religious person, I would happily make him my god. My blue-eyed, murderous god whose maddening cock strokes viciously inside my aching cunt. His hips slap against my ass, the sound so dirty and enticing, I grab onto his side with one hand, urging him to take more. His hand tightens around my throat, pressure growing both in my chest and temples from the air restriction, and I feel like calling for *my* god again, but all that comes out is unintelligible mumbles.

Pressure covers the bundle of nerves at the apex of my slit, his skilled digits circling with precise movements that send burning shocks through my core.

"No, no, no..." I chant, more to myself than him, hating that the heat is taking over me so quickly.

My knees tremble with each slither of pleasure cutting through me, and with one more deep stroke of his cock, I'm breaking apart. He releases my neck and covers my mouth in an instant, pressing over the lust-filled cry shattering through me. But he still fucks me through the orgasm, stroking that pleasure until it's almost unbearable.

When the shaking subsides he pulls out, and I think he's going to allow me a break, but I'm manhandled once more, flipped around, my back slammed against the wall just as soft, demanding lips crash against mine.

He kisses me like he couldn't care if I like it or not, taking his pleasure from me like he has every right to, and something deep in my core contracts in ecstasy at the demand. Only, he's gone before I can deepen the rough kiss, and with quick hands under my ass, I'm hauled up against him, back pressed into the wall for support. On instinct I grab onto his shoulders as I wrap my legs over his hips, and he adjusts me until he's holding me with one hand, the tip of his cock prodding at my entrance once more.

"Christ, you're too light."

I'm about to argue that it's not true, but he lowers me onto his cock, and all I manage is a lustful moan as I tighten my limbs around him. Before I know it, he's not just guiding me up and down, but I'm bouncing onto him too, seeking the delightful pleasure this man gives me with each stroke of his cock. He holds my neck in a comforting possessiveness, and it hits me then... I've never known this type of unconditional safety. Maybe once, amongst my family, but not like this. I could relinquish all control, all sense of self, and I know this man would build a fortress around me to keep me safe, comfortable.

"Please, slide your hand... higher... into my hair." The words are strained with the breathlessness of his thrusts, but also because they're not easy to speak out loud.

His movements falter for a few moments, then he picks up the rhythm again, fingers slowly threading into the hairline of my nape. An icy feeling follows in their wake and deep in my chest freezing stillness grips my lungs.

"Red," I speak quickly. "Just for the fingers. No further, hold them there," I add quickly before Finnigan stops moving altogether.

"Are you sure you want this?" he asks, his thrusts slowing.

I nod, and pull him against me, his chest flush to mine, as I force his lips to meet my own. I kiss him with as much passion as I can muster, because goddamn it, this man deserves it all. His movements quicken once more, his hips jerking upwards as I bounce harder onto him, his cock stroking feverishly against a spot inside of me that makes my muscles shake with each grind. The bones of my back hurt as he crushes me against the wall, his breaths quickening, and his fingers press harder into my scalp, fueling and soothing the panic inside my chest all at the same time.

He breaks the kiss enough to whisper, "Touch yourself, Evie darling."

My cheeks heat in an instant, my mind drunk on pleasure as I try to process what he's asking of me. I do as told, reaching between us until my clit is beneath the tips of two fingers, and I cry out from the sensitivity.

"That's it, my dirty little thing. Make yourself come with my cock stroking every bit of you," he whispers those sinful words on a low rumble.

I speed up the touch, adding more pressure as I assault the bundle of nerves, and threads of ecstasy bloom from that center, bursting all through my body as it shakes and convulses around the man who holds me so tight against him. I come hard enough that stars dance behind my eyes, and I'm worried I drew blood where my nails sank in his shoulder. But he doesn't sound affected. He holds me through it until the shaking stops.

I don't realize I'm smiling until he peppers kisses all over my lips, and the softest of laughs, coming from him, warms my soul. He eases me off of his cock and down to my feet, but he has to hold me through my shaky balance.

"But you, you haven't... finished," I protest when he pulls away, reaching for his cock through the darkness.

There's a pause that lasts too long as I squeeze the hard length that throbs in my hand.

"Make me, then." The grit in his voice turns the words to both an order and a plea, and I get an odd sense of power out of them.

The heat between my legs burns brighter and there's only one thing I crave to do right now. Something I've never done before. I drop to my knees, my hand wrapped around the base of his cock, and when my warm breath touches the tip of it, he mutters a series of curses.

"That's not what I meant, sugar. Jerk me off. You don't have to—"

But the next words lodge in his throat and come out as an unintelligible jumble as I suck the tip of him between my lips, surprised at the saltiness and slight bitterness of his pre-cum. Before he can protest further, I suck him inside my mouth as deep as I can take him, stopping when a strange gag reflex pushes him back out. Then I swallow him back in, curling my lips against my teeth and press my tongue against the underside of his pulsing length.

"Fuck, Evelyn! Goddamn it!" he swears over and over.

"Guide me," I whisper. "I've never done this." Then I swallow him again, bobbing up and down his cock.

"You're doing fucking amazing. *You* could do anything to me, and it would be the best I've ever had."

I whimper around his member at the compliment, and a rumble shakes through him.

"Follow with your hand what your lips can't reach," he says on a throaty whisper, and I comply, running my hand up and down his shaft. "That's it, Evie darling. Fuck, yes."

He's somehow even more rigid between my lips, and I finally understand the *rock hard* expression everyone seems to use.

"Faster," he urges softly.

And I do as told, quickening the rhythm as he struggles not to thrust forward in my mouth, his hips rocking gently.

"Move away now. I'm gonna come!" he warns.

But I've already made up my mind. I want it. I want him to spill into my mouth and drown me in the taste of him. It makes me feel dirty, and god I want to be so damn filthy right now. So I slap a hand over his ass and press him right back into my mouth.

He curses low in his throat as he grips my shoulder and

holds me there. I know his instinct craves to grab the back of my head, and the fact that even now he has the self-control to avoid triggering me, makes me want to reward him. So I press him deeper into my mouth, breathing through the gag reflex as the tip of his cock hits the back of my throat, and the sinful grunts that spill from his mouth are followed by the violent twitching of his cock as hot spurts of thick liquid hit my throat. I can't avoid the choking, but he pulls out gently, letting his cum fill my mouth rather than straight down my throat, and I swallow it down the more it comes.

I've never looked at the condoms he threw away after sex, but this seems like a lot of cum. Is it normal? My core tightens when I imagine it filling me, spilling out as he strokes inside of me, and drips down my thighs. I moan as I suck his cock one last time, and he shudders between my lips.

"I can't believe you just did that," he says, breathless. "You swallowed it all?" the man is genuinely surprised.

"Every last drop." I smack my lips together as he helps me up.

"Such a good fucking girl." He growls before he captures my lips with his, and kisses me until I'm panting.

Then he wraps me in his arms, my cheek pressed against his chest, as he rubs my back in slow, soothing motions. We stand like that for long enough that I start to worry what the others are going to say about our absence. Yet, I don't push away. This feels... important. I'm not sure why, but it does.

A few more minutes pass before he finally speaks. "Let's get you cleaned up."

He reaches somewhere to the side and light floods the space. I squeeze my eyes shut, grunting, but accept the fact that this has to happen. Oh, we're in the bathroom. I was so disorientated, I didn't realize this is where he shoved me in.

He moves me to the sink and reaches for some toilet paper

he quickly wets and presses between my legs. I wince, but he holds me there as he wipes gently before he throws it in the toilet. He repeats it a few times, and heat flushes me cheeks each time. This is nice... really nice. I fix my makeup and hair in the mirror as he cleans himself, his glorious cock, and this moment is so intimate. It makes me smile. I like it.

"You should go to the toilet," he says.

I cock an eyebrow as I look at him in the mirror.

"I'm serious." He laughs, "After sex, you should always go. Apparently it prevents UTIs."

"I'm not peeing with you here." I smile like an idiot, the prospect sounding ridiculous.

"I licked frosting off your asshole, but we draw the line at you peeing in my presence." He shakes his head, but the smile on his face is devastating. "Very well, my darling Evie." He presses a quick peck to my lips, then quickly straightens his clothes as he walks out of the bathroom, shutting the door behind him.

I drag my fingers through my hair as I focus on myself in the mirror, looking all sexed up and satisfied. At least I'm not going to have to be the one to explain to the others why we both disappeared at the same time. Though the gleam in my eyes might betray us anyway.

CHAPTER 33
Evelyn

$\mathcal{E}$ITHER FINNIGAN TALKED TO EVERYONE, or they truly don't care, because the moment I return to the terrace, no one even bats an eyelid. They notice me returning but no one focuses on me, their conversations carrying on.

"Evie!" Maya jumps on the sofa next me, grabbing onto my forearm as she lands on her knees, a great big smile on her lips.

"Yes, pretty girl."

"Can I sleep here again tonight?" she asks, grinning from ear to ear.

"Darling, I think we should give them a break tonight."

"Pleeease. I already asked them." She squeezes my arm and throws the best puppy eyes she can pull off.

"She did, indeed." Annika startles me, appearing to my

left. "It's honestly fine. No bother at all."

"It's not quite fair to you, Ronan... or Vincent," I whisper to her.

"We're not here for much longer, and we all enjoy her company. From what I heard, you've had your hands full for a while now. You deserve a little break."

"It's not like that, I don't need a break," I say, feeling bad that she thinks she needs to do this for me.

Then her eyes flash somewhere beyond me before returning to mine. I don't know what or who she looked at, but from the heat searing the back of my neck, I can only guess.

"I understand, trust me, but you can still enjoy one," she answers.

"Please, Evie. It's been so fun with Aaro around. And Annika has been teaching me to paint!" Maya squeals.

"Is that right?" I turn to my sister, pleasantly surprised at her words.

"Yes! Wait here, I'll go grab them and I'll show you." She jumps off the sofa and runs away.

I watch her run inside the house, shaking my head and laughing at the girl.

"Look at that energy at this time of night. Are you sure you want to deal with more of that?" I ask Annika.

"It's honestly nothing. Mamaw June has been staying here for safety reasons too, so please, don't worry." She starts moving away, then stops and cocks her head. "So it's a yes, then."

I snort, shaking my head. "You're a saint, you know. Thank you."

She smiles and walks away. I'm going to miss Annika. Her presence here has had an incredible impact on me because it allowed me the space, the time to find out more about myself.

A moment later, my phone that I left on the sofa vibrates, and I fumble for it, noticing text notifications when I pick it up. I know no one here, who texts me? Oh, maybe it's Raven?

I open the notifications just as Maya jumps back on the sofa and I hear the faint rustling of paper being laid on my lap. Only, my gaze can't focus on anything else but the words screaming at me from the screen of my phone.

> Missed me?

> Tell your precious Sanctum about this and I will pull your sister's guts out while she still breathes. But I'll make sure you watch me rip into her first.

What the hell is this? Panic threads through my veins as Maya speaks words I can't hear, excitedly pushing colorful papers in my line of sight.

"Look! It's the forest." She shows me a thick piece of paper covered in various shades of green.

But I'm numb, struggling to pick the dominating emotion ripping through my soul, because I cannot possibly show my fear right now. I feign enthusiasm as my gaze drifts back to my phone and photos appear on the screen. A few dozens of them load, one by one, and as I catch the first few, a chill runs down my spine.

"Evie, are you looking?" I turn back to Maya, the very subject of the photo gallery currently loading on my screen, forcing my staggering breaths to level out as I gush about my sister's works of art.

"I told you! I'm pretty good." She jumps up and down. "Oh, Aaro's calling for me. I'll put these away."

I nod, squeezing her little body to mine. "You're my little genius. I love you, sweet girl."

She frowns for a split second, before kissing my cheek. "I love you, too."

Then she's off as quickly as she came, and I rise from the sofa, walking inside the house as calmly as I could muster at this moment. When I'm out of view, I rush into a guest bedroom, and close the door behind me, unlocking my phone for a better look.

There she is... my sweet sister... under fucking surveillance.

Frankie B has been watching her. Dozens of candid photos of her pop up one after the other. On the beach, in a store, in the back of a car. All in public. Some in front of our apartment building. I'm in there too, Annika, Mamaw June, but neither of us are the focus. Only Maya is. Every muscle shakes beneath my flesh and I drop down to my knees as I scroll through the images of the vulnerable girl lit up on my phone. The one I'm supposed to protect, shield from assholes like him. The words from that text run in a loop in my head, the nonchalant violence bringing bile up my throat.

Another text comes, like the son-of-a-bitch knew I read his messages.

Midnight, tonight. Dalton Pier. You may not see me, but I will see you every step of the way. And if you're not alone, it won't be just your precious little sister who will suffer.

I stare at my phone in pure disbelief, chest spasming as air fight's to reach my lungs through the staggered breaths I manage. The slither of light creeping through the cracked door blurs before my eyes, but there are no tears brimming them. Only despair. It shatters through the chaos twisting my heart, and the beats bring nothing but pain. It's relentless in its assault, gripping my memories in a sharp vice, and dragging them forward to my present.

I'm back in that dark room of the warehouse, my cheek pressed against the cold, concrete floor as muffled cries of children sound far beyond these walls. But I'm losing them. As poison fills my veins their cries turn too maddening, liquid sounds too distant for their notes to affect me. Except for one—a silent wail from a girl who shares our mother's eyes. Its absence affects me. I know she won't be crying. And she'll be waiting for the sister who will never rescue her, who will lie half unconscious on this stained floor, as the man with a lisp and tar-laced voice takes his pleasure from her pain.

The texture of the concrete scrapes the tips of my fingers as I try to drag myself away from him. I'm questioning my reality.

Maybe I was never saved.

Maybe I'm still lying on that floor. Maybe his dick is still ripping my ass. Maybe I dissociated and made up the last few months of my life.

Maybe Finnigan doesn't even exist.

I'm questioning how deep this panic goes. Which is the lie? The reality?

Laughter somewhere far away cracks the pain and a slither of light breaks through. There is so much effortless joy in that melodic sound, brimming with innocence. Familiar. With aching hands I grip the concrete beneath them harder, trying to drag myself toward that laughter and find out who it belongs to. A visceral need inside of me is screaming of its importance. I have to find out.

Then it comes again, not closer to me, but louder either way. It sounds... small. A tiny voice. Slightly high pitched. A little comical too. Joy blooms in the pit of my stomach. So familiar. The concrete scratches my palms, but I'm pulling away further. Frankie is losing his grip on me. Only, Bartiste appears in my periphery.

You might have to share this one.

His words bring a silent cry to my chest and tears fill my eyes as I struggle to move further away, but I'm not going anywhere. Then the laughter splits the darkness and fills it with colorful light that calls for me—Maya.

I blink frantically as air fills my lungs with vicious force, and fall forward on my hands, heaving. I'm alone, inside the dark, guest bedroom, the door cracked to the dimly lit hallway, and my sister's laughter filters through from somewhere in the distance.

I'm safe.

But she isn't.

My instincts aren't screaming at me, no matter how hard I listen, and I don't know what I should do. The Sanctum can help me. Finnigan can help me. But if what Frankie said is true, that he will see me coming, and considering the surveillance photos he sent me, it's highly likely, then I will be risking Maya's life. How can we protect her if we didn't even know we were being watched?

What if I ask for help... and she will pay for it?

What if I do nothing... and they'll take her from me?

On my phone screen the time seems to scream at me in that bright white—nine forty-eight p.m. I have plenty of time to make a decision, though there's too much time for me to fail to act normal and not get away with it. Maya will get what she asked for and stay here. At least for tonight, Annika and Ronan will watch her.

What about the other nights that will follow? Without me...

Oh, god. I cannot fathom not being part of her life, her growing up without me. Would these people take her in if I'm not here? Would they keep her safe or put her in the system? They wouldn't, would they? No. I can trust them. But I'll leave a note just in case, or maybe I'll text before I meet with Frankie and ask them to take care of her.

Yes. That feels right.

Fuck! No, it doesn't!

None of this is right, but I don't have a choice.

I wrap a strand of my hair around my fingers, nervously rolling it as I force myself not to visualize what consequences I'm going to face. Surrendering myself to Frankie is a terrible idea. Mentally I haven't escaped him yet, but I'm also not trapped in his clutches like I used to be. This will physically bring me right back there. He'll destroy me.

Picking up my phone I go back to his message and the photos of my sister—if I don't do this... he'll destroy *her*. There is no other way, no other choice.

I push myself back up to my feet and walk over to the window, then slowly pull the blind up, revealing the moonlight touching the tops of the trees.

Will I ever see this again if I make this choice? Will I see the outside?

Will I be alive for it?

No!

I cannot think like that. Plan—I need a plan. Finn will want to take me back to the apartment tonight. How am I going to sneak out? There are so many variables, the man has security everywhere in that building, Katya lives there too, people have started knowing me there. However, before they even come into play, it's Finn I have to worry about. There's no way I can sneak out without him hearing, noticing, or searching for me, and I have a feeling he won't be asleep in time for me to leave.

I'll have to sneak out from here. Even with Vincent's cameras or the men patrolling the vicinity and the rest of his forest-covered land, it's not the same as an apartment building. So I tell them I would like to stay tonight with Maya too.

The peculiarity of this situation dawns on me—I'm planning my demise. In my gut I know that this will be my end, because there is no way I will allow a man like Frankie B to own me. No one can own me. I will find a way to escape him, even if it will mean my end.

Now, I just have to act normal in front of the others for another hour and a half.

Deep in my chest a stabbing pain cracks everything I managed to build in the last few months, the shield I formed around the visceral emotions I allowed myself to feel for Finnigan. I love the others too, but Finnigan... what he built inside of me happened gradually. It has a foundation and serrated claws embedded in the edges of my heart, one by one until he became fully seated there. Part of me.

He isn't wrapped around my heart, he *is* part of it. Right next to my smart, silly little sister.

And I'm about to rip my own heart out and abandon them both.

* * *

I counted twelve more breaths after my decision was made, each of them on the rhythm of my slow, dragging steps, but I haven't changed my mind. It's time to walk out of this room so I don't arouse suspicion. Just as I grip the doorknob, steps sound on the other side, on the corridor, and I freeze.

"He's with a woman." That's Carter's calm, leveled voice.

"With a woman?!" Finnigan exclaims.

"That's what I said, yes."

"You can't possibly imply that Frankie is currently on a date. That's not what you're telling me, right?!"

They found him! Pure excitement grips my chest, spilling into goosebumps over my skin, and I cover my mouth to keep from crying out.

"That, or he plans on taking her. It's irrelevant," Carter

answers, nonchalant.

"Let's go get him then." *Maddox*.

They're all here, but they're still walking and their voices are starting to lose volume. They must be going into the office at the end of the hallway.

"How many men did he have with him?" Finnigan asks.

"Cameras showed three."

"Three?! Fucking hell, the man is bold. His confidence is ridiculous if he thinks three is enough to protect him. Why the fuck is he feeling so untouchable?" Finn curses.

"The old Dalton Pier isn't exactly populated, as you know. The beach is too close to the industrial area, so he probably thinks he has plenty of privacy there, and it's easy to see someone coming," Carter answers.

Dalton Pier, where he told me to meet him.

Confidence blooms in my veins at the image of the bastard walking calmly on the dark beach, hand in hand with his *date*. Though, I believe in the *victim* theory much more. This is a curveball. But I can catch it. I have to catch it, because this is so much better than the alternative. The result might be the same, and I will probably still end up in his clutches, but... what if I don't? I'll have the element of surprise on my side.

A door closes and snaps me back into the present. Slowly, I open this one to find the corridor empty, and muffled voices coming from Vincent's office. I sneak to the door and listen.

"For what he did to Evelyn he will pay tonight."

"What if it's a trap?" someone asks.

It must be!

It would be perfect timing, taking The Sanctum out before my *meeting* with him. That way, no one would come to my rescue. And if it isn't a trap, I'm still not willing to take the risk.

I'm rushing in the opposite direction before the decision

made it into my consciousness. There will be no trap. I refuse to allow these men to fall into one because of me. Even if I have doubts. it is because Frankie just seems like the type of man to have far too much confidence for his own good, I will not risk Finnigan and his Sanctum. I won't risk anyone.

The house is still quiet, voices and laughter only filtering from outside, everyone huddled around the fire pit. My sister too. She's cuddled up on a chair, laughter all gone as she lays there half asleep watching the flame with Aaro. It almost hurts that she looks so at home. So settled.

I want to scream for her, yell my love, but they can't know what I'm about to do. Passing through all of Vincent's security will be hard enough. But they're all distracted now, maybe they won't notice. Or at least not yet, and I'll have a head start.

My bag is still by the front door, and I open it to double check all is still there. Between my wallet, tissue pack, snacks, and random crap, there are two weapons I received as a gift for my protection. Hopefully all this training will mean something and I won't be as vulnerable as last time. I grab the bag and head to the closest room that has windows toward the front, because I know the front door triggers the security system and alerts them. The windows won't. Maybe it's because there is physically no way to open them from the outside, I don't know anything beyond the fact that whenever I've seen someone open a window, nothing has been triggered.

Slowly, I close the door behind me, and head straight to the window, unlatching it. My heart is in my throat as I slowly turn the handle and push it open, listening for the repercussions. None come. So I open it wider, and climb over, dropping outside the house.

I don't waste any time, swing my bag over my shoulder, and bolt through the trees, right at the edge of the road that leads back to the main street. I know there's security patrolling around here, so I stay in the shadows of the trees and run. There is no burn in my lungs, no strain in my muscles, only tension inside of me, questioning my actions tonight. But all I can think about is Maya. My sweet Maya threatened by this revolting asshole. The reservations, insecurities, the fear I had is slowly being replaced by rage. Pure, untapped rage for the man who took so much from me.

I refuse to let him take more.

I have been living in fear that he could be anywhere, lurking, watching, ready to ruin everything for me all over again. So I didn't quite live. His photos are confirmation that he was indeed out there, watching us.

Stopping for a moment, I pull my phone out and book a ride to meet me at the end of this road, beyond the last security camera Vincent has installed here, then I run again. I don't have long before the guys will set off too.

If not for the risk they would fall in a trap, I would let them deal with it. But I refuse to allow anyone to get hurt because of me. And Frankie isn't expecting me so early.

By the time I reach the main road and see the ride waiting for me, the soles of my feet burn from the uneven forest floor, but the adrenaline is keeping me from caring. The older driver gives me a reluctant look when he double checks the destination, but I don't dwell on whatever train of thought he's going through. I have my own to deal with. And currently, my brain is working on a plan for how to go through three men and reach Frankie B.

Fire rushes through my veins, fueling the anger and fear that mixes in a dangerous concoction and are breathing new life into me. My past is about to meet my present, and I pray that the anger will dominate the fear in the end.

I wonder if these men were one of the ones who were

with him *that* night... if they were the ones holding me down when Frankie was sticking the needle in my arm? When he pulled my jeans down. Were they the ones who watched? Who laughed? Who cheered him on?

My skin prickles with nerves as the car approaches the destination. There is no going back.

Tonight will end in destruction... and it's likely to be mine.

CHAPTER 34
Evelyn

I'M HIDING BEHIND SOME CRUMBLING parapet of an old industrial yard, peering over the ledge down to the beach. I agree with Finnigan—what a ridiculous amount of confidence Frankie B must have to think he is safe here. It's quiet, deserted, no soul in sight on the moonlit sand, or beyond. It didn't take long to spot him, even as he is further down the beach now, closer to the pier. From Carter's words I thought he was already at Dalton Pier, but he is actually walking toward it.

Toward our meeting spot, though it's technically supposed to happen in just over an hour.

My fists clench, teeth grinding as I watch him walk with a ridiculous swagger like he owns this beach. This is the man who broke me... how unbearably pathetic. More anger filters through my mind, my body too, fueling my muscles like it's priming them.

He took my sister! He took me! Used me... then passed me right over to his boss.

That anger hits the soles of my feet, my hands clenching around the strap of my small bag I crossed over my body to keep close. Red hot rage fills my vision, my steps quickening with the adrenaline it brings, and not even the constant rumble of the surf soothes me. Before I round the corner I grab my phone and open the text I already wrote on the car ride here—it's short, maybe heartbreaking—but it must be done. I'm ducking behind the parapet, right where it ends and beach sand begins to soften my steps, and I have a clear view of the man who will dictate my fate.

Squatting, I remove the bag off my body, drop my phone inside of it and pull out the knife I got from Maddox, sliding it in my boot. I grab the gun Finnigan gave me for protection, though the silencer I'm currently screwing at the end of it I stole myself from his office. I don't remember why I did it, maybe some unconscious instinct that ironically will come in handy right now.

Shadows swallow me next to this parapet, and Frankie B and his men can't spot me, but I can see them clearly. I waited long enough, checking my surroundings, the vicinity, and none of this looks like a trap for The Sanctum. Maybe I was wrong, maybe we were all wrong. But I'm not backing down. They're maybe fifty yards away from me, enough for clear aim, but the adrenaline coursing through my veins might affect the skills I've honed in the last few months. Maddox is not a huge fan of guns, but he taught me well. I'm not half bad, but tonight... I have to be better. Because there's no way I can stroll down that beach to get to Frankie if his lackeys are still moving.

Ice invades my gut as the realization of my intention hits

my rational thoughts—*am I about to kill these men intentionally this time around?* Frowning, I take a moment to acknowledge my feelings, but the ones I'm looking for never come. I feel no apprehension or remorse because the memories of me held down during my assault are filling me with the only emotions that matter right now.

So I lift the gun, aiming it in their direction, bobbing slowly up and down as I follow their movements. The moment one of the men stops walking I squeeze the trigger.

"Fuck!" I curse under my breath when the bullet whizzes past them and hits the sand.

Through the crashing sounds of the waves, only two of them notice the disturbance, but they don't look like they understand what it was. Gripping the bottom of the magazine harder, I inhale deep and aim again releasing it slowly at the same time I squeeze the trigger. The muffled pop is drowned by the rumble of the sea, and one of the men staggers back and reaches for his stomach. I shoot once more, aiming higher, and I expect a scream as he crumbles to the ground, squeezing his chest, but confusion is keeping them silent even as they whirl to look around.

The sea would swallow most of their pointless noises anyway.

As guns are drawn and their gazes search for me, the scene changes from calm to alert, but I force my anxiety back down my throat. I aim once more, not for the head since fifty yards is too far away for me to guarantee the accuracy, but for the chest. Only, the bastard moves just as the bullet flies. Slow panic threatens my muscles and focus, and only one of the next three bullets grazes one of them.

"Just stop moving!" The anger does something to me, and before they can spot my location, I squeeze the trigger once more, and the second man falls back on a piercing shriek. "Finally."

I take my eyes off of them for a moment, searching for the source of that shriek and find the woman Frankie took for a walk, now forcefully trapped in his arms, held away from the gruesome scene.

That brief moment was enough for the third man to spot the general direction the bullets came from, and several shattering pops ripple through the sound waves. I manage to duck before the concrete of the parapet takes the hits. I expected something akin to a boom when they made contact, but it's surprisingly quiet. I rise to find him moving closer, and more bullets strike concrete, one flying just above my head as I duck down.

"This is not how I plan to die." Not before I reach Frankie.

I slide down on my knees and forearms, inching to the edge of the parapet as low as I can go, since the bastard is shooting high. I peer past it as another shot hits the concrete—he's no longer fifty yards away. The sand is slowing him down, but he's covered half the distance to me. *Good.* My aim will be more certain. I squeeze the trigger and the bullet rips through his shoulder on a painful bellow, the sound like music to my ears, but he's not down yet.

"Who the fuck are you?" someone yells from the distance.

That's Frankie B.

I don't answer. He'll find out soon enough.

Pulling the trigger once more, I hit the man's hip, and he staggers, finally falling to the ground. My legs shake as I rise but the early moonlight hits his features, and for a couple grueling seconds I'm pinned in place, panic striking down my nerves.

"I know you." I whisper, focusing my pistol at him. The satisfaction at his fury-twisted pain rippling his features breaks through my fear.

He lifts his own weapon, but I shoot him right in that arm before he can aim, and the gun flies out of his hand.

"You fucking bitch!" he roars, screaming in pain he couldn't possibly hide.

His words don't touch me. I can hear them, but they mean nothing as they float somewhere in the distant places of my consciousness. This feels like a first step, because this bastard was there.

"You held me down." I seethe, stepping closer through the soft sand.

I'm only a few feet away, enough to see the pain-steeped rage marring his features. God, it looks so pretty.

What an odd thought.

Warmth fills my belly, satisfaction turning the adrenaline coursing through my veins into a surge of power.

"Evelyn!"

My gaze whips toward the voice, and I pinpoint Frankie's position—he's farther away than before, arms wrapped tight around the woman who struggles against him. He seems surprised that it's me he's looking at.

"He'll rip you apart," the man on the ground spits, "worse than he did the first time. And then he'll give you to all of us to share and break until all we're fucking is your empty carcass."

I look down at the man crumpled to the ground, spit falling between his thin lips as he attempts a seedy grin when I take aim once more. "But you won't be one of them."

The bullet hits right next to the bridge of his nose, blood and eye matter splattering all around him, and on me too. Then silence comes. Sweet silence amongst the crash of the surf, and when I look up at Frankie B, the smugness is broken by something else. It looks like fascination, but I think there's fear in there too.

Once again, I wait for the guilt and disgust for murdering

three people to crash down on me, but nothing comes. All I feel is contentment and can't help but wonder what's wrong with me. As I watch Frankie aim his weapon at me, I do feel a bit of fear too. Still no guilt though...

Is this it, the moment all will be over and he will no longer invade my dreams, turning them into endless nightmares?

I wait a few seconds longer, yet he makes no move to squeeze that trigger. Not even when I begin walking toward him. The blonde woman he forces against his body is shaking silently, trying but failing not to look at the bodies strewn across the beach as dark makeup streams down her pretty face.

I shouldn't waste time, but I'm curious. "How did you know my name?"

He grins and I want to vomit, "You told me. You probably don't remember though, you were off your head impaled on my dick at the time. "

Bile lodges in my throat and I tighten my grip around the gun. I shouldn't have asked.

"You're early, *Evelyn*. I wasn't expecting you yet." His lisp grinds my eardrums, and I would gladly make him eat a bullet just so I don't hear it anymore.

"Thought I would surprise you since you wanted me here so badly."

"The plan was to keep you for myself, but considering this"—he waves his gun around the beach and my handy-work—"taming will be necessary. And I'm afraid I'm not good at taming. I tend to kill them, accidentally of course. Lucky for you, I know a few experts at it. I want to say they'll take good care of you before you're returned to me, but the truth is... they'll break you apart. Bit by bit, split your mind in so many pieces, you won't even remember your *Sanctum*, and your body will bear no memory of anything other than their grueling training. You will be pliant, docile. And willing."

I swallow the acidic bile in my throat as I stop not even ten feet away from the man.

"Never." I fume, lining up my gun with his forehead.

I won't miss from this distance, but the asshole yanks the woman in front of him, using her to shield himself as she wails and squirms in his grip.

"Coward," I hiss, keeping my gaze off the intimidating barrel of his gun. "All those threats, just so you can kill me with a gunshot?"

"You stupid fucking girl! Who said anything about killing? I will maim, fix you later, or maybe just partially. Leave you with a limp or something as a constant reminder of your failure."

Failure...

Failure to protect my sister.

Failure to save us.

Failure to avenge us.

I will not be a failure! Not again.

I aim next to the woman's head and pull the trigger. Adrenaline breeds irrational strength, and she cries out, ripping out of his grip and drags herself away.

"Goddamn it!" he yells and shoots at the same time.

Piercing, hot pain slices through my left bicep, and with a shriek spilling off my lips, I squeeze the trigger.

It clicks. Empty.

What the...?

I do it again, but no bullets fly. Then I press it frantically a few more times, keeping my eyes on Frankie.

A sickening grin pulls at his lips, and he bolts toward me. My eyes widen as I step back and throw the useless gun at him. It hits his head but barely slows him down.

The instincts I've been honing in the last few months

kick in, and I duck to the right, slamming my right fist in his exposed ribs, then to his head when he bends in pain. He comes for me, staggering on the uneven sand, and I take the opening and kick the gun out his hand. But the asshole is quick, swearing as he throws punches that I manage to intercept and move away from.

I sidekick him low in the gut, then grind my teeth through the ache in my bicep as I throw a quick series of jabs to the throat and head, following him as he stumbles backward. Even so, he lands a couple clumsy but painful punches to my stomach, my legs staggering as I heave, and he takes the opportunity and tackles me to the ground. He doesn't pin me fully, but trying to push him off with that burn in my arm at the same time memories of him on top of me assault me, is almost impossible.

"I missed the feel of you under me," he spits at me with that lisp of his and the seediest of grins pulling at his lips.

When he bends his head to make some sort of contact with mine, I headbutt him with as much force as I can gather in this position. He barks out his anger more than his pain, but at this point I'm deep in a frenzy, half here, half in the memories of him laid over my body, and I use my good arm to land as many punches as I can, blocking his attacks as well. I only pause for one brief moment, but he takes the opportunity and wraps a hand around my throat, squeezing hard enough that pressure builds behind my eyes. I claw at his arms, his shoulder, back, neck, and everything else I can get my hands on, but the man doesn't budge. Instead, he squeezes tighter and panic surges deep in my belly as I bend my legs and plant my feet to try to haul him off.

"That's it, you look so much prettier when hope leaves your eyes and your life is in my hand," he says on a tone he probably thinks sounds seductive, but I want to throw up.

The edges of my vision blur, the haze spilling in further as the air catches in my lungs, but a cold slither of hope presses against my ankle, reminding me it's there, and I reach down to grasp it. A grin pulls at my lips, Frankie frowns, but the confusion turns to a gut-wrenching bellow when the blade of my knife sinks just under his ribs.

He releases my throat to check the wound, but I use his distraction to flip us over, straddling his thighs. I lift my arms high, holding the hilt with both hands, and as his eyes bulge and mouth falls open like a fish out of water, I slam the blade in his stomach with such force, the sides of my fist make him fold over, spitting blood.

The gurgled sounds coming from him scrape against the back of my throat threatening my stomach to turn over, so I pull the knife out and smash it right back in there. But the noise keeps happening, so I repeat the assault.

You're making me sick! Stop!

I slam it in again. Then once more, and the gurgling twists to a whimper. It caresses against my senses, it soothes.

I crawl backwards away from him, my chest tight with unshed tears that burn behind my eyes. He's still, his chest barely moving with weak breaths, mouth agape as he grasps to every ounce of air, and his gaze is fixed on me as he holds his palms over his bleeding abdomen.

"You were wrong... you're the one who looks pretty when hope leaves your eyes, Frankie B." I scoff, shaking my head. "What a stupid fucking name you get to bear while you die."

Utterly ridiculous, like some *guido* who ended up on the wrong side of the tracks. Through blood pouring slowly out of his mouth he manages a weak, taunting laugh.

"You'll die... a horrible death when he finds out," he mutters.

Frowning, I cock my head, but he continues anyway.

"I wanted you to myself... but you're worth less than cattle to him." He takes so long to spit out the words between blood and staggered breaths, I'm losing my patience.

He's referring to his boss, Bartiste. Killing his right-hand man will demand retribution, but The Sanctum is fully prepared to take him on.

"Save your breaths, Frankie. Your threats mean nothing." I gather my knees to my chest as I watch the man who changed my life, waste away. I'll sit here for however long I need to. I need to see this.

"My name..." He coughs, spluttering blood that looks black in the moonlight.

He whispers something, but through his dying breaths and the waves of the sea, I can't make it out. He blinks slowly, eyes staying more closed than open.

I slowly roll onto my knees, getting just a bit closer to the man to see if his moving lips actually spew any relevant words. When his gaze opens to me, I can see the dying light peering back, and I smile. It's the death of my nightmares.

"My name..." he says in a weak whisper, "is Franco *Bartiste*. He's my father."

He exhales one more breath as the light seeps out of his eyes, and my mouth falls open.

"Oh, my god." I just murdered Roberto Bartiste's son.

CHAPTER 35
Finnigan

I LOST COUNT OF HOW MANY times I called her. How many times I roared in her voicemail, screaming for her to answer her damn phone. Then I pleaded to her...

I prayed to all the gods I stopped believing in that she is okay, that he didn't do anything to her, that she hasn't left me.

But she did. After I bared my pain to her.

The guys and I were in the office, hashing out a quick plan to tackle Frankie, when a few trail cameras and sensors were triggered out in the forest. It's common, there are animals around here, too, and when we couldn't see anything, that's what we thought. But more were triggered, there was movement out of sight, through thick, tall bushes, and our minds were drawn to Bartiste and his men. Annika was already putting the kids to bed at that point, the others were safe tidying up through the house, but our security was on high alert and went to search. When they didn't find anything, Madds, Vin, and I went out there too. We had to be certain since we needed to make sure our family was safe.

But then tires screeched on the road, and Carter called for us. When we joined him, he told us Loreley noticed Evelyn was gone. We thought she was somewhere in the house, just like the others since we had absolutely no reason to think otherwise. Just after, Evelyn texted her, and when Carter showed it to me as we all climbed in his and Ronan's car, my heart sank.

I'm sorry, I wish there was another way, but it's between Maya and I, or you all and I. So, it isn't even a choice at all. I have to protect Maya, and if he is indeed setting a trap for The Sanctum, I can't let them fall in it. Not since it was set so no one could come and save me from him.

I know this could be a mistake, but I can't risk any of you. I hope you'll understand. All of you gave me more than I could ever repay you for, a life beyond my wildest dreams, and I love you for it. If I don't return, please, please make sure Maya is taken care of. I know it's selfish of me, but I can't let him win again.

I'm sorry.

I've re-read that text so many times, it's imprinted in my memory. A jagged claw has been shredding through the depths of my soul, its tip slowly slicing through my heart, and I didn't realize just how much of Evelyn seeped in until now. How much her absence hurts.

In that message she mentions protecting Maya. Us too. Like we've been threatened, being held as leverage over her. Is that the case? She thought her sacrifice would save us? Keep us safe?

The questions run rampant in my mind.

Even with her abandonment, I can't bear the thought of something happening to her. Losing her would be the end of me. I will not survive it. Somewhere through this strange journey we've had, she broke me apart, slicing the edges in patterns only she can match and put back together. And even if anyone but her would dare recognize the shapes, I would rather carve my heart out with bare hands than let them.

Carter weaves through the last of the streets that lead to the desolate beach, tires screeching on the asphalt as he takes that left. He tracked her phone the moment Loreley showed him the text, and knew exactly where she was. And she hasn't moved since. At all. It's both a good and a bad sign, and my stomach lurches with every bump in the road.

Through the whole car ride I wanted to scream at him to hurry the fuck up, but I didn't need to—he drove like a madman, the urgency not lost on him.

"There!" I point to the end of a building, right next to a parapet that edges the beach. "Stop."

I'm out of the car before the others stop behind us, and I duck behind the low wall, rushing to the edge of it. I'm so focused on taking in my surroundings, I almost stumble.

"That's Evelyn's," Maddox whispers behind me as I look down at the small bag dropped at my feet.

I peer in and the first thing I notice is her phone—that's why she hasn't moved. Well, that makes sense, but it doesn't make me feel better. Cocking the gun I peer out, and the first thing I notice is the man splayed out on the sand, dark blood splattered around him.

Did she do this?

Panic grips my insides, wondering how close he got to her. Is she hurt?

More fucking questions I have no answers to.

I look beyond the obviously dead man, down to the bottom of the beach, and mere feet from the crashing of the waves, I catch sight of a slim figure in the bright moonlight. From her hands and knees where she was leaning over the ground, she backs up and falls on her haunches.

Evelyn!

Wait, that's no ground she was leaning over—it's a person.

I'm running before any of these thoughts settle, noticing the other fallen bodies as I speed toward her. There's four in total, including the one she sits by.

She killed.

Again.

But this is not the same as when she protected Madds from getting shot. That was pure instinct, a spur of a moment decision to protect someone, and most of her destruction was driven by fear. Desperation, even. These four men sprawled on the sand weren't killed with the same drive. This was different. Very much intentional. Even premeditated.

I get to her just as she gathers her knees to her chest, staring at the ocean with tense shoulders, and a weak shudder raking through the rest of her body.

"Evelyn!" I shout for her.

But she doesn't even flinch. Maybe over the crashing of the surf she can't hear me.

My feet are sluggish in the soft sand, but I reach her nonetheless, stopping only a few feet behind her, my heart racing as I take in her delicate figure, so vulnerable in this moment. I open my mouth to call for her once more, but no words spill past my lips. Frankie, or better yet, his corpse, lies here, a knife buried to the hilt in his mangled chest. Nowadays, I barely blink when I take a life, so I can't imagine what's going through her mind right now.

But none of that matters right now because she's not

gone.

The breath I finally exhale is deeply charged with fear and anxious energy like I've never felt before, and I'm so happy to let it out.

I want to wrap her in my arms and scream at her in equal measures. I want to punish her for her stupidity, for not trusting me, and kiss her because she's still here.

Still alive.

Still *mine*.

Evelyn

THE INCESSANT BUZZING IN MY brain has quieted. Death brings silence, and not only for the dead. Yet, I find no peace. I feel no better, or worse. No relief...

I won. But no great feeling of victory has taken over me. The stories, the movies—they all lied.

"Evelyn?"

My name sounds distant, slow, like the fog it tries to penetrate is simply too dense to allow it to reach me. Yet it fights through...

"Are you okay?! Evelyn!"

Between each crash of the ocean's waves, the sand beneath my body vibrates. Their rhythm slows as the thumping loudens and the words that filter through the fog soften, carrying something that seems to be missing from my state of mind currently... something strange. Painful.

The vibrations stop as the man who's been soothing my nightmares plunges on his knees in front of me, gripping my shoulders harshly.

"Please, beautiful, please come back to me. Don't leave

me again..." The last sentence is spoken in the softest of whispers, carried away on the soft crashes of the waves like it never happened.

Fear.

That's what his words hold. And exactly what stares into my eyes from his striking blue ones.

Did I put that there?

"For the love of god, Evie, please! Are you okay?"

His touch is warm, and tight. He's holding me steady and only now I realize it's because I'm shivering. Am I cold? The salty, strong ocean breeze whips my hair around my face and goosebumps spread over my bare arms. Though, they may be due to Finnigan's possessive touch on me.

He arrived out of nowhere, like I wished him here once the madness ended. Or maybe that's why I took my phone with me, knowing Carter could track it.

I need him.

But will he want me after what I've done?

His eyes roam over my body, pulling at my limbs, petting me, like he's looking for seeping wounds while holding his breath. He hisses when he reaches my bicep, and mutters something about a flesh wound. Watching the foamy waves doing their calm dance as the moonlight shines brighter, higher in the sky than when I came here, I let him do it.

My muscles are weak. My will is even weaker. Numbness seeps through the fibers forming my being, an ominous gloom I can't escape, and they feel a lot like punishment. I deserve it all and not even for what I've done, but for feeling absolutely nothing about it. Nothing at all.

"Oh God, you're okay." He sighs, that sickening fear expelled out of his body as he rips the bottom of his T-shirt and wraps it around my arm.

What's wrong with me? Killing four people should rip my

soul apart, should break me, should shred it with guilt. Yet… there's nothing.

"Evie darling, we have to leave."

Why? The salty breeze soothes my skin, and if I don't move, I can keep enjoying it. A pure moment within the destruction I caused.

Not only the one on this beach and the dire consequences it will bring, but what I left behind. The people I so harshly abandoned, even if I did do it to protect them. One of them sits right before me, and I cannot bear acknowledging his presence. I had a tinge of hope that I would survive tonight, but I didn't actually think I would. Do they hate me? Does he hate me?

Distant footsteps shuffle through the sand somewhere behind me, and I flinch, but don't turn. No matter who it is, I know they won't touch me. Not with Finnigan here. He wraps one large hand over my bony knee, narrowing an assessing gaze on me.

"The others are here." He jerks his head toward the source of the shuffling without breaking eye contact. "A cleanup crew is on the way too."

Cleanup crew. Will they scrub my soul too? My thoughts drift somewhere in the distant parts of my mind where they seek the solace that should be there with Frankie's death.

Franco Bartiste actually.

"Are you okay? Say something."

Finnigan's harsher tone forces me to focus and I narrow my gaze on him. Not because of the question, but because of the kindness looking back at me. It holds a tinge of pity.

I don't need his damn pity.

"Christ, listen to me, you've been here for too long. We have to go." His tone grows colder. It doesn't match his expression.

"Go then."

Please don't. I'm scared. But I'm even more scared to be alone with him, to face him properly.

"I'm not fucking playing. Someone could have witnessed this, and if the police were called, you can't risk being seen."

I draw in a deep breath as his eyes narrow on me. He's losing his patience. Oh well. I shrug, but that angers him further.

"Fuck this!" He grips my good arm, pulls me up, and before I can register the movement, he dips down and throws me over his shoulder.

That snaps me right out of my trance, bringing me back to the reality I've been avoiding.

"Son of a—! Put me down, right now!" I smack his lower back, avoiding his annoyingly perfect-shaped ass as he moves to walk away.

"No. If I say we have to go, we have to fucking go."

"I'll walk!" I argue, as I plant my palms on his lower back and push myself up.

But a crack splits through the softening crash of the surf, and a sharp ache heats my right ass cheek.

"You didn't just—" the protest lodges itself in my throat when the last man I killed comes into view, lying on a bed of blood-stained sand with my blade stuck in his gut.

"Ronan, grab that knife."

Even his brother's here?

Embarrassment pools in the pit of my stomach, but I'm unsure why. Maybe it's because I consider the man normal since he's technically not part of this world anymore. And now he's a witness to my sins.

Actually, there's another witness.

"The woman!" I say on a loud gasp.

"We got her. She's fine."

The bobbing around on his shoulder is making me nauseous, and I grab onto him to steady myself.

"What will you do to her?"

"*With,* Evelyn. With her. We're not gonna do anything to her. Carter will question her to find out if she's a threat, and take it from there."

"Carter?!" I all but squeal. "He's going to eat her alive!"

"Only if he has to."

Finnigan ducks down and settles me back onto my unsteady feet, and I'm about to argue that his answer isn't soothing me in any way, but it only reaches his warm palm. Frustration pools in the back of my throat and bleeds through my eyes as the man holds his hand over my mouth.

"I said"—his tone lowers just as his brows do—"we have to leave. Get in the car."

He pushes me backward, and my legs hit something, but there's only empty space behind my ass.

"Le' 'e 'o." I mumble against his skin, and the bastard grins.

He actually grins. So I push my tongue out against his palm, licking it as surprise hits his brows.

"Get in the car, Evelyn." He says it with the softest, most soothing of growls rumbling deep in his chest, and the command spills through my body like syrup, driving my legs to bend and shift until I'm sitting in the car.

A few moments after the door shuts, he slips on the other side of me, and Maddox and Ronan climb in the front at the same time.

Reality sucks the air out of this enclosed space, and only the roar of the engine seems to save me. The man I... like, his brother who has been taking care of my sister, and the giant who has become like a brother to me, sit in an uncomfortable silence as we pull away from the bloodied beach.

I sneak a peek at Finnigan, and his gaze finds mine at the

same time. I cannot decipher the range of emotions burning through me. There's too many, too loud, some dark, and others unbearably light. I don't know what to say, if it's the right time to apologize. Will there ever be one?

Pressure builds in my chest and lodges itself in my throat as I lose control of my breathing, and prickles explode beneath every inch of my skin, urging me to scratch it bloody and get them out. Finnigan's gaze widens and his hands rush to me in a split second, just as a broken, sharp cry slips through the dam forming at the back of my tongue. He drags me on his lap, wrapping me in his warm embrace that feels more like home than anything I ever experienced, and presses my cheek in the crook of his neck.

Right here… in the arms of the man I can no longer deny I love, my soul breaks.

The dam opens, and my chest frees the fear and anguish that has plagued me since the moment Franco Bartiste stole me away. He tore so much from me, ripped me open and filled me with malice.

My cries bounce around the car, mixing with the rumble of the engine as I curl deeper into Finnigan's body, folding my arms against my chest as he tightens his hold on me, whispering soothing words against my hair. Even now, he doesn't dare thread his fingers through it—a gesture that would calm any normal person. Instead he keeps to my back, my neck, rubbing in circles.

There's nothing normal about me. I crashed so hard from my high horse, back when I used to judge Finnigan and his Sanctum for their crimes and violent ways. I could blame them for what I've done. For what I've become. But I would be a hypocrite. I was one back then as well.

Because this has been *me* all along.

Their violence hasn't impacted me, they haven't even

exposed me to it. It all comes from within, deep in my dark little soul that craves revenge as much as it does the love I feel in this man's touch.

My tears fall in waves, joining the desperate cries I can't control.

"I'm so sorry!" I mutter, repeating those words over and over again praying that the next time they come out, there will be no fear in them.

"Breathe, Evie darling, breathe." He soothes me with soft kisses as I shake against his chest.

Only, I cry harder, nightmares and memories spilling with every tear and broken sob, and through it all I realize... I still feel no remorse for the people I murdered. And the tears seem endless now.

"That's it... let it all out," Finnigan says as he strokes my back gently.

God, it helps. Why does he have this effect on me? I don't know how much time passes, how many roads we've swerved on, or how fast Ronan's been driving, but my chest finally fills with a full breath of air.

"I left!" I blurt out between the last of the sobs.

"You did." He says in such a calm tone, it scares me.

"Why are you...? You're not even upset. You don't care."

The car screeches to a halt at the same time Finnigan pushes me only far enough away that he can look into my eyes, and I hear a muttered *fuck* from the front seats.

"I. Don't. Care?"

Oh... I screwed up.

There is no trace of sweet baby blue in his eyes, only the menacing shade of destructive ocean storms, and they're pulling me in their vortex.

"I—"

"Don't!" he interrupts with a raised index finger, silencing me with a deep chill in my bones.

The car moves again and the echo outside of it reminds me of a parking garage. I dare peek past the man who still holds me tight on his lap and confirm it—we're home, in his building.

A few moments later, he maneuvers me out of his hold, then pulls me out of the car after him, but doesn't say a word.

The others are silent too, and even if I was just in the car with him, I dread looking Madds in the eyes. He's probably so pissed at me. When Finn takes a step out of the way, I'm faced with the giant that doesn't look all that gentle right now. Amber eyes regard me with so much fury, it could only be bred from love.

He grips my shoulder, nostrils flaring when he notices the strip of fabric wrapped around my bicep, but doesn't say a thing.

I drop my head, chewing on my lip nervously. "I'm sorry."

"Later," he mutters in response, giving my shoulder a tight squeeze, and I know I'm down for some serious telling-off.

But I guess *later* means he still wants to have me in his line of sight.

A warm hand wraps around mine just as Madds releases me, and I'm pulled away.

"We're going upstairs. Now."

"But—"

"I swear to god, woman." He growls deep in his throat as we hurry over to the elevator, where one of his men is currently waiting, holding it open.

"They're gonna know... about us, now," I whisper.

"That ship fucking sailed, Evelyn," he spits back as the doors close, sealing us in.

I'm left with questions I have no right to demand answers to, and the rest of the ride up to the penthouse is quiet, sizzling with tension, all wrong and right, heavy and soothing. But the anticipation of what's coming is killing me, because no matter what, it's not going to be good.

The *ding* comes too soon, and when the doors open and he steps out, I almost hope he'll leave me in here. But he plants a hand on the frame, and pierces me with his gaze. The order is silent, but I follow it anyway.

The penthouse is bathed in moonlight and the faint glow of two distant lamps, but they're enough to see the tensed, slow rise and fall of Finnigan's shoulder.

"Finnigan, I—"

"I don't care?!" He whips around, rage rolling out of his mouth like a shattering storm as he pins me in place with nothing but his menacing eyes. "You think I don't fucking care about you, Evelyn? Look at me, goddamn it!"

I don't understand, I am looking right at him.

He steps closer, the glow showing him in such an eerie light, he's godlike. Strong. Beautiful. Broken.

Broken.

His heaving breaths, tensed shoulders, fisted hands... oh god, the pain in his features, brimming his eyes, threatens to knock me on my knees.

"You think I'm not upset? Jesus Christ, Evelyn, how could you even say that I don't care?" His steps echo through the vast space as he nears me, and I tense when he grabs the side of my throat, tipping my head back with his thumbs under my chin, forcing my gaze to him. "Is that all you learned in the last few weeks? Hell, in the last few months?! I care, Evelyn. More than I've ever cared for anyone. Ever. I can't fucking breathe knowing I could have lost you before I realized... before I told you that I—I—"

With bruising pressure his lips crush my own, the kiss hungry, demanding, pained, forcing out of me solace and life-force to soothe his own.

I grip his waist, but the moment my fingers sink in, he pushes me away, holding me at arm's length.

"I can't believe you left me. Us. Your sister."

Tears return to my eyes as I gaze back into that pain that I put in his.

"I thought it was the only way. He threatened her. He had her under surveillance."

He shakes his head, releasing my neck, and grabs my hands, holding them between us. "You should have trusted me to help you. To make this right and kill that asshole. Now it's you who carries his blood on your hands."

Literally. As I glance down, my hands and arms are stained with blood, now dry and itchy.

"It will wash off."

He scoffs, shaking his head. "That's not what I mean. This kind of violence is something that stains your soul. You shouldn't have been the one to carry something like this. This was intentional, willing, premeditated, not like when you protected Madds."

I shake my head, tightening my grip on his fingers as I chew on my lip, the words too heavy to be spoken.

"Evie?"

Swallowing the lump in my throat, I take a deep breath and brace myself.

"My soul was stained long before I came to Queenscove."

CHAPTER 36
Evelyn

"WHAT DO YOU MEAN?"

I shake my head, steering the conversation away. "I'm sorry. I should have trusted you, but he threatened you too. All of you. After he messaged me, I heard you all talk about how you spotted him, that you thought it was a trap. It was the same location where I was supposed to meet him later, and it all sounded too good to be true. Why would he show himself there, just a couple of hours before our meeting, if not..."

"To kill us before he got to you," Finnigan finishes for me.

"It sounds silly now, knowing that it was just his ridiculous confidence, but I couldn't risk it. The thought of anyone dying for me was unbearable. I trust you, god, I trust you with my life. With Maya's life!"

He softens at those last words. He knows I value her much

more than I value myself.

"I understand, but please, for the love of god, never. Ever. Do that again. Trust me to protect you both. We haven't exposed you to our *ways* because it wasn't necessary for you to see any of that, but believe me when I tell you, as scary as Bartiste and his men sound, we are scarier. And more than ready to take them."

I sigh, watching him with regret I struggle to hold back. "I can't rationalize it more than I have. Not so deep down I know all of that to be true. But I think the fact that Bartiste has evaded you successfully scared me as well."

"Evie darling, what we share with you is at face value, because you don't need to know every single detail. You shouldn't. But trust me when I say, Bartiste and his men have not evaded us successfully. We are being smart about how we take them down. Bartiste is hiding, but to bring down a kingdom successfully, you start with the army. We've been picking hard at it, and today our soldiers took down more than half of the one he brought here with him. Which is how we found out where Frankie was. Bartiste has experience in hiding, I can admit that no matter how hard it bruises my ego, but he is no longer smarter or stronger than The Sanctum."

My shoulders fall on a relaxing sigh. So many people dead shouldn't be a soothing thought, but alas, they could burn alive in a mass grave for all I care.

Finnigan leads me further in the penthouse, setting me down on the plush sofa, and leaves me to watch the clear, starry sky through the floor to ceiling windows. Water runs in the kitchen, then he returns with a first aid kit and a bowl of water, holding his hand out for mine. I wince when he unwraps the small wound on my bicep, but I can't hold in the smile when pain skirts his eyes. It seems to hurt him more than me, and that does something to my little heart. We don't speak as he cleans the gash. He focuses there and I focus on him, unable to stare anywhere else.

I don't know how to process this. Good things don't happen to me. Instead, everything I touch seems to crumble.

"Okay," he says as he dabs the area. "I'm going to add a few adhesive stitches, but luckily, it's a graze. Albeit a little deeper."

I nod as he rises and disappears again, leaving me with my intrusive thoughts as I stare out the windows. I'm going to miss watching the horizon over the ocean if I do decide to return to Fleeton. This place calls for my soul. A brief time later Finnigan returns with a tray, a bunch of glasses clinking on it as he sets it on the coffee table.

"What's this?"

He points to each of them as he rattles them off. "Whiskey, vodka, rum and coke, vodka lime, water, and orange juice. To cover all... needs."

I puff out a stifled laugh, reach for the vodka lime and down half of it with a groan.

"What did you mean, Evelyn? When you said your soul was already stained before you came here?"

I didn't think I would evade this line of questioning, did I? Hence the variety of drinks.

"Remember what I told you about how I lost my mom?" I wait for his answer, but he frowns in disbelief and nods. "Sorry, I guess I just don't assume you hold onto everything I tell you."

"I remember everything. Go on."

"Maya and I were homeless not long after, but I did my best to keep an ear out for information about her murderer. I found out none of the men responsible were caught. When it comes to gang crime, they rarely are. The thing is... when you live on the streets, even in your car, you hear things. Homeless people are a wealth of information because people don't pay them any mind. They're almost invisible but hear so much. And sometimes they talk. That's how, about ten months or so after we ended up on the streets, I caught wind of this guy, a young one, who was bragging about the night of his gang initiation. Same month, same place, the exact shooting that took my mother. He bragged about how they escaped murder charges, and how *cool* it made him. Raised his street cred."

I pause as Finn wipes a hand over his face, releasing a staggered sigh.

"I followed that *breeze* for a while, until I learned more about him, the gang, who he was, and finally, I saw him. His face is still imprinted in my memory, but after that... I could barely sleep. He plagued my nightmares and pulled my mother into them too. It was always both of them, never just him. A grueling reminder of what he took from me, from us. Then one night, we were staying in this shoddy motel in the bad side of town. One of many, Maya was sleeping in the room, and I went out to get some food. Then our fates aligned, and I heard him..."

I draw in a deep breath and throw back the rest of the vodka sour. "He was in an alley, on the phone, smoking. All alone. Even through that darkness, I knew it was him. Nothing could have stopped me that night. Not Maya, not my dad, not the police. All I saw was shades of crimson, and all it took was noticing a rusty pipe on the ground. I grabbed it and ran toward him just as he ended the call. He didn't even see me coming. It wouldn't have mattered if he did. No one could have recognized him by the time I stopped. I didn't even scream as I did it. Rage consumed me. I'm not even certain he was dead when I left. He looked dead. Felt dead. What concerned me the most was that I didn't care. Still don't."

Looking at Finn, I expect to see more pity, but it's just

sadness gazing back.

"I'm sorry, darling. I really am. That shouldn't have been the aftermath of your mother's murder."

"No. The police should have caught him. All of them. I shouldn't have become a murderer and hated myself for it. But you see, Finn, I blamed you and your criminal world for destroying mine, when in fact... I'm projecting the anger and hate I have for myself. Because all I felt that night was a worrying sense of victory and satisfaction. No remorse. I'm no better, no different."

He watches me calmly, no judgment staining his gaze as he quietly sips his drink, keeping a possessive hold on my thigh.

"In some twisted way I understand. I realized it's what I'm doing with Ronan, and I'm definitely projecting on Aaro." He shakes his head. "And now? Do you have the same feelings about these men?"

I swallow the lump in my throat, questioning if sincerity is the right course of action. He cocks his head ever so slightly, urging me on.

"No," I answer.

He nods once, the movement free of hidden meanings.

"I will bother you with this question, over and over again for a while, Evelyn, and I'm not gonna apologize for it—how are you feeling, are you okay?"

I like that he doesn't dwell on what I've done, on the guilt or lack thereof, he doesn't insist.

"Better, honestly."

I thought I was handling my emotions well, especially with therapy too, but I was wrong. I was just seeping through the seams, letting out only enough to function, and held onto the full brunt of the heartache, pain, and the real tears that come from my hidden scars.

"I know you feel no regret for the men you killed, no

matter the impeccable job you did." The little smirk at the end of that gives me an odd sense of pride, "But what you did was still significant, because one of them was Frankie B. Talk to me about it. Don't hide or bottle up any emotions or conflicts you might feel. Something like this, no matter your past, can eat you up from the inside without even realizing. We're not all built to be killers."

Christ, this is a rather odd conversation. The crime lord is basically giving me *murder aftercare*. Well, how can I complain about that?

I nod, and grab the glass of straight-up vodka, drinking a quarter of it, following up with the orange juice to soothe the burn.

"Come here." He drags me against his side before he finishes the request, wrapping his arms around me and burying his nose in my hair.

It takes me a few breaths to relax into his hold. I'm not sure I deserve the comfort, but his warm body against mine feels so right. I wrap one arm around his middle, and when his dark chocolate and sea salt scent invades my senses, I nestle deeper into him.

Mmm... I could make a little tart that tastes like him. Cacao crust, dark chocolate and sea salt cream, piercing blue baroque swirls blooming around a skull in the center, to match his eyes. My mouth already waters. One deep yawn and my eyes drift close. The man is so comfortable. I could climb on top of him and fall asleep.

"I think it's time for a shower and bed." He shifts to rise, but I tighten my hold.

"There's something else." I stop him. "Frankie—it's just a nickname."

"Yes, I know. We haven't found out his real identity yet."

"I did."

With rigid, coiled muscles he leans back and looks down at me, loosening his hold as I tip my head to meet his eyes.

"His real name is Franco *Bartiste*."

Finnigan's eyes widen as his mouth falls open before he spits a long series of vulgar curses.

"I killed Roberto Bartiste's son," I add.

"His son..." he whispers, processing the information. "I guess this is when we find out if Bartiste gave a shit about him or not. It will either drag him out of hiding, or we simply continue with our plan."

He tries to downplay the magnitude, but it shadows over his features still. Before I can say anything else he grabs his phone, typing vigorously, then rises, pulling me with him and toward his bedroom.

I don't protest. My lids weigh heavy, and the dried blood is too itchy on my skin. I need to get rid of it and burn these damn clothes. The last thing I need is more Frankie B on me.

Finnigan

I LAY AWAKE FOR MOST of the six hours she slept, watching her like she was going to disappear on me once more if I blinked for too long. I thought I knew fear, experienced the broad spectrum of it, but I was wrong. This isn't fear of loss as I thought, of Evelyn being taken away from me. This is fear of abandonment. She *chose* to leave and take on Frankie B, no matter if she lived or died at the end. No matter if she saw me again. I'm afraid she'll do it again, not forced like this time around, but by her own volition.

That is fear.

Of course I've never felt anything like this before, how could I when I've never experienced this intense, heart-wrenching emotion for someone. I'm afraid to give it a name. What if I do and I'm left with just that... a name? No Evelyn. No object for my desires, for my heart to cling to.

She said she hasn't decided if they're going to stay in Queenscove. I'm struggling to understand why the decision is so hard to make. Do we frighten her so much? Do I? I'm trying to be a good man and allow her space to make her choice, but goddamn it, I'm not a good man! And I certainly don't want to give her a choice in this. She simply cannot leave. Evelyn belongs in Queenscove. With me.

Forcing her hand isn't quite the option, but I can offer an incentive. And it's landing in Queenscove in less than an hour.

I'm about to wake her up when a soft moan passes her lips and hits my cock in an instant. My muscles coil around the sound as a ghost of a strain tightens her eyebrows together. I want to dip right into whatever dreams she's having, because the moment the comforter shifts with her legs squeezing together, I know it's a good one.

Actually, I think I will do just that—dip into her dream and make it a reality. Rising ever so slowly, I climb out of bed, constantly looking back to make sure she doesn't stir or wake up as I go to the walk-in closet, grab a silk tie and carefully climb back into bed. This is going to be a challenge, but I'm intrigued to see if this little minx is a deep sleeper.

She's already laying on her back, only vaguely angled toward the right, so part of the work is already done. With the softest of movements and touches, I bring her wrists together, wrapping the tie around them until they're secure and she's immobilized. I do a quick check of her bullet graze to make sure it's not bleeding, but it all looks good. Reaching over behind the bed, I pull out the strap that hangs there unused since I installed it years and years ago, letting it drape over the padded headboard, the metal ring at the end glinting against the dark blue velvet. I lift Evelyn's arms over her head, the air straining my lungs when she stirs, and I'm expecting her eyes to pop open and see me like this. But she only moans again, her lips parting to let the enticing mewl out.

She's a goddamn dream.

I let her joined wrists rest against the headboard as I loop the remaining length of the tie around the ring, tying it into a bow. Breathing a little easier when she still doesn't wake up, I shift backwards on the bed, pulling the comforter with me, and expose her whole body. She looks so fucking pretty laying here deep in her sleep, completely unaware that she's about to be fucked until her tight little pussy has my name imprinted on its lips. My cock stirs, fully hard as my balls ache with the need to come all over her soft skin. Even in a tank top and underwear she still looks like every bit the sexual creature she's becoming.

She stirs, rubbing her thighs together in the softest of gestures, and the moment her back arches, I strike, covering her mouth with my palm. Her eyes fly wide open, fear laced through the silver and gold, and she shrieks against my skin, kicking her legs in a desperate attempt to free herself once she realizes her arms are bound.

There's only a brief pause in her frenzied writhing and it's the exact moment her gaze shifts, softening with awareness. Yet she holds onto her panic, nurtures it as I yank her tank top up, exposing her breasts to my hungry eyes and even hungrier mouth. I roll one soft bud between my fingers, grinning when she yelps against my palm at the flicker of pain, because her arching back and squirming betrays her pleasure.

"You're fucking beautiful just like this, tied to my bed, your eyes glazed with lust," I tell her as I reach over and start wrenching down her underwear.

She twists to try to stop me, but she exposes her taut ass to me in the process. With a sharp crack of my palm, she yelps again, pausing her writhing enough for me to yank the offending fabric off as she curses against my hand.

"Aaah! Let me go, you ass—!" she screams as I release her mouth, but her insult is muffled by the underwear I shove in her mouth.

"Look at that. How fucking devastating you look, gagged

and bound. Can you taste it, Evie darling?" I ask, but she frowns. "Can you taste the sweet wetness on your panties? How fucking drenched you get for me?"

She tries to keep the needy mewl from resonating through her throat, but she fails, and I'm on her in the next second, kneeling over her. She quickly shuffles back, bringing her knees up as she attempts to hide her pretty pussy from me, and my cock responds with a tight jerk. I'm impressed at how good she is at playing into this fantasy.

"You think you can stop me from feasting on that tight little cunt of yours? It's mine, Evelyn. All. Fucking. Mine."

I wrap my hands around her knees and pull her as far down the bed as the strap holding her allows, reveling on her muffled protests and cries. They turn to pure fiery screams when I dip down and suck one nipple into my mouth, nipping just to the edge of pain, as I thrust two fingers in her aching core.

"Your screams might spell *no*, Evie darling, but this pussy is weeping for my fucking cock. Are you gonna be a good girl and take it?" I say with a menacing grin.

She shakes her head in response, her eyes glassy with need.

I slide down in one swift move, enjoying her little cry when my fingers leave her core, but I replace them with my tongue, watching as her head whips back and eyes squeeze shut. She's so fucking sweet, a decadent feast as I roll my tongue inside of her, close to the spot that can tip her over the edge in mere seconds. I have to pin her by the thighs when I move to suck on her clit, because she's just about to shoot off the bed from the onslaught of sensations.

I'm not easing her into it. No, I want her to drown in fucking pleasure, cry out for release and reprieve all at once. So I thrust two digits back into her aching core as I assault her swollen bundle of nerves, sucking hard before I threaten it with my teeth, licking and rolling it between my lips. She's writing on the bed as her pussy pulses around my fingers, but when it grows in intensity, when she's too close to the cusp of her orgasm, I pull out. She cries out, and I can't help but smirk.

"Change your mind, by any chance? Are you gonna be a good girl and take my cock?"

She frowns, her chest rising and falling with her indecision, then shakes her head, violet hair whipping against her flushed cheeks.

"Okay then," I say as I dip back down, covering her core with my mouth.

Only this time I ignore her clit completely and lap the sweet center of her, massaging her walls as she squirms and whimpers. Words are being muffled by the makeshift gag, and I have a feeling they're all deliciously vulgar, because the woman is rolling her hips against my face, seeking the release she desperately craves. Her pussy tightens around my tongue, my face is drenched in her pleasure, but this is not happening on her terms.

Pressing a palm over her lower belly, I hold her down, but her eyes open so wide, I'm not sure if it's from pleasure or pain. She's not snapping her fingers, so I know she's still into this, but I snap mine with a question in my eyes, just in case she forgot the safe word. A brief shake of her head is my answer.

Licking my way up her body, I latch onto one nipple as I plunge three fingers inside her, smirking when her brows draw together at the stretch. But her body shudders under me and I realize that I never enjoyed holding a woman just at the edge of release, playing with her until she's a begging mess under me. As Evelyn bucks down on my hand, attempting to fuck herself with my fingers, she needs no words to beg, her body does it for her. But I push my fingers in as far as they'll go, pressing my whole hand over her core and pin her down.

"Last goddamn chance." I seethe. "Are you gonna be a good fucking girl and take my cock?"

I see the bratty, challenging denial in her eyes, before the first sweep of her head to one side, but before she can swing it the other way, I'm braced on one hand, my cock is lined up with the hot center of her, and I thrust forward. She cries out, a lust-filled moan as her head rolls back and legs widen to allow me more access.

"Fffuck!" I growl as I drop onto my forearms, caging her soft body beneath me.

I kept her pleasure on the edge, but I should have realized I was holding mine right along with it, because... Christ... I'm gonna come in two strokes. I better make them good ones then.

With harsh bucks of my hips, I fuck into her, turning her little yelps into wanton cries as she wraps her legs around my waist, angling her hips and allowing me deeper. Her muffled cries grow louder with each of my thrusts, but they're not enough for me anymore. So I rip the panties out of her mouth as I roll my hips on a deep stroke, and I almost come at the sound of her lustful moan. Such sweet music to my needy ears.

"Finn... oh god! I think—I think I'm coming," she whispers as she pants.

Meeting each of my thrusts with a harsh buck of her hips, she demands the pleasure she vehemently deserves.

"Eyes on me, Evie darling. Let me see you shatter," I demand when her eyes squeeze closed, and I reach between us to help her off the ledge to oblivion.

A ghost of a touch over her clit and she tumbles over, legs shaking as she holds onto me, pushing me even deeper into her spasming core.

"Fuck, I'm gonna—"

I try to pull away so I don't spill inside of her raw, but

she holds me so damn tight, lost in her ecstasy, that I can't possibly get out in time. Not when my own oblivion slams into me with devastating force and pulls me into the depths of pleasure.

When she arches her back and moans as my cum shoots inside her, I swear I come even harder, but I'm hungry for those wanton sounds, and I swallow them with a feral kiss. Pressing her deeper into the pillow as my cum spills in never-ending streams, she meets each thrust of my tongue with her own, stroking me as we both claw our way out of this hypnotizing euphoria.

"God, you're fucking perfect, Evelyn. So goddamn perfect. And mine," I whisper against her mouth.

"All yours," she murmurs, and my heart seems to shatter and piece back together all at once, only it feels different... like it's both mine and hers, and she holds most of the power over it.

All yours...

Maybe there is hope yet.

Maybe she'll stay.

Maybe she'll be *forever* mine.

CHAPTER 37
Evelyn

FINNIGAN'S SOFT KISSES STILL LINGER on my lips half an hour later, mixed with the words we spoke to each other in the heat of the moment. They sounded more like oaths... vows.

Mine...

All yours...

Until then, I never allowed myself to acknowledge how much I crave exactly that. I want to be his. God, I *need* to be his. Because this infuriatingly gorgeous and smart man has my whole damn heart.

"So you're okay?" Maya's little voice pulls me back into the car as Finn drives us through the bright streets of Queenscove.

"I'm perfectly fine. I'm sorry I didn't wake you up to say goodbye last night." It's a lie since I was gone before she actually fell asleep, but she doesn't need to know that. I'm also wearing a long sleeve shirt so she can't see the bandage wrapped around my arm.

"Okay, then," she says, seemingly satisfied. "So where are we going, Finn?"

"Asking me for the third time is not going to make me tell you, Maya," Finn answers, shaking his head with a smile on those enticing lips. He puts one on mine instantly.

He hasn't told me where we're heading either.

After he screwed my brains out and turned me into a mindless puddle of euphoria, he wrapped my arm and we took a hot shower together before he helped me get dressed. It's just a flesh wound, but he's been fussing over me like a mother hen. It's endearing really. Then he told me he had something to show me. My curiosity spiked since it was barely seven thirty in the morning.

He's been kind of jittery since, flexing his fingers around the steering wheel every time he lets out a heavy, charged breath. He dismissed my questions, insisting it's a surprise for both me *and Maya*, which only spiked my curiosity further. But I relented, it was a lost cause. On our way to pick her up we stopped at the pharmacy to buy the morning-after pill he suggested, and I strongly agreed with since I don't want any *surprises*, and drove to this mysterious location.

I don't know how close or far we are, but he wouldn't be so secretive if it wasn't big. Something about this whole affair both frightens and excites me.

"Are we close?" I give up and ask the question.

He slows down and takes a left on a tree-lined street, but apart from gates at the end of it, there's nothing else.

"We're here," he answers, stealing a glance at me.

My eyes widen and mouth falls open when the car slows down in front of a huge set of shiny black gates that are probably over fifteen-feet tall, surrounded by towering brick walls. That's not what makes my stomach jump with nerves, but the elegant, gold lettered sign screwed to the wall—*Queen Anne Sanctuary*. The cryptic name won't mean anything to most people, but to me, it does. I've looked into it. It's probably the most prestigious and expensive assisted living institute on the South coast, if not beyond, for both the elderly and those who require extra care. Above all, they specialize in a variety of conditions from Alzheimer to MS.

And it's beyond any scope of my imagination in terms of monthly fees. More money that I could ever dream of seeing, not just having.

"Finnigan, what are we doing here?" I ask, unable to keep my eyes off the gate as it opens to what pretty much looks like a well-kept park, filled with tall trees, and flowerbeds flanking the weaving paths that cross through.

I turn to him when no response comes, and he looks at me for a brief moment, then focuses back on the slow drive up the narrow street.

"Wow!" Maya exclaims behind me. "Look at that mansion!"

My head whips back ahead and a beautiful, massive house springs to life through the trees. The façade seems to be built in the same highly decorative period style of Lulu's building, with tall windows, and beautiful iron work. I've seen the place in photos, but it's something else in real life. Finnigan parks right at the front, completely ignoring the *visitors car park* sign that points to the right.

He exits first, signaling me to wait as he walks around the car and opens the doors for us.

I have to ask again. "Seriously, Finnigan, don't mess with me. What are we doing here?"

"Visiting." The cryptic answer spills nonchalantly off of his lips, and I would smack him if my sister wasn't here.

Instead, I follow him through the black double doors

looming over the few steps up to them, and we're immediately greeted by a stylish, black-haired woman, wearing a beige skirt suit.

"Mr. Hennessey, lovely to see you again." The woman shakes his hand with a wide smile, way too enthusiastic for my liking, then turns to me. "Miss Shaw, it's a pleasure to welcome you at Queen Anne's." She reaches over, delicately shaking my hand.

She knows my name? What in the hell is going on here?

"Evelyn, this is Ms. Campbell, the director of the institute."

Director? The woman runs the entire place. I nod, forcing myself to remain polite, but a lump quickly makes its way into my throat, urging me to scream my questions.

"Please, follow me." She turns, swiping a card over the access pad of one of the French doors that lead away from this foyer.

I briefly see the reception desk and a few people caught in conversation, but she ushers us through the door she holds open, and I don't have time to process. Dragging Maya along with me, we follow through the corridor lit only by the picture lights above replicas of famous oil paintings, and then through another locked door.

Only, this space is bustling with activity. A large common room with a mixture of normal tables and chairs, comfy sofas and armchairs around coffee tables, with lots of people caught in chatter and laughter as nurses watch over them or help them around. Everyone looks calm and happy. Content.

I can't help the slight smile pulling at the corner of my lips.

"This way."

Ms. Campbell directs us through an open door, down a corridor covered on one side with floor to ceiling windows, and I almost run straight into Finnigan's back when she halts.

"The meeting room is right here and, of course, privacy

is ensured."

What in heaven's name is happening? What is this meeting about?

God, I have so many questions.

She points delicately toward an open door, signaling me to walk in. I wait for Finn to take the lead, but he just turns and looks at me.

Laughter echoes past that open door, deep and rich, pure and so damn familiar my heart stops as my mouth falls open, prickles tingling the back of my eyes.

"Daddy!" Maya shouts, pulling free from my hold.

"What did you do?" I whisper to Finnigan, heat filling my chest, spreading through my nerves like wildfire, and I have to clench my fists, digging my nails in my palm to keep from letting it out.

I don't wait for his answer, even as his gaze softens, brows pulling together with a silent apology I can't bear to hear right now. Whipping around, I find my father holding his youngest daughter to his chest with small tears in his eyes as he kisses the top of her head.

Oh god, Daddy.

I'm running to him before I finish the thought, and wrap both of them in my arms, burying my head in the crook of his neck. His scent is so utterly him, even after all this time and through devastating memory loss, he still uses the same aftershave—musk and lemon.

"My sweet Evie, I've missed you so much. You changed your hair!"

"Daddy, are you okay?" I pull back, checking him all over, before I grip his cheeks to hold him to me.

"Perfect now."

His warm smile brings a fresh set of tears to my eyes. He puts Maya down and pulls me in the warmest, tightest hug, dropping sweet kisses on the top of my head.

"I'm okay, my sweet. Thank you for arranging the private plane. Jackie was squealing the whole way, and I think she ate all the peanuts."

Private plane?

"Jackie?"

"Hi, baby girl!" The melodic voice of the older woman sounds from somewhere behind him, and I pull back to find her standing with Maya in her arms, all smiles.

"Oh, Jackie! It's so good to see you!" Daddy lets me go and I rush to her, pulling her in a tight hug. "Are you okay? Is he okay? Were you—" I whisper on a rushed breath.

"We're fine, honey. He's fine too. The trip went by okay, he had a mild sedative at one point when he got a little confused, but it's all good."

I let out a charged breath clutching a hand to my chest.

"What about you?" she asks in a matching whisper. "I was told that it was going to be a surprise for both of you, but I must admit, I fought back quite a bit. At first I thought they wanted to kidnap us."

I stifle an awkward laugh. She has no idea.

"But all the paperwork checked out. I had an interview and everything."

Interview?

"Thank you for looking after him. For keeping him safe," I finally tell her.

"Safe? Evelyn, it was *them* who kept us safe." She nods toward where I know Finnigan stands. "It felt like a presidential escort. And I got a wonderful job thanks to Ms. Campbell."

"You work here now?" I ask much louder, turning to the door where Finnigan and the woman pause their quiet conversation. It explains the interview.

"She came highly recommended. Plus, we heard that

your father and her have a great bond, and at Queen Anne Sanctuary we believe in nurturing these connections. They help a great deal in certain cases," the Director confirms.

"Well, I, for one, am happy. Thank you very much for having us in this lovely place." My father nods his head in reverence to the woman. "Sweet Evie, did you see? They even have a fully stocked kitchen, like the ones you see in the movies for cooking courses, for us to use. We can make meringues again."

He's beaming, a smile so wide, I choke up. He's clearly having a good day today, his Alzheimer's allowing us some moments of beautiful clarity.

"Evelyn would love that. She's baking more and more these days." Finn steps up when I can't form any words.

"And who might you be?"

"Finnigan Hennessey, sir." The devastating man sports his softest smile as he extends his hand to my father and they shake. "We saw each other on video call, with the lovely Jackie, a few days ago."

I'm sorry, he did what? I'm going to strangle the man. Not now, though. Not when my dad is next to me. Happy. Safe. Maya clings to him now, looking up at him like he's the moon in the sky.

"Right. And to Evelyn?" my father asks.

"Sorry, sir?"

"Who are you to my sweet Evelyn?"

Finnigan's cheeks turn a lovely shade of pink against his blonde curls, and I'm stepping toward them to intervene.

"Oh, apologies, I'm Evelyn's boyfriend."

I stop dead in my tracks, choking on my own spit when I try to swallow the gasp.

"Need some water, darling?" The man turns to me, a devastating smile dimpling his cheek.

"Finally!" my sister says with a cheeky sigh.

"Maya! I swear... one of these days." I shake my head at her, but she giggles in response and clings tighter to our father.

"Well, it's nice to meet you, son. You're taking care of my girls, yes?"

"Of course. I hope you'll be comfortable at Queen Anne. I've inspected all the facilities and services personally."

"You did?" I ask, unable to hold back anymore of the shock.

"Thoroughly," Ms. Campbell says with a soft chuckle. "We've never been scrutinized quite like this before. Your father is in safe hands. If you'll excuse me, I'll give you some privacy. Please feel free to explore. Jackie here is starting to know her way around, but there are others to assist if you get a little lost. Mr. Hennessey has my contact details if you need anything at all in the future."

"Thank you," I say to the woman, still flabbergasted.

"My pleasure. Welcome to Queen Anne Sanctuary." Her smile is soft and warm as it touches her eyes.

This woman is genuine, and I wonder if she knows how much documentation Finnigan faked to get him here. Dad sits down, pulling Maya on his lap, and they start talking, and I grab Finn's arm and yank him out of earshot.

"What the fuck did you do, Hennessey?" I whisper in a hissed tone.

He cocks his eyebrow, probably at my use of his last name, but amusement brushes his lips.

"I wanted to surprise you—"

"Surprise me?!" I interrupt. "Is that another way of saying that you did something stupid behind my back and without my permission?" My nails dig into his bicep, but it's the only thing keeping me leveled. I don't want to make a scene in front of my father and Jackie.

"Depends how you look at it."

"Is this how you intend on manipulating me into staying in Queenscove?"

His brows lower, gaze darkening at my accusing question.

"Trust me, Evie darling, I have better manipulating techniques than this." He quirks an eyebrow, gaze drawing down my body before it meets my eyes again.

"Don't mess with me; I can see right through you."

He takes a deep, slow breath, cocking his head as he inches closer to me. I tense, but hold strong. Pulling this is completely out of order, though my father's warm laughter filtering through doesn't help my case, especially when it makes me unnaturally giddy.

"Listen to me, Evelyn"—Finn's tone shifts to a low rumble—"I did what I needed to see that beaming smile your father puts on your lips, the tears in your eyes at the sight of his own, and the sheer happiness on your beautiful face, that you can't hide even with your anger. You were devastated, and it broke my fucking heart. After all you've been through, you and Maya did not deserve to suffer through the pain of also being away from your father."

My lips part as I release my hold on his bicep, his declaration leaving me slightly stunned.

"This feels like bribery. I know how much this place costs, and you know for a fact I cannot afford this."

"Don't you even dare mention money to me right now," he argues as his eyes narrow to a straight line. "You don't understand how much I yearn to make you happy. It's fucking worrying, Evelyn, and I can't make sense of myself. But here I am... trying to make you happy. To make your life easier. Better. You can fight me all you want, but this isn't gonna stop. I'll do whatever I need to do to see that addictive happiness beaming in those gray eyes of yours."

I swallow a lump in my throat as emotions heat their way

through my chest at the declaration that feels a lot like he's baring his soul to me. Maybe even his heart.

So many possibilities turn from black and white to full color in my mind, dreams I didn't allow to surface; a high-school degree, my own business, Maya safe in a school, baking with Mamaw June, and regular dinners with all these people who have become family. All of this could happen now.

I just have to allow myself to experience them.

"Finnigan, I—"

"Now is not the time. Go, spend it with your father. Take as long as you want. I'll wait for you in the car."

I drop my gaze, chewing on my lips, and nod. There's plenty of anger and confusion inside of me, but his explanation almost urges me to apologize. Almost.

Turning, I smile once more at the sight of my father and sister beaming as they laugh together, and head over to them. But before I can join them, I halt, and whip back around.

"Stay."

The word spills from my lips like a plea. He answers with the sight of that stunning dimple on his cheek, and a slight nod. I can't deny it, he did make me happy. Devastatingly so because I missed my father more than I allowed him or Maya to know.

"My sweet Evie."

"Daddy," I say, pulling a chair next to his and leaning to press a peck to his cheek.

"How about we go for a walk on these beautiful grounds? I have yet to see them."

"Let's go then."

* * *

Apart from Maya's humming in the back seat, the whole ride to Mamaw June's house, to drop her off, was spent in silence.

Now, as he drives us back to his penthouse, the tension in the car is thicker, charged with unspoken words. I hope we're not making a habit of this, though I was purposefully keeping my mouth shut, so I didn't go off at him for crossing this line.

Only, my heart is full after spending all those hours with our dad. We had lunch there, went out to buy him a few things, like clothes, toiletries, and others, since I could barely afford more than thrift-store stuff before. He woke up from his nap and we spent even more time with him until the sun was setting and we could tell that it was becoming a bit too much for him. When the confusion started to hit, we decided it was best to let him rest.

Most of the car ride I spent thinking of when I'll visit him next, instead of being angry at Finn. Because I can do that now, I can see him whenever I want. And he's safe. Happy.

I'm still mad at *my boyfriend*, but I think I'm wishing the sentiment more than actually feeling it, because I think I have to. I should be furious. But the man did all of this for me and my sister. He talked to my father's main caretaker, a woman he knew I trusted, paid off god knows how many people to falsify documents, organized a private plane, and brought my father to one of the leading care homes in the whole country. All at his expense, without even batting an eyelid.

"Come on. Lay it on me. I can't take the damn silence anymore." He huffs, squeezing the steering wheel in his fist as we drive out of the forest road and back into civilization.

I take one deep breath, sifting through all the thoughts and questions I have. But after spending all this time with my dad, some of them don't seem as important anymore. One in particular does weigh on me, though.

"Do you think that by bringing my father here you're going to sway me to decide to stay?"

"No."

"Bullshit," I call out immediately. "You're trying to convince me to stay."

"I definitely *want* you to stay, Evelyn, but it's not why I brought your father. I wanted to eliminate that worry for you. Now that he's here you can focus on what you want for yourself. For Maya. Whether it's work, saving money, baking, or just enjoying yourself, you can do it without missing your father, or worrying about being able to pay for his care."

"You're saying all the right words, Finnigan, but I'm struggling to accept that there are no strings to this. That you're not forcing my hand to stay here."

Realistically, if this is what he was doing, he wouldn't admit it just because I asked. So this is futile. But I can't help but wonder if this gesture is going to sway my decision, regardless. Christ, I'm not even sure a decision was ever necessary. I think I've been governed by fear and lack of options. More and more I feel like there is a world of possibilities here, and it's all due to this man. His Sanctum, too.

But it's him who keeps my soul alive and my heart full.

Him who I want to wake up next to every morning and see each night before I drift off back to sleep.

It's him who I want to share my dreams with and the craziness of raising my little sister.

I want this man by my side.

I want to be his. But most of all, I want him to be mine.

All mine.

After a slow, deep breath, he finally answers, "The spot at the old care home in Fleeton is still reserved for your father. Until you make your decision, it will stay his. So if you wish to return there, he can also return with you without issues. Jackie too, of course."

"Oh, that's..." I trail off.

"Impressive?"

My head whips to him in time to see an annoyingly striking grin pulling at his lips, and I snort, shaking my head.

"Do you not see how worrying it looks to me that you were able to pull this off?"

He shrugs as he drives us through one of Queenscove's main boulevards. "It's nothing."

"Not in my world."

"*Our.*"

"What?" I frown.

"*Our* world, Evie darling. Fight it all you want, but you're one of us. You fit. More importantly," the car stops at some traffic lights, and he turns his gaze to me, "you're mine."

A shudder rips through me as goosebumps bloom over my spine.

"Will I still be yours if I decide to leave?"

His gaze sears through me, but no answer comes. As strange as it seems, I know why. If he answers the question, he'll risk doing just that—manipulate me. Even without trying.

He drives off when the traffic lights turn, and my breaths lighten as his attention shifts.

"Look in the glove box," he tells me.

"For what?"

Is this his answer to my question?

"An envelope. Open it."

Confused, I do as told and pull a large, brown envelope out. Parting the end, I start to pull out a bunch of papers and frown as I look at Finn. Something about the feel of the paper seems a bit too official. A little too thin, yet freshly printed. He nods, signaling me to keep going, even as my hands gently shake. I'm not sure where my reluctance is coming from, but it takes me a few seconds to look over the documents.

I gasp, my hand rushing to my mouth, blinking repeatedly like those words are a mirage and I expect them to disappear any moment now.

"This can't be," I mutter to myself, blinking excessively like that black-on-white ink is going to rearrange itself back to the real words.

Surely this cannot be.

But the words stay put.

Tears brim my eyes as they widen with every new sentence, every set of words, every single time mine and my sister's names are mentioned.

"How?" is all I manage to whisper, as Finn's phone rings, making me jump.

"We have *friends* in high places," he answers as he rejects the call.

I don't even care if what he means is that he blackmailed a bunch of people, or broke some legs, because these documents state, nice and damn clear, that I am Maya's official guardian.

"You did this for me. I have custody," I say in disbelief, heat flooding my soul and wrapping around my heart. *This man...*

His phone rings again, and he mutters curses as he presses a button on his car screen.

"Where are you?"

That sounds like Vincent barking on the other line.

"About a minute away from home."

"Turn the fuck around now! Your building is being stalked. Two of our men are down. They're waiting for you," Vincent urges.

"Shit. Where are you?"

"Loading up, underground. There's something else."

"What?" Finnigan asks, a deep frown settling between his brows.

"It's happening. Bartiste is coming for us."

CHAPTER 38
Finnigan

UCKING FINALLY!

This bastard evaded us for too long, and no matter how much of his operation we have destroyed so far, the satisfaction is never going to come until Roberto Bartiste is dead.

"Perfect!" I exclaim, stealing a glance at Evelyn who frowns at my reaction, her gaze switching between the phone screen, the paperwork, and me.

"Okay, I'm turning around."

"Morrigan and Loreley are joining Maya." Vin's avoiding saying where. I wonder if he thinks someone could be listening.

"I'm taking *her* too. Text me where to meet you."

"No!" Evelyn's words rush out as I end the call.

"There's no time to debate this."

She's pressed back into the seat as I turn the car around,

earning some angry honks from other drivers. I speed up, weaving through the evening traffic, and I head back toward the edge of town.

"Exactly. There is no time. Do not waste it by driving back to Mamaw June's." She shoves the paperwork back in the envelope and pops it back in the glove box.

I clench my fist around the steering wheel and press harder on the gas as I force myself not to raise my tone at her. "That's the best place where you can be right now—safe. With your sister."

"I appreciate that, but it makes no sense. Let's just go meet the others."

"You heard Vin, the others are going there as well," I retort.

"You know I meant Vincent and the others, not the girls! Why are you being like this?"

"I'm not discussing this anymore. There are loads of security around the forest and Mamaw June's, it's safe there."

"Security? I managed to sneak past them."

"Trust me, Vincent almost chopped a few heads because of that. No one goes through anymore."

"Oh, god," she whispers to herself, probably wondering if anyone's hurt because of her, then shakes the thought away. "It's too far, Finn. Please, we have to go after Bartiste." She wraps her small hand around my thigh as her eyes plead with me.

"No, *I* have to go after him. Me, not you!" Holding my tone back didn't last long, not when she insists on being so damn stubborn.

"Finn, plea—"

"Listen to me, Evelyn!" I roar, tires screeching as I pull over, turn in my seat, and grip her sweet face in my hands. "I will not risk your life! Over and over, you underestimate just how much you mean to me. What I'm willing to do to keep you safe. I can't lose you, damn it. Don't you understand? I fucking love you, Evelyn!"

Her plump lips part on a soft gasp, and her eyes are like saucers as she takes in my words.

"You mean too much. So fucking much..." I whisper now, brushing the tip of my nose to hers, and lean my forehead against hers.

"Yo—you love me?"

Pulling back, it's my turn for my eyes to bulge. I did say that, didn't I? Holy shit... I do. I love her.

Fuck me.

"I didn't stand a chance against you, Evie darling. You're a bright fucking star in a soulless world, and you burned right through the shackles that held me back."

Her gaze softens, the words sinking in slowly, caressing her soul as she clutches the back of my head and pulls me in. We kiss feverishly, allowing ourselves these stolen moments before the very thing that brought us together will end.

When we break apart, her eyes seem to sparkle even through this darkness. They spell overwhelming emotions I'm not going to make her put into words right now.

"We have to go, Finn. We have to get him. Please don't waste this shot. If he escapes again—"

"Is this why you're insisting? Evie, darling, he's not getting away. I promise you."

"I want... I have to—damn it!" the struggle is vivid in her features. "I *need* to be there."

Does she not trust me to do this? Or maybe, like me, she needs the visual confirmation that the bastard is dead.

I shake my head, pressing another kiss to her forehead. "Trust me to do this for *us*, Evie. Bartiste will die at my hands. I'll get you all the proof you want, just don't ask me to put you in danger."

Her chest rises on a slow, thoughtful breath, and after her eyes drift off for a moment, she finally nods.

"I trust you."

But no sooner she speaks the words, our world explodes into chaos, splintering pops hitting the trunk of the car.

"Down on the floor!" I shout as I put the car back into gear and drive off, the acceleration pressing me back into the seat.

In the rear-view mirror, headlights approach at dangerous speed. More bullets hit us and the shattering of glass sounds behind us as Evie slides as far down in the foot-well as she can.

"Finn!" she yelps, pleading but unsure for what.

"Goddamn it!" I swear as the passenger of the car following us holds a gun out of the side window. "Stay down!"

Another bullet pierces the back window, but this one passes through the front, too close to my head, and I floor it as I speed through the industrial estate. This is gonna be a shitshow. There are still civilians driving on these streets. Granted, not many, but it's enough for one to call the fucking police.

I press a few buttons on the car screen, and after two rings, Carter answers.

"We're taking fire in fucking traffic! Call the Chief to manage this bullshit!"

"Done. Where are you?"

"Edge of the business park in the industrial estate."

"Are you hit?" Carter asks.

"Only the car. I'll get rid of them."

"The plan is in motion, that's why they came for you."

"Shit, I thought I had time to drop her off." Another shot pierces the car body and I swerve, narrowly missing the curb.

"It's sooner than expected, but we're ready."

"Send the feed to my car. I'll meet you as agreed. And Carter..."

No answer comes as he waits.

"Bartiste's head is *mine!*" I warn.

He chuckles then disconnects the call.

"We're not going to June's then?" Evie asks as more bullets snap through the air, grazing the car.

"A bit fucking late now!" I shout over the roar of the engine.

We can't attract attention to Vincent's mom's house. We'll put everyone in danger.

"Where's your gun? I'll try to shoot them." My Evie is brave, but this is not the time.

"Stay down!" CCTV footage shows up on the car screen when I accept the notification that showed up there.

The warehouse is still empty, but not for long.

Tightening my grip on the steering wheel, I take a sharp turn on a high-pitched screech of the tires and Evelyn's yelp, and put my foot down once again, speeding through the quiet street lit by old, yellow lamps. The car behind us follows, but the bullets have paused, and they're further behind.

"Come on you bastard, come on," I mutter under my breath, my gaze snapping between the road ahead and the mirror.

"We're supposed to evade them, not will them closer!" Evelyn shouts from her makeshift hiding place.

"Evade them? I'm not running, darling, I'm fucking hunting!" I roar.

I lift the foot off the gas enough that they're starting to catch up. A few more bullets fly and I know they hit the back seat from the muffled sound.

"What's the plan?" she shouts.

"When I tell you, get up and hold the fuck on!"

She doesn't answer, but from the corner of my eye I can see how she's bracing herself. The road is quieter the deeper we drive into the estate and my gut is beaming with anticipation.

"Now!" I scream.

Evelyn whips out of her hiding place, plants herself in her seat, and manages to strap herself in as I swerve slightly to the left, and plant my foot on the brake. With a shriek, we're right next to the car that followed us, only I let us fall back just enough that my front lines up with their back, and pull a sharp right, catching their back with a crashing jolt.

"Gun in arm rest!" I shout as their car turns perpendicular to ours and I accelerate to carry them forward. The noise of blocked tires against the asphalt grits my eardrums, and I wiggle the steering wheel around to keep them in front of me.

Evelyn complies, and without further instruction, she cocks the weapon, lines it up out the window, and pulls the trigger on a loud pop.

"Good girl!" She hit the driver, and the shooter looks angry now. "Hold on!"

I press the foot on the gas and turn the wheel a few inches to the left, guiding them exactly where I want them, then slam my foot on the brake, screeching to a halt. Their car shifts straight into a concrete wall, windows smashing as it jolts.

Wasting no time, I grab the gun out of Evelyn's hand, and step out. On hurried, unfaltering steps, I reach their car illuminated by my headlights. The shooter attempts to pull himself out through the driver's seat, climbing over the man who's grunting in pain. Not dead yet, then.

Anger-driven adrenaline courses through my veins at the thought that the bastards could have fucking killed Evelyn. On echoing pops, I let two shots fly one after the other, and the men take their last breaths as blood trickles down their foreheads. Without a second thought, I whip around and go right back inside the car.

"What's happening, Finnigan? What are those?" Evelyn asks, eyes fixed on the car screen.

A smirk pulls at my lips as the infrared camera feed shifts between different locations inside the warehouse. Men are strewn all over, standing, sitting, laid down. A small army invades the space through the back entrance, arms drawn. Another group sneaks in through the back, trying to ambush the people already waiting there.

"Seriously, what is this?!"

"Bartiste's men. Coming for us," I answer, a calm quality to my tone.

"No! Finnigan, oh my god! We have to do something!" She shifts in her seat, hands trembling as she presses them to the sides of her head, brows drawn up.

She claims she might want to leave, but she cares so much about men she never met, men she only knows as being part of The Sanctum.

"Watch, darling." I nod toward the screen.

Bright green light flares on the feed as shots are fired, and Evelyn shrieks when the bullets hit the men, one by one caught in a frenzied attack.

"Wait, why aren't they fighting back?" she asks, her tone slow as she stops listening to her emotions and reads the scene before her. "Are they...?"

"Dead," I confirm before the question is asked. "They're shooting their own men. Ones we killed earlier."

"Bait," she whispers.

I nod watching the scene as it calms and confusion sets in. Putting the car back into gear I set off again, and Evelyn gasps just as the camera feed turns white with the flames that engulf the warehouse. Then it all goes black.

"What was that?"

"A culling," I answer. "We planted a seed that we have Frankie B."

"But he's dead."

"Aye. But his dear father has no reason to believe that. The beach was spotless clean within the hour. No bodies, no crime. All he would have known is that he stupidly came to get you, and disappeared. There's not much of a stretch from there to believing we protected you. But this was just a ruse, and we knew Bartiste would know that his son wouldn't be there. He thought he was going to kill us in our own ambush, but we used it to relieve him of some of his army. Sloan's men are in the perimeter, cleaning out the leftovers."

Sirens wail as we turn into another side street on our way out of Queenscove. It sounds like a fire engine, likely going toward the explosion we just caused, but I still don't want to attract attention with all these bullet holes piercing the car and the busted front.

"When we devised the plan, we were worried Bartiste wouldn't give a shit about his son. We didn't know anything about him until you told us. We thought he just popped up in the picture, like some bastard son. If that was the case, his emotional connection to the kid wouldn't have been strong enough. But one of our more recent captives shed some light on the situation after we tempted him with his family's demise. We wouldn't kill innocents unless attacked, but the poor idiot didn't know that."

"Jesus... is he still alive? Actually, never mind. I don't want to know." She exhales a heavy breath and shakes her head. "So what about Frankie?"

"His mother was Bartiste's ex. Not married, but a long-time partner. Abusive relationship from the sounds of it, and she took a page out of her baby daddy's book and disappeared, along with little Frankie. But it turns out that some evil is inherited, because in his early teens, the son forced them out of hiding. He sought his dad and swore his allegiance to him. Bartiste took the mom captive, but apparently was reluctant to trust him. Though, he was also desperate to have his kid back. After all, he was the heir to his disgusting kingdom, and already he showed signs to be as cruel as his daddy. He also became Bartiste's weakness, so he kept him hidden for a long time. This was still happening at the time Bartiste came to Queenscove last time."

She knows which time I mean now, I don't need to explain. Evelyn doesn't say a word, simply waits for me to continue, and I find that, after all I confessed to her, those memories from eight years ago feel... a little more distant. Not like fresh wounds any longer.

"The guy said that Frankie himself told some of his story. He saw what happened to his dad, what we did to him. He was the one who tracked him down in the hospital, he probably knew of the alias his dad would use. That's when the son nursed his broken father back to health, and stepped up in the business. He proved himself to his father, and to cement his commitment to *the cause* he killed his own mother. Stabbed her."

"Christ, that's personal. I mean—" Evelyn sighs. "A gun is quicker."

"Agreed. Frankie didn't just prove himself, he showed his father he's just like him. Which is how we were quite sure our plan would work."

"Rather ironic that Frankie died the same way he killed his mother." There's a tinge of amusement curling her lips. "Why wouldn't Bartiste just think his son is dead, since you captured him?"

"Carter. After planting the seed, Bartiste, or rather one of his men, contacted us. Proof of life was requested, and our resident genius created a deep fake using AI technology, and gave him the proof."

I chuckle at the memory. I saw it. It was fucking good. I

didn't even try to understand how Carter did it.

"He can do that? Why does Carter know how to mess with artificial intelligence tech?"

"Amongst other things, for the exact reason why he used it. In case someone does this, or other things, to us, he can learn how to spot it. Reverse the process. Fight back."

"Jesus... I must admit, he does scare me a little." she says running her fingers through her deep violet hair, "I guess we're lucky the man is on our side."

"Yeah. We're all well aware. We're even luckier *The Carver* is on our side."

"That's his nickname, right? What do you mean?"

"The man studies medieval torture methods as light reading. You've seen how brutal, how dangerous Madds can be. Carter is... different. He's silent in his brutality, a different kind of predator, but he feeds on life-force. On screams. On pain. And tears. And as the name suggests... he carves."

She grimaces at the mental image.

"Would he ever betray you since he's so... cold?"

"Never. I'm not sure if he can love. Maybe in his own way. But loyalty is important to him."

"Most times loyalty is better than love... So the agreed location mentioned to him was not this warehouse?" Evelyn asks, pointing to the now black screen.

"No. Different one. We're going there right now."

I grab my phone and shoot a text to Carter.

Still alone?

The response comes within five seconds.

On his way.

Bartiste is nearing. The adrenaline that has been slowly

leaving my body as we've been driving, is returning. We were only a few minutes away, but I was anxious that more of Bartiste's men could have followed us. I really wish I could have taken Evelyn to Mamaw June, but it's too late. Too dangerous.

"When we get there, I'm hiding you in a room and you have to stay there. I'm being serious, Evelyn. You cannot. Fucking. Move. Got it?"

I'm focused on the narrowing road as we pass through the old, wrought-iron gates of the abandoned sugar factory, and pull in by an old shed next to another one of our cars. She hasn't answered me.

"You got it, Evie?"

"Yes, yes. Stay hidden. Do not move. Got it." Her tone carries a bit too much stubbornness. I hope it's not a lie. "Why are we parking basically at the front, in plain view?"

I get out of the car and go to grab her. One kiss I steal before I usher her toward the looming, creaky building that hasn't seen much life in the last thirty years.

"Because Carter planted another seed that this is our hiding spot, a temporary center of operations. And also that we're under the impression we've successfully killed Bartiste," I answer with a chuckle.

"He thinks he's ambushing us."

"Exactly."

We pass through a secondary door since we've soldered shut the main one, and after a couple of corridors, we're in the main space of the factory. A projector screen lights up the space and its old machinery, as our men find their positions in the shadows.

"What is that?" Evelyn exclaims, pointing at the video playing on the screen.

I steer her in the other direction, toward the stairs, before she can see the gruesome scene projected there.

"Best not to look at that, Evie."

"This is a fucking bad idea!" Madds rushes to us, Jay, one of our men in tow.

"Trust me, brother. I know. There was no other choice. Jay, take her up to the archive room. It's far enough away, but still in decent reach. Take two more men with you. Protect her at all costs."

"Of course, sir."

Another one of our guys comes over with bulletproof vests for both of us, and I quickly strap Evelyn into hers, then throw mine on.

"No! Finnigan—"

But Maddox pulls her in a crushing hug, his lips a tight line as he looks at me. Yeah buddy, I'm fucking worried out of my mind too. She turns to me once she's released out of his grip.

"I want to stay with you, please Finnigan, I can't... what if something happens?"

I guide her pretty face to mine and press a deep kiss to her lips. When I move away, tears brim her eyes, squeezing my chest. I hope nothing happens to me so I can see her gorgeous face again.

"Jay will keep you safe while I deal with the bastard who wronged you."

"No, I mean what if something happens to *you*? To Madds?"

God, I love her. She's more worried about our safety. Leave it to Evelyn to think of everyone but herself.

"Then you'll nurse me back to health. We'll take Severin to a hospital." I grin, peppering kisses to the tears that are now flowing down her pretty face.

Finally she chuckles. "I'll be very angry and annoying in that case."

"I don't expect any less from you, Evie darling." I pull her in my arms one more time, then reluctantly let go of her. "Now go! Hide! And stay there."

She nods and slowly backs away, giving a chaste smile to Madds as she finally leaves with Jay up the creaky, metal stairs and disappears behind a wall.

"He's passed the gates!" someone's shout echoes through the factory.

We all disperse, hiding in the best spots we've already scouted when we assessed the place. Mine is next to Ronan. All but two access routes have been sealed shut, and blasting through those metal doors will be too much hassle, so we know exactly where Bartiste is coming from. We have the best view of the asshole's face as he'll walk into this space and see exactly what he came here to retrieve.

Maybe the anguish we're hoping for won't mar his features. But if it does, I don't want to miss it.

When the creek of the metal door echoes through the vast space, I know—it's finally time.

CHAPTER 39
Finnigan

I EXPECT THE STEPS TO RUSH in our direction, but they're careful instead. We don't attack, though. Not until most of them have entered the building. We don't want them to scatter. The snipers stationed out on the building have orders to count to five and if it looks like no one else intends to enter, kill all the ones remaining outside.

Ronan taps me on the shoulder and when I turn to him, he nods toward the left. The moment I look in that direction and aim my gun, watching the first men step in, is the same moment sound trickles in, echoing and bouncing off the heavy metal that forms this space. It's not coming from those men, but from the projector that was just unmuted by Carter.

Oinking and grunting stall their steps and they turn to the screen. Some of them don't react, but others cover their mouths, or turn around, unable to stand the vivid imagery of the *feast*. We wanted to hurt Bartiste, and Carter came up with the best idea how.

"What the fuck is this! It can't be..." Bartiste himself steps in on a slight limp, walking through the several dozen men who have flooded the space, eyes fixed on the screen.

A grin spreads over my lips with the deep shock and hint of sorrow tainting the bastard's features. There's a hint of disgust there too as he watches his one and only son, or better yet his naked corpse, be eaten by pigs. They're in no hurry though, enjoying this feast at a calm, soothing pace.

We don't make a habit of disposing of bodies in this way. Carter reserves his pigs for more *special* kills, and since this one wasn't his, he made an exception. The broken look on Bartiste's face was totally worth it.

"You will pay for this!" he bellows. "You hear me?! You will pay for this!" Spit flies out of his mouth as he turns around the space, blindly trying to find us.

The first shot splits through the sounds of the pigs and one of his men is down. That's our cue. Only a split moment later a shattering bullet-storm assaults my eardrums and Bartiste's men fall like flies around him. Everyone knows not to aim their guns at the man in question. My goal is clear, but it's too early to go straight for him. His men scatter, taking cover behind the old machinery, and I move through the shadows at the edge of the space, taking cover behind the thick concrete columns as I pick them off one by one.

Bullets screech against the metal machinery, howls are pulled when they hit their targets, grunts come from the people now in hand to hand combat, all a cacophony of overwhelming sounds that echo in this vast space. My bullets find home in the neck and forehead of two men who run for me, and before they hit the ground, I look back to where

Bartiste was taking cover.

He's not there.

"Watch out! They have armor-piercing rounds!" Vincent shouts from somewhere.

Frantic, I turn around and take cover behind another pillar, desperately looking for Bartiste. My fist clenches, teeth gritting as old memories of the asshole slipping through my fingers, assault me. Our men have strict orders—no one leaves the building. If they do, snipers will take them out. With one deep, slow breath, my pulse calms. Bartiste is not escaping. Even if the finger squeezing the trigger is not mine, he will not escape again.

With that calming thought, I spot him hiding behind some machinery, reloading the clip of his gun. My eyes sweep the perimeter and I jump into a sprint around the edge of the space, taking cover behind the pillars when bullets fly in my direction. It's sad, satisfying, and worrying all at the same time how many bodies I have to jump over to get to the man, praying none of them are ours. Out of nowhere someone leaps in front of me, and my breath whips out of my lungs as he elbows me straight in the sternum. My feet catch onto a body lying on the floor and my gun flies out. His is aimed straight at my head.

But he's too close to me and didn't realize it, so I swing my legs, scissor them around his ankles, and flip him onto the floor. My gun is somewhere behind me, but the time to look for it is not now. I scramble to the guy who's now looking for the same thing as me, but I slam my fist into his stomach, earning a few more seconds to lunge for his gun. Two seconds later, his brain splatters from the right side of his head, and I'm already up, grab my own gun, and rush toward my target.

He can't leave, by now the doors are shut from the outside. We were adamant no one, but us leaves this place tonight. One glance toward the stairs and I stop dead in my tracks—three bulky men rush up them. Aiming my gun, I shoot the one at the top in the back, and a split moment later one of our guys stationed somewhere above puts a hole in his head, and he tumbles back, taking the other two with him down the stairs.

When I turn back for Bartiste, the bastard's gone again, probably hidden somewhere or sick of seeing his son on that screen being eaten by pigs.

"Come the fuck out, Bartiste, you goddamn coward!" I holler, echoing through the sharp pops of guns, and collapsing bodies.

Looking back to the metal stairs, more of his guys rush up. Damn it, they can't get there, they'll be too close to Evelyn. One of them falls with my shots, the other by someone else's bullets.

Taking cover behind another pillar, I look around for Bartiste once more. The factory has turned into a massacre, bodies fallen everywhere, shots still being fired, though less than before, others are just punching or stabbing each other.

Madds is one of them. He prefers hand-to-hand to the bullets, and he's pummeling through men like they're nothing.

Vin is reloading god knows which number magazine into his gun, a devious tug at the corner of his lips. His thing is making people talk with his intimidating demeanor, with secrets and well-chosen words. But as it is with all of us... violence puts such a big fucking smile on his face.

Then there's Carter. His two guns are still fixed in his leather holster, but he's been doing a heck of a lot of damage with his knives. Blood is splattered all over him, and though I can clearly see the disgust contorting his features at the mess, he's fucking relishing in the violence.

But there's still no sign of Bartiste.

"Are you scared, Bartiste? Scared that you're finally going to pay for your sins?" I taunt, my laugh echoing through the vast space.

Goddamn it! Two more men are once again going up the fucking stairs. I aim my weapon but before I can pull the trigger, they're down.

"Take out the ones at the top!" someone shouts the order, and my blood runs cold.

"Where are you, you bastard?"

"Is she up there, *boy*? Is that why you keep taking out everyone who steps up those stairs?"

Oh, that's Bartiste alright. The way he says *boy* brings me back to all those years before, when he kidnapped Annika and Hanna and fucking taunted us. Now he wants Evelyn too? Over my dead-fucking-body and not even then. I'll come out of the goddamn grave and pull him down with me.

"It's me." Ronan alerts me as he slides next to me behind the pillar, taking down two more men. "Don't let him get to you."

"I'm not!" but my tone is snappier than it should be. "Watch out!" I whip my gun over his shoulder and shoot the man who was raising his weapon at him.

"Thanks."

"You need to go, Ronan. Take cover away from this. You have a wife and son at home."

"Now you're getting all protective? I'm not dying today." He grabs the back of my head and brings me down, kissing the top of it. "Besides, you have plenty to lose, too."

I shake my head and turn around.

"Oh fuck no!" I lift the gun, but it's too late. Two of our men stationed at the top fall, the other two take cover as more shots are fired.

Then I catch one more glimpse of Bartiste as he runs from

behind one piece of equipment to another, ducking as I let two bullets fly in his direction. The bastard is all the way on the other side of the space, too far for great accuracy, especially since there are no lights there. And I do want to be accurate, since I only want to maim, not kill, just yet.

I go to run, but bullets hit the concrete at my feet and I whip back, crashing against Ronan.

"Goddamn it!" I curse.

But I push away again anyway. And the same thing happens. When my brother tries to move out, bullets fly on his side too.

"They're trying to keep us here."

"Yeah, no shit." I huff out a breath. "Can someone fucking shoot the asshole?" I rage loud enough for the sound to vibrate over the flying bullets.

I can't shoot blindly, as much as it sounds like a pretty damn good idea right now, but I'm not gonna risk accidentally hitting one of our own. I sneak a look, and just as a bullet hits the concrete next to my shoulder, I see a group of Bartiste's men climb up those stairs again. Ice fills my veins as their steps get too close to the top and no one is stopping them. Two finally go down, but the rest turn out of my line of sight and shoot.

My ears ring, and a lump in my throat chokes me. I lunge, but arms catch me in a vice around my middle, pulling me back just as a sharp burn hisses against my forearm.

"They're gonna get to her!" I rage at Ronan's grip.

"You almost got shot, brother! You're no good to her dead."

"Someone go after her!" I shout and hope someone hears me.

I look down at the blood trickling off my forearm—it's just a graze.

A maniacal laugh bounces off the metal walls and I grit

my teeth at the sound.

"I'm gonna have her soon!" Bartiste shouts, "Again!" Then the bastard laughs once more.

"Cover me!" I leap out from behind the pillar, sprinting to the next one as bullets fly behind me, but I trust Ronan is taking the opportunity to shoot whoever's aiming their guns at me.

The space has quieted more or less, guns are still fired, but there are enough bodies on the ground to know that there aren't many of Bartiste's men left. Apart from the bastards upstairs.

I have to get to her.

"You're done, Bartiste! You're not getting out of here alive!" I sneak a look and see movement behind some bulky machinery. "Come out, *old man.*"

On careful steps I move from behind the pillar and moments later, the bastard comes out into view too.

"Don't worry now. No one here's going to shoot you." A grin pulls at my lips as I watch the forced expression on his features. "They all know you're mine to kill."

He's trying to cover the fear with made up malice. From the corner of my eyes I spot our men out in the open, guns aimed in several directions—I guess some of the asshole's men are still alive. But my focus is on their boss as more bullets fly and loud thumps hit the ground.

Hopefully those were the last of his men.

I lift my gun, aiming at Bartiste, but a flurry of gunshots split the silence. They're muffled, distant. My breath catches in my lungs—they're coming from upstairs. A heart-wrenching scream splits through the vastness of the space, and my heart stops.

Evelyn!

Evelyn

PAIN AND FURY BURST OUT of me in a bellow that bounces off these metal walls and echoes through my very soul. I took the last man down with the gun Jay threw at me, but not before he put a bullet through his chest. Tears spill freely down my cheeks, and my hand shakes as I brush my palm over Jay's eyes, shutting them. Brinn, his brother, is probably here too. I'll have to be the one to tell him. He died because of me, protecting me.

I wipe a bloody hand over my eyes, brushing the tears away.

"Don't shoot, we're with you." Two men hold their hands up in the doorway. "Finn sent us to protect—"

But I don't hear their words anymore, because others filter through from downstairs.

"Oh, shame. Waste of a good ass. Maybe I should have told them not to kill your bitch. Oops."

Dread spills through my soul at that seedy, disgusting voice that brings terrible memories, but mixed with the poison tainting me already, it turns to rage.

A deep, pained roar reverberates through the whole factory, and I flinch.

"I will string you by your guts through this goddamn factory! It will take you fucking days to die, you goddamn son of a bitch!" Finnigan. Oh god, my Finnigan! The pain in his voice brings me straight to my feet. *"She didn't fucking deserve it!"*

"But you do!" Bartiste shouts. *"You killed my fucking son!"*

I'm running before the thought touches my consciousness, pushing past the men standing by the door, clutching the gun as the metal platform vibrates with each footfall. My gaze finds Finn's wide one as I rush down the steps, shock and relief mixed in his gorgeous blue eyes.

"Nooo!" Finnigan shouts as a loud pop echoes sharply.

Something whizzed past me, but I don't stop even when the second pop sounds, and I slip the last three steps, jumping straight on the ground. I think the second shot came from Ronan who has his gun aimed somewhere behind me, but there's no time to thank him.

"Look at that, the bitch is still alive." The seedy voice still speaks, bile rising up my throat.

"This *bitch* is the one who killed your fucking son, you rapist bastard! I put a blade in his chest, slammed it over and over until he was close enough to death that I could see him try to reach for it and end his wasteful suffering. I watched him drown in his own blood, slow, painful, with a fucking smile on my face!" I rage at Bartiste, then shift my gaze to my gorgeous Finnigan who sprints toward me.

Ronan rushes toward Bartiste and knocks the gun out of his hand, pinning his arms at the back with a feral look on his face. He's holding the man who kidnapped his pregnant wife all those years ago.

"Kill her! Kill her now!" The asshole bellows when he realizes just how fucked he is.

Finnigan stops next to me, grabs my hand as our gazes meet for a relieved moment, then looks over to Bartiste. Only, his eyes fly wide before they land on the bastard. Someone yells. My lungs seize with Finn's coiling muscles. I catch the limping form moving out from behind some machinery, at the same time a boom of a discharged weapon sounds and Finn turns, stepping in front of me.

His brows draw together on a visceral shudder at the same moment his blood splatters all over me and I jerk. Searing rage drives me, the pain ripping through my shoulder not as strong as the one looking back at me from Finn's beautiful gaze, and I step to the side and find the bastard who pulled the trigger before the others can take him away from me. A banshee shriek bounces off the metal walls as I empty the magazine in him, pain tearing through the sound-waves. With the soreness in my throat, I realize the scream was mine.

On unsteady feet, Finn turns around and steps forward, aiming his gun at the man who caused so much sorrow to so many people.

Ronan jumps into a sprint, releasing Bartiste and rushes toward us just like the rest of The Sanctum, wide eyes laced with concern and fear fixed on us.

"Finn," I cry out when he staggers.

But this moment is the culmination of eight grueling years stolen from him by this man, and he pushes forward, steadying the gun with the other hand.

"You'll keep your guts in your belly, *old man*, but I won't grant you a quick death." He unloads the gun twice, in quick succession, and the bellow that follows crawls up my spine uncomfortably.

Bartiste clutches his abdomen, but his bleeding crotch is the wound making me happiest. Like his son before him, he will take a well-deserved long time to die.

But I won't get to watch him. I rip my gaze from him when Finnigan crashes to his knees next to me, and my heart stills in my chest.

"No, no, no! Finnigan, baby!" I follow him to the floor as he falls back, feeling for his chest, but the damn useless vest is in the way.

"He took an armor-piercing one..." someone says behind me.

I fumble around desperately, ignoring my own pain, but large hands push mine away and open the vest to find his shirt soaked in blood.

"Apply pressure!" someone shouts, and those same large hands press over his chest as I move to his face.

"It's gonna be okay, you'll be fine." My voice trembles as I grab him, brushing my thumbs over his eyebrows. "You stupid, stupid man! Why did you have to take the bullet for me?"

My vision clouds with tears I cannot stop from flowing.

"I'll be fine, Evie darling." But his voice is weak. It doesn't match his words, and his piercing blue eyes lost some of their brightness.

"Finn!" Those large hands are replaced by slightly smaller ones, and Ronan appears on the other side of me. "I only just got you back, you're not allowed to fucking bail on me." The concern in his eyes makes me more uneasy.

Finn chuckles, but the noise sounds wrong, gurgled and strained and I want to throw up at how horrific it sounds.

"I'm sorry for the last..." he says to his brother, but the words are slow, forced through the shallow breaths. "Now more than ever, I understand why you left. I regret pushing you away... losing all this time."

"Save it, Finn! Tell me when I can breathe properly, back home. Safe."

But he shakes his head gently. "I'm sorry, Ronan. I was an asshole... you didn't deserve it."

"Stop it, seriously, stop it! Don't talk like you're fucking going anywhere! I refuse to forgive you until we're out of this fucking place."

But Finn just smiles and a cry spills out of me at the lack of hope in his eyes. I want to scream at Ronan to forgive him, but I don't because I agree, Finn is not allowed to go anywhere.

"You're... you're hit." He grunts as his gaze turns to me, looking at my shoulder as he tries to rise.

"I'm fine. Stay down." I push him back.

I'm not fine. The searing pain in my shoulder is almost debilitating as the adrenaline slowly seeps out, but the man I love is dying on the floor before me and my heart hurts more than my flesh.

"I'm sorry..." Finn whispers as the others are trying to figure out how to get him to a hospital and keep his lungs from collapsing on the way.

"Stop, you didn't—"

"I did try to manipulate you... a little bit." He interrupts. "I hoped that... without worrying about... your father, you'll want to stay."

"You asshole! I knew it," I cry, dropping low to press sloppy kisses over his lips. "I never wanted to leave. I was scared, Finn. All I know is tragedy... I thought that leaving before another beautiful thing crumbles around me would be for the best. And now you—"

"You're wrong," he says, coughing weakly. "You... pieced me back together. I love..." His eyes drift closed.

"Finnigan!" I bellow. "Stay with me! Please, oh God, please!" I beg, pressing my forehead to his as my tears stain his beautiful, pale face.

I tap his cheek, gently at first, then harder when his eyes

still don't open.

"Brother, wake up!" Ronan's breaking too.

"Do something!" I roar to no one in particular. "Keep him alive or I swear to god…"

The threat dissipates as Finnigan grunts in my hands, and when I look down his eyes try to flutter open.

"Please, baby, stay with me. I promise I won't leave if you don't leave me either…" I'm crying so hard, the surrounding voices are nothing but background noise.

Finnigan's eyes drift close, but this time there's no flutter in his lashes.

"No! Finnigan, come back to me!"

Bellows burn their way through my chest, the pain tearing something embedded so deep inside my soul, it seems to shred every fiber that binds me.

"I'm yours. Forever… Please, come back…"

But there's only darkness, only sorrow, and too much silence.

CHAPTER 40
Evelyn

"DO WE HAVE MORE BUBBLE wrap?" Maya asks as she walks around the living room, looking between the half-packed boxes.

"Yes, in the corner by that empty bookcase there's a big roll."

She skips with a bit too much enthusiasm in her step for someone who's currently packing moving boxes. There's so much more left to do. I barely packed half the living room, and I'm already bored out of my mind. The ache in my shoulder and limited mobility isn't helping. Maya, though, she's treating it like it's the most fun activity ever.

I must admit it's endearing to see how she treats all these books. Layers upon layers of bubble wrap around them to make sure they reach their destination completely intact. She seems to take greater care of Finnigan's books, picking the older volumes out and wrapping them individually, like she's protecting memories, not bound paper. She insisted that the books are her responsibility, and she's actually made much more progress with them than I've made with the rest of this room.

"When do you think we'll be able to go visit Aaro?" Maya asks in her little voice.

Her friend left with Ronan and Annika only two days ago, returning to their home and leaving an open invitation for us. Considering the photos I've seen of the idyllic island paradise they live in, I'm keen to go as soon as we're settled in our new home and we're free.

"Next school holiday. You're back on a proper schedule, you know that."

"But that's not until Christmas!" she protests. "Ugh, fine... I miss not having to go to school."

"I'm sure you do." I laugh, shaking my head. "Now keep packing."

"Can I help?"

His warm, rich voice fills my chest with comforting heat, and I whip around to find Finnigan leaning against the wall, arms crossed against his chest.

"What are you doing up?" I rise to my feet and rush to him. "You're supposed to be in bed."

I look down at his torso, checking to make sure he's okay and hasn't ripped a stitch. Three weeks have passed since his surgery, the skin sealed by now, so I'm aware I'm being a bit over the top. It would take much more than rising from bed to tear it open.

"It goes both ways, Evie darling." He brushes his knuckles over my cheek, pulling a smile from my lips. "You know we have people coming who will pack everything."

"I know, but we wanted to focus on the more personal

things," I explain.

"Your shoulder needs to heal."

It won't take as long as his lung, but he's not wrong; the bullet that tore through him and lodged in my shoulder did some damage. Those armor-piercing rounds are absolutely ruthless. Madds and the others still feel guilty for missing the guy who shot us, and considering that one of their own almost died, it's probably not going to go away for a while. Finnigan has his own guilt about me, and I'm hoping to squash that soon, because I truly couldn't care less about a wound as long as he's alive and well before me.

Also, there is something creepily romantic about sharing a scar from the same bullet with Finnigan.

After the doctor came out of his surgery and confirmed he's alive, in critical condition but he was going to live, Sloan, Maddox and the rest of the guys apart from Ronan, left Queenscove and decimated what was left of Bartiste's organization. They kept prisoners who gave them all the details they needed, and along with Carter and his hackers, they found what was left of Bartiste's people. Which wasn't much. Turns out that due to the access to the ports in Queenscove, and some of the best trade routes, the asshole was set on taking the city from The Sanctum and establishing his trafficking empire here.

His dream crashed and burned. It died slowly, just like he did, bleeding out on the cold concrete floor while watching the video of his disgusting son being eaten by pigs. By the time we left the warehouse, the pigs were halfway done and Bartiste was dead.

We're free.

I'm free.

"She misses Aaro?" He quirks an eyebrow, gesturing to my sister who's wrapping up books in a corner.

I roll my eyes, shaking my head, "This is not even the first time she mentioned him since we woke up. The kid's only been gone for two days."

"Told you—*boyfriend*."

He chuckles and I would smack him if he wasn't seriously hurt.

"What about you?" I counter, "Do you miss your brother?"

On a deep sigh his gaze drifts out the windows, but there's no tenseness in his features. That puts a small smile on my lips.

"I think I do. I spent so long punishing him in my mind, blaming him, bashing him, but... it took a simple confrontation to realize it was me I was punishing. Retribution for my own failures. I guess being trapped on a hospital bed for days and not having any choice but to talk to him was all I needed to fully patch up my relationship with him."

I shrug. "Maybe, but it's not just that. You're not the same person you were then, Finn. The pain is not fresh anymore and you're older, more mature. You process these things differently now. Either way, I'm happy you have your brother back."

"Look at you, though." He turns his gaze back to mine. "You're younger now than I was when it all happened to me, but you're ten times more mature."

"Eh, I'm a woman. We're smarter."

He bursts into a full belly laugh, clutching his abdomen, and for a moment I freeze.

"Stop it." I hiss, "You'll hurt yourself. You know you can't strain your lungs."

"Yeah, yeah. Come on, smart-ass." He turns me and smacks my ass, urging me to move, but I don't miss the slight cough. "Come, sit with me."

He guides us on the sofa and pulls me into his side to

cuddle me.

"No, I'll hurt you," I protest.

"Stop it, woman. I'm not made of glass. Don't make me ask again."

Reluctantly, I comply and cuddle into his side as he wraps one long, powerful arm around me.

"Are you going to miss this place?" I ask, watching the sheer, white curtains flow in the breeze.

"Probably not. After Ronan moved out, it rarely ever felt like *home*."

I nod because, of course, I understand. After losing mom, Fleeton didn't feel like home, and it had nothing to do with being homeless.

"Are you sure you like the house I found for us?"

Whilst he was recovering in the hospital he was adamant about wanting a fresh start. For all three of us. A place to fill with memories and everything we missed out on. So I went house hunting. Maybe it was luck, maybe it was the hasty, exorbitant offer I made to the couple whose house wasn't even on the market, but it didn't take as long as I thought it would to find the perfect place.

"It's secure, on a private beach where I can go swimming whenever I want, and you assigned a giant room to build a library. What more can I want?"

I chuckle, remembering how his gaze twinkled when I told him about the double height space the owners were using for a tacky games room, which we could turn into a gorgeous library with a small spiral staircase and wrap around balcony. The prospect excited him so much, he told me I'm free to paint every room black and fill it with skulls and oddities, if I want, especially since he noticed I've been exploring my style more and more.

"Are *you* excited? Are you sure it's what you want?"

I snort in response. "I never allowed myself to find out what I want, Finn. This... this is beyond any dreams I ever had."

"You've dreamed of me though." He wiggles his eyebrows.

"Once or twice," I answer, trying to sound nonchalant and failing.

"The kitchen in that house helps, though. Right?" he says with a deep, rumbling chuckle.

"Okay, yeah, the kitchen helps."

It's gorgeous. Large enough to fit a decent size island in the middle, with a huge window stretching almost the entire length of the biggest wall, above the countertop, and two ovens already installed. I have plans to change the color scheme to deep violets and greens, but the configuration is fantastic. I can already see myself baking like a madwoman in there.

"Any reservations?" His tone is lower as he asks the question.

I hesitate for a moment. "It's quite a transition for you. From a 'one night only' kind of guy to living with your girlfriend and a kid. I guess I just wonder if you'll—"

"Stop wondering," he interrupts. "You're mine, Evelyn. Since the moment I laid eyes on you I knew you would be my end. I just didn't know what kind of end. Turns out it was of just... existing. I only ever started truly living once you came into my life. You are everything." He brushes his knuckles down my cheek, stopping under my chin and tipping it up until our mouths align.

His words hit so deep, goosebumps bloom over my skin, bursting from within my chest. He brushes his lips against mine in a ghost of a touch, then presses sweet, soft kisses to them.

"And your sister, she's the bonus I never asked for and could never, ever let go. She's part of you, Evelyn, which makes her part of me too. And I finally have someone to talk books with.”

“Thank you.” I whisper. My heart swells with his words. His acceptance of my sister, the one who is now officially in my custody because of him, means more than anything. “Though, she might grow out of reading at some point.”

“Eh, it will be good for as long as it lasts.” He shrugs.

“Are you talking about the new house?” Maya jumps on the opposite end of the sofa and nestles into Finn. No boundaries whatsoever. “I can’t wait for my little nook in the library. Can we build a tent? But like, inspired from ‘One thousand and one nights’, pretty and colorful, with carpets and pillows all over the floor.”

“How are you gonna earn the tent?” Finn asks her.

He knows I never give my sister everything she wants unless she earns it. I was never raised spoiled and I don’t plan on raising her the same.

She scrunches her eyebrows as she digs for the answer. “Umm... I’ll do well in school?”

“You have to do good in school anyway,” Finn says with a chuckle.

“Oh, okay. I’ll unpack the library after you build it.”

Finn turns to me with a surprised expression. “Actually, that’s pretty good,” he says, laughing.

“Yeah, not going to lie, I never planned on doing that myself. Plus, you know... bad shoulder and all.” I shrug, pointing at it.

“Aaah suddenly it’s a bad shoulder. Okay, I see how this will be.” He shakes his head, but the smile stays on his lips.

“So is that a deal?” Maya pulls at his forearm.

“No. You’ll *help me* unpack the library. It’s a big, slightly dangerous job, sweet girl. But you’ll be my assistant. How about that?”

"Yaaay! Thank you, Finn, thank you!" she wraps her little arms around his neck and hugs him tight, as I'm silently praying she's not going to accidentally fall on his healing chest.

But she pulls away carefully, jumping back off the sofa and disappears somewhere behind us.

Finn chuckles, turning his attention back to me, squeezing me just a little harder.

"Me and her, Evie... it comes effortlessly. Never worry. You gave me something I've been missing for so long, you gave me family. Different from The Sanctum, because you and Maya, you're all mine. Only mine."

"Forever?"

"And beyond."

Five months later

BRUSHED BRASS LETTERS SHINE OVER matte black background in the early evening light— *The Gothic Bakery*. Evelyn's dream has been slowly taking off.

I trusted her baking and creative skills from the beginning, but I didn't know much about the market to be assured there would be enough clientele for her. Turns out there is. Queenscove's elite especially seems to adore her dark, baroque motifs she makes out of sugar, fondant, and even icing. Her creativity is blooming along with her business, and she had to hire two more staff members, on top of the other two, to keep up.

To say I'm fucking proud of her is an understatement.

I stand outside, leaning against my Mercedes G-class that she pretty much claimed for herself now, waiting and watching as the deep plum walls turn black when she flicks the lights off, then steps out and turns to lock the door behind her.

"Ready?" I ask, extending my hand to her.

"Yup. You're driving, though, I need to retouch my makeup before we get to Midnight."

I nod and open the door, helping her up in the passenger seat.

"How was your dad today?" I ask. I know she went to visit him at lunch.

"Alright, I guess. It was one of those days. Harder. Twice he asked where mom is. But he's okay. Happy."

"I'm sorry." I know he's not been doing all that great, the moments of clarity rarer nowadays.

She shrugs. "He's here, and that's all that matters. Was Maya okay?" she asks.

"Happy to spend the night with Mamaw June, yes. Though she was apparently disappointed that it's too warm now to turn the fireplace on," I answer as I start the car and pull out into traffic.

Evelyn's shop is only a two minute walk away from Midnight. We could have walked there, but she already had the car here. She laughs, a soft melodic sound that always seems to travel straight to my cock.

"It's always too warm in Queenscove. Mamaw June was bloody sweating in January too, but she was still appeasing that stubborn girl."

"She's hard to resist, sugar," I say, snorting.

"Well, people should try harder. Y'all are spoiling her."

I say nothing because it's hundred percent true. Instead, I steal glances as Evelyn taps a small brush over her face, refreshing her extravagant makeup. We are a decadent contrast against each other. Her plum, sleek hair against my wavy, blonde curls, her bold, dark makeup against my golden skin—leather, velvet, and metal against my clean cut clothes. We're perfect. *She's* perfect.

She's a fucking goddess, and she's all mine.

Just as I pull into the secure car park at the back of Midnight, Evelyn's done retouching her makeup and looks at me with a pretty grin on her dark lips.

"Stunning," I say with a smirk. "I can't wait to smudge that lipstick all over your pretty face."

The flush to her cheeks breaks through whatever product she used there and my smirk widens, giving her thigh a squeeze. Exiting the car, I walk to the other side and help her out, then guide her inside the speakeasy.

We're not open for another two hours, so it should only be The Sanctum in here. As we walk inside the main barroom, I find Vin, Morrigan, and Madds lounging on the comfy sofas and armchairs around a coffee table. Low, warm lights illuminate the space, bathing the woodsy bar in a cozy vibe.

I slump into a winged-back armchair, pulling Evie onto my lap, my hand splayed over the fishnet tights barely covering her legs.

"Settle this for us, will you?" Morrigan asks. "Madds is the one who proposed that The Sanctum invest in Metamorphosis after half of it burnt down, and now it's been open for about three months, he has not stepped foot in it. Shouldn't he see what his money bought?"

Metamorphosis, her and Loreley's fetish club, was only open for a couple of months, before an intentional fire burnt down half of it. In the heat of the moment, Madds offered to front them the money to renovate, something that shocked pretty much all of us. I still think there is much more to it. Like the way he looks at Loreley sometimes, with both exasperation and uncomfortable curiosity. She was adamant she didn't want to be indebted to The Sanctum. Luckily, it all worked out, and the club is now reopened and stronger than ever. From what I heard, there's a fight for memberships, as the place is even more desirable now than it was before.

"Why don't you want to go, Madds?" Evelyn asks him.

He shrugs, turning his gaze toward the bar, pretending to focus on something. "I don't need to. It's going great from what I hear."

"It is, but it would be nice if you could see it. Be proud of me and all of that," Morrigan counters.

"I am. I know you both did a great job."

Evie turns to me. "Can we go?"

"No" Madds and I shout simultaneously.

"Hey, that's not fair. I want to see," Evie says.

"Well, other people might want to see *you* and that's a definite no for me."

Morrigan laughs and shakes her head. "Your possessiveness is refreshing, but you know first-hand that no one touches anyone in my club without permission. You know you can just come for a drink. And a show." She wiggles her eyebrows suggestively.

"Maybe just for a little bit." Evelyn leans in, whispering in my ear.

I don't answer, but the look in my eyes might be enough, because a cheeky smile spreads over her face.

"For the love of god, at least don't go when Carter's there," Madds tells her.

"Ever the big brother you are," she says with a chuckle.

"Speaking of the wolf. Where is he?" I ask.

"In the office," Vin answers. "I texted him that you arrived too."

Just on cue, Carter pops in through the back door, as

always, dressed in pressed trousers, a light shirt with rolled-up sleeves, and tailored waistcoat. He looks every bit the man who belongs in a speakeasy. Only, there's something different tonight. I can't put my finger on it.

"Carter?" Vin's tone sounds like he's seeing the same thing I am.

"I have to tell you something." Carter releases a slow breath that sounds too much like a sigh. Deeply uncharacteristic for the man.

"What?" I ask.

"I fucked up." His gaze sweeps over each one of us. "About six months ago, when we were looking for Bartiste, I was looking for one of his men, and I went after him myself. I tracked him down one night, cornered him in an alley and after I got what I could out of him... I killed him."

There's a pause. "So?" Vin shrugs.

"Someone saw me."

Vin leans forward in his chair, bracing his elbows on his knees, head cocked, as I guide Evelyn to go sit next to Madds.

"And?" I ask.

"I can't find her."

"*Her?!*" all of us say in unison.

"Sorry, a woman witnessed you killing a man, and in the last six months you haven't been able to find her?" Vin runs through the story.

Carter nods, sliding his hands in his pockets, his expression one of annoyance, and maybe, just maybe, slight embarrassment. Amusement is common on his features, but anything beyond that is extremely rare. Which makes this highly worrying.

"You don't know who she is?" Madds asks.

"No. Couldn't find her. I kept track of reports, of stories, of damn internet posts, and no one has talked about it."

"Maybe she recognized you, she's scared, and knows better than to talk," Vin adds.

"She certainly wasn't scared," Carter mutters under his breath, barely audible.

"What?" Madds asks.

"Nothing."

The others accept his answer and I seem to be the only one who heard what he said.

"Why wait until now to say something?" I ask.

"I thought I would find her by now. The challenge became greater and greater, but nothing popped up."

Vin leans back in his chair, shrugging. "Fine. If nothing has come to light in six months, I'm doubtful it will. I'm sure you'll keep an eye and ear out anyway."

"Yeah." Carter nods slowly, his gaze now fixed on a random glass from the table.

I think he does feel some form of embarrassment. How peculiar. Although, I think the man has an inherent need to know everything. This must be bothering him to no end.

"Was she pretty?"

"Morri, Jesus," Vin says, shaking his head.

Carter scowls in her direction, but she just curls her lips inward, as Evie looks away from him, clearly amused.

"Was she?" I quirk an eyebrow, because now I'm curious.

The Carver sets his gaze on me and I shrug, not even trying to hide my amusement.

"Right, I think it's time for a drink. If you don't mind, Carter, I'll do the honors. I don't trust you won't poison our women, or me, if you make them." I get up and head behind the bar, not missing how the man rolls his eyes before he takes my seat.

As I pour the spirits and mixers in the crystal glasses, I steal glances at my Evie, talking with Madds on the sofa. I know Madds is close with Morrigan; they've known each other since she was sixteen, but his relationship with Evie is completely different. They have a friendship that sometimes is lead in silence, because these two seem to share scars they don't talk about, but understand nonetheless. She had to do a lot of apologizing after the stunt she pulled when she went after Frankie B, but Madds felt so guilty that she got shot during the whole Bartiste thing, that he didn't take long at all to forgive her.

I'm happy for her. She didn't just find a new, better life in Queenscove, or love—she found friendship and family. And knowing that she has others here who are willing to protect her, go through hell and back for her, makes me feel so much better.

I'm shaking a drink when Evie rises from the sofa and my mouth goes dry at the slow, deliberate sway of her hips as her thick soled Doc Martens hit the wooden floor. The minx knows exactly what she's doing with those long legs barely covered in sinful fishnets, the dark green, tight velvet skirt hugging her frame, and the worn band T-shirt she tucked in and cut herself into a V-neck. But she had to add that leather harness over just to drive me crazy.

The tips of her hair graze the sweet spot where the neck meets the shoulder with each step she takes, and I'm jealous, because my tongue and teeth should be doing that.

Propping her forearms on the counter, she leans in, rewarding me with her most sinful smirk.

"So, Mr. Hennessey. Will you take me to Metamorphosis?"

Jesus, she's gonna kill me with that seductive voice. I lean in, grip her chin, and she parts her lips for me, but I barely graze them as I dip to the side, blowing a breath over the side of her neck, before I capture her soft lobe between my teeth, nipping it once.

"Only if you're a good girl. Prove it. Tonight." I brush the tip of my tongue over the sensitive skin just under her ear for a brief moment, before I pull back and continue making the drinks.

"Tonight? What are we doing?" Her flush is evident, even in this dim light.

"Having one stiff drink"—I slide a glass her way—"and then go home."

She cocks her head, biting her lip as she grabs the drink and turns around, her ass swaying as she walks away.

Oh yeah, she'll be a good girl alright.

The next hour goes by excruciatingly slow. No one needs that much time to finish the vodka sour I made, but the minx has been sipping it so fucking slow, each drop of liquid is a pawn in her erotic game. She's deliberate in her torture.

By the time we get in the car, my breathing is strained, just as my damn cock against my trousers is. She grabs my thigh as I'm driving, coaxing me on, but two can play this game. I keep her waiting, *wanting*, on the whole drive home. And since our house is just on the outskirts of Queenscove, down a private road that ends in our own, secluded little bay, the drive isn't all that short.

"Finnigan…" She says my name in a breathy voice that stirs my cock.

"Tsk, tsk, tsk, Evie darling. Good girl, remember?"

"But you like it when I beg," she purrs, sharp nails digging into the top of my thigh.

We reach our gate, secured between two small cliffs, the road looking like it was carved through, and I'm ready to blast through them if they don't fucking open quicker.

"I haven't even touched you yet."

"When has my craving for you ever needed your touch, darling Finnigan?"

Her words hit with a shattering lightning, the current

spreading goosebumps through my nerves, urging my foot to press harder on the gas. We're past the gates, and our two story beach villa, lit by beautiful, upturned lights, comes into view. From this distance, against the star-splattered sky and dark sea, it looks like a lighthouse, guiding us home.

Screeching to a halt in front of the detached garage to the right, that's exactly what I want to do—find home. Right inside the pretty pussy of the woman who has flipped my life the right way up, and turned me into a love-sick bastard who can't get enough of her.

With a tight grip on my hand, we rush through the front door and flip the moody lights on. Apparently the ceiling lights are a big no-no, and eventually I had to agree she was right. Funky lamps and picture lights are dotted all around, their glow bouncing off mismatched gold frames and rich-colored paneled walls, giving a deeply cozy quality to our decadent house. We aimed for comfort, and Evelyn added, as she calls it, a Gothic cottage-core vibe to it.

"You know what I've been wanting to do all evening, Evie darling? As you've been sipping that drink at snail speed just to get me all hot and fucking bothered?" I ask as I back her against a wall, caging her in.

She curls her lips inward, swallowing her amusement.

"I don't know what you're talking about." She shakes her head, but I grip her cheeks in my hand, forcing her lips to part as I hold her to me.

"Your pretty makeup running down your face as you choke on my cock."

She gasps, the hitch in her chest pressing her peaked nipples against my shirt, and I shift up just enough to graze them, teasing her.

I swipe my tongue over the dark crimson lipstick, getting a hint of cherries. "Tastes delicious, but I can't wait to see it smeared all over my fucking cock."

"Oh god…" she says in a breathy voice.

Releasing her face, I take a step back, then grip her T-shirt and pull it out from under the hem of the skirt.

"I have to take the harness down," she says pointing to the thick leather straps.

"No." I push her hands away as she rushes to unfasten it.

Ever so fucking slowly, I lift the hem until it passes the horizontal strap rounding her ribs, revealing the soft skin from the underside of her breasts. They're trapped between the leather framing them inside two triangle shapes, meeting over her sternum on a brass metal ring, and disappearing over shoulders. I pull at the side of the T-shirt, guiding her arm through the sleeve, then do the same with the other side at an excruciating pace, grazing the fabric over her hard nipples, relishing in her swallowed cry. Finally, I free her breasts, tugging the T-shirt from under the shoulder straps and over her head, then step back to admire her.

"My goddess…" I whisper.

She blushes a deep berry red that matches her lips so perfectly, her back straightening a fraction.

"Now, Evie darling. On. Your. Knees." She drops before me in an instant, her hands making quick work of the belt, then the buttons of my trousers, freeing my aching cock.

I'm on the larger side, but in her delicate hands it looks damn right huge. It looks even fucking better as she takes me right to the back of her throat in one swift motion.

"Jesus Christ!" I groan, fisting the bottom of my shirt like it can help me hold my balance through the whirlwind of sensations.

She ignores me completely, pulling back to reveal the crimson marks her lipstick left over the veined ridges of my cock, but she takes me deep once more before I can fully admire.

I pull my shirt over my head while I still have enough conscious brain cells to manage the movement, and look down at the pretty sight before me. She swallows me down and I push forward, smirking when she chokes on the tip, spit falling off her lips and over her tits. Finally, tears brim her eyes, starting to mess with her makeup. She hums deep in her throat and the vibrations make my eyes roll back.

"Ready?" I ask.

She looks into my eyes, giving me a slight nod of approval, and I thread my fingers through her plum-colored hair, like we've been practicing for months. With a grin pulling at my lips, I tighten my hold on her as she steadies herself on my thighs, and I pump my cock into her plush mouth.

Tears bring the dark makeup down her cheeks as I fuck between her soft lips, and the sight is enough to make me come right now. Tightening my fist, I dig my nails in my palm at the ecstasy that threatens to bring me to my knees, calling on some pain to keep me from spilling all my pleasure too soon. But God, it feels glorious inside her mouth, with black tears streaming down her face, and red lipstick smudged all over my cock.

"Fuck!" I roar, releasing her in an instant and pulling out of her mouth.

It's too much, too good, but not as good as sinking between her thighs, and it's there where I want to come. I help her up, capturing her lips with mine, our tongues tangling as I walk her backward until her thighs hit the back of the couch.

"You"—I tease a nipple between my thumb and forefinger—"are..."—I nip at her lip, soothing it after with my tongue—"divine."

I fall on one knee, kissing a trail down her bare torso, covered only with that sinful leather harness, and push the skirt over her hips. These fishnet tights are my fucking weakness. Every time she wears them I go feral. She could be dressed like a damn librarian, but if she had these tights underneath, I would still see her as the dirtiest little vixen.

Looking up at her with a smirk, she parts her lips when I grip the flimsy fabric covering her pussy, and pull harshly. She gasps, her brows drawing together, watching intently as I suck on two fingers, push her lace panties to the side then sink them inside her pussy at the same time I cover her clit, pulling it between my lips.

She cries out, the sounds tearing from deep within her chest as she grips my hair and grinds herself on my face. I pump my fingers inside her sopping core, deep and fast, exactly how she likes it, until her knees are shaking and she tightens around me.

"Please, please... Oh, please." She chants between the lust-stained panting, a decadent prayer for the pleasure only I can bring her.

She begs so beautifully. So I give her what she wants, rubbing the sensitive spot inside of her as I suck the bundle of nerves between my lips. She breaks on wanton moans that travel straight to my cock.

Rising, I flip her around while she's still whimpering, bend her over the back of the sofa, and guide the fat tip of my cock through the drenched seam of her pussy. Her spasms turn gentle, the orgasm still vibrating through, so I take my time as I push in to the hilt and absorb every tightening pulse of her sweet cunt.

"Divine..." I whisper, gripping the back of her leather harness as I dig my fingers into her hip, bracing myself.

The first few pumps are dragged and deep, following the rhythm of the soft waves that crash against the sand, beyond the wall of windows before us. I grunt as she whimpers each time my hips meet her ass, drawing out that pleasure from deep inside her as my own seems to coil around the base of my cock.

But it doesn't take long until the surf no longer dictates the speed of my strokes, and the feverish slapping of our skins pulls all matter of lustful sounds from our throats. Each thrust brings bolts of current up my spine, pleasure twisting harder, low in my belly, quickly becoming too much. Too close.

I lift Evie up by the harness, wrapping an arm around her and guiding her lips to meet mine, just as I reach for the needy bundle of nerves between her thighs. She jerks her hips against me at the contact, biting on my lower lip on a lewd whimper when I rub it, my cock stroking madly inside her weeping pussy. Our mouths fuck just as well, licking and stroking, sucking and biting on the thrusting rhythm of our bodies, and when the first spasm of her core chokes my cock, I press harder over the hood of her clit.

The moment she breaks, I swallow her cries, my own orgasm ripping through me with enough strength, my knees go weak for a brief moment. I spill inside of her over and over, wondering just when exactly am I going to stop. It's irrelevant, I'm in no rush to leave her warm core.

"I will never get used to this," she whispers between our slowing kisses.

"This?" I ask, peppering more around her lips, her cheeks, the tip of her curved nose.

"Pleasure." She relaxes into me as I wrap her in my arms. "What you do, what we do, it feels more like worship."

It really does.

"I've only ever worshiped *you*, Evie darling. Pleasure has never felt like this before."

Her cheeks flush and lips pull into a chaste smile.

"Let's clean up. I could do with cooling off with a late night swim."

She nods her answer, pressing another gentle kiss to my

lips, and I reluctantly pull out of her, chuckling when she drops down a few inches. She always has to stand on her tiptoes when we fuck like this, and for some odd reason I find it deliciously cute when she dips down to her normal height.

We head to the bathroom, and while I help her clean my cum that's dripping down her thighs, since it's become both my pleasure and my specialty, she removes her messed up makeup.

She's bare-faced now, and she looks so pure, so damn young. I beat myself up for a while, thinking I'm stealing from her years she could be spending making friends her own age, doing all sorts of crazy things, and experimenting like everyone else does at that age. Then I sat back and watched her go through her day-to-day life and those feelings dissipated. Even without me in her life she wouldn't have made those types of choices. Not with Maya by her side. Not with her dad weighing on her. Her personality doesn't fit.

She's different, and she fucking refused to let me go. I suggested it twice—living her youth and all that. The first time, she looked at me like I grew a second head, the second time she threatened me with the knife she was using to slice cake. I was gently advised to shut the fuck up and stop saying stupid things.

"Where did you go?" Her voice filters through the dangerously hot memory of her aiming a buttercream covered knife at me.

"Nowhere, sugar. Come, let's cool off." I lie because I would rather not end up getting stabbed.

We walk stark naked over the wooden patio and onto the soft, warm sand toward the ocean. Most nights, Maya is here and we can't skinny dip, but once in a while Mamaw June takes her for a sleepover and we spend hours out in the calm waters of the bay.

Evelyn hisses when the first slosh of the surf touches her feet and I laugh, shaking my head. "It's pretty damn warm."

"I'm surprised you think so. Your body runs at a hundred degrees. Celsius! This should be ice on your skin." she teases, gritting her teeth as she keeps walking forward.

"Yeah, yeah. You say this every time."

"Yup. Shows that it's true."

I snicker as I dive straight in, stroking underwater and reveling in the feel of it against my skin. When I finally emerge and turn around, Evie is floating on her back, eyes closed as the moonlight shimmers over her wet skin.

Goddess...

This is my life now. Every single day I wake up unable to fully believe that it's not a dream running in a sick loop through my head. It's not *too good to be true*, because we have our share of challenges, our own issues we're working through, failings we haven't fully overcome, but we're doing all of this together.

The two of us... my darling Evie. My moonlit goddess.

"You're doing it again. Losing yourself inside your mind."

Her silver eyes seep into golden sparkles as she turns to me, and I realize I've been drifting over to her without thinking. She drops her legs underwater, swimming gently toward me, and I reach for her. Gripping her waist and guiding her legs over my hips, I tread water for the both of us.

"You're mine..." I whisper, pressing a salty kiss to her lips.

The corner of hers quirks as she brushes the hair back from my face. "You sound surprised."

"Every day." I nod. "I wish you wouldn't have gone through all that pain to get here. I wish I wouldn't either. Yet..." I let the word drift away.

"I know. It's funny, really. We condemn the terrible people who destroy us—our lives. We punish them, hate them, and yet... they created the connection between us, our moment, our opportunity for two to become one. They formed the basis of our love story. Without them I wouldn't have been in that container, and you wouldn't have been on the other side of it. I wouldn't have sacrificed myself for those children, and you wouldn't have looked at me with that gut-wrenching pain in your eyes you didn't even realize you were bleeding all over the room. There wouldn't have been an opportunity for us. We would have never met. This heartbreakingly beautiful, fucked up love would have been wandering all alone, drifting through the universe, crying for a loss that it never gained in the first place. Without the pain they caused us, we wouldn't have felt this... serenity."

I shake my head, a lump in my throat at the harsh words that make so much damn sense. I hate them nonetheless, but they are the harsh truth.

"I can't picture a world without you in it. Without you by my side."

She brushes the tip of her nose against mine, then presses a kiss to my lips.

"You will never have to. You are mine, Finnigan Hennessey."

"All yours, Evie darling."

* * *

Thank you for reading Evelyn and Finnigan's story.
Carved Obsession is up next. Pre-Order to discover Carter's story and the woman who brings him to his knees.

AKNOWLEDGEMENTS

My amazing readers, thank you for giving me and my words a chance. You reactions, your graphics, your reviews, and amazing paperback photos are the encouragement that keeps me moving forward in this incredible career. Thank you.

My darling Jackdaws and Sirens, having you all in my Content Creator and ARC teams is something I'll forever be grateful for. Thank you for all you do for me! You are all so amazing.

May, I will forever be grateful for your help with each and every book. You've been with me right from the start and my stories are better because of you. Thank you for everything, I'm so very grateful to have found you.

Thank you to Victoria and Michele for your work in editing and proofreading this book baby.

Of course, I have to acknowledge my hard-working husband. You do so much for me, or instead of me, and I'm grateful to have found such an amazing, supportive man like you.

And last, but never least, Jess... I couldn't have written Manacled Hearts without your support and shoulder to cry on. You are there for me when I need it the most, and I'll never be able to thank you enough. You trust me, encourage me, hype me up, and you make me a better writer. Thank you, always. I love you!

Love,
Lilith

ABOUT THE AUTHOR

Lilith Roman is a romance author who lives with her husband and fluffy bear-dog in the UK, where she writes stories laced with a little danger, intense passion, and dark themes, always ending in a Happily Ever After.

She's an introvert with an addiction for pretty hardbacks she never reads. A lover of anything with chocolate, cursing, and steamy books. And her love for horror movies convinced her without a shadow of a doubt that... even the monster under the bed needs a love story.

For exclusive insights, join her Newsletter, or
Lilith Roman's Corrupted Souls Facebook group.

scan the QR code

ALSO BY THE AUTHOR

Dangerous Strokes, a Dark Mafia Romance
(The Sanctum Syndicate #1)

Reckless Covenant, a Second Chance Mafia Romance
(The Sanctum Syndicate #2)

Carved Obsession, a Dark Mafia Romance
(The Sanctum Syndicate #4)

My Kind of Monster, a Dark Contemporary Romance

Even in Death, a Romantic Horror Novella

Blissful Perdition, a Lesbian Romance Short Story